WHITE
ANGEL

Gary Gottesfeld

FAWCETT GOLD MEDAL • NEW YORK

A Fawcett Gold Medal Book
Published by Ballantine Books
Copyright © 1995 by Gary Gottesfeld

Library of Congress Catalog Card Number: 95-90028

ISBN 0-449-14879-3

Manufactured in the United States of America

First Edition: June 1995

10 9 8 7 6 5 4 3 2 1

The capillaries lining the pouches under Ben's eyes began to twitch uncontrollably.

Nothing he had seen in his twenty-two years on the police force prepared him for this. . . . The couple had been mutilated, ripped apart by something Ben silently prayed wasn't human.

James Rico, as if he were still asleep, was lying on his side in a fetal position. He wore only Jockey briefs. There were deep, jagged gorges indiscriminately crisscrossing his torso like earthquake faults. The right arm and leg were completely severed.

"What could have done this?" Nani whispered through a fogged voice.

Ben just shook his head. He didn't have an answer. His eyes turned to the nude body of the woman. A small groan escaped from his throat. . . . Ben took his eyes off the woman and looked up at the blood-splattered wall in back of the couple.

No, nothing human could have done this.

By Gary Gottesfeld
Published by Fawcett Books:

THE VIOLET CLOSET
BLOOD HARVEST
TRIBAL SHADOWS
WHITE ANGEL

For Nancy

This book could not have been written without the painstaking work of Daniel "Kaniela" Akaka and his beautiful wife, Anna. They've helped keep this book honest and taught me about the extraordinary culture and generosity of Hawaiians. Many thanks to them and their wonderful children, Kalei, Kina, Yosha, Kalá, and La'akea.

PROLOGUE

1974

Hāmākua District, Hawaii

DISTRICT POL. CAPT. Ben Lopaka tightened the muscles around his tired eyes, forcing them to stay on the dead *haole* and his Hawaiian wife sprawled under the bloody bedsheet.

Paul Nani, the coroner from Hilo, ducked his towering Samoan torso under the yellow police tape strung across the bedroom door and walked over to him. "What do we have, Ben?"

"Nothin' good," the captain said.

Nani put his thick hand on Ben's shoulder to move him out of the way. *"Auwē!"* he murmured, looking down at the bed. "Who the hell would do something like that?"

Ben didn't answer.

"Know them?"

"Slightly," Ben said, keeping his voice tight to control the quiver. He had grown up on the island and knew all the locals, especially the ones in his district. "The man's name is James Rico. He works for the Honokaá Sugar Company. That's his wife, Loke. When I was a kid . . . her father and me used to be friends."

The water dripping off Ben's rain slicker formed a small puddle next to his feet. He looked around the room. Clothing and other bedroom articles were spewed across the floor. The bureau drawers were all open, so was the closet.

"Robbery?" Nani asked. He removed his raincoat and draped it across the chair.

"Maybe," Ben said quietly. "How long do you think they've been dead?"

Nani leaned over the bed and lightly touched the stained sheet. He rubbed his fingers together and showed Ben the glis-

3

tening wet blood on their tips. "Still fresh. Maybe forty ... forty-five minutes tops." He wiped his hand on his gabardine pants.

Ben nodded, his gaze turning back to the victims' faces. James Rico's eyes were closed, his head angled to the side. Loke's were open, staring straight up at him, her lips frozen in a frail smile.

Strange ... smiling when she knew she was about to die, Ben thought.

"They were killed while they slept," the coroner said.

Ben shook his head. "Maybe he was, but she wasn't. She saw her killer." To emphasize his point, he reached down and closed her eyes with his fingers.

"Let's see what we got here," Nani said. He grabbed the torn sheet and pulled it away. His head immediately jerked upward, as if a foul odor had leapt up from the bed and burrowed through his nostrils. "Oh, man," he muttered under his breath.

The capillaries lining the pouches under Ben's eyes began to twitch uncontrollably. Nothing he had seen in his twenty-two years on the police force prepared him for this—not the ninety-mile-an-hour car crashes on Queens Ka'ahumanu Highway or the beer-bottle fights in the Puna bars. Nothing!

The couple had been mutilated, ripped apart by something Ben silently prayed wasn't human.

James Rico, as if he were still asleep, was lying on his side in a fetal position. He wore only Jockey briefs. There were deep, jagged gorges indiscriminately crisscrossing his torso like earthquake faults. Chunks of raw meat, splintered ribs, and organs were showing. Some of the wounds cut right through the body and continued down into the mattress ticking. The right arm and leg were completely severed.

"What could have done this?" Nani whispered through a fogged voice.

Ben just shook his head. He didn't have an answer. His eyes turned to the nude body of the woman. A small groan escaped from his throat when he saw that she was in the last months of pregnancy. Her swollen belly was split open like a ripe melon, exposing the womb. Encased in the membrane, he could clearly see the placid face of the unborn child sucking on its thumb.

Breathing heavily, Nani opened his black bag, removed a pair of plastic gloves, and put them on. "Move, Ben. Let me do my job," he said, trying to regain his composure.

Ben took his eyes off the woman and looked up at the blood-splattered wall in back of the couple. Its indiscriminate design reminded him of a De Kooning painting he once saw at the art museum in Honolulu.

No, nothing human could have done this.

Ben went toward the door, being careful not to step on the footprints with the small diamond patterns stamped on the blood-soaked floor. He had also noticed the odd-shaped imprints in the hallway and living room. Did they belong to the killer? As he was about to duck under the tape, he spotted a small stuffed animal lying in the corner. He picked it up. It was a hand-sewn horse made of blue felt, with yellow ribbons for the mane.

It belonged to their daughter, he thought. Seeing the condition of the bodies in the room made him almost forget about her.

In the living room, he saw two of his officers powdering the furniture for fingerprints. Everything in this room was in its rightful place—no drawers opened, nothing thrown about. Was it robbery? He glanced down at the floor. His eyes followed the trail of the bloody diamond patterns leading out the front door and disappearing into the rain-filled night.

He turned his troubled face toward the window. Through the darkness and rain, he could just make out the small figure of the four-year-old girl sitting in his truck, which was parked by the shoulder of the flooded road. The coroner's van and three other police vehicles were next to it.

He drew the hood of his rain slicker over his head, sidestepped the footprints, and went out into the heavy downpour.

In the middle of the sugarcane field surrounding the house, Ben caught a glimpse of that gangly teenage boy who lived up the road from the victims. The boy nervously twisted one of the cane stalks in his hands while watching him.

A strange boy, the police captain thought. He would question him after he talked to the girl. When Ben first arrived on the scene, he found the boy kneeling by the edge of the ancient, man-made pond in the field, attempting to get the little

girl out. She had concealed herself in the water to hide from
the killer.

Ben made his way to the truck and opened the door. The
girl was sitting in the backseat with one of his men. She was
soaking wet, wrapped in a brown army blanket. Her body was
shaking and her teeth chattered uncontrollably from the cold.

Lopaka's heart went out to her. He knew she was in the
room when her parents were killed because their blood was
speckled across her golden-colored face. He wanted to leave
her in peace but knew he couldn't do that.

He told the officer with her to go down to the house and
help with the removal of the bodies, then squeezed in next to
the girl and closed the car door. His body felt ice-cold, but he
couldn't tell if it was from the wet night or from what he had
seen in the bedroom.

"You saw what happened, didn't you?" he said softly, putting his hand on her small knee, which was shaking like a
frightened deer.

She looked up, her terrified eyes searching for a face that
went with the gentle voice. Suddenly, fireworks from the city
of Hilo—celebrating the anniversary of Hawaiian statehood—
cracked through the stormy night, lighting up the car. For a
brief moment the girl could see his features: stooped, rounded
shoulders; sad, pouched eyes; thinning black hair; Polynesian
skin the color of pancakes.

The girl was too scared and cold right now to fully understand what happened, he thought. He silently prayed the chill
would stay with her, freezing out the hurt and anger that
would emerge later on.

"What did you see?" he asked.

As the night began to replay in her memory, her dark, hollow eyes opened wide. "An—an angel," she stuttered through
cold, quivering lips.

Ben looked confused. "You saw an angel in your mommy
and daddy's bedroom?"

Again she nodded, then wiped the wet strands of black hair
from her face with her tiny fingers.

"Are you sure it wasn't just a man?"

"Y-yes."

Ben knew he had to go slow with her. "What did this angel
look like?"

"White . . . with big wings."

"Where was it standing?"

"Over Mommy and Daddy's bed." Her eyes took on a murky glow. Then she added, "It was holding a red sword."

"A sword?"

"It was on fire."

"Were your parents asleep?"

"Da—Daddy was. Mommy saw it."

"Did she try to do something? Yell? Scream?"

"No."

"Nothing?"

"She just looked up at the angel and smiled."

Lopaka's eyes narrowed. "Why do you think your mama did that?"

The girl looked down at her lap, clutching the corners of the blanket, thinking about his question. After a moment, she shrugged and said, "Maybe she thought it was going to take her to heaven to meet God."

The chill in his bones began to bite deep into his marrow from her innocent remark. Nothing was right about any of this. What had she really seen in that room? Better talk to the boy. He looked over toward the sugarcane field for him, but he was no longer there.

Ben heard a tapping on the truck's rear window, turned and looked out. Paul Nani was bending over the glass, motioning to him. After fixing the blanket around the shivering girl, the police captain left the truck.

He and the coroner walked quickly over to a large banyan tree to take shelter from the rain. Ben took out his pipe from his breast pocket and stuck it in his mouth with the barrel pointed down. He rarely lit it anymore.

"I didn't want the girl to hear any of this," the coroner said.

Ben sucked on the stem. "What did you find?"

"You're not going to believe it, but I think a shark killed that couple."

The police captain probed Paul Nani's face to see if he was serious. He was. "What the hell are you talking about, man? The ocean is a half mile away."

The coroner handed him a small, blood-covered object. "I dug this out from one of the wounds on the woman. The abrasions on both bodies seem to match it. I'll know better when I examine them back at the hospital."

Ben turned his flashlight on it. It was a curved tooth from a great white.

"One of your men also found this neckerchief on the floor outside the bedroom." He held a red-and-black bandanna up to the light.

Paul and Ben stared at each other. They both knew who it belonged to.

"That's Panali's," Ben said. "What's it doin' here?"

"You better find him and ask him that," Paul said.

Ben didn't relish finding him. Panali was a crazy man. He was also his brother-in-law. The cold inside Ben Lopaka deepened. First an angel, then a shark . . . now Panali. No, nothing was right about any of this.

White, red, and blue tracers began to streak through the night sky, shattering the stillness with sharp, snapping noises, throwing the darkness into an array of colors.

Ben turned back to the girl in the truck. Her eyes were staring out at him through the windshield, but her sight was turned inward. He was willing to bet that whatever she was seeing right now had to do with what went down in that house tonight.

Somewhere inside that girl was the answer to all this. Ben wondered if it would ever come out.

1994

Chapter One

New York City

THE MOMENT MALIA saw Tom Wolfe walking out of Antibes in his white suit she knew she'd worn the wrong thing. She stopped at the door of the restaurant and tried to straighten out the wrinkles in the 1920s crepe dress she'd bought at a secondhand shop in Soho. It was useless. She made a mental note never to wear crepe on a hot day again.

Malia entered the restaurant. She squeezed her way through the well-dressed drinking crowd at the bar and over to the tuxedoed maître d' standing behind his station. He was busy talking to a couple waiting for a table. She leaned over the podium and cleared her throat, trying to get his attention.

The maître d' turned his head and peered down at the golden-skinned young woman with the thick black hair twisting into natural dreadlocks. His eyes narrowed into disdainful slits.

"I have a lunch appointment with Ciji Brown," Malia said quickly, hoping to squash his attitude.

His face immediately softened and his thick lips curled into a forced smile. "Yes, she's here and expecting you." His thick accent had a Marseilles nasality.

Malia glanced up at the clock on the wall and frowned. She was ten minutes late. *Damn!* Not a good start. She had totally forgotten about the transit strike.

She followed him into a small VIP room at the rear of the restaurant reserved for the literati of publishing. She couldn't be sure, but she thought that was Umberto Eco over by a window table huddling with Norman Mailer.

The maître d' abruptly stopped at the end of the room, causing Malia to almost climb up his back. He swooped his hand

11

toward an attractive, middle-aged woman sitting by herself at a corner table.

"Voilà," he said.

Malia knew it was Ciji Brown, the editor in chief of Baronin Books. She'd seen her photo many times in *Publishers Weekly*.

Ciji didn't see her right away. Instead, her impatient eyes were scanning the room as she sipped a glass of white wine. She was dressed in a white linen Valentino suit. Her blond hair was a bit unkempt and frizzy, held in place by a few bobby pins.

Malia sized her up as being a hard worker who had no time for beauty parlors or facials. She brushed her own thick hair back from her face and tried pushing the wrinkles down on her dress one more time before going over to her.

Ciji looked up and saw Malia. The lines in her brow deepened in surprise. "My God, I heard you were young, but not *this* young," she whispered in a slight New York accent. She didn't stand up, nor did she extend her hand. "Sit down," she said in a brusque voice.

The maître d' pulled the chair away from the table to make room for her.

"Sorry I'm late. I forgot the buses weren't running," Malia said, sitting down.

Ciji quickly brushed her hand in the air to say it was not important. "Would you like a glass of wine?"

"Burgundy," Malia replied.

Ciji smiled in amusement. "In the afternoon?"

Malia smiled back. "*Especially* in the afternoon."

The editor looked the young woman over for a brief second, appraising her, then motioned to the maître d' to get her the wine.

A baby-faced young man who'd written a best-selling novel about growing up privileged and miserable on Long Island's Sag Harbor, whose name Malia had forgotten, waved to Ciji from another table. Ciji winked back at him, then turned her attention back to Malia. "Malia Rico. An interesting mixture of names," she said.

Ciji pronounced Malia wrong. Most *haoles* did. She no longer bothered to correct them. "Malia is Hawaiian for Mary.

My mother was Polynesian, my father was French ... from Corsica."

"The two cultures seemed to have merged quite well with you." There was a hint of sarcasm in her tone.

Malia ignored it. "I was a little bewildered by your phone call this morning."

Ciji leaned forward, put her arms on the table, and drew her long, milky-white fingers to her chin. "I offered you a potential deal. One that most writers would sell their firstborn for. What was so confusing about that?"

"Why me?"

"Good question. I asked the same thing of General Steinway. You're the one he wants to meet."

Malia arched her eyebrows in surprise. "He said that?"

"Yesterday. It seems he read an article you'd written on some World War Two general and liked it."

"Which one? I've written many articles on generals. They're my hobby."

She paused, then said in her subtle mocking tone again, "Someone I've never heard of before. A General Mortimer Crowe."

Malia squinted her eyes, thinking. "My God ... I wrote that right after I graduated Columbia. It was for a small military magazine in the Northwest." She laughed. "I don't think the magazine had more than ten subscribers."

Ciji didn't laugh with her. Instead, her lips tightened as she swirled the wine around in her glass. "How fortunate for you that Steinway was one of the ten."

Again Malia heard the contempt. "You seem concerned."

"I'll be honest with you, I am. Right now General Steinway is riding a crest of popularity in this country. There's even talk that he'll be running for president on the Independent ticket in two years. We paid him seven million dollars for the rights to his autobiography. He needs a ghostwriter. He's already fired the first one we sent him."

"What's that have to do with me?"

Ciji gave her a hard look. "That writer was Jasper Rhodes. He's a best-selling author with a Pulitzer Prize under his belt. You, on the other hand, sold ten copies of a magazine article about a general no one's heard of. Understand my concern?"

Malia realized she wasn't Ciji Brown's choice, that she was

being forced into making her this offer. "Why not use some-one else then? This town doesn't have a shortage of writers."

The editor emitted a small sigh. "As I said, you're the one he wants to meet."

"I may not have a Pulitzer, but I am a professional writer," Malia said emphatically.

Ciji compressed her eyes, not quite convinced. "I read some of the articles you wrote for the *Village Voice* criticizing our military-industrial complex."

"Criticism is healthy."

"Not when seven million dollars is at stake."

"Steinway obviously wasn't disturbed by the articles."

"Obviously not. For the life of me, I don't understand why."

She reached for a breadstick in the basket, broke it in half, and popped the piece in her mouth. "Maybe because I didn't include him in my criticism. I like the man. Most generals are somewhere to the right of Attila the Hun. He's not. There's something real about him."

A smile of relief crossed Ciji's face. "That's what I want to hear. *If* he hires you, the job pays seventy-five thousand. Interested?"

Malia slowly chewed the bread, thinking. She knew that amount was low. Just a token compared to what the other writer must have gotten. But she was broke, almost to the point of having to sell some of her jewelry to meet next month's rent. "I'll be interested to see what he has to say," she said finally.

Her red wine came, along with the oversized menus. Malia opened hers up. It was all in French, written in unintelligible calligraphy. She ordered something called *du steak haché*, hoping it was a hamburger. Ciji picked the *spécialité de la maison*, also another glass of white.

When the waiter left, Malia asked, "*If* I get the assignment, and *if* I accept, who will be my editor?"

"Me. You're still too wet behind the ears to go with anyone else. A seven-million-dollar deal doesn't come along every day." She raised one eyebrow. "Now what do you mean, *if* you accept?"

Malia sipped her burgundy. It tasted thick and harsh, the way she liked it. "I don't know if writing someone's white-washed life story is something I want to do."

"How altruistic of you, darling."

"Maybe it is." Malia quickly finished off the other piece of breadstick. She was beginning to get irritated by this woman's attitude.

Ciji moved the vase filled with flowers away from the middle of the table, so she could see this young girl better. A knowing smile spread across her face. "You haven't worked in three months. Unless you have a trust fund, which I don't think you have, I'd say seventy-five thousand dollars should make your mouth water right about now."

Malia was more impressed than angry that Ciji had rummaged through her private life. "When can I meet the man?"

"Would tomorrow evening be too early?"

"You don't waste time."

"Not with the kind of money we're putting out."

"Where do I meet him?"

"At his ranch on the Big Island of Hawaii. He just bought a spread there last year when he retired. We'll fly you over first-class for the interview." She suddenly noticed Malia's skin turning pale. "Are you all right?"

Malia felt the blood draining from her face. "I'm fine," she whispered. "It's the heat." She brushed her damp forehead with her napkin.

"Are you afraid of flying?" Ciji rolled her eyes. "I don't think I could handle that."

Malia waved her hand. "I'll be fine."

"Good. If he wants you, we'll send you the contracts with the first part of the advance. Who's your agent?"

Malia shook her head. "I don't have one."

Ciji let out a deep breath. "Do you at least have a credit card?"

"What kind?"

The woman's lips tightened around her teeth again. "The kind you don't leave home without."

"I have one somewhere," Malia said. She picked up her shoulder bag from the floor and pulled out a handful of crushed tissues, old receipts, and a package of Wrigley's spearmint. Dropping them on the table, she continued the search.

Ciji brusquely waved her hand to stop her. "Find it later. Use it for expenses while you're there. Use it judiciously and send us the receipts. Your airline ticket will be messengered to you later on this evening." She looked the young woman over once more. "And do something with your hair for God's sake . . . pull it back or straighten it. There are no Rastafarians living in Hawaii."

Malia smiled. "Would the Marilyn Quayle flip make you happy?"

Ciji forced a return smile. "I don't think it would work on you, but *do* give it a try." She glanced down at Malia's antique dress. "Also think about treating yourself to a new wardrobe. You're meeting the next president of the United States, dear. You are not going to a barn raising for Bonnie and Clyde."

After Malia left the restaurant, she found her American Express credit card at the bottom of her bag and went to Saks to buy that wardrobe Ciji suggested. When she finished shopping, she caught a cab downtown. The transit strike was squeezing the life out of the city and it took her over an hour to get back to her loft in Tribeca.

Malia spent most of the evening packing and calling friends to see if one of them would take care of her Siamese cat while she was gone. Eventually she found a hesitant taker, her old boyfriend, and told him she'd leave the key under the mat for him.

After writing out her usual two-week-post-dated rent check, she went downstairs and slipped it under the super's door, tiptoeing away before he came out.

At nine o'clock, the airline ticket, as Ciji promised, arrived by messenger. Malia opened the envelope and saw that it was only a one-way ticket. Ciji told her that it was going to be an interview with Steinway, not a definite job offer. What if she decided not to take the assignment or Steinway didn't want her? How was she going to get back? At this moment, Malia realized that she didn't have much of a choice—there was no money in her bank account to cover the post-dated check.

By ten o'clock she was in bed, with the cat snuggled under her arm. She had a big day tomorrow. She wanted to be at the New York Public Library the first thing in the morning to research everything she could find on Steinway.

Sleep didn't come easy. Stroking the cat, she lay awake and thought about Hawaii. She hadn't been back since she was four years old . . . not since that terrible night. Perspiration, caused by her own fear, began to trickle down her neck and underarms. Would she be able to handle being on the island again? Would it bring back that old dread she thought she had put behind her? It had taken a long time for the night terrors to fade, even after she found out the police had shot and killed the man who'd murdered her parents.

Eventually she fell asleep. The white angel entered her dreams, something that hadn't happened in years. He was chasing her through the rain-swollen sugarcane field, holding a flaming sword above his head, trying to kill her.

She let out a small, terrified sob and wrapped her arms tightly around the sleeping cat.

Chapter Two

THE PRETTY BLOND stewardess smiled down at Malia. "Anything to drink?"

Malia looked up from the thick mass of Xeroxed papers on her lap. "A glass of Burgundy. Also a couple bags of peanuts."

"Peanuts are for tourist class. Try the cheese platter," the stewardess said, pouring the wine into a glass goblet.

Malia peered at the rolling tray filled with tired-looking Brie and other dried-out cheeses. "I think I'll stick with the peanuts."

Smiling, the stewardess whispered, "Good choice." She handed Malia the wine and two bags of salted almonds.

Malia tore one of them open with her teeth and poured half the contents into her mouth, downing them with a swig of Burgundy. Her eyes were tired. She'd spent most of the ten-hour flight going over the information she'd got on Steinway from the New York Public Library.

A fascinating, colorful character. An honest-to-God war hero. The American people adored him, putting him on a pedestal with the likes of Eisenhower and Schwarzkopf. He'd retired from army life last year as a four-star general and worked now as an occasional troubleshooter for the State Department. A condition of his retirement, one the army happily accepted, was that in case of an impending war, he would be returned to active duty.

Malia dug through the material on her lap and picked up an old newspaper clipping that had previously caught her attention. There was a photograph at the top of the article. It showed Steinway in army fatigues, with his arm around a primitive young Montagnard in the Vietnamese jungle. They were both smiling for the camera. The boy wore a brief loincloth that barely covered his groin, and his teeth were filed down to points. Steinway seemed to tower over the short, squat boy. The caption under the picture read:

COL. FELIX STEINWAY OF THE 175TH AIRBORNE DIVISION AND HIS PROTÉGÉ, TAANG

Malia read the article. It told how Steinway, a colonel then, while leading a reconnaissance mission against North Vietnamese insurgents, found sixteen-year-old Taang barely alive in a secluded area of the mountains. He was the only survivor of a remote village, and until now, never saw a white man. The Vietcong killed everyone, including his parents and the girl he was going to marry. Steinway took the boy under his wing and made him his orderly, then brought him back to the States.

She had heard about this strange mountain dweller. He was Steinway's constant companion, always standing somewhere in the background whenever the general appeared in public.

Something in the article touched her. Taang's parents were savagely murdered, like her own. He was also taken away from his natural habitat and reared in an alien world of concrete—like she was.

The more she read about Steinway, the more she realized his complexity, and the more she began to respect him. He wasn't made from the same cookie cutter that produced most West Point graduates, meaning he wasn't afraid to speak his mind. Being an outspoken critic on the way the Vietnam conflict was handled by the Pentagon didn't stop him from being a brilliant, deadly warrior on the battlefield. His tactics were swift and ruthless, causing a high enemy casualty rate—and earning him the salty nickname of "Pit Viper" by his men. The Cong feared him more than the napalm that fell from the skies. Yet, with his virulent reputation, he still found the time to save the life of a native boy and raise him as his son.

Malia finished off her wine, wondering if she'd be able to handle a man of such epic, conflicting proportions. Well, she'd soon find out.

When the island of Hawaii passed by the wing of the plane, she leaned back in her seat and stared down at the green island. A nervous tinge passed through her. After all these years, she was coming home.

She was met in the terminal by Thomas, the general's driver. He was a friendly, potbellied Hawaiian in his early sixties. His face broke out into a gapped-tooth grin. *"Aloha 'auinala,"* he said.

Not understanding, Malia just returned his smile. The man had mistaken her for a native because of her Polynesian features. She was a *hapa haole*, part Hawaiian, but she knew nothing of her mother's language, nor of the culture.

Thomas grabbed her bags from the conveyer belt and carried them to the Jeep parked out in front.

Having grown up in a smog-infested city, she was not used to the blinding tropical sun. She slid gratefully into the cool leather seat of the air-conditioned car.

As the Jeep turned north on the highway, she put on her sunglasses and looked out at the miles of black lava rock that made up this part of the island. Its dark, porous fingers spread over the earth as far as she could see. The landscape was eerie, like that of a dead, charred planet. Once again, the restlessness gripped her body, as if the white angel had come down from the sky and brushed her face with its wing.

The barren Kona Coast soon gave way to lush pastures, surrounded by Norfolk and Australian pines. Cattle and Hawaiian cowboys—*paniolos*—dotted the flourishing fields.

Her mood began to change. She became alive. It was all so familiar, yet totally unfamiliar. She rolled down the car-door window and inhaled deeply. The visual memories of her homeland were gone, but her primal senses somehow remembered the warm, sweet smell of jacarandas and heliconias. She caught a glimpse of herself as a small child running through these fields, picking the colorful, fragrant flowers. In the background, her mother was watching, laughing.

Malia suddenly felt lost, as if she no longer knew who she was or what part of the world she belonged to. She quickly rolled up the window and sat back in the seat.

An hour later, the general's ranch came into view. The large house hugged the rim of a cliff that overlooked the Pacific. Brilliant green pastures surrounded it on all three sides. It was a sprawling compound of Spanish architecture, built over a hundred and forty years ago. Brightly colored bougainvillea clung stubbornly to its walls, making the house warm and inviting.

The sun was beginning to touch down on the water, causing the sky to erupt in splashes of yellows and oranges.

Thomas pulled the Jeep into the driveway. Malia stepped out of the car and walked toward the ranch.

A dinner table, surrounded by several chairs, was set up on the lawn. Standing over it was an attractive, copper-skinned Hawaiian girl. She appeared sluggish as she placed the proper silverware around the dishes.

Then Malia saw the general and her mouth went dry.

He was standing by a pit at the corner of the house, getting ready to remove a cooked pig wrapped in taro leaves. Letting out a loud grunt, he picked up the dead carcass in his huge hands and placed it on a metal table.

The general was a much larger man than he seemed on TV—at least six foot five. His jowls hung loosely on his face, and his tall, stooped frame made him look like a palm tree bending in the wind. The tropical breeze from the ocean was blowing his thinning hair in all directions. He had on baggy, khaki pants and a bright green golf shirt.

As she walked up the pebbled pathway, the general turned in her direction. His eyes tightened for a moment, then his face cracked into a large, pleasant smile. He wiped the pig fat from his hands onto his pants and went down the steps to greet her.

"Malia Rico, right?" he said.

"Yes, sir. That's me."

He held out his hand and she shook it. It felt wet and greasy. She had to stretch her neck up in order to see his face.

The name "Pit Viper" didn't seem to go with his warm smile, she thought.

"I'm glad you came," he said cheerfully. He gave her shoulders a small squeeze, engulfing them in his long fingers.

She tried to hold in her nervousness, but she knew it was registering on her face.

His eyes, filled with intensity, beamed down on her. "Peachie is in town. When she gets back, I want you to meet her."

Malia knew Peachie was the general's wife.

"I hope you like steamed pig."

Her smile turned to confusion. "I don't know."

He chuckled loudly. "Hell, I thought all Hawaiians liked to eat pig. You are Hawaiian, aren't you? Ciji told me you were."

"By birth."

"I cooked this sow especially for you, so you'd better eat the damn thing." There was a mischievous scowl on his face.

She glanced over at the dead animal. Its mouth was frozen in a silly grin and its cloudy eyes stared lifelessly back at her, as if waiting for her answer.

"Does it get served with the eyes?" she asked.

Again the chuckle. "Hell, it's the best part. Why don't I have Lupe take you to your room. We can talk later on." He winked at her.

She nodded, suppressing the feeling to wink back.

Steinway motioned to the sullen-faced girl setting the table. She shrugged and came over. With her dull eyes focused on the ground, she gave Malia a short, bashful smile.

Steinway then turned and walked back to the pig and began to peel the leaves off its pink skin.

Lupe's shapely hips sashayed from left to right as she sauntered toward the house. Malia followed her inside and up the wood-planked stairs. At the end of the hallway, the girl opened the door to a small bedroom. Malia went in.

The oak bed and the furniture had to be as old as the ranch, Malia thought.

Standing by the door, Lupe asked, "Can I get you anythin'?" She spoke in the guttural, pidgin English of the island.

"I don't think so," Malia said.

The girl's lips pursed into an obligatory smile, then she slowly turned and went back downstairs.

A minute later, Thomas walked in carrying her bags. He set them down on the floor and opened the drapes. "Good room. To the *makai* side," he said. "The man must like you to let you have it. The general don't give this room to many people."

"What's *makai*?" Malia asked.

The driver smiled at her ignorance. "Everythin' on the island is either to the *makai* side or to the *mauka* side. *Makai* is to the sea. That's where you want to be," he said, pointing to the ocean outside the window. "*Mauka* is everythin' else." He made a face and brushed his hand in the other direction.

"How long have you been working for him?"

"Since he came to the island a year ago. Good man. He treat everybody well. If I didn't work for him, I'd be servin' Mai Tais to Japanese tourists at some fancy hotel in Kona." He grimaced. "Not a good way to make a livin'."

Malia caught a glimpse of the servant girl outside the window. She was working at the table again, putting napkins in water glasses.

The driver looked down at Lupe and smiled in acknowledgment. "Pretty girl. Not much up here." He pointed to his temple. "She got plenty *pilikia*." Again realizing Malia didn't know Hawaiian, he said, "Means the gal got a lot of problems. Don't talk to nobody around here. Got a boyfriend that treats her mean. Sometimes he beats her. How smart could she be, if she lets him do that?"

The man had a point, Malia thought.

When he left, she opened up her suitcase. Uncertain whether she'd get the job, Malia only unpacked a few things. She hung a light cotton, sleeveless dress up on the door of the closet to air out; it was one of the ones she'd bought at Saks. It was too conservative for her taste, but when in Rome . . .

God, was she tired. The down mattress on the bed called out to her, but it would have to wait. First, she needed to do a lot more boning up on the general if she was going to get through their interview. He came off like a country bumpkin with her just now, but she knew he was no easy mark. The man was supposed to have a 175 IQ.

After taking a long, hot shower to wash away the fatigue of

the ten-hour plane trip, she wrapped a towel around her body and sat on the small couch next to the window. Opening up her attaché case, she took out a handful of papers that she hadn't read yet, along with her yellow notepad.

The evening sun was flaring directly into her eyes and she stood up to close the drapes. Glancing outside, she saw the short, gnomelike figure of someone standing by the black boulders of the cliff peering up at her window. By the time she cupped her hand over her eyes to get a better look, he had disappeared.

Malia already knew who it was. Steinway had his arm around that odd little body in the news clipping she saw earlier today. It was the Montagnard, Taang.

Chapter Three

MALIA AWOKE IN darkness to the sound of laughter and voices coming from outside on the lawn. Groping for the lamp on the table, she turned it on and glanced at her watch. Eight-thirty. Shit! She didn't mean to sleep that long.

Stepping over the newspaper clippings scattered on the floor, she quickly changed into her new dress and put on a pair of sandals that she'd also bought at Saks. The straps were stiff and rubbed against her ankles. After hastily passing a brush through her hair, she went downstairs and out onto the lanai.

Torches lit up the area surrounding the dinner table on the lawn. Steinway, along with a slightly horse-faced woman and three other men, was already seated and waiting for her.

Malia knew the woman was Peachie, the general's wife. She'd seen her on several talk shows and remembered her as being bright and articulate, a person who was deeply loyal to her husband.

Seated next to the general was a short, squat man, with thick-boned Asian features and large white teeth.

Taang, she thought.

The Montagnard was wearing a bright Hawaiian shirt with jeans, and his hair was pulled back into a chignon. A small, bone-handled knife jutted out from the knot.

A well-groomed, middle-aged Japanese man wearing a police uniform sat directly across from Taang. Next to him was a good-looking Hawaiian with the mixed blood of a *hapa*.

The conversation stopped when Malia approached. The men, except for Taang, stood up.

"Sorry I'm late," she said.

"Nonsense, we haven't even started yet," Steinway said, putting his arm around her shoulder. "Damn, you look beautiful in that dress! What did I tell you, Peachie?"

The general's wife put down her wineglass and scanned Malia's figure with slightly reddened eyes. Her skin was sallow, making her red hair even more pronounced. "You were too modest in your description of her, dear." The woman held out her hand and shook Malia's with a loose grip.

The good-looking *hapa* man smiled sheepishly. He was dressed in a khaki summer suit with a blue polo shirt opened at the top. "I have to agree with Peachie. You downplayed her beauty, Felix."

"Sit down. Sit down," the general ordered Malia, pulling out a chair from the table.

She quietly slid into her chair across from Steinway and placed her napkin on her lap.

"This is Professor Daniel Keahi, an anthropologist from UCLA," the general said, motioning to the *hapa* man.

Keahi's handshake was warm and friendly. His name was familiar to Malia, but she couldn't place it. Perhaps she had read an article of his somewhere.

He introduced her to Isaac Yamaguchi, the district police captain, then to Taang.

The Montagnard did not shake hands with Malia. He sat studying her face for a moment, then opened his mouth and smiled, exposing large white teeth. His intelligent black eyes faded into the fatty pouches around his lids.

An unexplainable chill ran down Malia's back when she realized those big teeth of his were false.

Lupe, standing over the serving tray next to the table, was cutting up the pig. Malia watched carefully to see what she would do with the eyes. When Lupe discarded them into a plastic bag along with the innards, she suddenly realized the general had been teasing her this afternoon.

The conversation between the men continued where it left off. Only Peachie and Taang did not join in. The general's wife, with a bored expression, sipped her wine and stared hazily out into the dark night. Taang, his brow furrowed, was busily scrutinizing his forks, trying to remember if he was supposed to use the small one or the large one with the vegetable salad.

Malia listened, piecing together what the men were talking about. It had something to do with ancient Hawaiian customs.

"The Polynesians, before Cook discovered the islands, were brave, primitive sons of bitches, the kind of fighters I'd like to have with me in battle," Steinway said.

"They were also a violent people," Keahi quickly answered back. "Legend says, after they killed Cook, they peeled back his head and ate his brain."

Peachie's face paled. "My God, why would they do that?"

Keahi shrugged. "It was a sign of respect. If you ate the brain of an esteemed enemy it would make you smarter."

The general laughed. "I could live with that if they were good warriors."

"I also don't know if I would consider them primitive. A bit bloodthirsty, perhaps," Keahi said.

"Why bloodthirsty?" Malia asked, feeling foolish that she didn't know much about her own people.

"They were a highly structured society divided up into classes. If you weren't from royalty, your life wasn't worth much. The *ali'is*, or chiefs, put taboos, known as *kapus*, on everything. When they were broken, the punishment was usually death."

"What kind of taboos?" Malia inquired.

He turned to her and smiled. "Two hundred years ago a woman couldn't eat at the same table with the men like we're doing now, nor could she share the same food."

An incredulous expression lined Malia's face. "And they were killed for that?"

The smile lingered on his face. "Absolutely."

Peachie, tired of the conversation, sighed with weariness. She refilled her wineglass once more.

When the sow was sliced up, Lupe put pieces of pork on everyone's plate. She then tied up the plastic bag containing the uncooked organs and took them into the house.

"What does she do with them?" Malia asked curiously.

Peachie frowned. "They're for Mr. Taang's breakfast. He loves munching on little animal parts."

Malia looked over at Taang. He was staring at Peachie with vacant eyes.

"His preferences are different than ours," Steinway said, glaring at his wife. There was a warning tone in his voice.

"And so they are," Peachie answered back, with a bitter smirk. She took a large swallow of her wine, then put down the glass and wiped her ruffled lips with her napkin. "He's our little mascot," she said, turning to Malia. "The pet store ran out of pit bulls, so we got him instead."

"Enough, Peach," Steinway said. It was now an order.

Smiling sarcastically, she put her hands up in surrender. "Sorry, Felix. He's all yours."

The table grew silent.

Again Malia looked at Taang. His expression hadn't changed, but the blackness of his eyes seemed deeper, like pits of boiling tar.

Malia suddenly turned to Daniel. "What kind of anthropology do you teach, Mr. Keahi?"

"Polynesian anthropology," he said, appreciating her attempt to break the stillness. He put some poi on his plate, then gave the tray to Malia. She took a look at the chalky paste, wrinkled her nose, and passed it on to the general.

"I grew up on this island," Daniel said. "My parents moved to the mainland many years ago."

"What brings you back?"

"An ancient *heiau* was uncovered not too far from here. It's a human sacrificial temple that was used to appease the god, Kūka'ilimoku. I'm here to examine it. We think it has to be at least a thousand years old."

His voice was pleasant and his smile sincere. She found herself drawn to him.

He continued. "My expertise is in Hawaiian warfare. The ancient islanders were a very sophisticated killing machine."

"Excellent tacticians, too," Steinway said. "Glad it wasn't me who had to fight them. The Montagnards would have given them a good run for their money, though. I never saw such fierce, devoted soldiers like those mountain people." Beaming, he put his hand on Taang's shoulder. "This man here was the best. In Vietnam, I once watched him crawl on his stomach over to a unit of VCs in broad daylight and disembowel them one by one. The bastards never knew what hit them." He let out a raucous laugh.

Peachie pursed her mouth as if she'd tasted something bitter, then filled her glass once more, this time to the rim.

During dessert, Malia turned to the police captain. "I used to live on this island. I remember meeting a man who had your job."

"You must mean Ben Lopaka," Isaac Yamaguchi said.

"I never knew his name."

The captain nodded. "He was a good man."

"What happened to him?"

"A terrible tragedy. It broke apart his family . . . almost destroyed him."

Malia could sense a darkness coming over the policeman. "What happened?"

"There was a terrible murder on the island twenty years ago. A man and his wife. I'm originally from Maui. I just got out of the army and decided to make this island my home. I took a job with the district police. I'd only been on the force for a month when it happened."

He was talking about her parents, Malia realized. She forced down the rush of emotions that were sweeping over her.

Isaac cut the cake on his plate into small, exact bites with his fork. "The man was a *haole* from the mainland, his wife was pure Hawaiian. They both worked at the sugar mill. The killings took place on the anniversary of Hawaiian statehood. I remember because there was a fireworks display that night. I was on duty when I received a call from the victims' neighbor saying that she'd heard a small child crying out in the nearby sugarcane fields. It was in the Hāmākua District and very isolated. It was a bad night, the rain was coming down in buckets. When I arrived, the people who'd made the phone call told me the couple down the hill had a small girl. I listened carefully through the heavy rain, trying to hear her cries." He looked at Malia. "Eventually I heard them. A child's cry is unlike any other sound."

Malia looked away from his eyes.

"I first went to their house. The door was open and I entered. When I discovered the dead couple in their bed, I called for backup. Then I called Ben Lopaka, who was our district captain at the time."

Malia bit down on her lip and glanced at everyone's face. All eyes, except for Daniel's, were riveted on Isaac Yamaguchi.

"Did you ever find the girl?" Peachie asked.

"Lopaka did. He discovered her in the fields, hiding out in an old, unused fish pond. A teenage boy, the neighbor's son, was bending over the pond, trying to get her out."

Peachie put her hand to her mouth and gasped. "That poor thing."

Isaac took a sip of his coffee, dabbed his lips with the napkin, then said, "The girl was in the bedroom that night. She saw it all."

These people, total strangers until tonight, were talking about her, Malia thought. She forced down the urge to say something. She glanced over at Daniel Keahi. He was staring down at his plate, looking uncomfortable.

"How were they killed?" Steinway asked. He seemed fascinated by this story.

"A good question," Isaac said, stabbing a piece of cake with his fork and putting it into his mouth. He chewed several times, swallowed, then said, "The bodies were mutilated, especially the woman's."

"What kind of weapon was used?" the general probed.

The policeman shook his head. "We don't know if it *was* a weapon. The contusions were made from the teeth of a great white shark. One of the incisors had broken off and was found in the wound of the female victim."

Malia never knew this. "Was sea water found in their lungs?" she asked.

"No. They were killed on land."

"Then how could a shark do that?" she said.

"I didn't say it did."

"And the killer?" Steinway said. "Was he ever caught?"

"He was caught all right. Lopaka shot and killed him. We found boot imprints on the floors of the house and by the edge of the pond. They were the kind of imprints found on rubber galoshes that *paniolos* wear."

"Oh, my!" Peachie blurted out. "If the imprints were next to the pond, then he must have been trying to get to the child."

Isaac nodded.

"What happened to the girl?" the general asked.

"She left the island soon afterward. I heard she went to live with relatives on the mainland, somewhere back East. I don't know what happened to her after that."

"How did you find your killer?" Daniel asked, pouring himself a cup of coffee.

Isaac meticulously wiped the corners of his mouth again with his napkin. "It wasn't very hard. There was a *paniolo* named Panali who worked at a cattle ranch nearby and had a reputation for violence. He'd been in trouble with the law many times. We found his neckerchief, a red bandanna, on the floor of the victims' house. When I went to the bunkhouse where he lived, he'd already fled. I did, however, find a gold bracelet under his bed that belonged to the murdered woman. We got a search warrant. His car turned up in the town of Honokaá. We went through it and found a pair of soiled rubber boots. The imprints on the soles and the boot size were an exact match to the ones found at the murder scene."

Malia tried to control her voice. "Why did this affect Ben Lopaka?"

"It was an unfortunate situation. Panali turned out to be Ben's brother-in-law. After we found the boots and the bracelet, he felt he should be the one to arrest him. We got word that Panali was holding out in this bar in Puna and was drinking heavily. Ben went inside by himself. That was a mistake. Panali was a wild man when drunk. When Ben tried to read him his rights, Panali attacked him with a knife. Ben shot and killed him. The man was his wife's brother. She never forgave him. She left Ben, taking the children with her. He became a drunk and lost his job. He now lives in the Waipìo Valley and grows taro to survive."

"How sad," Peach said, clucking her tongue.

Malia's eyes grew clouded with confusion. "What did this Panali know about sharks if he was a *paniolo*?"

Isaac shrugged. "The man is dead. We'll never know."

The general abruptly stood up and put his arm on Malia's

shoulder. "I hate to break this up, but this gal and I have some talking to do." Holding up his hand, he said to his guests, "Sit. Finish your coffee. We'll take ours in the study." For a brief moment his expression grew grave when he noticed Peachie eyeing the bottles of after-dinner drinks on the portable bar, then he took Malia's arm and walked her toward the house.

Oak furniture and a dark, well-worn leather couch filled the den. Every inch of wall space was covered with framed photographs taken of Steinway along with leaders from many countries.

He sat down on the chair and motioned for her to take the couch. There was nothing hokey-looking about him now. His face was set and his eyes were fired with shrewdness.

She forced down the fear banging around in her stomach.

Steinway was in no rush. He took out a long, fat cigar from the humidor on the desk and slowly lit it.

"Cuban. I get them from Canada. The only kind worth smoking," he said. He blew out a long trail of smoke, then stared at the cylindrical roll of tobacco in his hand. "I hate Cuba. The only man who ever bullshitted me and got away with it was Castro." Steinway grinned. "One day Cuba will be part of the free world and we'll be doing business with them again." Winking, he said, "I could wait until then or smoke it now."

At first the interview went well. He asked simple questions about her background. She responded with answers she'd rehearsed on the plane.

They were interrupted by Lupe walking in carrying a tray holding a silver coffee urn and a quarter-filled glass of Maalox. She placed it on his desk, poured Malia a cup of coffee, then gave the antacid to the general. When she leaned over him, he grabbed her arm and whispered something in her ear. She nodded and left.

After Lupe closed the door, Steinway grumbled, "Lousy ulcers. I have to drink a quart of this stuff a day." He quickly downed the Maalox, wiped his mouth with his hand, let out a small belch, and set the glass down on the lamp table.

Then he brought up the article she had written on General Mortimer Crowe. "He was a damn decent man," he said emphatically.

"I thought so, too," she said.

"Very underrated. I knew him when I was a boy. He was a good friend of my father's. They went to West Point together. He came to my house quite often, used to bounce me on his knee. You caught his soul, captured the man like I remembered him. That's a rarity in biographies. Most of them are nothing but glazed-over crap."

"Thank you," she said.

Then his eyes narrowed. "Some of your research, however, I found questionable."

Malia could feel the mood change in the room. "What did you find questionable?"

He turned the cigar over in his fingers, studying it. "You made some serious allegations about Crowe."

She knew what he was alluding to. "Are you talking about his homosexuality?"

His lips tightened. "Yes, I am."

She took a deep breath. "My research was accurate."

"Was it? Homosexuals were not allowed in the army during that time. The few that got through certainly didn't rise to the rank of general."

"Mortimer Crowe was *the* exception. The army needed him. He was a brilliant covert strategist with the OSS. He understood operative warfare better than anyone. The reason he was so underrated by the military was *because* of his homosexuality. Instead of giving him a ticker-tape parade down Broadway when the war was over, they give him a desk job in Berlin."

His face reddened. "That's a bunch of bullshit!"

The words sprang from his mouth like darts, startling her. What was this all about? Ciji Brown told her that Steinway liked her article on Crowe. Wasn't that why he was interviewing her? "I only wrote what I believed was factual and could be substantiated."

"And we can't ask General Crowe about this nonsense because he's been dead for forty years."

"That's correct."

"Murdered, according to you."

She shook her head. "I never used the word *murdered*. I said he died under suspicious circumstances. That was the belief of the German detective who was assigned to the case. I traced him down and interviewed him."

Steinway grunted at her story. "The entire German police department and the U.S. military said it was a broken gas pipe that killed him while he slept. One man says it was murder, and you go along with his version. Very objective reporting."

She held her ground, refusing to be intimidated. "His story made sense. Berlin was going through a heat wave. There was no air-conditioning in those days. The temperatures were well above ninety, yet all of Crowe's windows in his bedroom were closed. The gas pipes were recently installed and made of copper. I checked with a mineralogist. Copper piping, especially when new, just doesn't break for no reason."

"You mentioned Crowe's orderly in the article."

"What about him?"

"Do you remember his name?"

"No. He was an Italian boy Crowe found in Rome. He eventually took him to Berlin with him."

Steinway stared hard at her face, studying it. "His name was Giuseppe Rigutini. You should read what you write."

Malia had a blank expression. "I don't remember his name. I wrote the article three years ago. What about him?"

"You said he disappeared right after Crowe died."

"He did. I tried to find him. I couldn't."

A blue vein bulged from Steinway's temple. "Do you think he was diddling around with the general? Maybe they had a lover's quarrel and Giuseppe killed him."

Malia was confused. "Maybe," she said. "I don't know about their personal relationship. That wasn't the reason for writing the article."

Steinway's eyes were searing through her like hot embers. "I think you've ruined the name of a great general just to get published."

She stayed locked on to his face. "I wrote the truth."

"Did you now?"

"Yes."

"And if I gave you the freedom to write *my* book, what would you say about me? That I was also a goddamn pansy?"

Oh, Christ. She saw the job slipping away. "If it *was* the truth, I suppose I would write about it. However, I wouldn't put it in a derogatory context the way you just did."

"I read some of your other articles on the military. You write about generals, but you don't seem to like them much."

"I simply questioned why a man would choose that profession."

"And why would he?"

Drops of sweat trickled down her neck. "Perhaps he felt the need for absolute power."

"Power?" He smiled sarcastically. "Is that what your fascination with generals is all about?"

"Power has a lot to do with it."

"There's another reason you're overlooking," he said.

"What's that?"

His eyes became alive. "To protect and serve one's country." He stood up and moved toward her, then bent down until his face was inches from hers. "My God! Why the *hell* would I want to use someone like you?"

She could smell the mixture of milk and tobacco on his breath. "Maybe because the book wouldn't be that kind of glazed-over crap you seem to detest so much."

"No, it would probably be slanted immature babble, written by a self-absorbed little girl who never saw a soldier die and who doesn't understand the first thing about devotion and patriotism."

There was no reason she had to take this any longer. She leapt off the couch and tried to open the door. It was locked. She shook the knob several times, then looked back at Steinway.

His expression was placid now, showing no traces of anger. He was calmly puffing away on his cigar. "I asked Lupe to lock the door on her way out," he said tranquilly.

Was that a smile etched around the corners of his mouth? Then she understood. "You were testing me, weren't you?"

That charming glow was back on his face. "Bet your sweet ass I was. If I continued asking you stock questions, you would have continued giving me rehearsed stock answers. That's not what I'm looking for. Ciji Brown wants a book about the great American hero—the man who gave respectability back to this country after the Vietnam fiasco. Hell, there're plenty of those goddamn unauthorized biographies like that about me right now. I don't need to add my name to another one. What I want to do is tell it straight. And I need someone to help me do that—someone who doesn't turn into mashed potatoes every time I look at her." His teeth clenched down on the cigar.

"What happened to the first writer Ciji sent you?"

"Jasper Rhodes! That yahoo! A worthless hack. He peed in his pants every time I walked into the room."

The general went over to his desk drawer and pulled out a bottle of French cognac. He took out two paper cups, half filled them with the brandy, and handed her one. "To a partnership," he said, tapping his cup against hers. He smiled. "You got balls. I like that."

She took a sip. The liquor burned her stomach.

Steinway finished off his drink in one gulp. "I don't know about Crowe's death, but you were right on the money about his homosexuality, sweetheart. He may have been queer, but he had one of the best military minds I ever ran across. He was also a great patriot. The army did a terrible injustice to him."

"Can I quote you on that in the book?"

"Hell, yes! Say that I admired that faggot even more than I did that pistol-toting egotist, Patton." A loud guffaw erupted from him. "That should make the toes of the Pentagon curl." He filled his cup again.

The anger she felt for him a few minutes ago ebbed. She liked his outspokenness. Not many generals she met had that quality. "I hope I keep the job longer than your last writer."

"So do I," he said quietly. With his sharp eyes focused on her face, he sat back in the chair, put his feet up on the desk, and blew steel-colored smoke rings from his circular lips. "I want you to go over the reams of documents the other guy, Rhodes, collected about me before I canned him. There're a couple of thousand pages sitting on your desk waiting for you. See what you can use. You have three days to do it in."

"Is this another test?"

"Bet your sweet ass." He stared out the window and emitted several more perfectly formed rings from his mouth.

Malia found it hard to sleep that night. The ungodly quiet of the island was louder than the worst street noises of New York. Tired of twisting in bed, she got up, put on a pair of shorts and a T-shirt, and quietly walked barefoot downstairs. The lights were off. Everyone in the house was asleep.

The French doors leading to the cliffs were open. She went out into the balmy air and walked toward the moonlit green fields overlooking the steep cliff. The night was so clear that the millions of stars overhead burned her eyes.

Stars. Something else she wasn't used to. The only time she saw them in New York was when the city was in a "blackout." She strolled over to a lava boulder jutting out of the earth next to the precipice. In the darkness below, she could faintly hear waves lapping gently against the rocks.

If she kept the assignment, she would be on the island for at least eight months. A long time to be away from New York. Then she thought about the man she'd met tonight, Daniel Keahi. Where had she heard that name before? There was something about him that she liked. It was more than his looks. There was an air of confidence about him. When he spoke, even Steinway listened with respect.

Her mind suddenly went back to that night of her parents' murders. She was in the room, saw everything—only she had so little memory of it. But it was there—a dark, heavy mass lying in the pit of her stomach, waiting to get out.

Right after their funeral, she was sent to live on the mainland with her uncle on Staten Island. Like her father, he was also from Corsica. He was an abusive, illiterate man, not nearly as admirable as Taang's general.

She remembered Ben Lopaka, the kind district police captain, wrapping her in a blanket. He told her the angel was only a bogeyman. "Fears of a four-year-old."

Several years ago she went through hypnosis to help deal with this dread that wouldn't go away. Bits and pieces of that night emerged from those sessions:

> *Running madly through the sugarcane field to get away from the white angel ... hiding in a cold, murky pond ... feelings of total terror ... hands reaching out to her ... water filling her lungs ... gasping for air.*

That was all. The segments were never put together to form a total picture.

To this day she believed Ben Lopaka was wrong—the angel she saw in the bedroom was real.

Noises coming from behind some rocks about fifty yards

away interrupted her musing. She arched her head in that direction. They were human voices, heavy and guttural. The sounds of lovemaking. Embarrassed, she got up and started to walk away.

The grunting abruptly turned into angry voices. She didn't understand what they were saying because they were talking in Hawaiian. The words became louder and more argumentative.

Then she heard a slap, followed by the woman sobbing. There was another slap, then another. The woman let out a muffled scream every time she was hit.

Concerned, Malia walked toward the rocks, kicking her feet into the sand, making noise. Perhaps if they knew she was here, the beating would stop.

It worked. The argument subsided. There was a deadly stillness on the other side of the rocks now. Then Malia saw the dark shadow of someone darting out from behind the boulders and racing across the pasture. The moon caught the figure in its muted light. It was Lupe. She was holding the ripped portion of her muumuu up to her chest.

Malia watched her run into the servants' quarters of the house. Then she looked back toward the ominous black boulders. Whoever Lupe was with, was still behind them.

The back of her neck prickled in fear. She knew the man was watching her. She could practically feel his heat emanating from the darkness. Every instinct in her body told her to move away, and to do it quickly.

Without taking her eyes off the rocks, she walked back to the ranch house. Only when she was safely inside, and the French doors locked, did she finally feel secure enough to look away.

Chapter Four

"**S**AY, *BRAH*, HOWZIT?" Thomas said, slapping Ben Lopaka on the back, making the ex–police captain spill part of his coffee on the bar counter.

Ben looked up from his half-finished plate of stew and saw the general's driver sitting down next to him. "Howzit yourself, Tommy? *Pau* for the day?"

"*Pau* for the day . . . all done. The general is tucked in his bed, nice an' comfy, drinkin' his milk and watchin' TV." He ordered a draft and waved to several men sitting at the other end of the bar.

The saloon was a local hangout in the town of Hāwī. Neon signs advertising PABST BLUE RIBBON and BUD hung over the bar wall. Men, contemplating a shot, surrounded a worn felt pool table in the back. There were no *haoles* here. Most of the patrons were *paniolos* who worked the cattle ranches nearby, or hotel employees from the Kona Coast.

"You still farmin' taro?" Thomas asked Ben.

"It's a livin'," Ben said.

"What kind of livin' is that, breakin' your back all day, trudging through a muddy *lo'i*, baggin' leaves into a sack?"

Lopaka's wrinkled brown face cracked into a grin. "A livin' that don't require me to sit on my fat ass all day, drivin' some bored ol' man 'round his property."

"*Shaka, brah.*" He high-fived Lopaka, then broke into laughter, exposing his gapped teeth. "The big man is bored as hell. He don' know what to do with himself. Half the time he walks aroun' in his bathrobe starin' out at the *paniolos* or out at the ocean." His beer came. He drank half of it down in one gulp, then wiped the foam from his mouth with the back of his hand. "They say he gonna run for president of the country someday."

"That's what I hear. I also hear he's writin' a book."

"He ain't writin' it, *brah*. He got some young *hapa* girl doin' it. A real nice *wahine*. So fine she could make the snow on Mauna Kea melt. I picked her up at the airport a couple of days ago."

"She a local?"

"Was. I think you know her."

Ben looked up from his cup. "I do?"

"*Ae*. Remember that killin' twenty years ago?"

"Which one?"

"You know, man. The *haole* that was married to the pure-blood. You should remember. You killed your brother-in-law for it."

An old pain that was lodged in Lopaka's stomach resurfaced. "Who's the girl, man?"

"She was their daughter."

Ben moved his dinner plate away and edged closer to Thomas. "Her name Malia Rico?"

"*Ya, ya, ya*. That's the one. I don' think the general knows what happened to her parents an' I didn't say nothin' to him."

The ex–police captain quickly finished off his coffee and stood up.

"Where you stay go?" Thomas said in pidgin talk.

"Home, man."

"Stay, *brah*. I buy you another cup. Coffee's cheap."

Ben slapped a few dollars on the bar for his dinner. "Got no time."

"The taro ain't goin' nowhere."

Ben didn't answer. He was already out the door.

It was raining outside, like it always did on this side of the island. Ben got into his bright yellow, twenty-five-year-old Land Cruiser and sped down the road toward Honokaá.

He lived alone in a small house in the Waipi'o Valley. The road down was narrow and steep. Tourists weren't allowed to drive it without experienced guides. That was all right with him; it meant that it was one part of the island that couldn't be developed.

He thought about that frightened little girl who sat shaking in his truck twenty years ago.

How his life had changed since that night. He'd lost all he'd had because of it.

Everything pointed to his brother-in-law, Panali. He didn't want to believe it at first, but he had no choice. The evidence was overwhelming: Panali's neckerchief, the woman's bracelet found under his bed, his boot prints all over the place.

His brother-in-law was a mean bugga. Always high on Maui weed and alcohol. He'd had to lock him up several times for fighting and stealing.

Panali was his wife's younger brother. Her favorite. When her mother died, she raised him like he was her own son. She would plead with Ben to leave him alone. "The man doesn't mean no harm," she'd say. "He's just wild. He'll settle down one day."

The police captain didn't share his wife's belief. The man was beyond wild, he was mean and vicious. Ben always knew he would die violently. He just didn't figure he would be the one to help it along.

He'd had no choice.

Panali was drunk and pulled out a knife.

Panali, his eyes glazed over with hate and alcohol, told him, "Fuck you, man! You ain't gonna put me in no jail for killin' nobody."

Ben held out his hand for the knife, something he shouldn't have done.

Panali lashed out with it, cutting Ben's palm, severing the muscle between his fingers. He then came at Ben, with the knife raised above his head.

No, he'd had no choice.

When he told his wife he shot and killed her brother, she screamed and hit him as hard as she could, then collapsed on the floor and cried. She locked herself in the bedroom for days, refusing to let him sleep in the same bed with her. He camped out on the couch at the police station. After Panali's funeral, she moved to Kaua'i, taking his six children with her.

Without family, he couldn't feel whole. His life spiraled downward. Alcohol took the place of the emptiness inside him. He could no longer do his work, and sometimes didn't even bother to show up. The district council eventually had him replaced. After a year of hard drinking, he sobered up and found himself dead broke. With six children to feed on Kaua'i, he began to grow taro on his small piece of land to earn some money.

That was twenty years ago.

No, nothing had been the same since that night.

Ben parked the truck outside his house and ran for the door. He had forgotten to take his raincoat and he was soaking wet.

His walls were filled with photographs of his children at various ages in their lives. Four sons and two daughters.

The youngest daughter, Aka, one of the twins, died in a car accident several years ago. She was buried on the island next to his wife, Sarah. His other children, now grown, were doing well. David was a doctor in Boston; Ruth, a history professor at Kansas University. His oldest son, Keith, was a police lieutenant in New York City. Aka's twin, John, lived on O'ahu and managed one of the big hotels on the island. Jerome, his middle son, flew commercial airlines for American.

They were all successful, and his heart filled with pride every time he looked at their pictures. It also filled with sadness because he hardly ever saw them. Except for John, they all lived thousands of miles away.

He looked at the large painting of Sarah in the center of the wall surrounded by the photos of her children. It was done when they were still living together, when she still loved him.

Ben made some hot tea to warm up. The aches in his bones were working overtime tonight. He had arthritis in his legs, and the dampness didn't help. A few years ago his doctor suggested he move to Arizona, where the climate was dry. He went out and bought a magazine on the state and looked at the pictures. Nothing but lizards and rattlesnakes. He figured he could live with the pain a lot better than he could live in a place that catered to those kinds of critters.

Ben took the tea into the bedroom and opened up the top drawer of his dresser, where he kept his socks and underwear. He dug around inside until he found what he wanted. It was Panali's old, folded bandanna. He slowly unfurled it, until the shark's tooth was exposed.

What did Panali use to kill the two people with? This tooth belonged to a great white. The coroner's office and the FBI had come up with nothing.

None of it made any sense, including Panali committing the murders. There was no question that the son of a bitch was capable of doing it. He was *pupule*—crazy. But the man would do it with a knife or a broken beer bottle. How did they die from shark bites?

Everything was so easy to find—the bandanna, the gold bracelet under his bed, the boots in his car. It was almost *too* easy. A blind man could have found them. Panali was stupid, a real *lōlō* head, but even he would get rid of that kind of incriminating evidence. Why didn't he? There were not too many crazies in this small district. Didn't he know that he'd be the first one the police would suspect?

That question had bothered him for twenty years.

Now the girl was back. Thomas said she was a real *wahine*—a pretty woman. That didn't surprise him. She was also a pretty child.

Ben wrapped the tooth in the bandanna and put it back in the drawer.

The girl said she saw a white angel with a flaming red sword in her parents' bedroom. He dismissed her story then because she was scared and in shock. After Panali's death, he began to have second thoughts.

Maybe he'd pay a visit to Malia Rico tomorrow. Hopefully, she'd remember him.

Chapter Five

THE GENERAL GAVE Malia a small crowded office adjoining his own. It was filled with boxes of memorabilia from his years in the army. There was just enough room for a desk and a couple of old file cabinets.

For the next three days she locked herself inside, reading and taking notes on the mounds of data Jasper Rhodes had collected. Rhodes may have been mashed potatoes, but he was a damn good researcher, Malia thought.

The pages were in numerical order. When she reached page

726, it jumped to 833. What happened to those missing pages? she wondered.

She spent eighteen hours a day in the office, sometimes forgetting to eat. When she did, it was usually alone in the kitchen or in her room. At two in the morning, exhausted, she'd go downstairs and fall into bed with her clothes on. She had little contact with the general or the rest of the household. Occasionally she could hear Steinway's blustery voice on the phone in the next room, but he never came in to see her.

Every morning she'd look out the small window in the office and see Steinway and Taang jogging together. Sometimes they took horses up in the hills. They'd ride through the cattle and disappear into the pine and eucalyptus trees. The Montagnard was almost comical, with his short legs clutching the sides of the horse and his rear bouncing up and down in the saddle. The only thing that kept Malia from laughing was remembering what Taang did to the enemy in Vietnam.

Ciji Brown nervously called several times from New York to see how she was doing. Malia, trying to calm her apprehension, told her she was still sifting through Rhodes's material, highlighting the parts she could use. "Jasper did a good job. All I have to do is put it in chronological order," she said to her editor.

On the third day, Lupe walked into her office with a carafe of coffee. This was the first time Malia had seen the girl since that night on the cliffs.

As Lupe leaned over the desk to pour the coffee, the top part of her blouse opened. She wasn't wearing a bra. Deep purple welts and teeth marks were embedded on her breasts.

An old anger erupted within Malia as she remembered the beatings her uncle inflicted on her as a child. "Why do you let him do that?" she abruptly asked the Hawaiian woman.

Lupe's head perked up and her listless eyes took on a suspicious glow. "What you talkin' about?"

"I was on the cliffs a few nights ago. I know what happened. I heard everything."

The girl pushed her top up and quickly put the cover back on the carafe. "Should I leave it?" Her voice was hard.

Malia sighed. "Yes, please."

It was useless. The girl wasn't going to talk about it.

Lupe, her beautiful face flushed with anger and embarrassment, put her head down and silently left.

Useless. Malia rubbed her tired eyes. Well, she'd tried. Hopefully the girl would get it. *Christ!* Who was she to tell someone to get it? Did she ever get it? The few men she had relationships with never hit her, but they were abusive in other ways. Perhaps her old shrink was right: you always go back to what you know best, what is comfortable. *Shit.*

Malia drank the coffee, waited for the caffeine rush, then went back to work.

She took down old photograph albums that were stacked on top of the files. Jasper Rhodes was supposed to go through them, picking out snapshots for the book to send to the publisher. He obviously never got around to it.

She started with the oldest album first. It contained photos of the general's ancestral family in Austria before the turn of the century. The binder was broken and the black-and-whites stacked inside were all disorganized. She removed the pictures and placed them on the floor, putting them in chronological order. They were yellowed and cracked with age. The men, wearing knee-length suit jackets and bow ties, posed stiffly for the camera. By their sides sat their unsmiling wives.

The next album had photos of Steinway as a boy in Iowa. These snapshots would tell more about the general's early life than any anecdotes he'd relate to her later on.

She slowly went through them. They were like flashes of time frozen in a young man's life. At first glance, they showed the kind of childhood found only in Norman Rockwell paintings: sleeping baby Felix in the arms of his mother; teenaged Felix laughing and wrestling in a snow-covered cornfield with his friends; proud-looking Felix wearing the uniform of his military academy; a staid Felix in a tuxedo, sitting with his father at a formal affair.

Something she saw in the snapshots caught her interest. Something very subtle. She went over the photos again. Malia segregated all the close-ups of Steinway and the ones with his mother in them.

She glanced at each one carefully, until she saw what she was looking for.

Young Felix had his mother's eyes—sensitive and melancholy. It almost pained her to look at them. William Blake would have called them the eyes of experience.

There were several old photographs of his father, Otto Steinway: some were taken with the general's grandparents, others were of him alone. In most of them, he wore a somber expression—not even the hint of a smile.

Tucked away in back of the album she found a photo of Otto Steinway holding a toddler in his lap. From the other photographs, she knew the child was Felix. Otto was dressed in knickers, surrounded by several men of all ages. With their arms around one another, they were holding beer steins up to the camera, laughing. In the background, a banner hung over a picnic table: THE BAVARIAN MEN'S CLUB OF IOWA—1934. She knew Steinway Sr. had emigrated to the United States when he was a boy. The club must have been a gathering place for men of Teutonic lineage.

Malia put the picture back in the album. She picked up an eight-by-ten sepia photo of Steinway's father from the floor and took it over to the window to see it better. This one was done by a professional photographer. The older Steinway, a lieutenant then, was wearing a World War I uniform. Unlike his son's, his eyes were hard and uncompromising. He was staring directly ahead, square-jawed, with a stringent look that said he was a man with a mission.

It was his mother's eyes Felix inherited—definitely not his father's, she thought.

She felt someone in the room with her and turned around.

It was the general. He was standing by the door.

"Whatever I've accomplished in life I owe to that man," he said softly, staring at the photo. He just came back from riding and was wearing worn Wrangler jeans and cowboy boots.

The general went over to the coffeepot and poured himself a cup.

"I'm looking for photos to put in the book," she quickly said, hoping he wouldn't think she was prying.

He waved his hand in the air to reassure her. "Use that one." He pointed to the picture she was holding. "Everything you want to know about him is right there. Look at the man's face. Righteous ... honest ... a deep sense of purpose. He was all that and more." His lips began to quiver and his eyes misted over.

Malia saw him get emotional like this on television. He once wept openly on Capitol Hill when the Senate gave him a standing ovation after he announced his retirement. It was a sincere emotion that inadvertently became his trademark, endearing him even further to the public.

Trying to get his feelings under control, Steinway slowly sipped his coffee and gazed at the book titles on the shelves. He was quiet for a long time.

Malia waited for him to break the silence.

Eventually he did. He wiped his eyes on his sleeve, took a deep breath, then said, "Do you know how he died?"

"Your father?"

He nodded. His sad eyes now mirrored his mother's in the old photographs.

"I could find nothing in the other writer's notes about it," she said.

"That's because that idiot Rhodes didn't bother to ask me about him." He paused, then said quietly, "My father was run over by a garbage truck. Happened twenty-five years ago. The man survived three wars on the front lines. Received four Purple Hearts, also the Distinguished Service Cross."

Again he was silent. Then he muttered, "A goddamn garbage truck. Talk about injustice. Makes you wonder if there's someone out there keeping the planets from banging together, doesn't it?"

She could see the anguish lining his face. "I'm sorry," she said, standing up. She opened up the album and removed the photo of Steinway Sr., along with the other men drinking beer. "I also found this." She handed it to the general.

A warm smile came over Steinway's face. "My God. I haven't seen this one in years."

"What was the Bavarian Men's Club?" she asked.

"A group of German-speaking immigrants formed the club. It lasted for a few years, then disbanded. Unfortunately, when Hitler came into power, anything with a Teutonic name on it was suspect."

He put the picture in his pocket and changed the subject. "When are you going to be finished sifting through that trash heap?"

She forced a smile, looking down at Rhodes's notes on the desk. "I'm through."

He put his cup on the bookshelf and clasped his hands. "I have a meeting at Fort Ord tomorrow, and I'll be gone for a couple of days. So let's get moving, okay? I've wasted enough time."

Malia realized she'd passed his damn test. She took out the tape recorder from the drawer and put it on the desk.

Steinway sat down on the window ledge and removed a cigar from his shirt pocket. He tore the end of it off with his teeth, leaned back against the frame, and spit the tobacco bit into the basket. "Where do you want to start?" he snapped.

Realizing that his bark was a lot bigger than his bite, she no longer felt unnerved by him. Turning on the tape recorder, she sat on the end of the desk and said, "Let's start with the day you first slid down the birth canal."

He cocked his head and looked at her strangely. "Are you serious?"

"You wanted a writer, General. Well, you got one. By the time we're through with these interviews, trust me, you'll remember that experience."

"What the hell did I get myself into?" he growled.

"An autobiography that people won't throw out with yesterday's garbage."

He stared out the window for a long time, puffing his cigar. "I was a breech baby," he said finally.

"That's a start," she said, smiling.

Chapter Six

THE NEXT MORNING Malia heard noises coming from the driveway and glanced outside her office window. It was Thomas putting the general's luggage in the Jeep. She knew Steinway had a nine-thirty flight to Fort Ord.

She turned on the tape recorder and listened to the conversation she'd had with Steinway yesterday.

After playing the tape several times, she picked up subtle differences in voice tones when Steinway described his family: warm when he talked about his mother, protective and fearful when he brought up his father.

Tears welled up in his eyes yesterday when he spoke of him. But listening to the tape now, she heard something else. She'd love to talk to him about this. Too bad he was going away. She needed as much time with him as possible to gain his trust.

Her office door opened; she turned off the recorder.

Steinway walked in.

Malia let out a silent breath when she saw him. Steinway was wearing a blue pin-striped suit and his hair was slicked back. He walked with a powerful strut. This was the man the world knew.

"I'll be leaving in a few minutes," he said.

"What's going on at Fort Ord?"

"Business." His voice was abrupt. "Can you use anything from our talk yesterday?"

This was her opening. "Most of it. Your stories were colorful. I want to hear more about your father when you get back."

He looked at her, hard. "Why?"

"He was a general in the army. He must have had an immense influence on you."

"He did. I thought I made that clear."

She could sense his uneasiness. Yes, there was definitely something there. "Did you always get along with him?"

"That's a hell of a question. Of course I did. I already told you that."

His bark was back, but she held firm. "It's a question that needs to be answered if we're going to do this right."

He stared at her, thinking, patting his breast pocket for a cigar that wasn't there. "No, we didn't *always* get along. I suppose I fudged on that one." His face softened. "I'll be back in three days, and we'll talk about it."

"There's something I've been meaning to ask you. You're a man of immense importance to this country. Why isn't there any security? The house is in an isolated area. Aren't you concerned?"

He let out a small chuckle. "You lived in New York too long. Why would I need guards when I have Taang?"

She now understood the reason for the Montagnard's presence. "I never see him," she said.

A mischievous smile crossed his face. "That doesn't mean he doesn't see *you.*"

Her skin began to crawl from his wry remark. "Will he be going with you to Ford Ord?"

"No, not this time."

"Your wife doesn't seem to care for him very much."

"She just doesn't understand our relationship. It's a special one. The Montagnards have a belief that many primitive cultures share—if you save their skin, they're committed to saving yours. Taang has done just that on many occasions. I'd rather have him watching out for me than an army of Secret Service men."

"Where does he sleep?"

"He lives in a room in back. Most times, though, he sleeps out in the open." The general turned to the wall mirror and straightened out his tie. "I have to go. Peachie will be off the island for a couple of days." He smiled. "It'll be just you and Taang." He gestured toward the computer on her desk. "Get busy. We'll have lots more time to talk when I get back."

He walked out of her office and closed the door.

From her window, she watched his car disappear down the road toward Hilo Airport.

The house seemed deathly quiet without him, like a mausoleum.

She rewound the tape and tried listening to it again, but the news photo of that savage-looking boy with the filed-down teeth kept reappearing in her head. Knowing that she'd be alone with him in this house made her feel on edge.

Two hours later she heard a car badly in need of a tune-up pulling up to the driveway. Malia looked away from the computer and peered out the window.

She saw a small Hawaiian man in his sixties get out of a dented yellow Land Cruiser and slowly walk up to the front door. He was dragging his legs, as if he were in pain.

A moment later Lupe knocked on her door, telling her the man was here to see her.

"Who is he?" she asked.

The girl shrugged. "I don' know his name. He used to be the police captain 'round here."

Ben Lopaka. She turned off the computer and went to the front door to meet him.

Ben was standing on the veranda. His back was stooped from years of picking taro, and his long arms hung down past his knees.

She opened the screen door for him.

He looked up at her face, studying it, then he smiled and said, "I don' mean to bother you, miss. My name's Benjamin Lopaka. Maybe you remember me?"

She returned his smile. "Of course I remember you."

He had the look of a shy man, but his eyes were alert, taking in everything. "You were jus' a baby then. You've grown into a beautiful woman," he said.

"Thank you."

"I know you're busy, miss, workin' for the general. You think you can spare me a few minutes?"

Actually Malia was delighted. She hadn't spoken to anyone *but* the general in the last several days and she could use the break. "Why don't we go out to the lanai," she said, moving out of the way so he could enter.

She went into the kitchen, asked Lupe to bring them some coffee, then took Lopaka around to the back of the house.

They sat on white metal lounge chairs overlooking the ocean.

Lupe brought out the coffee, along with a plate of *'ulu*, a sweet breadfruit. She avoided Malia's eyes as she put the tray on the table.

Malia poured Lopaka a cup.

He shook his head no to sugar and cream. "The one thing we grow on the island is good coffee. You mainlanders seem bent on ruinin' it with all that sweet stuff."

Malia agreed. She also took hers black.

"You like workin' for the general?" he asked her.

"I think so. It's too soon to tell."

"He employs a lot of *paniolos* from 'round here. God knows, they could use the work. Most Hawaiians are dirt-poor." He looked out at the ocean, sipping his coffee. "I think of you often," he said softly.

"Do you?" She was surprised.

"*Ae*. I think 'bout that night with you in my truck, shiverin' and frightened. Do you remember?"

"That was a long time ago, Mr. Lopaka."

He waved a hand at her. "Call me Ben."

She nodded that she would.

"You were tellin' me about an angel that night."

"I remember that," she said. "Is that why you're here?"

He scratched his gray, three-day beard stubble. "Actually, yes."

She eyed him curiously. "What about it?"

"Do you still figure you saw it, miss?"

"Call me Malia, Ben."

He smiled. "Agreed," he said.

"Yes, I still believe I saw it. Why, I don't know. I can't give any rational explanation. I just know it was there."

"It was night. Darkness and fear play strange games in a child's head."

"You told me that twenty years ago. I was a very pragmatic child, not the kind that indulged in fantasies."

"You never talked to dolls or had any imaginary playmates?"

"No."

"Can you tell me about this angel again?"

Malia arched her head. "Why do you want to know about it now?"

"I just want to hear what you have to say. I didn't listen to you back then."

She was somewhat baffled by his request. "I don't remember much. Just a white angel standing over my parents' bed."

"Was it wearing boots?"

She eyed him quizzically. Was he making fun of her? No, his face was serious. "Why are you asking that?"

"The angel that killed your parents was wearin' boots. I'm just wonderin' why that little cherub would need boots when God gave him wings to fly?"

"I don't know anything about boots. I just know what I saw. Are they important?"

"Very. I'll tell you why. There were imprints from boots found 'round the muddy edge of the fish pond and in the house."

"I know about that," she said.

"Do you remember the fish pond?"

"I remember the coldness of the water and a sense of drowning. Not much else."

"We found the boots in the trunk of a local's car. The size and the imprints were the same."

"Yes, I know. He was your brother-in-law. Isaac Yamaguchi told me about him."

Ben looked surprised. "You met Isaac?"

"At the general's house."

"Nineteen seventy-four was a bad year for everyone," he said, shaking his head.

"Why?"

"You lost your parents, I lost my family, and Isaac lost his son."

"He died?"

Ben nodded. "Leukemia." Talking about Isaac's dead son reminded him of his own daughter who'd died. He quickly changed the subject. "You said the angel had a flaming sword in his hands."

"A big one. It was on fire," she said.

"Your mama was lookin' up at him, smilin'. That's what you tol' me."

She moved her eyes away from Ben, thinking. "Yes, I remember her smiling."

"You said she was smilin' because he was goin' to take her to see God."

Her eyes quickly darted back to him. "Is that what I told you? I don't remember that. I was so young."

"That's what you tol' me," he said reassuringly. "Did this angel have a face?"

That was a question she asked herself many times. "I'm sure it did. I don't remember." She stroked her arm, thinking. "It's all so fragmented." She turned to Ben, looked into his tired, gentle eyes, and felt as if she could trust him. "I used to have nightmares about that night when I was a child. My aunt and uncle were devout Catholics. I was forced to go to church. When I was twelve years old, my church group visited St. Patrick's Cathedral in New York. On the wall inside, there was a fresco of a white angel with blond hair and large plumed wings. It was holding a flaming sword over the body of a blood-soaked Christ on the cross. I was mesmerized by it. I couldn't take my eyes off the angel's face."

Malia's skin lit up with an inner glow as she remembered. "I don't know how long I stood there staring at it. After a while I felt its eyes moving in my direction. They were black, like olive pits. It looked at me as if it knew me. I remember starting to scream, then I passed out. Our family physician told my aunt that my fears were deeply rooted in my subconscious and that I should see a psychiatrist."

"Did you?"

"Yes . . . much against my family's wishes." Malia grinned. "They didn't believe in psychiatry. They felt that God, if I believed strongly enough, would take away my fears."

Ben shook his head. That kind of ignorance was also rampant on the islands. "Did anythin' come out during those sessions?"

"Bits and pieces under hypnosis . . . that's all."

"Did you continue to go back to church?"

"No," Malia said. "After that incident at St. Patrick's, I began to believe that angels were evil creatures, the harbingers of death. When my aunt and uncle got ready to go to church on Sundays, I would go up to the rooftop and hide. Eventually, they saw it was useless and left me alone."

Ben moved his body closer to her. "What about the angel's hair coloring? Do you recall if it was blond and curly, like the kind you found in that religious painting?"

She thought about it, then shook her head hopelessly. "I don't remember anything about the hair."

The frustration he lived with for so long returned. Reaching in his pants pocket for his empty pipe, he removed it and stuck the shaft in his mouth. He leaned back in the chair and sucked on the stem, trying to calm himself down. "What happened after you left your house that night?"

"I remember running through the sugarcane fields."

"Was the angel chasin' you?"

"Yes."

"Were you frightened?"

"Yes." Talking to the old man made the dread return.

"How'd you get into the pond?"

"I suppose I jumped in. I don't know."

"You said you felt like you were drownin'."

"Yes. I remember hands reaching out to me, then water filling my lungs. I couldn't breathe."

"Interestin'," he said. He grabbed some breadfruit from the plate on the table, broke a piece off, and ate it.

"Why interesting?"

"The pond you were hidin' in was man-made." He saw the confusion on her face and tried to explain. "The ancient Hawaiians used several kinds of fish ponds. The main one was basically a natural inlet next to the ocean. The name for it was *loko kuapa*. It was cordoned off from the sea by wooden poles called *mākāhā* . Small fish would swim into the inlet through the spaces between the poles and feed on the algae. When it was time for the buggers to go back into the ocean, they were too fat to fit through the spaces. That's how our ancestors trapped fish. The kind you hid in, known as *loko wai*, was built away from the sea. It was fresh water. Do you remember how tall you were when you were four years old?"

Malia shrugged. "Maybe three . . . three and a half feet. Why?"

"The pond was only two feet deep. How could you be drownin' in it?"

"Good question." Ben Lopaka might be old, but he was sharp and cagey, she thought. "I was always able to swim, even as a toddler. Yet, for some reason, I couldn't get my head out of the water to breathe. That *is* strange," she said.

"Are you sure nobody was tryin' to help you do just that?"

She thought about the hands reaching out to her when she was hiding in the pond. It came out during her sessions with the psychiatrist. "No, I'm not sure," she said slowly.

He smiled. "There was a teenage boy bendin' over the pond when I arrived. Real skinny. I always thought him a bit odd when I used to see him hangin' 'round town. He was a kid that lived up the road from you. I questioned him later on. He said he was jus' tryin' to get you out. It was his parents who called the police when they heard you screamin'."

Yes, she *did* remember an older boy who lived near them. Thin, with big hands and thick glasses. He was always standing in his backyard, hanging around, staring at their house. "Are you suggesting that this boy was trying to drown me?"

"I'm not suggestin' anything, miss"— he corrected himself— "Malia."

"What's this all about, Ben? Are you telling me the *paniolo* didn't kill my parents? That maybe this kid did?"

"Look, I knew this *paniolo*. He was my wife's brother. The angel you described didn't look anythin' like him."

"Neither did the boy."

He put the pipe back into his pocket, took a long breath, then said, "Everythin' about those murders was so open an' shut. Everythin' fit together so easily. Perhaps *too* easily."

"You don't believe he did it, do you?" she said.

He took a long look at her concerned face. "Do you?" he said finally.

Her hand went to her cheek, as if to brush away an imaginary fly. Deep inside her, she always had doubts. If she believed the killer was dead, why did she still have all these fears?

"I heard my mother's bracelet was found in his possession," she said.

"Under his bed. He may not have known it was there."

She looked at him skeptically. "You think somebody planted it there?"

"Could be. Your father came to the island in the sixties an' worked for the sugar mill in Honokaá. He helped organize a strike 'gainst the plantation. The workers were underpaid and had no benefits. The owners of the plant tried to put it down. Sometimes they used violent means to do it. Lots of people got hurt."

"My parents were murdered in seventy-four."

"I know. After the strike, he met your mama, married her. He became a supervisor on the plant's assembly line. A few years later, another strike 'gainst the sugar mill was bein' planned. Your father was goin' to lead that one, too. Your parents were murdered jus' a couple of days before the strike went into effect. Without him, the workers didn't have a leader. They didn't walk out."

"You think the owners of the sugar plantation hired someone to do this, then blamed Panali?"

"It's a thought. Panali was the most likely person to pin it on. With his reputation, no one would think any differently. That teenage boy I tol' you 'bout, he worked part-time for the plant baggin' sugar."

"So what? The whole town worked for that plant," she said.

"Times were hard then. His family was poor. Sometimes they didn't even have food on their table. People do crazy things for money."

"You've been thinking a lot about this, haven't you?"

"Nothin' else for the last twenty years." He took another piece of breadfruit and began nibbling on it.

"Why were they killed in such a barbaric way?" Her voice was bitter.

Ben Lopaka took out the bandanna from his back pocket, unfolded it, and removed the tooth. "This is what killed your parents. It was taken from your mama's body. Her blood is still on it. It belongs to a shark. A great white. There's a small hole in its base, see? If you look closely you can just make out a small piece of *olonā* lodged in the opening."

"It looks like human hair," Malia said pensively.

"No. *Olonā* is fiber taken from a native shrub. Wrap several of them together and it makes a strong cord." He held the tooth up to her.

She saw the rust-colored blood on it, and her body instinctively recoiled away.

"The hole was drilled out," he said. "Man-made. The coroner first thought it was a shark that killed them. I had to remind him the ocean was a half mile away."

"Isaac told me there was no sea water in their bodies."

Ben smiled shrewdly. "That's right. So what do we have here? A hole in a tooth with a strand of cordage made from coconut sennit inside. One tooth couldn't have done the damage I saw that night. There had to have been more teeth."

"If it was a weapon, I heard it was never found."

"No, it wasn't. This is where it gets crazy. Panali knew how to use a knife, but that's 'bout all. He wouldn't have known anythin' 'bout this."

The old fear was back again, consuming her body this time. "What happened to the boy?" she asked, almost inaudibly.

"Shortly after the murders, he and his parents moved to California. His father needed work. Unless you like pickin' pineapples or waitin' on tables, jobs are scarce 'round here."

"Where is he now?"

Lopaka shook his head. I don' know. I haven't seen him in twenty years."

"Do you remember his name?"

"That I do," he said, wrapping his gnarled fingers around the stem of the coffee cup. "Daniel Keahi."

She swallowed hard a couple of times, trying to wet her dry throat. No wonder his name was familiar. He used to be her next-door neighbor. "I've got news for you, Ben. He's back."

As he brought the cup up to his lips, his eyes widened in surprise. "How do you know?"

"He's no longer skinny *or* odd. He's an anthropologist, a friend of General Steinway's."

Ben put the cup down slowly without drinking from it. He closed his eyes for several seconds, as if he were in a trance. Then he opened them and said, "You both comin' back to the island at the same time . . . hell of a coincidence." He reached for his pipe in his pants pocket again and put the stem back in his mouth.

"That's probably all it is, Ben. A coincidence."

He gave her a dubious look. "I hope you're right."

"I met him. He's no murderer. Besides, he lived next door to me. I would have recognized him in the bedroom that night."

"He could have been wearin' a disguise. As I said, I hope you're right."

So did she. A couple of nights ago she'd spent most of the evening sitting next to him at dinner when her parents' murders were discussed. He never once brought up the fact that he used to be their neighbor or tried to save her life.

"You know what kills me more than anythin' 'bout this?" he said sadly.

She shook her head.

He put his face close to hers. "Your daddy was cut up bad, but nothin' like what this animal did to your mama." He paused, trying to find the right phrase, then said, "She was eight months pregnant."

Malia's face turned white.

"This sick bastard did most of his work on her belly."

Her hand went up to her mouth in horror. "I didn't know she was pregnant." Her voice was barely loud enough to be heard.

"I'm afraid so," Ben replied. Seeing her reaction, he started to get angry at himself for telling her.

She needed to know the answer to the next question. "What *was* it?"

This was hard for Ben. He looked away from her and down at the breadfruit. "A girl. You'd've had a sister now."

Her hands began to tremble. She locked her fingers together to keep them still. "Are you planning to reopen this case?" There was an immediacy in her voice.

Ben shook his head. "I been tryin' to do that for years. If no one would listen to me when I was a policeman, why would anyone listen to me now? I'm known as *pupule* 'round my district. That means 'crazy one.' "

"Why?"

"Because I went around sayin' that maybe I killed the wrong man, that maybe Panali didn't murder your parents."

"That's no reason to call you crazy."

He smiled as he chewed on the breadfruit. "It is when you say an angel might have done it."

She was amazed. "You actually believe me, don't you?"

He nodded. "*Ya, ya.* I jus' wish I did back then."

Chapter Seven

AFTER BEN LOPAKA left, Malia went over to the cliffs and stared out at the ocean, thinking about a sister that never had a chance at life. In one night, this white angel had destroyed her family and shattered her own childhood, which was just beginning to bloom. Anger raged through her.

Was this angel still alive? Where was he now? All she could think about was his face that had no features, a face that lay hidden in the dark recesses of her mind for all these years. Thoughts of vengeance began to swirl around in her head. She needed to rid herself of these feelings or they'd consume her.

She went to her room and put on her running shoes and shorts. Her fingers were trembling so hard she could hardly tie her laces. She left the house and ran down the path, then leapt a fence and raced into the sloping green hills.

She thought about her parents. The few images she had of them were like faded watercolor paintings: her mother slowly brushing her thick Polynesian hair as she stared whimsically out the window; the smell of tobacco on her father's shirt; and the roughness of his beard as he kissed her good night and called her *mia bambola*.

As she grew into womanhood, the memories became more translucent, like a rainbow slowly fading in the sky after a storm. Soon they'd all be gone.

Her pace quickened.

She ran through meadows of grazing cows, while *paniolos* on horseback looked on. The lime green pastures turned into brown, desolate fields of dormant lava cones. She raced up one of them. The soft earth filled her shoes. When she could no longer run, she dug her feet and hands into the dirt and continued to climb. Her lungs were on fire, as if saturated with the white-hot lava that once flowed from this small volcano.

At the top of the cone, she dropped to the earth, clutching at the infertile ground, gasping for breath. She lay there for several minutes, unable to move. Her arms and legs felt limp, like appendages of a rag doll. But the hate inside her was still very much alive, like a burning ember that refused to be extinguished. Nothing would put it out, nothing except the truth about that night. It was there, buried somewhere in her mind. If she had to claw away at the walls of her own psyche, layer by layer, she would find it.

Eventually her strength returned. With her body covered with brown earth and volcanic ash, Malia stood up and began the long trek back to the ranch.

When she reached the main road, she saw the figure of Taang squatting down by the shoulder next to a parked car. He seemed to be waiting for her. At first she wanted to go through the pastures to avoid him, but she knew that was the long way back and she was dead tired.

As she came closer, she could see he was wearing a Camp Pendelton T-shirt. His thick, chunky legs protruding out of his khaki shorts resembled gnarled tree stumps. Once again his eyes were lost in his fatty cheeks as he produced that strange grin of his. He was holding a big cigar, turning it around in his fingers the same way the general did.

"You run very well," he said.

This was the first time Malia heard him speak. She was surprised that he spoke English with only a small trace of an accent. In fact, there was almost a Midwestern twang to his words. Why was he here? Had he been following her?

"You look tired." He pointed to his car with the cigar. "Let me drive you back."

The stories about him still unsettled her. She didn't want to be alone with him. Too exhausted to talk, she shook her head and waved her hand in the air.

He shrugged and said, "It's about five miles to the ranch. Turn left when you get to the macadamia nut factory. It's the shortest route." He stuck the rolled tobacco in his mouth and clamped his teeth over it.

She walked about a half mile before her legs cramped up again. Malia dropped to the grass and sat there, massaging her calves, trying to get life back into them. In the distance she could see Taang's car slowly making its way toward her. He had been following behind.

He pulled up next to her. Peering out the driver's window, he said, "A hell of a nice day for exercising." He sat back and waited, smoking his stogie, his eyes staring dreamily up the road.

He emphasized *hell* the way the general did. *The man not only blows cigar smoke like him, he imitates his voice patterns as well,* she thought.

There was no way she could walk any farther. She slowly rose up, hobbled over to the passenger seat, and got in. The car was filled with the thick, bitter aroma of Cuban tobacco. She grimaced at the stench.

"A good cigar helps the digestion," he said, as if reading her mind.

She knew that had to be something he heard Steinway say. He was the ape mimicking the master.

Holding his hand out the window, he crushed the lit end of the cigar between his finger and thumb, then put the half-finished portion on the dashboard. Taang started the car and drove slowly back to the ranch.

He was only five feet tall, and his feet barely touched the

gas pedal. To see above the steering wheel, he had to tilt his head upward.

At first he drove in silence, then he broke it by saying, "I run, too. Halfway up Mauna Kea and back every morning. I don't use shoes. Hurts the feet."

If she wasn't so agitated right now, she would have been impressed. Very few people could make that run. Looking down at his massive legs, she could see that he wasn't lying. The gnarls in his thighs were actually solid, rippling muscles.

"What made you want to run like that?" he asked offhandedly.

She knew he was trying to pry. There was no reason to tell him the truth. "Stored-up energy. It happens when you sit in an office all day." She closed her eyes. Damn, she was tired!

He glanced over at her face. "You looked fairly peaceful before Mr. Lopaka came to see you."

"You don't miss much, do you?" She tried to make her voice sound pleasant but didn't succeed. If he was aware of her annoyance, he didn't show it.

His driving was erratic, and he had a hard time staying inside the yellow line. Malia clutched the door handle.

He laughed at her nervousness. "I didn't learn to drive until a few years ago. The first car I ever saw was a Jeep at a field hospital in Da Nang. I come from Mbur, a remote area in the mountains. I heard about white men, but I never saw one until I was sixteen years old."

She noticed the small knife tucked deep into the knotted portion of his chignon. Does he always have it with him? she wondered. "Do you have a last name, Taang?" she asked, refusing to let go of the handle.

"Montagnards don't have last names until they get married. Then they take on the name of their wife and add it to their own."

Malia saw his eyes dull over, as if he were remembering something from long ago. She knew he'd lost the woman he was supposed to marry when his village was destroyed. Was he thinking about her now?

"Have you ever gone back?"

"Back to where?"

"To the mountains where you came from?"

He took his eyes off the road for a moment and looked at

her. The pupils peering out of his tiny slits were almost reptilian. "There's nothing to go back *to*. My tribe was wiped out during the war."

"I know. Were you on the side of the South Vietnamese government?"

A bitter smile emerged on his face. "Side? We didn't even know there *was* a side. We heard stories from travelers that came from other villages that there was some kind of war being fought many miles away. We didn't know what it was about, nor did we care. They'd tell us about white warriors wearing hard hats, from another land, helping to fight the people from the North. My grandfather fought the French and wore a beret taken from a soldier he killed. He'd smoke his pipe and laugh, saying these white men must be pretty stupid, like the French, to come so far to die."

"Did the Vietcong think you were helping the Americans?"

Taang shrugged. "They must have thought that. Why else would they have wanted to kill us?"

"How did you survive and no one else?"

For a brief moment there was a trace of sorrow etched around his eyes, then they became hard and indifferent again. "I was the best man with the crossbow in my village. I got up early that day to go hunting. I had just killed a wild dog when I heard loud noises I never heard before. They were mortar shells. I could see fire and smoke coming from my village. I ran back. When I got there, everything was burned and my people lay dead."

"Including the woman you were going to marry?" Malia asked, with a quiet tone.

Again the sadness in his eyes for a second, then it was gone. "Her name was Piing," he said finally. "The mortar had demolished her hut. The only way I knew it was her body was from the bracelet she was wearing. I had made it for her."

"I read that when the general found you, you were barely alive."

"There was nothing left in my village. I wandered through the forest for days, not eating or drinking. I wanted to die and go to the spirit world; I wanted to be with my people again. Eventually I laid down on the ground and waited for death. I don't know how long I laid there—maybe a week, maybe two. Then I woke up in a large tent with strange white men staring down at me. One of them was the general. At first, I was angry and tried to fight them. I told them in my language that I wanted to die, but they didn't seem to understand. They tied me up so I wouldn't run away. The general would come and sit with me every day, forcing food down my throat because I refused to eat. He learned my language very quickly and we began to talk. We became friends. Because of my hunting skills, he asked me to help him weed out the Cong." Taang's lips spread into an angry smirk. "I was more than glad to oblige. When the war was over, the general went back to America. He promised to send for me. It took him two years, but he kept his promise."

"I heard that many of your people came to the United States to live. They have their own community," Malia said.

"They are not my people, and I don't call that living," he caustically replied, shaking his head. "My people are dead. These people have houses in the suburbs. They cut their hair short and eat at McDonald's. I'd rather live here. At least the rain forests on the island resemble the mountains I grew up in."

He was a man caught between two worlds, she thought. "Does the general try to westernize you?"

He let out a loud, raucous laugh, not unlike Steinway's own guffaw. "Hell, the general and I, we belong together. He lets me be."

Perhaps they did belong together, she realized. They were alike in many ways. They differed only in appearance. His voice—even his behaviorisms—were patterned after the general.

Taang was an enigma, she thought. His personality came from mimicry now, not from within. Thousands of years of his culture were wiped out in a bloody war that had nothing to do with his people. Taang could no longer be a Montagnard, but he had to anchor himself to something or he would float away in a sea of nothingness. He chose to be the general. Taang may have been a ruthless killer in the war, but she felt sorry for him. He was a man desperately trying to transplant himself in a soil that would never truly nourish his soul.

This man lost his family in the same violent way she had. She wanted to tell him about it. Glancing over at him, she thought she saw a trace of understanding wash across his face.

It was a perceptive look, almost as if he knew what she wanted to say.

Once again she felt that wintry chill seeping through her body. The Montagnard reminded her of her own rootlessness. She leaned against the door, trying to keep a physical distance between them. She stayed that way until they reached the ranch.

After Taang dropped her off at the main entrance to the house, she went to her room and took a long hot bath to soften the pain in her leg muscles.

Lying in the bathtub, she began to think about the other reason she came to the island. It had nothing to do with the general's book. Perhaps it was time to take care of it.

Putting on a pair of jeans and a tank top, she left the room and went into the kitchen. Lupe was mopping the wood floors. Malia asked her if there was an extra car on the property she could borrow.

The girl stopped her swabbing. She wiped her brow and pointed to a set of keys on a hook next to the door. "It's the Buick in the garage. It belong to Mrs. Steinway."

She took the keys off the hook, then looked over at Lupe. The girl's eyes were cast down on the floor as she mopped, avoiding her once again.

She drove to the leeward side of the island, toward Ka'ohu—the town where she'd lived as a child.

The farther she drove, the thicker the foliage became, eventually turning into a rain forest. Bright sunshine gave way to dense clouds, then finally to rain. The houses lining the road became farther apart and more run-down—roofs were made of corrugated metal and rusted shells of cars were parked on front lawns, covered over by fungus. This was the real Hawaii, not the one the tourists knew.

When she reached Ka'ohu, a crumbling village with just one street, she pulled into a gas station and asked directions to the cemetery. The attendant pointed her toward the edge of town.

She found it with no trouble. It was a small graveyard, with about a hundred tombstones jutting out of the ground. Most of them were old and decaying. When the sugar factory closed down fifteen years ago, many of the people left Ka'ohu to earn money in the cities of Kona and Hilo. The cemetery was only used now for the ones who stayed behind.

She found her parents' graves in the last row.

Loke Aka Rico	James Sean Rico
Born January 4, 1954	Born March 7, 1932
Died August 21, 1974	Died August 21, 1974

MAY THEY FIND PEACE FROM THEIR GRIEVOUS DEATHS

Grievous deaths. She held back her tears. It was a time for anger, not mourning.

Malia looked at the date of her mother's birth and was surprised to see how young she was when she died. Twenty years old. That meant she was only sixteen when she brought her into this world.

Malia saw an old Hawaiian woman sitting on the ground next to the cemetery selling leis for the departed. She bought two. The Hawaiian custom was to place them around the stone cross on top of the graves.

She wished she knew the Hawaiian prayer for the dead. Right now, she wished she knew *any* kind of prayer. Religion was just not her thing. Death, to her, was final. She didn't believe in an afterlife or some great white light that spirits floated into. At this moment, she hoped she was wrong. She closed her eyes and talked softly to her parents, telling them that she'd never forgotten them.

The memory of her mother smiling up at the angel suddenly drifted into her head. When she was a child she'd told Lopaka that the angel was going to take her to God. That was only naïve, wishful thinking. Looking back now, she was beginning to think that perhaps her mother was smiling because she *knew* the angel. It's possible, she thought. If only she could remember more about that night.

The clouds ripped open and it began to pour. She ran back to the car and drove away from the cemetery. As she headed toward the ranch, she realized that the house where she once lived had to be only a few minutes from here.

She drove back to the gas station and asked directions to Akoni Road. It was past the outskirts of town and not hard to find.

At the bottom of the dirt road, she saw her old home. Part

of the corrugated roof had long caved in and wild vines and moss covered most of the house.

Not caring about the rain and mud, she got out of the car, climbed over dead logs and wild palms sprawled along the ground, and made her way to the house. When she reached the rusty, broken screen door, an uncontrollable fear stopped her from entering. What was she afraid of?

She wiped the wet hair off her face with the back of her hand, took a deep breath, and pushed the door open. It gave way from its one hinge and clattered to the floor. She stepped over it and went inside.

Stained mildewed wallpaper covered the hallway walls. Patches of it had ripped away, or were eaten by insects, exposing waterlogged, yellowed baseboard. The pungent odor of stale wet air filled her nostrils.

She touched a piece of that familiar flowered wallpaper and it crumbled in her fingers. Excitement and dread raced through her veins. There was no doubt that she had once lived here.

She stopped when she came to a small room. The walls inside were painted a pale yellow. It was her bedroom as a child. Her bed was still there, but the mattress was gone. Probably taken by locals, she thought. The springboard was hanging off the bed, rusted and broken.

Her foot touched something and she looked down. It was the head of a Barbie doll floating in three inches of water. She emitted a small cry as she suddenly remembered it. It used to have a pretty blue dress. She saw the rest of the body trapped by the leg of the bed. The dress was now a muddy, indefinable color.

Where's Poni? something inside her suddenly asked. My God, she hadn't thought about her in years! Poni was her favorite stuffed animal, a horse with a mane of yellow ribbons.

She left the room and walked slowly down the hallway, stepping over masses of slippery wet trash littering the floor. Her feet, as if having a mind of their own, knew where they were going. She couldn't stop them now, even if she wanted to. They were leading her directly to her parents' bedroom. When she reached the threshold, she grabbed onto the rotted doorjamb, trying to prevent herself from going in. Her heart was pounding and her breath was short.

What was she afraid of? The killings took place twenty years ago.

Malia forced herself to look inside. The roof had caved in, exposing most of the bedroom to the elements. The oak bed was still there—so was the mattress. The islanders, a superstitious lot, probably didn't take it because her parents were murdered on it. The walls, covered with green fungus, still had dark brown spots on them: bloodstains. By the side of the door, she saw the decomposed remains of Poni lying in a pool of water.

Pieces of that night began to play in her mind:

She was standing by the door like she was now and hugging Poni. Fireworks from Hilo faintly lit up the night sky, and for a brief moment she could see her parents asleep in the bed.

The room went black again, only to be illuminated once more by Roman candles and flashes of many-colored lights. Then she saw the angel standing over them, with its flaming sword raised above its head, its plumed wings jutting from its back.

Darkness again, then more light. Her father was now lying on his back in an unnatural position. The sheet around his body was covered in red.

She could see her mother's smiling face looking up at the angel. There was confusion on her face, but no fear.

Darkness again. More fireworks. The angel was now bringing his sword down on her mother. Everything in the room was turning red. Warm liquid splashed across her face.

Blackness again. When the fireworks came overhead once more, the white angel was now looking at her.

Malia turned away from the room where it had happened and held onto the wall, gasping for air.

A sudden feeling of immense guilt and shame overtook her. Why shame?

Then she remembered.

Her parents sent her to bed early that night. They wouldn't let her stay up for the fireworks because she'd said a bad word—a word so insignificant that she could no longer recall it. She was furious. Lying in bed, clutching Poni, she wished them both dead.

"Oh, Jesus," Malia whispered.

The putrid air inside the house was stifling. She had to get out. She ran through the hallway, which was quickly filling up with water. The current was going against her. As she leapt over floating debris, she slipped and fell down. Her knees hit a jagged piece of window glass lying on the floor. A sharp pain shot through her leg. Glancing down, she saw raw bleeding skin protruding from her jeans.

As she started to get up, something long and furry scampered through her arms from under the rotted beams. A mongoose. The creature jumped up on the log, let out a high-pitched shriek, and scurried under a mound of pulverized bricks in the corner.

Heavy rain splashed down on her head from the open ceiling. She frantically rubbed her eyes, trying to see through the torrid downpour.

Somewhere down the hallway she saw the figure of a man standing by the doorway. "The water's rising fast. Keep moving or you're going to be swept away," he yelled at her.

Malia fought the current, making her way to the door.

Through waterlogged eyes she saw the blurry form holding out his hands to her. He grabbed her by the waist and pulled her toward him. Then he picked her up in his arms and carried her outside on the lanai.

When he put her down, she pushed the matted hair away from her eyes and looked up.

Daniel Keahi was staring down at her, grinning. "I hoped we'd meet again, but not like this," he said.

Chapter Eight

DANIEL KEAHI TOOK Malia's arm and moved her under the eaves of the roof, which offered some shelter from the downpour.

"What are you doing here?" she shouted, trying to be heard over the deafening sound of water crashing onto the metal roof above them.

He shouted back. "I'm staying at my old house up the road. I saw you drive past. Are you okay?" He saw the rip in the leg of her jeans and the blood flowing out of it. Daniel knelt down to get a better look. "You've got a nice gash. Let me take you back to my house."

She moved away from his touch. "Thanks, but I have to get back." Her voice was distant.

He looked quizzically at her, then stood up. "I don't think you'll be going anywhere for a while." He pointed over to the road. It was now a raging river. The water was rising over the Buick's hood. "You need a four-wheeler on this part of the island. These rains come sudden and fast. The house flooded because the drainpipes are all clogged up."

"How the hell am I supposed to get out!" she screamed over the din.

He cupped his hands over his mouth and yelled, "You're going to have to wait until the rain stops. That should be in about an hour. The grounds are porous, the water will sink down. I'll be able to dry off your spark plugs, and you'll be able to leave."

Malia, glaring at him, folded her arms against her chest. "I'll wait here."

He looked at her as if she was crazy. "You can't wait here. The water's rising."

"I'll take my chances."

He screamed in her ear: "What's the matter with you?"

"You knew who I was when we first met, didn't you?"

"Yes, I did. So what?"

"Why didn't you say something that night?"

"What difference does it make? You didn't say anything, either, when Yamaguchi was talking about you."

The *rat-a-tat* clamor on the roof was getting louder as the rain came down harder. She could barely hear him. "I want to know!"

Daniel angled his head, again looking at her queerly. Then he laughed. "Is that what's bothering you? Look, unless you were going to say something that night, I wasn't. I was respecting your privacy. I thought I'd wait until the proper time to talk to you. Listen, you can't *stay* here. Come on back to the house. We'll talk there."

She thought about her options. There really weren't any. If she stayed, she'd be swept away by the mounting flood.

They went around to the back of the house and climbed up the hillside, away from the rampaging water.

When she reached the top, she could see his wooden house sitting on the slope about two hundred yards away. They pushed through the wild sugarcane to get to it. Daniel was in front of her, walking with a slight limp.

When they reached the house, they climbed the staircase to the back porch and entered through the sliding glass door that led into a barren living room.

Daniel slammed the door shut. He was wearing a T-shirt and shorts. Taking off his saturated Topsider loafers, he tossed them next to the threshold. "Let me get you something to wear and see if I can do anything about your leg. Stay here." He hobbled up the stairs.

Watching him move, Malia realized there was nothing wrong with his leg. He was favoring the left side of his back, which caused him to limp.

She stood by the glass door and looked around the stark room, rubbing her arms to keep warm. Sheets covered the couches and the shelves were devoid of books and knick-knacks. The faded bare walls had dark rectangular patches on them, suggesting that paintings used to hang there.

It was as if no one lived here, she thought. A blazing fire in the hearth was the only sign of habitation. She went over to it and sat on the brick ledge, letting the heat warm her wet body.

Daniel came downstairs carrying a bath towel, work shirt, jeans, and a roll of gauze. He handed her the towel and clothes. "Dry yourself off and change into these. Don't worry about getting blood over anything. I'll wrap your leg up afterward. Yell when you're done." He turned and quickly walked back upstairs.

She removed her drenched clothes and put on Daniel's. He was a big man, and the shirt hung over her like a tent. She had to roll up the legs of the jeans, then hold on to the waist, so they wouldn't fall down. "Okay," she yelled when she was finished.

Daniel came downstairs. He had also changed into dry clothing: a pair of Levi's 501s and a long-sleeved, light blue shirt. Going over to the credenza, he poured two glasses of brandy and handed her one. "This should help," he said. "Sit down. Don't mind the house. Nobody's lived here for twenty years."

She sat on the covered couch next to the fire. Sipping her drink, she looked up at Daniel unrolling the gauze. She could see his face a lot better in the daylight than she could that night at the general's ranch. He was more rugged-looking than she originally thought. His black hair was cropped short, and there was a small jagged scar on the right side of his forehead running down his temple. He hadn't shaved in a couple of days and the dark beard stubble helped emphasize his rough-hewn appearance. His *hapa* features were not so much Hawaiian, she realized, but a mixture of Caucasian and Asian.

He finished unrolling the gauze and caught her studying him. He smiled.

Embarrassed, she looked away.

Daniel knelt down next to her and rolled up the leg of her jeans. It was a deep cut, but most of the bleeding had stopped.

"Nothing serious," he said.

"I'll be all right." Again her voice was cold.

Daniel paid it no mind. He wrapped the gauze tightly around the wound several times. After he was done, he put his mouth up to her knee and tore the bandage off with his teeth.

When his lips touched her skin, she flinched—not so much because of the physical contact, but because it felt pleasant.

He put the unused roll on the floor, then tied the end of the gauze into a knot. "That should hold you," he said.

She rolled down her pant leg. "Thanks."

He took his drink off the coffee table and sat down on the ledge. "That mongoose scare you?"

She nodded. "It isn't every day you see one running loose on the streets of Staten Island."

He shook his head and grinned. "They were brought here from India to keep the rat population down. Unfortunately there were no natural predators to keep *them* down. Nobody to this day can figure out how to get rid of them."

"Are they dangerous?"

He laughed. "That little guy was probably more frightened of you than you were of him."

He had a warm, seductive laugh, and she found it infectious.

"Feel better?" he asked.

She ran her fingers through her knotted, damp hair and motioned that she did.

"I remember you as a kid. You were pretty much of a brat," he said.

"Who me?"

"Uh-huh. Sometimes you'd cut across my backyard and make these weird faces at me."

"Give me a break. I didn't do that."

"You sure did."

"What kind?"

"You were missing your two front teeth. You'd put your tongue in the gap and wiggle it at me. You looked like a Maori warrior just before he went into battle."

"I never did that!"

"Sure as hell did. I'd call you *papuka*, and you'd run back down to your house crying."

"What does *papuka* mean?"

"Ugly."

She wrinkled her face in mock displeasure.

"Hey, I was a teenager then. You certainly didn't turn out that way, that's for sure."

"The only thing I remember about you was that you always stood in your backyard, pacing and staring at our house. What did you find so interesting?"

He looked a bit flustered. "Your family were the only living things around here other than mongooses and sugarcane fields. Staring at those fields all day was like watching paint peel. I was bored."

"Did you ever come over?"

"No. I was very shy then. I was tall and bony for my age, with arms like a chimpanzee's. Not exactly the kind of qualities that made for an outgoing person."

"I also remember that you used to wear thick glasses. Do you still?"

He laughed. "No way. It turned out to be a stigma. I had it cleared up when I was in the army." He stopped laughing and suddenly grimaced in pain. Letting out a small groan, he began to slowly massage his left side.

"Are you all right?" she asked.

"Yeah. I had a skiing accident last winter in Aspen. Tore up a muscle. The damn thing likes to act up now and then."

That explains the limp, she thought. Looking around the austere room, she asked, "Are you sure you live here?"

"I'm sure. It just doesn't look that way yet."

"Where do you work?"

"I have an office upstairs, but most of my work is done at the excavation. Sometimes I sleep there. My parents never sold this place."

"Why not? Didn't they need the money?"

"Absolutely. We were dead broke." His face got serious. "The Hawaiians are very superstitious. Nobody wanted to buy a house on the same street . . ." He stopped talking and looked down at his glass, rolling it in the palms of his hands.

She finished the sentence for him. "Nobody wanted to buy a house on the same street where people were murdered. Is that what you were going to say?"

He nodded. "They tried to sell it. There were no takers. After a while, my parents just closed it up and took their losses. I reopened it a few months ago when I returned to work on the excavation. It needs some fixing up, but I like it. I'll get around to it one day. It's quiet and secluded here. Not another human being for at least a half mile."

"I didn't know we were that isolated," she said, beginning to feel uneasy. She remembered Ben's apprehensiveness about Daniel.

He saw the shadow of suspicion cross her face. His lips

stretched into a vague smile. "Why are you so distrustful of me?"

Her body tensed. "Am I?"

"Yes. I saw that look on your face just now. It's the same one you had at your house just before. Does it have anything to do with a man named Ben Lopaka?"

She felt the dread returning. "What about him?"

"He called me about an hour ago. Asked if I remembered him. He wanted to talk about the night I tried to fish you out of the pond. He seemed tentative when he questioned me, same as you are now."

Once again her arms went around her chest. "What did you say to him?"

"That it all happened a long time ago. I told him I remembered trying to grab your hand, but you were too frightened to give it to me. Every time I managed to get hold of you, you pushed me away. Then Lopaka came over to the pond. He jumped in the water and got you out. That was it. I'm not quite sure what he thinks I'm omitting."

She took a strong sip of the brandy to steady her nerves. "What were you doing at the pond that night? How did you know I was there in the first place?"

"I heard you screaming." Daniel turned his head toward the fire, thinking. "I was under a canopy on my roof—watching the fireworks—when I saw a car driving down the road. It was going to your house. The motor was off, so were the head-lights. The car was gliding down the hill. Whoever was in it didn't want to be heard."

"What kind of car?" Her voice had a slight quiver.

"I don't know. It was too dark. I saw it parked on the side of the road. Someone got out and went around to the back of your house."

"What did he look like?"

Daniel shook his head. "I couldn't see him. It was too dark and it was raining hard. I told Lopaka that twenty years ago, and I told him the same thing today." He was beginning to sound defensive.

"You were sitting with Isaac Yamaguchi at the same dinner table. How come he didn't remember you? He was there the night of the murders."

"Ben Lopaka questioned me that night, not him. Isaac was

new to the island. He didn't know me and didn't recognize my name when we were introduced at the general's house. We're talking about something that happened twenty years ago."

She studied Daniel's face by the light of the fire. He seemed to be telling the truth. She was glad about that. "Where is this pond?" she asked him.

Daniel rose from the ledge and went over to the window. He pointed toward the sugarcane field. "Midway between my house and yours. You really can't see it from here."

"I'd like to go down and look at it," she said.

"Fine. I'll take you. But how about waiting until the rain lets up? The pond's been there for hundreds of years. It's not going anywhere."

She agreed.

Daniel seemed unnerved. "I don't know what this is all about. First Lopaka throwing questions at me, now you."

He was standing close to her. She could feel his breath tickling her cheek. Again, the sensation was not unpleasant. "I'm sorry," she whispered. "There are just so many unanswered questions. Ben doesn't think the murderer was that cowboy. He may be right."

Putting his hands gently on her shoulders, he said, "Hey, I was trying to save your life that night. That's all."

"I believe you," she said.

A spirited look suddenly came over his face and he clapped his hands together. "Are you hungry?"

"Actually I am. I haven't eaten anything since breakfast."

"Let me see what I can dish up." He went into the kitchen and came out a minute later with mangoes, bananas, nuts, and a sliced pineapple. "I ran out of poi. Hope you don't mind."

"Not at all."

He grinned. "It's really quite good once you get used to it."

"I'll believe that when I see it on the menu at the Carnegie Deli."

"For a Hawaiian you're really a New Yorker at heart, aren't you?"

"All the way."

Daniel placed the platter on the mantel, then opened up a bottle of white wine. He poured two glasses and handed her one.

"How did you meet General Steinway?" she asked.

He grabbed a handful of nuts and cracked them open in his strong hands. "Actually, he was the one who got in touch with me. He sent me a letter when I was teaching at UCLA. Turned out he was a big fan of mine. He'd read every paper I'd ever written on the ancient Polynesians. We corresponded on and off for several years. When I found out he bought a house on the big island, I wrote and told him I was coming here to work on the unearthing of the sacrificial altar. We never met before that. He invited me to his ranch, asked if he could come and take a look at the ancient *heiau*. I could tell he needed something to keep busy. He comes all the time. Always brings Taang with him."

"I don't think retirement was something he took gracefully," she said.

He sipped his wine. "I think the old man misses the action."

Malia quickly devoured a banana and half a mango. She had no idea she was this hungry. "If he takes the offer to run for president, he'll have more than enough action."

"I suppose you're right," Daniel said.

"You seem close to him. Have you talked to him about it?"

"A little bit. He feels the country is going down the tubes."

"Who doesn't?"

"He believes very strongly that he knows how to get it on the right track again. Running on an independent ticket, without the major parties backing him, means he doesn't have to answer to anyone."

"Is that healthy?"

"Not having to answer to anyone?"

"Yes."

Daniel shrugged, popping another handful of nuts into his mouth. "I don't know. I'm an anthropologist, not a politician."

Twenty minutes later the rain stopped as quickly as it began. Malia asked again to see the pond.

He went upstairs and brought down a belt to keep her pants up, then they went outside to the back porch and into the sugarcane fields. They tramped through the mud, pushing the thick stalks aside. About a half mile from the cliffs, he stopped.

"Here it is," he said, motioning to a small circular mass of water surrounded by black lava stones. The area was camouflaged by sugarcane.

She looked down. The water was dark and murky, filled with greenish algae.

She knelt by the edge and skimmed the water with the tips of her fingers. It felt slimy and menacing. Once again that vague fearful feeling returned.

The chill of the water ... the feel of her naked feet on the slithery bottom ... the sound of cane stalks being chopped down around her.

"Are you okay?" Daniel asked, bending down next to her, putting his arm around her shoulder.

She continued to look down at the pond. That soft, methodical hacking noise! It was loud and lucid in her head, as if it were happening right now. She could feel the angel close by, like she did then. He was cutting down the sugarcane with his sword, trying to find her. The *whack*ing got stronger. He was coming closer. Then she suddenly saw a pair of black boots standing at the water's edge. They were the boots Lopaka was talking about.

Something pressing on my head ... can't breathe!

Daniel put his hands on her terrified face and turned it toward him. "Malia!"

The memories broke apart and scattered to the corners of her mind. Her eyes returned to the present and she saw Daniel's concerned face staring down at her. "I want to get out of here," she said.

Back at the house, Daniel took a set of jumper cables and a dry rag from the garage, then drove Malia down to the road to get her car. The water subsided, like he'd said it would. He dried off her spark plugs and attached the cables from his battery to the one under the hood of the mud-covered Buick. The car started up on the first try.

When she got in, he leaned over and put his arms on the edge of the driver's window. "Are you going to be all right?"

She didn't know the answer to that, not at this moment. Her body was still shaking. When she stood by the pond, it was like twenty years ago was only yesterday.

Malia forced herself to look at Daniel. "I'll be okay. I just need to get away from here."

"Look, the general's out of town. It's got to be a bit lonely at the ranch. How about dinner tonight?"

She liked Daniel, liked talking to him. The urge to say yes was great, but she had a book to write.

"Some other time," she said.

"Promise?"

"Promise."

He stepped away from the car, smiled at her, and waved. "I'll call you soon."

As she drove away, she could see him standing in the middle of the road watching her, the boyish grin still on his face.

Chapter Nine

FOR THE NEXT three days Malia tried to concentrate on the book, but questions kept nagging at her—if the *paniolo* didn't kill her parents, then who did? *And why?*

Lopaka thought the upcoming strike at the sugar plantation in '74 may have had something to do with it. He'd phoned her yesterday, saying that he had an appointment with the ex-owner, a Mr. Kamakani, sometime this afternoon. The old man was now retired and living in Hilo. Lopaka said he would call her after he talked to him.

She told Ben the visit would probably lead nowhere. Too much time had passed. The plant was torn down and a small housing development was erected on the property fifteen years ago. Why would Kamakani say anything now and incriminate himself?

Lopaka disagreed. "When a man kills, the act stays in his mind like a weed. You can cut it down, but the roots are still alive, waitin' to come out. If it's there, I'll find it."

Daniel also called yesterday to see if he could hold her to her dinner promise. Again she was tempted, but she turned him down. She had only eight months to finish the first draft of the book. That wasn't much time, and her lack of experience wasn't helping any. Malia was becoming more and more

thankful for the research Jasper Rhodes did before he was
fired.

Coming back from a five-mile run this morning, she spotted
Peachie lying on a lounge chair by the pool, sipping a glass of
orange juice.

She must have just returned from Honolulu, Malia thought.
Lupe had told her that was where she went when the general
was not on the island.

Peachie was wearing sunglasses, with an ice pack draped
across her forehead. She looked as if she'd been on a three-
day binge: her skin was pasty and her body seemed small and
lost in the chair. The general was due back today, and Malia
knew she was trying to sober up before he arrived.

From Rhodes's notes, Malia discovered they were married
right after Steinway graduated West Point. It was a whirlwind
courtship. He, a general's son; she, an heiress to a supermarket
chain. It should make good reading. When Peachie was in better condition, she would schedule some interviews with her.

Taang was nowhere to be seen, but Malia knew he was
around. Whenever she went into the kitchen or into Steinway's
study to get some papers, she smelled faint traces of cigar
smoke in the hallway.

Lupe also kept her distance. Malia's meals were waiting for
her in the dining room at the proper time, but she always ate
them alone.

She enjoyed the quiet and the seclusion. Without interrup-
tions, the work went smoothly. The general's early years
seemed to fly out of the computer.

On Sunday afternoon, the serenity was broken by the loud
fluttering of helicopter blades overhead.

Malia got up from her desk and looked out the window. An
army Huey was hovering above the ranch, eventually setting
down on the driveway. The hatch door opened and Steinway
stepped out wearing combat fatigues. He was not alone. Several men, also in uniforms from different military branches, accompanied him. Most of them were carrying attaché cases.

Something was happening, she thought.

Ten minutes later, she heard heavy footsteps on the plank
floor coming her way. Her door opened and the general
walked in.

"You work on Sundays, too, Rico? I like that," he said,

closing the door behind him. His eyes were bagged from little sleep.

There was something different about Steinway, she realized. It was his demeanor, the way he carried himself. He seemed alive with nervous energy. "How long have you been on the island?" she asked.

"Since early this morning. I've been at Pōhakuloa Military Base most of the time." He walked over to the window and looked out. His eyes were fired with excitement. "How's the book?"

"Coming along well," she said.

"Good. That's good."

She wanted to show him the first two chapters, but his mind seemed elsewhere.

"You're going to see some men coming and going around here."

"I've already seen them."

"Don't pay them any mind," he said.

She nodded. Steinway would tell her what was happening *if* and *when* he got around to it.

"I'm going to be busy for a while. Our private talks will have to take a backseat."

"The first draft is due in eight months," Malia said, concerned.

His jaw tightened with impatience. "You'll have it. I intend to honor my commitment." He leaned over her chair. "I want you to write out a list of questions for me every day and give them to my aide. You'll have my answers on a tape cassette by ten that night. Is that all right with you?"

She was disappointed. "I'd hoped we could talk in person."

"Too bad. Some things take precedence over a book."

She saw the determination in his face. It matched his father's in the old World War I photograph. He was now a man with a mission. She wondered what kind.

When the general left, she found it almost impossible to work. Sounds of doors banging, hurrying footsteps, and gruff voices barking out orders caromed off the walls of her office.

Her phone rang. It was a private line, not connected to the house.

She picked up the receiver. It was Ben Lopaka.

"I talked to Kamakani," he said sullenly. "Can you get out of the house to meet me?"

"You picked a good day. I don't think anyone would know I was gone. Where are you?"

"At a gas station in Waimea. I could meet you at the macadamia nut factory about three miles east of the ranch. Do you know it?"

"I know where it is," she said, then hung up.

Malia changed into her running clothes and ran the three miles. When she reached the old factory on the outskirts of Honokaá, she was covered with sweat and her legs felt rubbery. She opened the door and went in.

It was an old plantation-style structure, built over a hundred years ago. Tourists on their way to Hilo would stop here for lunch and buy Hawaiian candied nuts for the folks back home. It was empty now, except for the employees working behind the glass wall sealing up boxes. The rumbling of ancient machinery crushing nuts was overpowering.

She saw Lopaka sitting at a back table, hunched over a cup of coffee. He looked up and waved at her. Grabbing a can of orange soda from the large refrigerator next to the counter, she paid the cashier, went over, and sat down next to him.

Lopaka smiled. "You run all the time?"

"Only when I'm not in a relationship." She took several napkins out of the metal container on the table and wiped the perspiration off her face.

"The man is innocent," he said.

"Kamakani? How do you know?"

"He's dyin' of lung cancer. Got six months to live. If he was involved, he would've said somethin'."

She popped open the lid and gulped down half the can. Wiping her mouth with her fingers, she said, "Not everyone believes in the confessional box."

"This guy does. He's Roman Catholic. The man's leavin' for O'ahu in a few weeks so he can spend the time he has left with his family. I asked him what he knew 'bout the strike that was goin' to hit his factory back in seventy-four. He said it never was goin' to happen. They had plans to stop it."

"What kind of plans?"

"He wouldn't tell me. He jus' said murder wasn't one of them."

"Why would he tell you if it was?" She grunted. "I knew seeing him would be pointless."

"I said *he's* innocent. I didn't say his partner was."

She looked up from her soda can. "The man wasn't sole owner?"

"No. I didn't know that. Everyone on the island thought Kamakani was the main man. He wasn't. In fact, he was nothin' more than a front for a big corporation."

"Why would a corporation need a front?"

"It happens on the islands. You see, Kamakani was Hawaiian. State laws favor businesses owned by Hawaiians. They get all kinds of perks and tax breaks. It's the same kind of thing you do for Indians on the mainland. The sugar plantation was registered in Kamakani's name, but he wasn't the one calling the shots."

"Then who was?"

"He tol' me it was a company called Comport. Ever hear of it?"

She knew it well. When she first started out as a reporter, she did an exposé on Comport for an environmental magazine. "It's a German conglomerate. During World War Two they made munitions for the Axis. After the war, they emerged as a powerhouse in Europe. They own companies all over the world, ranging from newspapers to oil tankers. They've had trouble in the past with the EPA in the United States for playing fast and loose with waste-disposal laws. Who did Kamakani answer to at Comport?"

"The chairman of the board himself. He's the one who wanted the strike broken."

She tried to unscramble the name of the CEO in her mind. Finally she remembered. "Was it Franz Hauptmann?"

"That's the name he gave me," Lopaka said.

"How many people did the sugar plant employ?"

Lopaka rubbed his grimy fingers through his hair, thinking about it. "Maybe two hundred people," he said finally. "Why?"

"That doesn't make sense. The plant had to be table scraps to a conglomerate as big as Comport. Why would the chairman involve himself in a strike of that small magnitude? It wouldn't have had any effect on Comport's stability." She suddenly remembered the research she had done on the company. It was in her computer back in New York. She quickly finished her soda and slid off the chair. "I need to look something up. Let me call you in about an hour."

"You plannin' on runnin' all the way back in this hot sun? You won't find a Hawaiian doin' anythin' as dumb as that."

"I'm not Hawaiian . . . I'm a New Yorker," she said, heading out the door.

When Malia arrived back at the ranch, she went into her office, sat down at her desk, and turned on the computer. She hoped it had a modem and communications software. It did. She dialed her modem number in New York, found the file on Comport, and downloaded it. Within seconds, the data appeared on her monitor. She scanned through the mounds of material until she came to Comport's acquisitions, which included over one hundred companies worldwide. Many of them were in the United States. She was surprised to find that they even owned Baronin, her publishing house.

Honokaá's sugar plantation, however, wasn't on the list. If they actually owned the factory, then that was a major violation of federal law.

It still didn't answer the question of why the CEO implicated himself with the strike. She hit the Down button on her keyboard, passing over Comport's records, looking for— What? At this point, she wasn't sure.

Forty minutes later she found something. It was just a few quotations from an article in the French newspaper *Le Monde*. If she blinked, she would have passed right over it. She printed out the information and called Lopaka back.

He answered on the first ring.

"I think I know why the strike was so important to Hauptmann," she told Ben. "In February of seventy-four, a small winery in the Loire Valley in France went on strike. It was a bloody one. Three workers were killed."

"Was this winery owned by Comport?"

"Yes. I told you, Comport is a worldwide conglomerate. It happened six months prior to the impending walkout at the sugar plantation. Hauptmann was called before the World Court to explain why such brutal action was taken to quell the

French strike. He and his company were reprimanded. Comport's stocks plummeted. With the Environmental Protection Agency in the U.S. investigating them, and another strike on the way, the company would have been in real serious trouble."

"But no one knew they owned the plantation. They also had a boycott in sixty-eight, which your father was involved in, and got away without anyone finding out about them."

"True," she said. "In 1968, the world could have cared less about two hundred Hawaiians going out on strike. But in 1974, Comport was in the limelight. They had the EPA pulling them from one end and the United States Congress and European agencies pulling from the other. If the strike happened, and it turned violent, someone would have nosed around and found out that Comport illegally owned the plantation. Comport could have been demonopolized."

"When you cut off the head, the body dies," Lopaka said pensively.

"Is that a Hawaiian colloquialism, Ben?" she said impatiently.

"It means your father was the brains behind the walkout. Kill him and you kill the strike."

She was beginning to believe he might be right.

"Is this guy, Hauptmann, still in control of Comport?" he asked.

"He was three years ago. The man has to be well into his eighties by now. I don't know if he's even still alive."

"I'll find out. Let me get back to you," he said.

Again she felt hopeless. "He's a very insulated man. A loner. Never been married. He doesn't talk to anyone. I tried contacting him in Berlin when I wrote the article about his company. He wouldn't take my calls."

"He'll take mine," Lopaka said.

She shook her head at his naïveté. "Ben, Comport is a global industrial complex, not a roadside fruit stand."

He chuckled. "I may be from the sticks, *wahine,* but when it comes to doing business, big or small, there ain't really much of a difference. You buy something at one price and sell it for another."

"Good luck," she said, hoping her voice didn't sound mocking.

After she hung up, she deleted the material about Comport from her computer, put the printed files into a folder, and placed them in back of her drawer. Her computer was a terminal that hooked up to the one in Steinway's office. She didn't want him to know what she was doing. This was not what she was being paid for.

Just as she started working on the book again, she heard the general's blustery voice coming from his office next door. He was throwing a tantrum, yelling a string of obscenities at someone at the top of his lungs.

Eventually he lowered his tone, but the anger was still there. Most of what he was saying was unintelligible, but she could make out phrases and words like: "Yellow Sea . . ." "You're all idiots! . . ." "I told you so . . ." Something that sounded like "Nampa," which she knew was a city in Idaho. What did Idaho have to do with the Yellow Sea in Asia? she wondered.

There was a map of the world pinned to a corkboard on the wall across from her desk. She went over to it and found the Yellow Sea tucked between China and Korea. Her eyes scanned the coastlines, stopping when they came to the city of Nampo in North Korea. She'd misheard the general. He wasn't talking about a city in Idaho—he was talking about a port outside of the capital, Pyongyang.

A moment later, she heard Steinway's door open, then close. Footsteps quickly led away from his office.

Peering out the door, she saw one of the general's aides, a red-faced, bald-headed man with a thick mustache, holding a stack of papers as he raced up the steps.

The intercom light from Steinway's office lit up on her phone. She picked up.

"Get in here," he growled.

She took a deep breath, then opened the door that connected their two offices.

He was hunched over his desk, rubbing his tired, angry eyes. Traces of foam clung to the corners of his thin lips. His rumpled fatigue jacket was strewn across the couch.

His eyes, like a hawk searching out prey, suddenly swiveled in her direction. "Pack your bags. We're leaving for Pennsylvania in the morning," he said.

"What's in Pennsylvania?"

"The Army War College. I have to give a goddamn speech there tomorrow night. I totally forgot about it, and they won't let me postpone the damn thing!" He slapped his hand angrily against the desk, sending papers scattering to the floor. He didn't bother to pick them up. "Those go-by-the-book ass lickers at the State Department don't understand priorities."

"I guess North Korea wasn't on their 'A' list," she said.

Steinway snapped his head her way. "You have your bags packed and be ready to move out by six-thirty in the morning."

His voice was low and threatening, making the fluids in her stomach curdle. She had never seen him this irate. "How long will we be gone?"

"*You* for a couple of days. *I'll* be flying to Ford Ord from there, then to Washington."

"Will Peachie be going with us?"

A disdainful look crossed his face. "No. She has too many important functions in Honolulu that need her attention." He didn't bother to explain what they were or hide his sarcasm.

She waited for him to continue. When he didn't, she perceived that the conversation was finished and turned to leave.

"Rico," he growled.

She turned around.

"Whatever you hear in this house about North Korea, stays here. Do you understand?"

"Yes, sir," she said, quelling an urge to salute him.

By ten o'clock her bags were packed and she was in bed. She just finished writing out a list of questions for Steinway and would give them to him tomorrow.

Not feeling tired, she turned on the news. A grim-faced anchorman, wearing a Hawaiian shirt, sat behind a prop desk. The country of North Korea was chromakeyed behind him.

Malia immediately grabbed for the controls on the nightstand and raised the sound.

"A navy minesweeper is being detained in the port of Nampo by the North Korean government—three hundred men are on board. The United States military is on full alert. President Claiborne is furious . . . The lights are on at the White

House ... The president is meeting with top officials right now to see what type of action may be warranted." References were made to the *Pueblo* incident.

So that's what the hullabaloo around the house was all about today, Malia thought. She wondered if the United States was planning some kind of military strike. If they were, she didn't doubt for a second that Steinway would be one of the men spearheading it.

"What perfect timing," she muttered to herself. Ciji Brown must be jumping with joy right about now. A military engagement for Steinway, followed by his memoirs hitting the bookstores only months later.

In a million years, no P.R. firm could have thought up this one, she somberly thought.

Chapter Ten

A N AIR FORCE 727 sat on the runway of Pōhakuloa Military Base with the engine running, waiting for Steinway and his entourage. Minutes after they embarked, the plane was skyborne.

Malia sat in front of the plane. The general and his aides were seated around a table in the back, going over maps. Taang stood over Steinway's shoulder, his hands clasped behind him, also looking at the charts. The atmosphere on the plane was tense. Tobacco smoke hovered over them like a rain cloud.

Malia had transferred her files to a laptop computer early this morning so she could work on the plane, but she was finding it difficult to concentrate. She kept looking over at the solemn faces of the men seated in the back. They were huddled together, speaking in low, grave voices. Every so often she could hear North Korea mentioned.

If she couldn't write, then at least she could try and edit the first two chapters of the autobiography. She took the manuscript out of her attaché case and went over it once again.

The story seemed to flow. Everything was there except for one thing: Felix Steinway's relationship with his father. The man seemed to be a shadow, without personality or substance. Steinway told her he was the most important influence in his life, yet she couldn't feel the connection between them. Whenever she tried to talk to him about it, he became evasive. What was he guarding? Feeding her cassettes every night wasn't going to give her an answer.

Four hours into the trip, Steinway, with a cup of coffee in his hand, came over and slumped down in the seat next to her. He looked tired and drawn.

"I can give you ten minutes," he said. "Make your questions short and to the point."

She grabbed her yellow pad and a small tape recorder from her attaché case and turned it on.

"I have to ask you about your father again," she said.

He nodded slowly, rubbing his eyes. "You seem to have an obsession with him."

"The last time we talked you told me that you two didn't always get along."

"Most children don't *always* get along with their fathers." After a pause, he said, "The man was a great soldier."

"I know that. That's not what I'm asking."

He emitted a deep, long sigh. "It wasn't anything insurmountable. He just had a problem differentiating between being a soldier and being a father. He was stern, demanding the best from me . . . the same thing he demanded from his troops. In reality, there was nothing wrong with that. When you're a child, however, you don't see it that way. I needed more from a father than a disciplinarian."

"Is he the reason why you didn't have any children?"

He chuckled. "Don't get Freudian on me, Rico. We didn't have any children because Peachie couldn't have any."

"Was your father ever affectionate to you?"

A sad smile slowly crept over his face. "When I was a boy, he was warm and doting. When I grew older, our relationship changed. He was the general and I was his junior officer. Those were the roles we took on. It was hard to live up to his expectations. I tried but never seemed to succeed. Actually, when I reached my teen years, I never saw him very much. He was gone most of the time. He spent four years fighting the Germans and the Japanese, then went to Europe after the war to help rebuild it."

"Did you ever visit him?"

"He was stationed in Berlin. My mother and I went to see him a couple of times." He bit down on his lip. "He was a busy man . . . didn't have much time for us. When he finally retired and came home, I was already at West Point. I then did five tours in Vietnam. He died when I was still there." He turned to her. "Not very exciting, is it? Anything else?"

It all seemed to fit. The son trying to please the father, and failing. Playwrights and novelists made their living by writing about this sort of thing. Yet she knew her man was holding something back. She could see blurry images of Steinway Sr., but she couldn't feel his pulse.

"He was home during the first twelve years of your life, right?"

"That's correct."

"Was he ever angry with you?"

"I told you, just stern."

"Did he ever punish you?"

"Why would he do that?"

"You were a boy. Boys get into trouble. It happens."

"Yes, I suppose you could say he punished me."

"How? Give me an example."

He gave her a suspicious look. "Are you trying to titillate the readers with this kind of stuff?"

"No, just trying to make them understand who you are."

He sipped his coffee, thinking. Finally he said, "He had a sword hanging over the mantelpiece."

"Your father?"

"Yes. It was given to him by a general who surrendered to him after a bloody battle in World War One. I was told never to touch it. It was a beautiful sword, inlaid with gold and silver. I took it off the wall one day when he was at the base and brought it outside to show a couple of my friends. We decided to play a game of cavalry and Indians. Since I had the sword, I was the cavalry. I became General Custer at Little Bighorn, chasing those little bastards all over the neighborhood. In the end, I lost them in the woods. I began testing the sword out on the branches of trees. It was sharp as a razor; cut clean through the wood. Except I nicked the damn thing up pretty bad. Eventually I went home and hung it back on the wall before my father returned. I thought everything would be just fine and dandy. It wasn't. During dinner that night, I saw him glancing up at it. Talk about rotten luck! That was the first time he looked at the sword in years. He went over to the mantel and took it down. I remember him running his hand slowly over the jagged edge. Then he turned and looked at me. I kept my head down and continued to eat, but I wasn't hungry. I was never so scared in my life. He asked me if I touched it. I lied and said no. That was the worst thing I could have done."

She saw the pain in his eyes. "What did he do to you?"

"Do? He did nothing. He put the sword back, sat down at the table, and ate his dinner."

"I thought you said he punished you."

"He did. My father wasn't the type that hung men up by their balls. There were other forms of punishment." He looked at her. "Do you know what 'silencing' is?"

"No."

"It's an unwritten code at West Point. If a cadet is accused of an honor violation, like lying, his classmates don't talk to him for the entire time he's there. They act as if he doesn't exist. It's the worst form of punishment a man can go through."

"Is that what your father did?"

"Yes. My father believed in codes and in honor. He lived by them. I had lied. A man of honor doesn't do that."

"How long did the silencing last?"

"For two years."

"Two years! How old were you when it happened?"

Biting down on his lip, he said, "Eleven." He then crumpled the empty Styrofoam cup in his hand and got up. "I have work to do." The softness in his face evaporated. "When you write about that incident, and I'm sure you will, don't portray him as a bastard. He was just a man bound by honor. That's all he knew."

He then went back to the other men seated at the table. She watched him pour a glass of Scotch, grab his cigar butt out of the ashtray, and point to an area on a map with it.

Steinway Sr. might not have a pulse yet, she thought, but at least he was beginning to have some of the chemical properties that made up life. His son didn't see him as a bastard. Malia didn't share his feelings. Imposing a code of silence on an eleven-year-old child was a shitty thing to do in her book. She rewound the tape. Turning it to a low volume, she put the recorder up to her ear and replayed the conversation.

That night, General Steinway spoke in front of two hundred high-ranking senior officers in the dining room at the War College. It was a passionate speech on how morality and modern-age warfare can coexist. When he finished, he got a standing ovation.

Although Malia had trouble understanding most of the technical jargon in his speech, she couldn't help but be moved by his fervor and charisma. He held the audience in the palms of his hands. The presidency was only a stepping-stone away, she thought.

She was sitting at the front table, next to Maj. Gen. Thomas Brinks, the president of the college. He was a tall, thickly built man with a stark white crew cut. Earlier, over dinner, he'd told her that he and Steinway had been friends since their plebe years at West Point. She asked him if they could meet tomorrow to discuss his life at the academy. He agreed.

She met Brinks in the dining room for breakfast at eight-thirty the next morning. Steinway had already left for Fort Ord, California, before dawn.

"Do you mind a tape machine being on?" she asked him.

"As long as the conversation pertains to the time Steiny and I were at the academy."

"Of course." She turned on the recorder. "Steiny? Is that the general's nickname?"

"Only to his friends." He snickered. "I wouldn't try calling him that if you weren't."

For the next forty minutes Brinks talked about Cadet Steinway at West Point. He was his roommate for the entire four years. His memories of him were glowing: captain of the football and debating team; honor student; class leader; a brilliant scholar; an inventive military planner.

"With all that, you wouldn't think he'd have time for women," Brinks said, chuckling.

Malia was surprised. "Steinway was a ladies' man?"

Brinks laughed. "There was none better. He wasn't exactly Tyrone Power, but you'd never know it. Once he turned on the charm, the girls dropped like flies."

"Was he dating anyone in particular?"

"No. The poor guy just couldn't make up his mind, there were so many to choose from." Again Brinks laughed. "He quit going out with women and hanging out in bars when he became a first classman."

"Why?"

"I was his wife. That's Point lingo for roommate. I used to spend most of my time sleeping in the bathroom because the bedroom was always occupied. One day, the girls stopped coming around. I asked him what happened. He said he no longer had the time. That wasn't like Steiny. He was always the life of the party. The first one in a beer joint and the last one to leave. And when he left, he was never alone."

"Was it because his grades were suffering?"

"Steiny? Not a shot. He was a fileboner at the academy—the best of the best."

"If he stopped seeing women and going to beer joints, what did he do with his free time?"

"First of all, you never had too much free time at the Point. Sometimes he'd just disappear for a couple of hours. He never told me where he went."

"You said he was a leader."

"He became regimental commander. There was no higher honor you could bestow upon a cadet."

"How did he treat the lower classmen?"

"They respected and feared him. If you were a good cadet, studied hard and did your work, he was like a father to you. If you were a 'goat,' or if he didn't like you, then your stay at the academy could be pure hell."

"What's a 'goat'?" she asked.

"A screwup. Someone who's at the bottom of his class."

"What constituted him not liking you?"

He scrunched up his eyes. "Weakness. He hated that more than anything."

This was a part of Steinway she didn't know. "How would he make life pure hell?"

"A hundred different ways. Steiny was very creative in that area."

"Was 'silencing' one of them?"

Brinks turned to her. "Absolutely not," he said emphatically. "Silencing was only given in extreme cases. In my four years at the academy, I never saw it." He wiped his mouth and put his napkin on his plate. "There was a plebe, his name was Steve Bankroft. He was the kind of guy who had two left feet. Couldn't do anything right. Bad academically, even worse at sports. He never should have been at the Point. I think he had some kind of pull to get in. Steiny hated him. Made his life miserable."

"You still haven't told me how."

He looked nervously down at his plate, as if he'd already said too much. "I really don't think it's important for the book," he remarked. Then he looked at his watch. "I have a meeting in ten minutes. I'm afraid we're going to have to end this." Brinks stood up, dropping his napkin on his plate. The conversation was over.

He walked Malia to the front lobby, then had one of the officers drive her to the airport to catch a noon flight.

On the plane back to Hawaii, she thought about her conversation with Brinks. He seemed ill at ease, and had abruptly ended their meeting when she wanted to know more about the cadet Steinway hazed at the Point.

She couldn't remember the plebe's name and had to look through her notes to find it. Steve Bankroft. What creative tortures did the general think up for him? She felt a tinge of disappointment. Before today, she was led to believe Steinway was a man filled with compassion—not someone who'd persecute a plebe because he was weak.

In many ways, he was very much like his father, she concluded. Strict and unbending.

Chapter Eleven

WHEN MALIA GOT off the plane, Taang was waiting for her at the gate. He seemed sullen, with his head down and his hands in the pockets of his shorts. The Montagnard must have taken an earlier flight, she thought. Why wasn't he with the general?

Without saying a word, he gestured impatiently for her to follow, then quickly scuttled toward the exit. She tried to keep up, but his small legs moved too fast. By the time she walked out of the terminal, he was already seated in the Jeep.

It was raining hard and the winds were tearing the leaves off the palm trees around the airport.

She tossed her bag in the back and got into the car. Before she could get her safety belt on, Taang hit the gas hard, causing the tires to squeal and her head to bang up against the backrest. He sped through the airport, toward the main highway.

She clutched onto the dashboard. "Having a bad day, Taang?"

He answered her by taking a sharp left at fifty miles an hour. Again the tires whined, burning rubber over the wet road. Cars moved out of the lane to let him pass.

"Why aren't you at Fort Ord?" she asked.

Once again his response was to step down on the gas pedal.

Then she understood. Steinway had sent him back to Hawaii to be with the women. In most primitive cultures, that was a job reserved for old men.

The hour trip was made in less than forty minutes. She let out a sigh of relief when the car finally came to a stop at the ranch.

* * *

After unpacking, she went down to her office and found three messages on the answering machine: Daniel; Ciji Brown; and Ben Lopaka.

She looked at her watch. It was after one in New York—too late to call Ciji. She put off phoning Daniel until she talked to Ben.

After several rings, the old man picked up.

"It's Malia. Are you in bed?"

"Hell no. Too early. 'Jeopardy' is on. Oh, by the way . . . Franz Hauptmann is very much alive."

"How do you know?"

"I talked to him yesterday, that's how I know. The man speaks perfect English for a German. He stepped down as chairman of Comport two years ago, but he still controls the major shares of stocks."

She was amazed. "How did you get to him?"

"No problem. I called Comport's number in Berlin. It was listed. Then I asked for Hauptmann's private secretary. Nice people, the Germans. They put me right through. Did you know he owns a home on Diamond Head? He visits there several times a year."

"No, I didn't," she said, still stunned that he'd pulled it off.

"His secretary tol' me he just got back. I tol' her that I was from the Hawaiian branch of the EPA, and that I was investigatin' an ol' environmental claim 'gainst a sugar plantation in Honokaá that Comport once owned. She put me on hold. Hauptmann got right on the phone with me."

Malia smiled. She had totally underestimated Lopaka.

"At first, he denied that he ever owned a sugar mill. I tol' him the figurehead owner, Mr. Kamakani, was on his death-bed an' he says differently. I tol' him that this dyin' man showed me papers provin' Comport owned the plant."

"Were there papers?"

"No. But Hauptmann didn't know that. Before he could deny it, I said I wasn't interested in who owned what. I tol' him everythin' was off-the-record, that I jus' needed to clear up some paperwork. The agency didn't care about a small plantation that went out of business fifteen years ago. He agreed to listen without ownin' up to anythin'. I first made up a story about some chemicals being spilled into the ocean by the mill and that I had to look into it. Then I got 'round to askin' him about the strike that almost happened in 1974. He said he knew nothin' about it."

"Was he lying?"

"You bet. I also asked if he ever heard of your father, James Rico. He said no, but I knew he was lyin' there, too. I ran down the murders to him. He acted surprised. He said he had nothin' to do with any of it. Then he got suspicious about why any of this should concern the EPA. I tol' him I had to go and hung up."

"Do you believe anything he said?"

"I'm not sure. You don't become head of a big company by tellin' the truth." He hesitated for a second, then said, "I also asked him if the name Daniel Keahi meant anythin' to him."

"Ben . . ."

"I had to ask."

"What did he say?"

"He said no."

"You're off on that one, Ben. Daniel had nothing to do with it."

"You sure 'bout that? I hear he's a real charmer."

"What does that have to do with anything?"

"Hopefully nothin'. Maybe I'm just a warped ol' man that don't trust anyone. I'm sure it was jus' a coincidence that Keahi was bendin' over the pond with you in it."

"He was reaching out to save me."

"Right."

"I have to go," she said irritably.

"I understand. You're not in the mood to hear this." He paused, then said softly, "Go slow with him, *wahine*."

After hanging up, she looked for Daniel's number in her phone book, then suddenly closed it and pushed it aside. Ben's warnings kept knocking around in her brain. *Damn him!* Why was she so enraged at that old man? Maybe because he was right: Daniel *was* a charmer.

Like it or not, she was drawn to him.

The rain outside was coming down heavier now. It was almost hurricane conditions.

Instead of going to bed, she began to write out a list of questions for the general, as he had asked her to do.

Halfway through, she heard soft music coming from another

room. Someone singing. She listened. It was Frank Sinatra crooning "Only the Lonely."

She left her office and walked down the hall to the other end of the house. At the entrance to the living room, she stopped and looked in.

Peachie, with a vodka glass in her hand, was slow-dancing on the balcony with an imaginary partner. She was wearing a sheer nightgown that exposed the dark nipples on her small, sagging breasts. Her eyes were closed, her head tilted to the side, as if resting it on her companion's shoulder. With her hips gliding in rhythm to the music, she swirled around and around.

Malia, feeling as if she'd intruded on a private moment, turned to leave.

Peachie opened her glazed eyes and saw her. She quickly stopped dancing, put her hand to her mouth, and let out an embarrassed giggle. "Oh, my. Caught in the act." Her words were slurred.

"I heard music," Malia said, feeling uncomfortable.

"Come on in. Join the party." She moved into the living room on legs that were none too steady.

"I think I should get some sleep."

"Nonsense. I've been alone all day. I could use the company. Let me make you a drink." She walked over to the stocked bar by the fireplace.

"I thought you were in Honolulu," Malia said.

"I got back early." She turned to Malia. "What's your poison?"

"Orange juice."

Peachie made a face. "One of those." She tossed ice in a glass and poured in the juice, spilling some of it on the counter. Then she refilled her own with vodka, this time not bothering with the ice. She handed Malia the drink, then plopped down on the couch, gesturing for her to sit.

Malia was tired. She just wanted to get some sleep. Instead, she sat down directly across from her.

"What's New" was now filtering out of the stereo.

Peachie closed her eyes, her head swaying back and forth to the music. "He was the best," she said. "Nobody could sing ballads like Ol' Blue Eyes. We had dinner with him once in Las Vegas. He was an admirer of my husband."

Malia nodded. Growing up in a different era, she was more inclined to go with Harry Connick.

"He can't sing like that anymore. His voice went. Christ, nothing lasts," Peachie said wistfully. "Felix and I, we used to dance to this album. He knew all the lyrics to the songs. When our cheeks were together, he would sing them to me." A sad smile crept over her face. "No, nothing lasts."

Feeling uncomfortable with her drunkenness, Malia shifted her body on the couch. "Do you miss him when he's away?" she asked.

"He's *always* away, even when he's with me. Felix is married to his work. When he was in the army, he preferred a tent to a home with solid walls and a fireplace. Always has. Not his fault. It's mine. I knew what he was before I married him."

Malia's fingers were cold from the ice cubes in her glass. "How did you two meet?"

With her tumbler resting in her lap, Peachie threw her head back, thinking. "How did we meet? God . . . so long ago. We met at a hop. That's what the cadets at West Point call a dance. Do they still call it by that stupid name?"

"I don't know," Malia answered.

"I was dating a cadet at the time. A lovely man. We were dancing the lindy. Suddenly, there he was, standing by the punch bowl. My legs almost gave way. Steiny was so big and handsome. He was sipping his lemonade, watching me with those green eyes of his. Later on, I went out on the balcony to get some air. He followed me. I think I knew he would. He asked me for my number. Before I knew what I was doing, I gave it to him. I was in a trance." She peered at Malia. "Felix can do that to you."

Malia remembered Brinks, the president of the War College, saying the same thing about Steinway and women.

"We met clandestinely for the rest of the year. After Felix graduated, we married."

"Was Felix an upper classman when you two met?"

"Yes."

Brinks told Malia that Steinway stopped going out with women sometime during his senior year. Now she knew why. He'd met Peachie. Why didn't he tell Brinks, his roommate and friend, about her? "You used the word *clandestine*. Was your relationship with him a secret?"

Peachie's half-shut eyes looked down at her glass. She leaned forward, putting her elbows on her knees to steady herself, and took a long sip of her drink. Smacking her lips, she said, "I came from a very wealthy family. Changing beaux in midstream was not considered the proper thing for a young woman to do. They felt it was best not to go public with our affair until after Felix graduated."

"Did your parents like him?"

"*Everyone* liked him. Felix had a way." A slight smirk came over her face. "I'm sure you've seen it." Her head was beginning to bob from the vodka.

"You must have met his father," Malia said.

She let out a breath. "Oh, God, yes. What a rigid son of a bitch. He had a stare that could turn you into ice. His insides were made of granite. Felix idolized the man. I don't know why. Getting a kind word from him was like squeezing water out of a stone." Peachie's elbows slipped off her knees and she almost fell. She dropped her body back on the couch, sunk down in it, then pulled up her nightgown and spread her white fleshy legs. Her eyes were almost closed.

Sinatra was singing "One for My Baby" now. With her head tottering to the music, Peachie began to mouth the lyrics . . . something to do with being true to your code. She then emitted a small, private laugh, as if those words had a special meaning to her. "That's my Felix . . . true to his code, all right, just like the song says. Just like his goddamn father was true to his."

Then she passed out. Her chin touched down on her chest and a light snoring sound whistled up from her throat.

Malia went over to Peachie and took the glass from her limp hand and placed it on the coffee table.

She had been a beautiful woman once—before the booze and the loneliness, Malia thought. Her legs still showed traces of sensuality.

She lowered the nightgown past the woman's knees, lifted her legs, and swiveled them onto the couch so that her whole body rested on the pillows. After putting a blanket around her, she turned off the lights and went up to her room.

Lying in bed in the darkness, Malia listened to the huge thunderstorm raging outside. She thought about Peachie, a woman living off memories and old songs. No one would ever suspect, but there were deep chasms in her marriage. She and Steiny came across to the world as the perfect couple.

Malia's lips curled into a bitter smirk. *Christ! Families were never what they seemed on the outside.*

Her own childhood, with her aunt and uncle on Staten Island, floated through her head. To everyone in the neighborhood, they were also the perfect family. But in that apartment on Richmond Avenue, with the door closed, it was a different story.

Her uncle Vincente was a crude man with a large black mole on his nose. He worked as a subway engineer for the New York transit system. His back was stooped and his eyes were bloodshot from sitting all day in a dark, tight cabin watching lights flickering by. When he came home, he'd take off his shirt and pants, sit on the kitchen chair in his Fruit of the Looms tank top and boxer shorts, and drink a six-pack. With a load on, his mood turned sour. Sometimes he'd look at her with hate, saying that she had nigger hair and nigger blood. In his thick Corsican accent, he'd curse his luck that he was strapped with taking care of his dead brother's daughter.

Other times—the times that frightened her the most—his eyes would become glassy and take on a different kind of look. He'd get up off the chair and sidle over to her, putting his lips next to her ear. The stench of beer on his breath would nauseate her. Whispering how beautiful she looked, he'd begin stroking her arms and back with his thick, sausage fingers. They felt like cold worms crawling over her body, and she'd quickly move away. Her aunt, frightened of his moods, would turn on the tap water and begin to wash dishes, pretending not to see.

One hot July night, when Malia was twelve years old, a man on her uncle's train went berserk—pulled out a gun and shot three passengers. When Vincente opened his cabin door to see what the commotion was about, the man shot him in the stomach. The bullet tore through his spleen and exited his back. He spent two months at home recuperating.

Malia's aunt went to a church function one evening, leaving Vincente alone with her. He sat in the living room drinking heavily, watching a Johnny Carson rerun. Occasionally his red eyes would glance her way, with that look coming over his face again. Feeling uneasy, Malia went to her bedroom and closed the door. A few minutes later the door opened and he entered. He wasn't wearing a shirt. Vincente walked unsteadily over to the bed and peered down at her through droopy eyelids.

Smiling bitterly, he suddenly ripped the bandage from his side and showed her the stitches surrounding the purple circular scar. "That's what you get for workin' twenty-five years for the transit system," he said. "A fuckin' bullet in the stomach."

Though it was a hot night and there was no air-conditioning, she quickly pulled the covers over her.

He sat down next to her on the bed and began to stroke her hair. She could smell the acrid aroma of stale beer emanating from his sweaty pores. Terrified, she tried to move her head away. Before she could, he put his hand over her mouth and held her down. He tore the covers off her and forced her legs apart. His rough hands were grabbing at her breasts, her buttocks, squeezing them hard, hurting her. Then he thrust his fingers inside her vagina, breaking her hymen. She moaned from the pain. Pulling down his boxer shorts, he tried shoving his penis into her bloody vulva, but he was too drunk to get an erection. Cursing, he rolled off her small body and yanked up his shorts. He looked down at her terrified face. Swaying, he told her what he would do to her if she said anything to her aunt.

When he finally left, she turned her face into the pillow and cried. She was lucky this time. But what about tomorrow night and the next? He would be back. She was on her own and would have to deal with this herself.

A week later, when her aunt wasn't home, he came into her room again. He grabbed her by her hair and forced her down on the bed. She could feel the large bulge in his shorts pressing up against her thigh.

This time she was ready for him.

As his thick lips locked onto hers, she slid her hands over his hairy body, feeling for the bandage on his stomach. Finding it, she ripped it off and dug her long nails into the bullet wound, tearing at the stitches. He let out an agonizing scream and tried to get up, but she held on tight, refusing to let him go. How she hated him! Her nails burrowed in deeper. She could feel his pain; his raw skin and the wetness of the blood gushed down his side. With a loud roar, he managed to pull away and leap off the bed. Holding his hand over his open wound, cursing, he reached out for her, but she had already slid off the bed and ran into the bathroom, locking the door behind her. Screaming, he kicked at the door several times, then left the bedroom to dress his lesion.

She stayed in the bathroom until she heard her aunt come home. Malia knew he'd never do anything to her while she was there. She quietly washed up, then took the bloody sheets off her bed and hid them in her closet. After putting on fresh ones, she crawled back under the covers. It was hours before she could fall asleep.

He never came into her room again, but the lines had been drawn in blood between she and her uncle.

When she turned eighteen, she left home and went to live in Manhattan. She supported herself at odd jobs while putting herself through college. The only contact she had with her family was a Christmas card sent every year from her aunt. The woman died several months ago, so now she wouldn't even have to deal with that.

Malia's memories were interrupted by footsteps creaking on the floor outside her room. Seconds later, she heard the metal sound of a latch turning. Someone was opening the French doors. Had Peachie awakened and gone outside?

Malia rose from the bed, went over to the window, and looked out into the darkness. Bolts of lightning ripped open the thunderous sky and she saw Lupe's silhouette crossing the meadow, going toward the black cliffs. Her body was arched low, as if wanting to avoid being seen.

Malia looked at her clock on the night table. It was after one. Where was the girl going at this hour?

Then she remembered her boyfriend. She hoped the bastard wouldn't hurt her again.

Chapter Twelve

SEVEN O'CLOCK THE next morning, Malia dragged her tired body out of bed and got dressed. When she went into the kitchen, she found that the coffee wasn't made. Odd. Lupe always had it prepared in the morning.

Perhaps she'd overslept. Malia went into the servants' quarters and knocked on her door several times. When there was no answer, she turned the knob and peeked in.

Lupe's bed was made up and her nightgown neatly folded across the covers. No one had slept there last night.

Malia saw her climbing up on the cliffs in the rain. The girl must have spent the night with her boyfriend, she thought.

She noticed the dresser mirror had photographs stuck into the sides of the frame. They were snapshots of Lupe cuddled up to a coarse-looking Hawaiian man with long hair. He had a thin, droopy mustache and tattoos running down his beefy arms. Above the mirror, a withered flower lei hung down from its post.

She closed the door and walked down the hall to the living room. Peachie wasn't on the couch where Malia had left her last night. The blanket she'd covered her with was lying on the floor. Had she gone upstairs sometime during the night?

She went into the kitchen and brewed a pot of coffee, then toasted two slices of bread and brought them down to her office.

While munching on the toast, she called Ciji in New York.

"Where are we in the book?" the editor asked as soon as she got on the phone.

"Chapter three."

"Send me the first five when you finish. I want to see them. Any difficulties so far?"

"Maybe. The general's wife has a drinking problem."

"That's another book," Ciji said gruffly.

"I also don't think their marriage is all that stable."

"Whose is? Concentrate on Steinway's heroics. That's what we shelled out seven million dollars for."

"I think his private life is also important for the book," Malia said.

"Not to me it isn't." Ciji's voice cracked with impatience.

Malia's other line began to ring.

"I'll send you the five chapters at the end of next week," she told Ciji.

When they hung up, she pressed the button on the second line. It was Daniel.

"You playing hard to get?" he asked.

"Sorry I didn't return your call. I just got back from Pennsylvania last night." She tried to control the rush of contradictory feelings erupting inside her when she heard his voice.

"How about lunch?" he said. "I have to come over to the ranch anyway—to pick up a book Felix borrowed from me."

She thought about it. "Okay. But it can't be a long one."

"No sweat. I'll have you back in a couple of hours, I promise."

"What kind of book is it? I'll see if I can find it for you."

"It's on Maori war clubs and other sundry weapons. The general is a collector of Polynesian artifacts."

She already knew that. Every wall and shelf in the house was crammed with ceremonial masks, pottery, and other hand-carved relics.

"He was thinking about purchasing some of their clubs at an auction. I told him to go through the book so he could get a better idea of what they're worth."

"I'll look for it in his office," she said. They agreed to meet at noon.

Malia worked on the autobiography for two hours straight. When she finally looked up from the computer, it was past ten. She rubbed her neck, trying to get the kinks out, then went into Steinway's office to get his West Point graduating yearbook. She wanted to look through it to get the feel of what the academy was like in the fifties.

She saw Daniel's book on the desk as soon as she walked in. The general's yearbooks, almost thirty volumes in all, were on the top shelf of the bookcase. They started from the year he graduated up to the present.

She took down the first volume, dated 1952, and leafed through it, stopping when she came to his graduating class. Being regimental commander, his photo was larger than the others. He was a good-looking man in his dress uniform. His jaw was square then, and he had all his hair. No, he wasn't Tyrone Power, but he came damn close. She could see how women would be attracted to him.

Most of the other pages exhibited different cadet activities at the Point. She came upon a collage of photographs showing students eating at the cadet dining hall. Steinway's unmistakable frame was seated at the head of one of the tables. Listed under the photo were the names of the cadets sitting with him. She scanned the roster. Thomas Brinks, now president of the War College, was seated to Steinway's left. To his right, she recognized Billy Doyle, the present head of the National Security Council.

An impressive array of dining companions, she thought.

The figure of a plebe seated directly opposite Steinway caught her eye. He was sitting straight up, head bowed, with his hands at his sides. Everyone else at the table seemed to be eating except him. Her finger went down the list of names, stopping when it came to his: Steven S. Bankroft.

He was the plebe that Brinks had told her about, the one who Steiny detested.

She took the general's magnifying glass off the desk and put it up to the picture. Enlarged, the faces suddenly became alive. She saw young cadets at the table, laughing and talking to one another. Bankroft was the only one who seemed as if he didn't belong. His sullen eyes were cast down on his plate.

She didn't know this man, yet she felt a compassion for him. What happened to Bankroft? she wondered. If he was a plebe in '52, then he should have graduated from the academy four years later.

She took down the '56 yearbook and looked over the list of graduates. Bankroft's name wasn't among them. If he was weak like Brinks claimed, then he probably dropped out or was asked to leave. It was a known fact that life at the academy was not for the feeble.

She looked at her watch. It was almost noon. Daniel would

be here shortly. She'd better change into a decent pair of shorts.

As she got up from Steinway's desk, she noticed a stack of books piled chaotically on the bureau across from her. They'd been taken down from the packed shelf directly above the cabinet. Not characteristic of the general, she thought. The man thrives on order. Perhaps Lupe moved the books so she could dust and forgot to put them back.

She grabbed several volumes and started to return them to the shelf.

That's when she saw the cylinder-shaped wall safe inside the ledge. It was cut deep into the partition, with the steel edges flush against the oak panel. These books were supposed to be up there, hiding it. The steel door was open, exposing stacks of old letters inside. Some were in manila files, others were separated by rubber bands.

She'd asked the general several days ago where he kept his old correspondence from prominent people. They could be used in his book. He said he would go through his boxes of papers and find them. Had he left the safe open so she could sift through these letters?

When he called later, she'd ask him. Malia closed the safe, being careful not to lock it, and put the books back up on the shelf.

Malia went to her room and changed into a new pair of linen shorts and a Saks T-shirt. When she finished, she heard the doorbell ring. She raced out the room to the front door and opened it. Daniel stood by the threshold, smiling. He was wearing a khaki shirt with rolled-up sleeves and matching shorts.

"I have your book," she said.

"Thanks."

She took the volume off the vestibule table and gave it to him.

He shoved it under his arm. "Ready for lunch?"

"Ready," she said. "Where do you want to go?"

"Oh, an interesting little place I know. It's about a twenty-minute drive."

They took his Jeep and drove west on Highway 19, past the small local towns of Onomea and Pāpa'ikou. He veered south on a small dirt road, driving several miles into the jungle. The foliage began to overtake the road, making it difficult to follow. Finally the trail disappeared altogether, and a swampy field took its place. When they reached a thick mass of trees, Daniel stopped the truck.

"We walk the rest of the way," he said. He got out and grabbed a weaved bamboo basket from the trunk.

Malia looked around. The area was overridden with wild tropical growth. "This must be some exclusive restaurant you're taking me to."

"Not many people know about it," he said, smiling.

She followed him into the jungle. They trekked about a half mile, meandering their way through dense vegetation, until they came to an abrupt clearing.

Malia immediately saw several young people excavating a mound of black stones that jutted twenty feet up from the ground. The thing was massive, about a city-block long.

"The *heiau* I was telling you about," he said. "These people are anthropology students from the University of Hawaii."

The *heiau* didn't look like much to her. Just a large, rectangular rock pile.

He grabbed her arm and helped her scale the huge mass of stones. When they reached the top, she looked down into the interior of the deserted ancient temple and saw walls made of stacked rocks crisscrossing one another like a giant labyrinth. He took her hand once more and they climbed down into it.

He stopped next to a six-foot-long clump of flattened stones resembling a plateau. He opened the basket, pulled out a tablecloth, and spread it over them.

"Sit down," he said, pointing to the ground next to the makeshift table.

"I didn't know we were going on a picnic," she said.

"You looked like you could use the sunshine."

She sat down and looked around. "How long did it take them to build this monolith?"

"Years. Hundreds of commoners worked on it. The stones come from the crater on top of Mauna Loa, about forty miles away. They carried them here by hand." He took out several ham-and-cheese sandwiches, different kinds of fruit, and put them out on the stone table. Reaching back in, he brought out a bottle of red wine and held it up. "I heard you liked Burgundy."

"You heard right," she said.

He uncorked the bottle, poured two glasses, and handed her one.

She took a sip, then bit into the sandwich. "Is this the temple where the ancient Hawaiians performed human sacrifices?"

"Right." He spread mustard on his sandwich with a plastic fork.

"Where did they do it?"

"At the altar."

"I don't see one," she said, looking around.

"That's because you're eating on it."

Malia peered down at the tablecloth covering the flattened rocks. She wrinkled up her face. "You really know how to show a girl a good time."

A wry smile played on his mouth. "You don't think about it in my business. Now you know what I do for a living." He fingered his glass, thinking, then said, "Actually, I had a reason for asking you out."

"What was that?"

"To help put your mind at rest about me."

She blushed. "Look, it's rested. Don't worry about it."

"Too bad your friend Lopaka doesn't feel the same way. He's been asking questions about me in Honokaá."

"He used to be a policeman. They don't trust their own pets."

Daniel grinned.

A shadow suddenly passed over her face and she looked up. A tall, thin Hawaiian man, with his body blocking out the sun, was standing on top of the *heiau* looking down at them. He had a scraggly beard with patches of white in it and his eyes were covered by sunglasses. When Daniel saw him, the grin disappeared and he immediately stood up.

"Who's he?" she asked.

"Roger Alika. He's a colleague of mine from UCLA. I'll be right back." He disappeared into the maze.

A moment later he came back into view, climbing the escarpment toward the man. When he reached him, they began to talk. Every so often the thin one would glance down at Malia, push his glasses up the bridge of his nose with his index finger, and give her a curious look. Eventually they separated. The man went down the other end of the *heiau* and Daniel came back to her.

"A problem?" she asked as Daniel sat down again.

"Not really. Just business." He tore into his sandwich.

"He looks nervous," Malia said.

"Roger's *always* nervous." He changed the subject. "You engaged or spoken for back in New York?"

"Neither one anymore. What about you?"

He grabbed his wineglass from the altar and lay back, propping himself up on his elbows. "I was married once. It didn't work out. I was gone most of the time, digging up temples like this all over the South Seas. I came home one day and found someone else sleeping on my side of the bed."

"Did you hit him?"

He smiled. "No. Actually, he was a nice guy. A gynecologist. He loved her. Said he wanted to marry her and give her the kind of life I couldn't. What could I say? I wished them well, packed my bags, and moved out. They married the day after our divorce was final."

"Do you have any children?"

"One. A daughter. She's eight now. They all live together in a nice big colonial in the suburbs of Marin County."

Malia grabbed a slice of pineapple and popped it in her mouth. "Do you ever see her?"

"My daughter?" He smiled gently, as if he were picturing her face in his mind. "Sure. When I'm in the neighborhood. That's not very often. She considers the other guy her daddy now. It's no one's fault but mine. I chose this nomadic life." He turned to her. "You said not anymore? What happened to the love of *your* life?"

She finished her sandwich and lay down on the stones next to him. The sun felt good beating down on her face—so did Daniel's arm, which was pressing up against hers.

"I once lived with a man who I thought I was going to marry. He was an artist. Very cocky, but quite talented. Unfortunately, he was frightened of success. He did everything he could to avoid it."

"Was he temperamental?"

"Yes. How did you know?"

"Under an arrogant guy is usually a frightened little boy."

Malia laughed. "You sound like you know him. He used to thrive on throwing tantrums."

"What kind?"

"The usual. Destroying his paintings because he didn't feel they were good enough ... getting drunk before a show and making an ass out of himself. The drama got too much for me, and I moved out."

"Who got the cat and the Springsteen collection?"

She grinned. "I got the cat. He got Springsteen. I also let him keep the torn couch and a beat-up bed from Pier One."

"That was very decent of you."

She nodded. "I thought it was."

Malia opened up and talked about her relationship. Daniel listened intently. An hour later she looked at her watch. "Oh, Christ! I've got to go." She stood up.

"Why?"

She brushed the black sand off her shorts. "I have three more chapters to write by the end of next week or I'm history."

He laughed as he got up from the ground. "Okay, I'll let you go."

She helped him clear off the make-do table, putting the unfinished food and wine back into the basket. When she tried to remove the tablecloth, Daniel grabbed her hand and brought her toward him. She didn't resist. He lifted her chin with his fingers, bringing her face close to his, and kissed her. She found her arms going around his back and her body pressing up against his. He brought her down on the altar. His weight was against her torso, his knee edging up between her long, slender legs.

She suddenly moved her lips away from his. "I don't think it's the right place for this," she said, trying to catch her breath.

He quickly glanced up and looked around to see if any of the students saw them. No one did. They were all on the other side of the *heiau*. He rolled off her body and lay on the altar, his chest heaving up and down. Then he turned on his side, reached out, and began stroking her hair.

She let him, bringing her head into the fold of his arm.

"Sorry about that little outburst. I just couldn't resist," he said.

She let out a small giggle.

He lifted his head and peered down at her. "What's so funny?"

"I was just thinking. This altar seems to serve many purposes. You can slaughter on it, eat on it, and now you can even make love on it."

Daniel grinned. "Our Hawaiian ancestors were very resourceful people."

He said *our* ancestors. Daniel was including her in his culture. She was more at home with the Italians and the Irish in New York than she was with the Hawaiians on the islands. Once again, that sense of not knowing who she was began to play with her equilibrium.

"I really have to go," she said, moving her head away from his arm. She hopped off the altar and grabbed the basket.

Daniel stood up. "I think we need to do this again," he said, holding her shoulders in both hands.

Tracing the scar on his forehead with her finger, she said, "I think we probably will."

When they reached the entrance to the ranch, the road was blocked with several police cars. Up on the bluff, policemen were milling about in groups. A helicopter suspended above them was lowering a harnessed paramedic and a gurney down to the rocks below.

Malia and Daniel got out of the car and made their way to the cliffs. Before they could get to the edge, a young officer stepped directly in front of them, preventing them from going any farther.

"You live here?" he asked.

"I do," Malia said. "What happened?"

"An accident. A woman who works here fell off the cliff."

Malia brushed past the officer and ran over to the edge. Looking down, she saw the twisted form of Lupe three hundred feet below. The girl's skin was the color of eggshells. She was wedged in tightly between two boulders, thwarting the mammoth swells that were trying to wash her out to sea.

Chapter Thirteen

BEN LOPAKA PARKED his yellow truck in back of the county building on Aupuni Street in Hilo. The steel sky over the city was threatening rain again, but so far it hadn't come. Ben was thankful for that; his legs couldn't take much more pain. He hobbled around to the front of the two-story structure and went in.

Most of the offices, now empty, were occupied by city employees. The bottom floor belonged to the coroner's department.

He took the stairs down to the basement and walked past several enclaves until he came to Paul Nani's office. The door was open.

The pathologist's huge frame was slouched down behind his desk. Black-framed reading glasses rested on the bridge of his squat nose. He was using his two index fingers, laboriously typing out a report on a computer. At the University of Hawaii, he was an all-star defensive back and a third-round draft pick for the Chicago Bears. After a crushed kneecap ended his career, he went on to medical school and became the pathologist for the district of Hilo.

When he saw Ben's head peeking inside his door, he stopped typing and waved him in. "Aloha, *ahiahi*," he said.

"Aloha, *ahiahi*, yourself, Paul." Ben went inside the office, looked down at the computer, and smiled. "You've become a modern man. I remember when you didn't know how to stick a plug in an outlet."

Paul waved his hands in disgust. "The damn thing scares the shit out of me. It seems like every ten minutes the county's purchasing a new gadget for me to learn. I spend more time tripping over wires than I do dissecting corpses." He turned the computer off. "I'm glad you could come, Ben."

"I waited twenty years for you to invite me."

"Well, it just may have been worth the wait." He lifted his big body out of the chair and came around the desk to shake Ben's hand. He was over a foot taller than the old police captain.

"What do you want to show me, Paul?"

"A fresh body that came in this mornin'."

"You talkin' 'bout Lupe Maile, the one who worked for the general?"

"*Ya ya.* Do you know her?"

"Knew her family," Ben said. "Nice people. Terrible accident. The entire district's talkin' 'bout it."

Paul stooped his shoulders, so he could be on the same level with Ben. "Maybe it wasn't an accident. Did you bring what I asked?"

Lopaka patted his back pocket. "Sure did."

"Come with me," Paul said.

He took Lopaka into the lab next door. A body covered with a sheet lay on a gurney in the middle of the room. Paul lifted the sheet, exposing the broken form of Lupe. Since she'd struck the cragged rocks headfirst, her facial features had no semblance to anything living or dead.

"She white like this from the salt water?" Ben asked.

Paul shook his head. "No, it's because she doesn't have an ounce of blood in her."

"She hit the rocks that hard?"

"That's what I thought, too, at first." Paul grabbed Lupe's stringy hair and tilted what used to be the head to the right of the body. He pointed to the neck. "See that deep cut by her jugular?"

Ben looked up at Paul. "You don't think the rocks did that, is that what you're tellin' me?"

Paul nodded.

Ben looked at the skin around Lupe's breasts. They were scraped and raw, but he could see the teeth marks. "Someone bit her," he said to the pathologist.

Paul nodded. "I saw those. Let me show you something." He went over to the counter, pulled out the top drawer, and took out a small plastic bag. He opened it up and turned it over. A tiny red sliver dropped into a metal tray. "It's wood. I found it in her hair, next to the wound."

Ben peered at it. "What kind?"

"I don't know yet."

"What's so important about it?"

"Maybe nothing. The girl's hair was freshly washed and there were no trees on the bluff where she fell."

"You think it came from the weapon?" Ben asked him.

"Could be." He then went over to the terminal monitor sitting on the corner table and turned it on. "It took me a month to learn how to use this thing." He removed a four-inch glass slide from his counter drawer and placed it under an optical magnifier. "Look at the monitor."

Ben did. At first, the picture on the screen was jumpy and blurry. Then, as Paul focused the lens, the image sharpened. It was something gray and square, almost transparent. The top edge was jagged, the other three were cut in unwavering lines.

"It's a tissue sample, enlarged several times. I've taken it from the neck wound," Paul said. He traced the ragged edge with his finger. "Whatever cut into her jugular made that. Notice how the lines are angled like pyramids."

Ben moved his weak eyes closer to the screen. "There's no pyramid here." He pointed to one area on the tissue.

"Right. It skips one, then the triangle shapes continue."

Lopaka's eyes brightened as he began to understand what Paul was leading up to. "I bet I know what should have gone in there," he said, reaching for Panali's bandanna in his back pocket. He unfolded it and removed the shark's tooth.

Paul took the tooth from Ben and held it up to the monitor, positioning it on one of the pyramids. It fit perfectly in the grooves, like a piece from a picture puzzle. Then he put it to the area where the triangle was missing. *"Auwē no ho'i e!"* he uttered.

"Boy oh boy, is right, my friend. The tooth belongs there," Ben said. His body was pulsating with excitement.

Paul grabbed an old manila folder off the counter and opened it. He removed several colored photographs of tissue samples and handed them to Ben. They were similar to the image on the screen. Some of the photos included the missing triangle, some didn't.

"I went into my old files in the storeroom and dug these out. We didn't have computer enhancement back then when I was coroner. I shot these twenty years ago. These were taken from the wounds found on Loke and James Rico. The lacerations on James Rico had the complete set of teeth. After this tooth broke off in Loke's body, we get the missing triangle. See?" He pointed to the photo of Loke Rico's tissue sample. "At the time, I swore a shark killed the couple."

"I remember you tellin' me that," Ben said. "It wasn't a shark. It looks like it was some kind of weapon made from sharks' teeth."

He held up the tooth to one of the photos. It fit in the same area as the one missing on the screen.

"It's the same weapon, used twenty years apart," Paul said, amazed.

"If it's the same weapon, then maybe it's the same killer."

"Maybe. Maybe not. But if you're right, then I'd say this island owes you one hell of an apology."

"No apology needed. I jus' want to make sure I kill the right bastard this time. When you examined the Rico woman's body, did you find any human teeth marks on her?"

Paul opened the file and looked through his notes. A minute later he looked somberly up at Ben and nodded. "On her left shoulder."

"Did you make an imprint?"

"I didn't think it was necessary," Paul said. He looked embarrassed. "You'd already killed Panali. The case was considered closed."

"Make your call," Ben said.

Paul went over to the phone and dialed the district police captain, Isaac Yamaguchi.

Ben sat down on a chair to rest his legs and listened to Paul reporting to Isaac about his findings. For twenty years they'd called him *pupule* for telling them that the killer was still out there. He wanted to feel some kind of elation. Yet, for some strange reason, he felt no vindication, only a growing sense of apprehension. It lay in his stomach like a lead weight.

The angel had returned. For what purpose? he wondered.

At five after ten that night, a messenger came to the ranch house and handed Malia a package pouched from Washington. It was the cassette promised by the general. Steinway had flown to Washington from Fort Ord this morning. She put tomorrow's questions in the sack and gave it to the messenger. It would go out tonight.

Unfortunately, Steinway was not reachable by phone or fax. The reason was becoming more clear to her as time went on. North Korea had dominated the news again all day. The president had issued another strong ultimatum demanding the release of the naval vessel. Once again, the Korean government refused, stating that the boat had violated their sovereign waters. Steinway, she knew, was somewhere in the Pentagon, helping prepare plans for an invasion or a strike.

Malia, trying to take her mind off Lupe's tragic death, took the cassette into her office and played it. With her feet propped up on the desk and a notebook in her lap, she listened to Steinway's voice. His answers to her questions were humorous and insightful, filled with good character information about himself and several of his close associates.

Most of the questions she wrote down for him for tomorrow were about his senior year at the Point and his years before Vietnam. One query she threw in was about the plebe, Steven Bankroft. She made it casual, saying that she saw his name and picture in the yearbook and wondered who he was. Would Steinway be honest about his dislike for the cadet?

She went through Jasper Rhodes's notes one more time. There was nothing on Bankroft. Again she wondered what happened to the hundred pages that were missing. Were they something he threw away—or had Steinway edited the manuscript himself?

She turned on her computer and began to incorporate the general's responses into the new chapter. It was going to be a long night. All work on the book today had to be put off because of Lupe's death. Isaac Yamaguchi had questioned her, like everyone else who lived on or was employed by the ranch. She'd told him that she had seen the girl going toward the cliffs, probably to meet her boyfriend. When Isaac asked who he was, she said she didn't know his name, but the photos in her room might be of him. She'd told him about the fight she'd overheard between them several nights ago and the bruises and teeth marks on her body she had seen the following day.

When he'd finished questioning her, she'd looked for Daniel, but he wasn't there. He had left before the police could talk to him.

By two in the morning, Malia stopped working and stretched her tired arms. Her mind was fried, but she knew she had to continue if she was going to make up for lost time. She crouched down into the chair, put her long legs on top of the desk, crossed her ankles, and rubbed her bloodshot eyes.

When she opened them again, her line of vision was on the bookshelf directly across from where she was sitting. She speculated about the letters in the safe behind those books. Was it left open for her? She couldn't ask the general because he was unreachable at the moment.

Why not take a look? she thought. If the letters were useful, she could at least come up with some ideas on what to do with them while waiting for Steinway to call. If not, then she would put them back and forget about it.

Malia removed the books from the shelf and opened the safe. She grabbed a handful of the files, went back to the desk, and began to sift through them.

None of the old letters were in any particular order. There were a couple from Peachie, written to her husband when he was in Korea, then in Vietnam. She read them. They were long and emotional, filled with concern, praying he'd come home safely. She put those aside, thinking they'd play well in the later chapters.

She got up to get more files. Most of the letters in these were of the same type. When she came across a stack marked WEST POINT, she undid the rubber band and spread them out on the desk. She immediately saw an envelope with the name of Rosemary Bankroft on the return address. Was she related to the cadet, Steven Bankroft?

The envelope was powder blue, faded with age. She removed the letter and read it:

January 11, 1952
First Classman Felix Steinway,
My son, Steve, was home for the holidays last month. He broke down and told me what you've been doing to him. He told me about the incident with the peas and the other horrors you've put him through. I understand that hazing plebes is part of an upper classman's right, but the torture

*you're inflicting on him goes beyond hazing. It's cruel and
sadistic.*

*He's beside himself, fraught with worry and self-doubts,
which you've instilled in him. Before you came into his life,
he was a happy, patriotic young man who worked hard to
get accepted to the academy. The boy I saw last month was
not the same person who grew up in this house.*

*I've taken the liberty of writing to your superintendent,
Maj. Gen. Ronald Cherney, and told him what has been going on. If you can't stop yourself from committing these mer-
ciless, unprovoked attacks on my son, then I'm sure the
general will take action to help you stop.*

Rosemary Bankroft

Malia folded the letter and put it back in the envelope. This
was a strong accusation against Steinway. Rosemary Bankroft
was accusing him of committing mental cruelty against her
son. She then wondered about the pea incident in the letter.

She scanned the rest of the envelopes. Two more were from
Steven's mother. She read them. These were dated in March
and were even more desperate. Obviously the general hadn't
stopped the hazing. Malia was perplexed. Were these letters
about the same man she knew and admired?

Then she saw a small envelope in the pile. It had the raised
West Point crest on the left side. There was no stamp on it,
meaning the letter had been hand-delivered to Steinway. She
opened it up. The letterhead on top was Gen. Ronald
Cherney's, the superintendent of West Point. It was dated
April 14, 1952.

Reg. Comdr. Felix Steinway,
*I want to see you in my office at eleven hundred hours re-
garding the death of plebe Steven Bankroft.*

Supt. Ronald S. Cherney

Bankroft had died. How?

She put the letter back, then wrote down the address of
Rosemary Bankroft, which she'd copied from her envelope.
The woman lived in Holyfield, Virginia. After rewinding the
rubber band around the stack of letters, she returned them to

the safe, closed the steel door, and stuck the books in front of it.

Malia sat down at her desk and put her hand on the phone, tapping it with her finger. *Do I leave it alone or not?*

I just can't.

She got the area code of Holyfield, Virginia, from the long-distance operator and dialed information.

"Do you have a listing for a Rosemary Bankroft?" she asked her.

After a minute, the operator said, "I see no Rosemary Bankroft, but I do have listings for three other Bankrofts."

Malia asked for the numbers and wrote them down. Holyfield was a small town. Perhaps they were all related.

When she hung up, she looked at her watch. It was six o'clock in the morning back East. Too early to call these people.

What the hell was she doing anyway? she thought. This was not her job. This could be opening up a whole can of worms. Again she wondered if she was supposed to look at the letters. If Steinway was cruel to a plebe, Ciji certainly would not want to see it in the book.

"Better wait on this one," she said out loud. How could a day that started out so good, turn this bad?

Malia switched off the lights and went up to bed.

Chapter Fourteen

THE NEXT MORNING Ben called Malia and explained about the wounds in Lupe's neck matching the ones found in her parents. He told her to meet him and the police at the bluff where she died.

Malia walked out on the cliffs, folded her arms, and stared somberly down at the rocks where Lupe's body was found. The fear inside her returned in full force again.

She looked up when she heard the four-wheel-drive police vehicle driving over the field. It came to a stop at the edge of the escarpment. Ben and Isaac got out, along with two other police officers.

Ben smiled at Malia. "I think you two know each other." He gestured to Isaac, who was standing next to him.

Malia shook hands with Isaac. The police captain's face was taut.

"What are you looking for?" Malia asked Isaac.

"Blood. Signs of a struggle," Isaac replied. "Was this where you saw the girl the night of the argument?"

She shook her head no and pointed to the large rocks higher up on the bluff. "That's where I interrupted her, and I assume her boyfriend, last week. She was also heading in that same direction the night she died."

They left the two policemen searching the ground by the cliff and climbed to the spot. When they reached the boulders, Isaac swept the grass around the area with his foot. He shook his head. "Nothing," he said.

"Maybe you'd better come over here, then," Ben called out.

Isaac looked up. Ben was somewhere behind the rocks. They went over to him.

The tops of the two boulders where Ben was standing arched inward, forming a small cave. The old man got on his knees, staring down at the ground. Most of the area was covered with grass—except for a three-foot spot in the middle where the ground had been churned up.

Ben scooped up the dirt with his hands and tossed it over to the side. When he reached the bloodstained grass underneath, he stopped digging.

Ben looked up at Malia and Isaac. "The bugga killed her here, but threw her off the cliff a hundred yards away." He poked a finger at the bluff just a few feet from them. "It would have been a lot easier to toss her here."

Malia walked over the cliff and looked down. "Here's why he didn't," she said.

When Ben and the captain reached the precipice, they also understood the reason. The land was higher here, but the ground wasn't vertical like the cliff farther down. It sloped on a forty-degree angle to the small beach below. If she was thrown from here, she would have only rolled down. Her body wouldn't have been smashed beyond recognition and the wound on her neck would have been immediately spotted.

Ben went back to the boulders and continued to comb the ground next to the makeshift cave. Without looking up, he said, "Her jugular was cut open. It should have pumped a trail of blood leadin' to the spot where she was thrown off. I don't see any trail." Ben stood up slowly. His knees were on fire from kneeling on the wet grass. "The killin' had to be planned. He must have had somethin' with him to wrap her body in. He carried her over to where there was a straight drop, so it could look like an accident."

One of the officers came up the hill waving his arms in the air. "I think you'd better come down here, Captain. We found something," he said. His voice was animated.

They climbed down the hill and went over to where the second officer was lying on the ground, peering over the cliff. He motioned for Isaac to get down and look.

The captain dropped to the earth and slid his body halfway over the precipice. About twenty-five feet below, he saw a four-foot-wide ledge jutting out from the sheer bluff. There was a large, ovular rust-colored stain on it.

"Is that blood?" the officer lying next to him asked.

"It looks like it," Isaac said. There were deep crevices in the dirt wall leading down to the ledge. It was as if someone scaled the cliff using only their hands and feet.

He stood up and wiped the dew from his uniform. Looking at Ben, he said, "There's a small bluff protruding from the side of the cliff. You can't see the damn thing unless you lean over it. I don't think the killer saw it, either. When Lupe was thrown over the side, her body got lodged on its rim. Looks like he had to climb down to finish the job."

Ben poked his head over the edge. "He must have been one hell of an athlete. It's a steep drop, without anythin' to grab on to."

Isaac turned to Malia. "You told me yesterday that Lupe Maile had a boyfriend."

"There are photos of him in her room," she said.

"I want to see them."

They crossed the field and headed toward the servants' entrance.

Inside Lupe's room, Malia took the photos of the Hawaiian

and the servant girl out of the frame of the mirror and handed them to Isaac.

"Sam Pua," Isaac said, nodding.

"Who's he?" Ben asked.

"A small-time drug dealer. I arrested him a couple of times. I know where he lives. I'll have him picked up."

Ben stared hard at the picture. "When you talk to him, I want to be there," he said quietly.

In a small file room in back of the police station, Sam Pua, wearing only undershorts, was seated at a table with his hands cuffed behind him. His chin was resting on his chest and his shoulder-length hair clung to his sweaty face. He was full-blooded Hawaiian, big and stocky, with a gut that hung over his briefs. A motif of women's names, entwined by the bodies of two fanged snakes, were tattooed on his huge arms. Wiggling down the side of his back, like the fault line of an earthquake, was a thick knife scar.

Isaac and a young *haole* police officer were sitting at the opposite end of the table from Pua. Ben, fiddling impatiently with his pipe, was leaning against the wall.

An hour ago the police broke down Sam Pua's door and found him in bed. Before he could fully awaken from his drugged sleep, they had him handcuffed and led away.

"Wha' I do, *brah*?" Sam said, looking up at Isaac.

"I ain't your *brah*," Isaac said, leaning into the table, putting his face next to his. "You murdered Lupe Maile."

Sam's eyes arched in fear and disbelief. "Lupe? She *stay make*?"

"*Ya, ya,* she *stay make*. She's dead. You don't know anything, right?" Isaac said.

Sam shook his head vigorously. "No. No. I wouldn't hurt her. What you mean, dead?"

The police captain growled, "I mean dead, like *dead, brah*."

The Hawaiian let out a groan, then wailed, "Not Lupe! Not Lupe!" He said the girl's name over and over again, banging his forehead on the table.

Ben stuck his pipe back into his pants pocket, walked over and grabbed Sam by the hair, lifting his head up. He could feel the man's blubbery body shaking as he sobbed. "What did you use on her, *brah*?"

Sam didn't answer. He pulled away from Ben's grip and lowered his head into his heaving chest once again.

"You killed her the same way you killed that couple twenty years ago," Isaac said coldly.

"I ain't killed nobody," Sam managed to mumble between whimpers.

Isaac looked at Ben, smiled. "I think you finally got your boy."

"He didn't say he did it yet," Ben said.

"Give him a night in jail, he will," Isaac replied confidently.

Ben scratched his jaw, thinking. Then he turned to the Hawaiian and slapped him on his brawny arm to get his attention.

Sam snapped his head up.

"How old are you, son?" Ben asked.

"Twenty-six," he said.

"Twenty-six, *ae?*"

Sam nodded, then kicked the table with his bare foot. "I didn't kill no one! I want out of this fuckin' place!"

Ben sighed. "I see we got to get an understandin' goin' between us, boy." He grabbed Sam's droopy mustache between his fingers and pulled the Hawaiian's face toward him until their noses were touching.

"Aw, Jesus! You're hurting me!" Sam cried. He tried pulling his head away, but Ben's grip was like a steel vise.

"You like great whites, Sam?"

The Hawaiian grimaced in pain.

Ben tweaked the hairs harder, twisting his lip up to his nose. "I asked you if you liked great whites."

The Hawaiian's mouth dropped open in agony and confusion. "What the hell's a great white?"

"A big shark. The kind that would chump your *huas* off thinkin' they were party mints."

Knowing *huas* were Hawaiian for testicles, Sam involuntarily closed his legs. "I don't know nothin' 'bout sharks. Oh, Christ! You're killin' me!" His face was coated in sweat, and his nose was running from the pain.

"What about angels? You like angels with big white wings and red swords?"

Not comprehending, Sam's eyeballs raced from Ben to Isaac, then back to Ben.

"You starting that angel stuff again?" Isaac said irritably to Ben.

Ben let go of Sam's mustache. His hot eyes glared at the captain for a second, then he turned back to the frightened Hawaiian. "Were you with her the night she was murdered?"

"Fuck, no! I ain't seen her in months!"

"When you did see her, where *did* you meet?"

"At my place, sometimes at a bar. Why?"

"You ever meet with her up on the bluff at the general's ranch?"

He shook his head emphatically.

"Don't lie to me."

Sam moved the upper part of his fat body toward Ben. "I swear, man. I never met her there."

"The *hapa* woman who's workin' for the general says she was up there one night an' heard you and Lupe fighting behind some boulders. She said you were talkin' Hawaiian an' slappin' her around."

"The bitch is lyin'! I never was up there."

"There are witnesses who say they saw you beat Lupe on several occasions. One time the police were called to stop you," Isaac said to Sam.

He shrugged. "Yeah, maybe. That was a long time ago. I got drunk a few times. Those things happen when you're drinkin'."

"Not always," Ben said. He resisted an urge to punch the overweight Hawaiian in his mouth. "You ever bite her?"

A confused look came over Sam's face. "No, why the hell should I?"

"There were teeth marks on her stomach and on her breasts."

"What would I bite her with, goddamn it!" Sam opened his mouth and showed Ben a black cavern where his three front teeth should have been.

Ben put his finger to his lips. "Keep your voice down, son. You said you hadn't seen her in months. Why?"

Sam wiped his running nose on his shoulder. "I think she was seein' someone else. I accused her of it a few times. She denied it. Even after I beat the shit out of her, she denied it."

"What made you think so?"

"Things started changin' between us. Nothin' she said. I

jus' could feel it. She used to come over every night. The gal liked gettin' high on weed an' playin' 'round in bed. Know what I mean? Then she started havin' headaches or didn't feel well. Soon she jus' stopped comin' over altogether. Always gave me a bunch of dumb excuses. One time she said she was tired of bein' poor. Said if she played her cards right she was gonna have money."

"When did this start?"

"Maybe six, seven months ago."

"You have any idea who this other guy might be?" Ben asked.

He shook his head. "I'm not sure. At first I thought it was one of the *paniolos*. They're always hangin' 'round the ranch, starin' at her. 'Cept those guys never had no money."

"Anyone else who hung 'round the ranch that maybe did have some money? Maybe someone who Lupe talked 'bout?" Ben asked.

Sam bit down on his mustache, sucking the tip of it in between his thick lips, thinking. "Yeah," he said, after a while. "She used to tease me 'bout this good-lookin' guy that came over all the time to see the general."

Ben suppressed a smile. "This good-lookin' guy have a name?"

She never tol' me. She said he was some kind of professor workin' on that new *heiau*. Kept tellin' me how nice he was to her. Sounded like she had a crush on him."

"I think I know him," Ben said.

"You think he killed Lupe?"

"Could be, Sam."

"Look, I didn't kill her." Sam's voice was shaking from desperation.

"I know that."

"Then tell that to the captain. Tell him to let me out of here!"

Isaac gave Ben a disbelieving glance, then stood up. "I need to talk to you, Ben."

Ben held his hand up to Isaac, telling him to wait. "Gettin' you out may take awhile, Sam. We're on Hawaiian time. Nobody does anythin' in a hurry 'round here." He began to move to the door.

"You're gonna tell him, aren't you?" Sam's eyes were frozen in fear.

Ben leaned over the Hawaiian, until their faces were almost touching. "Look at my eyes, son. These pouches under them come from the stress of doin' what's right. If I say I'll take care of it, I'll take care of it."

"When?"

"When I get 'round to it. You like beatin' up women, Sam? I think the women of this island deserve a break from you for a while."

Ben walked out of the holding area with Isaac and closed the door.

"Come into my office, Ben," Isaac said. He sounded angry.

Lopaka followed the captain into the small office that once was his. Isaac closed the door and turned to the old man. "Look, Ben—"

Ben stopped him short. "What you got is a third-rate drug dealer here, Isaac. Nothin' more."

"I don't buy that. He admitted he used to beat up Lupe Maile."

"Come on, Isaac. Sam Pau is twenty-six years old. Accordin' to my calculations, that should make this bad guy 'round six when he killed the Ricos. A six-year-old with the strength of a two-hundred-and-fifty-pound Samoan? Give me a break. 'Cause that's the kind of muscles you'd need to create the damage I saw that night."

Isaac pointed his finger at him. "Okay. Maybe he didn't kill the Ricos, but he sure as hell killed the girl."

"You saw the guy. He's fat an' out of shape. How'd he climb down a sheer cliff to push Lupe Maile off the ledge? He couldn't scale a picket fence, let alone a twenty-five-foot wall."

"Fear of being caught can make you do things you never thought possible."

"That's bullshit, Isaac. You got the weapon he used?"

"My men are back in the house looking for it."

"How'd you like to bet your entire pension that they don' find it."

"He'll talk," Isaac said confidently.

"Coincidence, ain't it? The same mysterious weapon used twenty years apart by *two* different killers."

"That may be what it is, Ben. Two different killers."

"An' they both liked to bite women?"

"I don't have any imprints of the bites found on Loke Rico, so I can't compare them to the bites on Lupe Maile."

"What did Pua bite Lupe Maile with? His gums? You saw yourself he got no teeth. Isaac, this guy don' know nothin' 'bout nothin'. He may be a low-life drug dealer that beats up on women, but he don't know jack shit 'bout those murders."

Shaking his head in amazement, Isaac went behind his desk and sat down. He began to shuffle some papers in front of him, trying to look busy.

"It's got to be the same man," Ben said, leaning over the desk.

Isaac glared up at him. "You're starting to sound even crazier than people say you are."

Ben tried to shrug off his remark, but it still hurt. "He's still out there. I suggest you keep looking, Isaac."

The police captain smiled sympathetically at the old man. "Any idea who I'm supposed to be looking for, Ben?"

"*Ae*, maybe I have."

Crossing his hands on the desk, the captain smiled, not bothering to hide his sarcasm. "Who? This professor friend of General Steinway's? Is he this angel now, Ben? How many other people are you going to accuse before this is over? We have our man. Now hang it up and go home."

Ben shook his head slowly. "You were jus' a pup when you came on the force. I thought I trained you better than this." He turned and stomped out of the room, slamming the door behind him.

Chapter Fifteen

Lupe Maile's funeral took place on a day when the trade winds offered no relief from the crushing heat. The dampness hung over the northeastern part of the island like wet rubber over skin.

Inside the white wooden church the locals huddled together in the back pews. They swept at the thick air in front of their faces with newspapers, trying vainly to stir up a breeze.

Lupe's father, a *paniolo*, sat up in front next to the altar. He was rocking back and forth, his hands covering his grief-stricken, weather-beaten face. Peachie, wearing large sunglasses that covered her impassive expression, sat next to him.

The parish priest, with sweat trickling down his bald head, glanced at the coffin while reciting from the Book of St. Peter: " 'All flesh is as grass ... the grass withereth, and the flower thereof falleth away: but the word of the Lord endureth forever.' "

Malia sat next to Daniel in the third pew. Her eyes were locked on the carved wooden statue of a smiling, naked angel with fat rosy cheeks by the coffin. Its arms were outstretched toward the congregation. Malia felt they were held out only to *her ... beckoning.*

Daniel turned his head and saw Malia's pale complexion. He reached out across her lap, took her hand, and squeezed it gently.

Her eyes immediately bolted from the figure to his concerned face. She gave him a weak smile. From her angle, she saw Ben sliding into the pew across from them. The old man wore a threadbare brown suit with a dark knit tie hanging crookedly from his frayed collar. He raised his knobby hand to her in acknowledgment, but his pouched eyes were zeroed in on Daniel.

When the service ended, the mourners drove to the same cemetery where Malia's parents were buried. The sky was turning dark with rain, threatening to break the stifling heat.

The priest, sensing the oncoming downpour, quickly said a few words to Lupe's anguished father as he made the sign of the cross over the grave. Leis were dropped onto the coffin by the mourners, then the order was given to lower the casket into the ground.

The crowd began to disperse. Daniel took off his jacket and loosened his tie. His shirt was stained with sweat. He put his hand on the small of Malia's back and guided her to his truck.

"What happened in the church?" he asked, opening the door for her.

"What are you talking about?"

"You were frightened to death."

"I felt faint from the heat," she said, getting in.

Daniel kept the door open. "You looked like you saw something."

"Saw what?" she snapped. "You were sitting right next to me. What the hell could I have seen?"

"No reason to chew my head off," he said, with a hurt tone. He slammed the door closed, got into the front seat, and threw his jacket in the back.

She wiped the sweat off her brow with her hand. "Sorry. It's this damn heat." Glancing out the window, she saw Peachie getting into her car. The woman was as emotionless as she had been throughout the service.

The road leading out of the cemetery was gridlocked by a line of vehicles trying to leave. Daniel put his clutch into neutral and waited impatiently. He closed the windows and turned on the air conditioner.

Ben hobbled over to the truck. The old man, wearing his shrewd smile, tapped on the glass with his callused knuckles. Daniel rolled down the window.

"Hate to bother you," he said to Daniel, "but I left my car 'bout a quarter of a mile down the road. Think I can have a lift?"

Daniel frowned, then leaned his arm over the seat rest and opened the back door.

Ben grunted and his knees crackled like crushed glass as he slid slowly into the truck. "Really 'preciate this," he said.

"Anytime," Daniel answered coldly.

Ben leaned forward and put his arms on Daniel's headrest, his lips only inches from the man's ear. "Nice service, didn't you think?"

"If you like funerals," Daniel replied.

"I ain't seen you in twenty years," Ben said to him.

"Time does fly," Daniel said caustically.

"I been thinkin' a lot 'bout you."

"So I've heard. You've been asking enough questions about me—like I was your long-lost brother." Daniel found an opening in the jam-up and gunned the motor past several cars in front of him until the road was clear.

Malia turned and scowled at Ben. She knew he left his car down the road on purpose.

The old man ignored her stare. "I need to ask you somethin'," he said to Daniel.

"About what?"

" 'Bout fish ponds."

Daniel's shoulders stiffened. "I thought we talked that one out over the phone."

"Yes—yes, we did," Ben said vigorously. "Problem is, every time I put it to rest, another question pops up."

"Like what?"

"Like how come you were watchin' the fireworks up on your roof that night? It was pourin' out."

"There's a canopy on the roof. Besides, I like rain."

"That's where we're different. I hate rain. Kills my legs."

"Where's your car?" Daniel asked.

"My car?" Ben scratched his face, then pointed his thumb in back of him. "Oh, we passed it 'bout three hundred yards back."

Infuriated, Daniel did an immediate U turn, squealing the tires.

"That yella' one over there." Ben motioned to his dented truck over by the side of the road.

Daniel jammed on his brakes. He gripped the wheel tightly while Ben made all kinds of hissing and groaning sounds as he slowly made his way out of the vehicle.

Before Daniel could drive away, the old man went around to the driver's side and tapped on the window again. Daniel rolled it down.

"It was rainin' pretty bad that night and there was no moon. You couldn't see two feet in front of you," Ben said. "How'd you see a car go down a hill without headlights and park in front of the Ricos' house, which was over a hundred yards away? Not only that, but actually see someone get out of the car? You got special kind of vision or somethin'?"

Daniel's eyes strained at the man. Punctuating every word, he said, "There was a fireworks display, remember? The whole sky was lit up."

Ben smiled at Daniel and shook his head, like a father watching his son drop a fly ball because he didn't follow instructions. "The fireworks came from Hilo, 'bout forty miles from your house. I was watchin' them, too. There was only a dim glow in the sky; it wasn't lit up like you said. The only way you could see somethin' a hundred yards away in that downpour was if someone dropped a napalm bomb outside your house." Ben backed away from the truck. "We'll talk again soon, Daniel."

Before Daniel could respond, Ben turned his back on him and crossed the road to his truck.

Daniel closed the window and drove toward the general's ranch in silence. His lips were pressed tightly against his teeth.

Malia was furious at Ben for doing that. But the old man brought up a good point and she couldn't ignore it.

As if reading her mind, Daniel said, "I saw what I saw."

"I believe you," she said. Her voice was not too convincing.

"Lopaka is a smart man," Daniel said, with sarcastic admiration. "Too bad he drank himself out of a job." He turned to her. "Want lunch?"

She shook her head. "I have to work," she said coldly.

When they reached the entrance to the ranch, Daniel stopped the truck. She started to get out. He reached over and grabbed her shoulder, stopping her. "You don't believe me, do you?" he said.

"Look, it has nothing to do with what Ben thinks. I need some time, okay? You're moving too fast with me. You were not the reason I came to the island." She got out of the car and stormed up the porch steps.

A sad look came over his face and he clucked his tongue. "You're right. Sorry. I just thought— Hell, I don't know what I just thought." He drove away without saying good-bye.

Goddamn you, Ben! she said to herself as she went inside the house.

She changed out of her dress, then went down to her office. A pouch from Washington was on her desk. She opened it up. It was an audiocassette from the general. Her heart raced. She hadn't heard from Steinway since she'd sent him the list of questions a couple of days ago. Malia stuck it in the recorder and listened:

There's a four o'clock flight on United from Kona to New York. Take a shuttle to Washington. You'll be picked up at the airport. (Pause.) I see we need to talk.

That was all.

Malia removed her heels, stuck her legs up on the desk, leaned her head between them, and ran her fingers through her hair. *Damn, damn, damn.* She knew he wanted her in Washington because of the question she'd asked about the plebe, Bankroft. Why the hell had she started this in the first place? Steinway hadn't even bothered to answer any of her other questions. This was putting her further behind in the book. *Damn!*

Ben Lopaka parked his truck by the shoulder of Queen Ka'ahumanu Highway on the outskirts of Kona, got out, and made his way around the dead chickens scattered over the road. The smell of gasoline singed his nostrils. A poultry truck had skidded out of control, crashing into an oncoming car. The surviving chickens, still trapped inside their cages, were cawing loudly, frantically trying to get out. Next to the smoldering remains of the car, two bodies covered in sheets were lying on the blacktop, waiting to be loaded into the coroner's van.

Paul Nani was talking to a policeman by the side of the road when he saw Ben. He went over to him, grabbed the old man by the shoulder, and led him away from the accident. They stopped by the edge of a coffee field.

"I got your message and called your office," Ben said. "They tol' me where you were."

Paul took out a cigarette from his pack and lit it. He inhaled deeply, letting out a stream of smoke. "We ran tests on that red sliver of wood found in Lupe Maile's hair. It's koa."

Ben's eyelids narrowed.

"Koa trees are only native to the Hawaiian islands," Paul said.

"I know. The ancient Hawaiians made their knives and clubs from koa. You think a piece might have chipped away from the weapon an' got in her hair?"

"I think so," Paul said.

The old man's eyes suddenly lit up. "Malia Rico said she saw a flaming red sword in the hands of the killer. Maybe what that little girl saw was the bright red wood of the weapon." A slight smile suddenly broke on Ben's face.

"Did I say something funny, Ben?"

"No, Paul. I was jus' thinkin' 'bout an anthropologist I know who happens to be an expert on Polynesian weapons." He tapped Paul on the shoulder, thanking him, then walked sprightly around the bloody carnage toward his truck.

Ben sat at a dimly lit desk in the Hilo library turning pages of a book on Hawaiian folk art. Several other volumes about ancient weaponry lay scattered across the table. Glancing up at the clock on the wall, he saw that it was seven forty-five. He had fifteen minutes to find what he was looking for before the library closed. He shut the book and reached for another one.

Ten minutes later, he found it. *"Christ Almighty!"* he said out loud. The weapon that was used in the murders was right here on this page all these years.

He took the book over to the librarian sitting behind her desk. "Excuse me, Mrs. Pono. You mind, I need to check this out."

The Hawaiian woman looked up at him and smiled. She took the book from him, glanced at the title, and read it out loud. *"Folk Weapons of Ancient Hawaii.* I've known you for over fifty years, Ben. Since when did you get interested in Hawaiian weapons?"

" 'Bout twenty seconds ago," he said.

Ben walked around the desk and turned the pages until he came to a photograph. It was a thirty-inch club formed like a paddle: the outer rim was surrounded by sharks' teeth curving in the same direction; the inner frame was carved out. "It's called a *lei o manō*," he said to her, poking his finger at it.

"That means a lei made of sharks," she said.

"That's right. A good name for it, too."

Looking at the picture, her face wrinkled up in revulsion. "What a horrible-looking thing!"

"But a hell of a weapon. It was made from the root of the koa tree. The teeth, 'bout forty-two of them, were attached to the frame by coconut cordage.

"According to the book," he continued, "there're only two *lei o manō* clubs still in existence. One is in a museum in New Zealand. The other is in the Natural History Museum in

O'ahu. Only the chiefs were allowed to carry them. They were used primarily to carve flesh from the bones of human sacrifices at the *heiaus*."

"You mean like the one they're digging up near Honokaá?"

Ben smiled. "*Ya ya*. Exactly like that one, Mrs. Pono."

The next morning Ben Lopaka caught the 7:30 puddle jumper to Honolulu. When he landed, he grabbed the shuttle bus going toward the museum in Makalapa Center, across from the Arizona Memorial.

Looking out the window, he could see rows of garish, neon-lit strip joints stretching across the breast of the city. Busboys were standing by their doorways, hosing the vomit and urine off the sidewalks from last night's horde of drunken sailors. To the east was Waikiki Beach, with its human blanket of tanned, slippery bodies.

The old man hated Honolulu. The real Hawaii, what was left of it, was back in Honokaá, where he came from. He was determined to do his business quickly, then leave.

The bus let him off at Aloha Stadium. With the frayed library book tucked under his arm, he walked the two blocks to the museum.

Inside the marbled halls, he made his way to the War Room. The walls and glass cases were filled with ancient weapons from the South Pacific: war clubs from Tonga; spiked hammers and throwing clubs from Fiji; engraved human bone toggles from the Marquesas Islands; Samoan diamond-shaped knives; wooden staffs from the Easter Islands. One of the cases contained a Hawaiian dagger made from a swordfish bill that was thought to have killed Captain Cook.

Ben slowly strolled through the corridor looking for the *lei o manō* club. When he came to the last case, he still hadn't found it. He opened up the book and looked at the photo of the shark weapon once again and read the information under it. Yes, it was supposed to be here. He went over to the tourist desk and showed the photograph of the club to the information clerk behind the counter.

"I'm lookin' for this weapon. Accordin' to the book, this museum is supposed to have it," Ben said to him.

The clerk lowered his head, squinting through wire-rimmed glasses to get a better look. Seeing the photograph, he nodded in recognition. "This club used to be part of the collection. Not anymore."

"What happened to it?"

"Stolen."

"By who?"

"Don't know. Real professional job. Cut the glass around the case with a razor. Didn't even set off the alarm."

"Anythin' else taken?"

The clerk shook his head. "That was it. There were other things in the museum more valuable. A couple of Gauguins were on the second floor. The robber just wanted that club. The police thought a private collector who was an expert on Hawaiian weapons paid someone to have it done."

Ben slammed the book closed in frustration. "How long ago did this happen?"

The information officer answered immediately. "Twenty years exactly."

"How do you know?"

"I'd been working here for three months when the robbery took place. Four months ago I celebrated my twentieth year here."

A nice round number, Ben thought. Twenty years ago was when James and Loke Rico were murdered with the weapon.

An hour later Ben landed in Kona. He shuffled out to the parking lot, found his truck, which he'd left under the shade of a banyan tree, and drove home.

The information clerk thought it was a collector, an expert, who took the club. He began to get excited. The only expert he knew was Daniel Keahi.

Danny Boy . . . he was only a hop, skip, and jump from the museum in Honolulu. The officer said it was a professional job. Ben laughed at that one. He knew the layout of that museum. It was so unprotected, and the alarm system so antiquated, that a three-year-old could have pulled it off.

Daniel Keahi . . . *His name just keeps comin' up all over the place,* he thought.

Chapter Sixteen

IT WAS ALMOST six-thirty in the morning when Malia arrived at Dulles Airport. A nervous army captain was waiting for her by the passenger desk. Without smiling, he tipped his cap to her, then hurriedly grabbed her overnight bag. She followed him outside to a bland, government-owned Ford sedan that was parked in the Tow-away Zone.

Forty minutes later they pulled into a section of the massive underground area of the Pentagon not allocated for civilians. A silent electric cart, driven by a corporal, pulled up to them. She and the captain quickly got into the backseat and drove through dimly lit, endless gray corridors that showed no signs of life.

The tunnels got darker, almost to the point of blackness, illuminated by small-watt bulbs planted every fifty feet. Eventually the cart pulled over to a steel door.

"Wait inside there. The general will be with you soon," the captain told her. He handed Malia her overnight bag. As soon as she got out of the cart, the soldiers drove off, disappearing into one of the dark capillaries.

She opened the door and went into a windowless, twelve-foot-square cubicle made of concrete blocks. A small, gray metal table was in the middle of the room, holding a goose-necked lamp and a phone. Two chairs were placed around it. She put her bag against the wall and sat down. The only sound she heard was the low, steady hum of a generator somewhere in the building.

She massaged her eyes, trying to get the fuzziness out of her brain. It was two o'clock in the morning Hawaiian time.

The door opened twenty minutes later. Steinway entered the room. He shut the door, sat on the edge of the table, and looked down at her. She attempted a smile, but that soon faded when she saw the staid look on his face.

"Why am I here, General?"

"Because I asked you to be here. Did you bring your tape recorder along?"

"Yes," she said.

"Get it. I haven't had a chance to answer the questions you posed to me. We'll do it now."

Confused, she got up and went over to her bag. She unzipped the side pocket and took out the small machine. "I thought you were going to pouch me the answers," she said, sitting down again.

His face reddened. "Do you have a problem with a change in the itinerary?"

"Not at all," she said. She knew better than to argue. She put the recorder in the middle of the table. As she started to turn it on, the general reached out and stopped her.

"I'll tell you when." His voice was cold and flavorless.

Malia looked up at him, puzzled.

"You wanted to know about a plebe who went to West Point when I was there. Why?"

Here it comes. She let out a nervous breath. "You mean Steven Bankroft?"

"That's who I mean."

"Just curious, that's all. I saw his picture in your graduating yearbook. He was seated with you in the cadet dining hall."

He folded his arms. "What about the other men seated at the table? Didn't you notice *them*?"

"Yes, of course."

"One of them is the head of the National Security Council. Another, whom you've met, is the president of the War College. Two of the others are three-star generals. I didn't see their names in your questionnaire. Weren't you also *curious* about them?"

"Yes, I was."

"Then why didn't you ask about them?"

Lack of sleep was making it hard for her to think. She'd give anything right now for a cup of coffee. "I intended to ask you about them later on. I saw Bankroft's picture. He seemed distant from the others. I just wondered what his relationship was to you."

"He had no relationship to me," he said flatly. "He was a man who used his influence to get into the Point. He couldn't make the grade. If he hadn't died, he would have been weeded out."

"He died? I didn't know that. How?" she asked.

He looked doubtfully at her for a second, then his jaw tightened. "You didn't know?"

"No. How could I?" She had a habit of biting down on her bottom lip when she lied. She hoped she wasn't doing that now.

"What does Bankroft have to do with my book?"

"Nothing."

He had a bitter smile on his face. "Just curious, right?"

"Yes."

"The pathetic fool killed himself. It happened during the Easter break. His roommate came back from the holidays and found him hanging by his dress belt in the closet. He'd been dead for almost a week."

Malia sat there for a second, stunned, then asked, "Look, do you think I could get some coffee?"

He picked up the phone and whispered into it. She couldn't make out what he was saying.

When he put down the receiver, she asked him, "Why would he kill himself?"

"Because he was a washout. The boy was unstable. He never would have lasted. I tried to help him, but he wouldn't follow directions. Some of the other cadets were a bit harsh on him, and he couldn't hack it."

"Are you talking about hazing?"

"Yes, I guess you can call it that. It's a necessary tradition at West Point. It separates the weak from the strong."

Malia tried not to let the shock she was now feeling show on her face. According to the letters from Bankroft's mother and the tone in Superintendent Cherney's note, Steinway was the one who was doing the hazing. The man was lying to her.

He pulled out a cigar from his breast pocket and lit it. The smoke hung over them. There was little circulation in the room and her eyes began to burn. Steinway didn't seem to notice or care. "Anything else you want to know about this plebe before we get on to more important business?"

He made it obvious that there was only one answer she'd better give. "No, I don't think so," she said finally.

"Good." He smiled down at her. "Were you thinking about putting that plebe in the book?"

"I see no reason for it," she said quickly.

"Nor do I," he uttered, with finality.

The corporal came in with a thermos of coffee and set it down on the table. Malia eagerly poured herself a cup and took a sip. It was decaffeinated. The general knew she was tired and wanted to keep her that way.

"I know what happened to your parents," he said, looking down at his cigar, twirling it around in his fingers.

Her head jerked back in surprise. "You do?"

He nodded. "A shame. Sorry to hear about it. I didn't know Isaac Yamaguchi was talking about you when we all had dinner together. You should have said something."

"I saw no reason to."

"I've been told that the old police captain ... What's his name?"

"Ben Lopaka," she answered.

"Yes, Lopaka. He's been coming around, filling your head with stories."

"How do you know?" Taang must have said something to him, she thought.

"I know everything that happens on my property, little lady. This man has been taking up valuable time that should be put toward the book."

"Not that much," she said.

"I think differently. I don't want him around the house anymore. Is that clear?"

She forced down her anger. "I hear you," she answered.

"Good. I heard about Lupe. A terrible tragedy. If I knew she was seeing a man like that, I would have put a stop to it. Are the police finished with their investigation?"

"I don't know," she answered.

"I hope so. I don't need them coming around the ranch, disturbing you any more than they already have." He continued to puff on his cigar, then turned to her. "I also heard you've taken up with Daniel."

"My God," she whispered.

"I like Daniel. I think you two make a fine pair. Go with

God's speed." He leaned in until she could feel his breath on her cheek. "But go after the book is done."

"Look, General . . ." She attempted to stand up, but his brawny hand reached out and grabbed her shoulder, forcing her back down.

"You have a book to write. There're millions of dollars involved, not to mention my reputation. What you do between the sheets is your business, but do it on your time. According to the contract, *your* time begins eight months from now. Is *that* clear?"

She tried to stand up again, but his hand pressed firmly down on her shoulder.

"I've talked to Ciji about it and she agrees. She's not a happy camper at the moment." After waiting for this to sink into her head, he said, "Now that we've taken care of all this unpleasantness, turn on your recorder." The smile lingered on his face. He put on his bifocals, then opened up his attaché case. He took out the paper containing the list of questions she'd sent him and scanned through them slowly. Clearing his throat, he grumbled, "I see we're going to be here for a while."

Two hours later, an exhausted Malia turned off the machine. They were finished.

The general stood up and stretched his gigantic arms outward, then massaged his sides. He looked at his watch. "I have to get back."

Malia rubbed her eyes and looked up at him. "Are you here because of what's happening with North Korea?"

Steinway gave her his now-familiar wink. "If I am, then we'll add it in as a postscript to the book. There's a room waiting for you at the Watergate. Get a few hours' rest." He removed a handwritten list of names from his case and handed it to her. "These are the people I want you to interview while you're in Washington. They know me well. At seven tomorrow morning you'll be picked up by one of my men and driven to your appointments."

She took the list from him. It contained several prominent senators and the secretary of defense. The appointed times for each interview were written next to the names. Her schedule would be demanding for the next three days.

"On Monday evening you're taking a flight to Fort Bragg,

South Carolina, to meet several important senior officers who know me. One of them is Billy Doyle, head of the Security Council. You're to interview them, then take a ten o'clock plane back to Hawaii. You have a lot of work ahead of you. Daniel and this retired police officer will only add to your already overburdened agenda." He started to leave the room, stopped, then turned to her and said, "I expect the next set of questions waiting for me tomorrow morning." He walked out, closing the door behind him.

The anger she held inside of her suddenly erupted. The man was a ball-busting, controlling bastard! This was not the same person who'd greeted her with open arms when she'd first arrived on the island.

All this time she'd thought she had a free hand in writing the book. What a crock! With the schedule he'd just given her, he'd made sure she'd barely have time to breathe! This was only the beginning, she knew. There'd be other lists from him. He and Ciji were no different—they both wanted the same damn kind of book. The son of a bitch was arrogant, a master at manipulation. And up to now, she had fallen for it.

Except this time *she* had the edge: Steinway wasn't aware that she knew he'd lied about the hazing of Bankroft. *Now what the hell do I do with it?* she thought, putting the recorder back in her suitcase.

Christ, she was tired. She'd been up for over twenty-two hours. Malia grabbed her bag by the handle, dragged it across the floor, and left the concrete shelter.

Outside, she looked down the empty, darkened corridor for the electric cart. She waited a few minutes, but it didn't show. Another one of his games, she thought. What was she supposed to do now? *Goddamn it!*

She hitched the strap of her bag over her shoulder and began walking through the tunnel. The sound of her leather soles ricocheted like firecrackers off the concrete walls. About a hundred yards down, another hallway cut across the one she was in. Which way had the cart turned when it brought her? Left? Right? Straight? *Christ!* Why hadn't she paid attention? Her bag was getting heavy. She swirled around looking for help. There were no signs posted on the walls giving directions. Anyone who came down here had better damn well know the way. A person could walk these labyrinths for weeks and never be found. She tried listening for voices, but the only sound she heard was that of the rumbling generator.

She decided to turn left. As she began walking, she heard a sound coming from behind, intermixing with her own footsteps. It wasn't the generator. More like a flopping, shuffling noise. She stopped and listened. It was coming from one of the intersecting corridors.

It sounded like footsteps. Someone wearing rubber soles. Was it her imagination? Again she listened. No, it was real. She started walking again. The squishing, dragging sound continued. Only this time it was closer, coming her way.

Rubber soles . . . *rubber galoshes.*

The vision of the angel flared up in her mind. She suddenly saw the sword raised above its head, its eyes looking down at her.

Eyes!

She hadn't thought about its eyes before. Suddenly she could see them in her mind now the same way she had in her parents' bedroom that night. They were hard and cold. What color were they? Blue? Black? She couldn't remember. Her memory still clung to the darkness.

Terror numbed her body. She began to walk faster.

This is crazy, she thought. *This is the Pentagon, for God's sake!*

Another corridor angled into the one she was in. Without thinking, she took the hallway on the right. The second she made the turn and saw the black tunnel, she knew it was a mistake. Most of the bulbs on the walls were burned out. She wanted to turn around and go back, but the shuffling noise was right behind her now, blocking her path.

Black, shiny boots coming toward her. Squishing as they walked through the swampy grass. Stopping by the edge of the fish pond . . .

The wings of the angel loomed over her mind, blocking out all reasoning. The *whoosh* of the sword swept through her head as it cut deep into her mother's flesh. The sound was sharp and clear, like it was happening now instead of twenty years ago.

Those eyes!

She turned around and saw two blinding bright lights com-

ing toward her. Relief flowed through her body. It was the
electric cart.

Just as she was about to raise her hand and yell, she heard
the shuffling again—the dull sound of sloshing rubber. It was
coming from where the lights were.

Then she heard the corporal's voice call out, "Don't move.
Stay where you are!"

The lights were upon her now, blinding her. She raised her
hand to her eyes, trying to block out the glare.

"You okay, miss?" the corporal said, bringing the cart to a
stop.

"I'm fine," she answered. "What happened to you?"

"The cart got a flat on my way to pick you up. Slowed me
down. You shouldn't be walking around here. This is a classified area."

Malia climbed up on the cart. "I didn't know. There are no
signs."

The corporal grinned at her. "This is the bunker, ma'am. If
there was an invasion you wouldn't want signs posted, pointing out where the most important men in the military were
hiding, now, would you?" He began to drive through the tunnels toward the exit.

Once again she heard the sloshing sound of rubber. Fear
gripped her. Then she realized it was the flat tire flopping
across the floor.

The corporal laughed. "Sounds like a drunk staggering
home, doesn't it?"

Malia didn't think it sounded like a drunk. It sounded like
those rubber boots going after her in the stormy field twenty
years ago.

For the next three days Malia saw little sleep. She worked
fourteen hours a day interviewing the people on the general's
roster. When she got back to her hotel room at midnight, she
had to write out the next list of questions for Steinway and
leave them at the front desk to be picked up. After that, she
worked on the book for another two hours. By 4:00 A.M., she
dragged herself into bed. At 7:00 in the morning, the corporal
was waiting for her in the lobby to take her on the next round
of interviews.

* * *

After her appointment with the secretary of defense on Monday, Malia arrived back at the hotel and called Fort Bragg to cancel her interviews set up by Steinway. She then hurriedly packed her bag and went down to the lobby. At the front desk, she left a note for the corporal, who was supposed to take her to the airport. It said that she had to leave for New York on personal business. She checked out of the Watergate, using the back entrance.

She hailed a cab and took it to a small motel adjacent to the airport. Using her own credit card, not the one Ciji gave her, she booked a room for the night.

She ordered a bottle of Burgundy and a couple of premade sandwiches from the local market, asking for them to be delivered. While waiting, she took a quick shower to wash away her fatigue. By the time she was finished, the delivery clerk was knocking on the door. She took the paper bag from him, tipping him well. Using the drinking glass from the bathroom, she filled it with wine, sat on the bed, and wolfed down both sandwiches.

The silence in the room was exhilarating. This was the first time she had been alone in three days.

When she was finished eating, she lay on top of the bed covers, closed her eyes, and balanced the glass of wine on her stomach.

In the semidarkness, the eyes of the angel suddenly appeared in her thoughts. They were bleak, cold. Almost inhuman. After all these years, she had remembered them.

She pictured Daniel's eyes. They were warm, filled with life whenever he looked at her—not the kind of eyes that she'd seen in her parents' bedroom. Only once had she seen Daniel's eyes turn into black, dead stones. It was the day of Lupe's funeral, when he was angry and hurt.

She sipped more wine. Christ, was she exhausted! The general had run her ragged. He didn't want her probing into the dead plebe from West Point. Why? The man lied to her about him and God knows what else. It was time to find out the truth, then decide what she was going to do.

She slowly finished her glass of wine, then picked up the phone and called the information office at West Point in upstate New York and asked if Superintendent Ron Cherney was still alive.

She was told that he was and had a suite at the Hotel
Thayer across the street from the academy. The old man lived
with a full-time nurse.

Malia got the number of the hotel from the operator, dialed
it, and asked for Cherney's room.

A young woman answered.

"General Cherney is taking his daily walk. He always does
at this time," she told Malia. "Who's calling, please?"

Probably the nurse, Malia thought. *Be vague.* "I work for
General Felix Steinway. I'm doing research on his autobiography. I need to ask him a few questions about the general's
days as a cadet." She gave the nurse her number at the hotel
where she was staying.

"He should be back within an hour," the woman said.

After Malia hung up, she looked at her empty glass, refilled
it, and leaned back on the fluffed pillows. He'll call, she
thought. *The man will call.*

Fifty minutes later her phone rang. Malia leaned over and
grabbed the receiver.

"This is Ron Cherney," the gruff voice said.

Malia quickly put her wineglass down on the night table.
"Hello, sir," she said.

"The nurse mentioned you're doing some work for Felix
Steinway. What can I do for you?" His voice became filled
with caution.

"I've been commissioned by the general's publisher to help
write his book."

"How nice," he said caustically. "What does that have to do
with me?"

"Steinway was a cadet at the Point."

"I'm aware of that. Are you checking his references? He
was an exemplary student and had the makings of a fine officer. Is that what you wanted to hear from me? Now you have
it."

The man was sarcastic as hell. Why? Malia wondered. "No,
sir. I really wanted to discuss a cadet that went to the academy
at the same time General Steinway was there."

"His name?"

"Steven Bankroft."

There was a long silence on the phone, then he said, "You're the second one. Who the hell are you?"

"I told you, sir. I'm a ghostwriter for the general."

Another long pause. "I don't know you," he eventually said. The line went dead. He had hung up.

Malia dropped the phone on the cradle, picked up her wineglass, then brought up her legs and hugged her knees. *What the hell was that all about?* Bankroft's name touched a nerve in the old man, the same kind of nerve it touched in Steinway. Cherney said she was the second one. Who else was asking about the general?

No, you don't know me, Mr. Cherney, she thought. *But you will.*

Chapter Seventeen

MALIA TOOK THE shuttle from Washington to Newark Airport. Using her own credit card once again, she rented a car from Budget and followed the Hudson River north to West Point.

By the time she arrived at the Hotel Thayer it was two-thirty in the afternoon. It was an old hotel, located across the street from the entrance to the academy. The lobby was rich in tradition, with dark wood walls and floral, billowed couches.

Malia took a room for the night. It was small, but comfortable, designed in Victorian motif and overlooking the Hudson.

Before she'd left Washington, she'd rescheduled tomorrow's appointments at Fort Bragg. In the morning she would take a plane to North Carolina from Kennedy Airport, charging the tickets to Baronin Books. When they looked over her expenses, they'd think she was in Manhattan for the day.

According to Cherney's nurse, the old man exercised around six o'clock every evening. Malia glanced at the brass timepiece on the wall. It was almost three in the afternoon. She could get in a good two hours of work before she went down to the lobby to wait for him.

At five o'clock Malia went downstairs and sat in the entrance hall, hoping Cherney was up for his walk. Malia had seen the retired superintendent's photo in Steinway's yearbook. He had to be in his late forties then, which would put him well in his eighties now. Would she recognize him?

She grabbed a magazine off the rack, sat back, and waited.

At 5:50 the elevator doors opened and an old man, holding a walking stick and wearing a golf hat, hobbled sprightly out of the lift. He made his way across the lobby, only inches from where Malia was sitting, and walked outside.

It was Cherney, she thought. The face was withered and hollow now, but it had the same steely expression as the one in the yearbook. The man was so small and gaunt, it was hard to imagine that he once was a four-star general, with thousands of troops under his command.

She got up from the couch and followed him outside. He was walking fast, toward the gates of the Point. She quickened her pace, trying to catch up.

Once inside the academy, Cherney dug his stick into the ground and took Thayer Road past the cadet barracks and the library. Malia kept a hundred feet in back of him, wondering when she should approach him.

When he reached the parade grounds known as the "Plain," he stopped and looked over at a regiment of cadets practicing rifle drills on the field. He veered off toward the wooden bleachers by Sedgwick Monument and sat down.

Now or never, Malia thought. She walked over to the benches and sat down next to him.

Without taking his eyes off the field, he said to her, "Do I know you?"

"No, sir, you don't," she said.

"Then why are you following me?"

"I didn't know you saw me."

"I saw you sitting in the lobby when I was leaving."

"I called you last night."

"I figured it was you." His voice had a Tennessee nasality.

Malia looked out at the field. The cadets were lined up in several rows, flipping their rifles around their bodies and in the air like syncopated toy soldiers. Turning back to him, she said, "I'd like to talk to you about General Steinway, sir."

"He's an officer and a gentleman. I told you all that before. You could have saved yourself a trip."

"I don't think he's all that much of a gentleman, sir—neither do you."

He looked at her for the first time. "What is it you want?"

His dead stare touched her skin like cold tentacles. "I want to know what General Steinway did to the cadet, Steven Bankroft."

He snickered. "Is this for the book?"

"No, it's for me."

"For you? Is this what the great general is paying you for?" She shook her head.

"You're just ethical, is that it?"

"No, just confused. What he did to Bankroft doesn't go with everything I've been hearing about him."

He snickered. "Doesn't it? Maybe what you've heard isn't really who he is. Well, what's done is done," he said decisively. He then looked back to the cadets on the parade ground. The rifles were twirling around with such speed that they looked like wings of hummingbirds in flight.

"Tell me about the pea incident," she said after a long pause.

He turned back to her and glared. "What do you know about that?"

"I discovered a letter from Bankroft's mother addressed to Steinway, begging him to leave her son alone. She mentioned an incident with peas. What was that about?"

"It happened many years ago. Forget it. Go about your business and write his damn book. Make him look like America's sweetheart. That's what you're supposed to do, isn't it?"

"That's exactly what I'm supposed to do," she answered. There was a bite in her voice.

"Whatever happened, happened a long time ago. It's forgotten."

"I don't think so," she said.

He studied her face for quite a while. Then: "Why do you care?"

She looked away from his eyes, thinking about his question. "I don't really know," she eventually said. "I wish I didn't. I wish I could just do what everybody wants me to do—write that Steinway was the next best thing to vanilla ice cream, collect my money, and go home. Something inside me wants to know the truth about the man."

Cherney clutched the top of his walking cane and leaned his chin on it. "That man will someday be the president of the United States. Nothing you or I can do will change that. Go home."

"I'm not looking to change that. Steinway did something to Bankroft. Perhaps he caused his suicide."

"Perhaps? Hah!"

Malia's jaw dropped open in surprise. Cherney believed that Steinway *was* responsible. "Tell me about the pea incident," she asked again.

There was a long pause as Cherney mulled it over in his mind. "I will not be quoted as your source," he said finally.

"I accept that."

"See those cadets out there?" He pointed his stick at the men performing the rifle drill. "Not one of them is a half second off. They could do that in their sleep. That's how West Point runs, and that's how it *should* run—like a finely tuned clock. Everything about the academy is regimented . . . even the way the cadets eat. At the cadet dining hall there are ten men to a table. At the head of the table is the first classman. To his right is another 'firstie.' The pecking order after that consists of second classmen called 'cows,' then third classmen—'yearlings.' At the other end are three plebes. These plebes are at the mercy of their superiors at the table. Certain rules govern how they eat. They can only sit on the front half of their chairs. They are supposed to keep their eyes cast down on the West Point crest in the middle of their plates at all times. Their chins are always pushed inward toward their Adam's apple. Lunch and dinner is a half hour. When eating, a plebe can only take small thumbnail bites of food. During that time a first classman can ask a plebe to recite the answers to any of the thirty questions regarding the legends and traditions of the corps. A plebe cannot eat when answering."

His face became as hard as granite as he spoke. "First Classman Steinway would ask Cadet Bankroft to recite the answer to his question, then would give him time to eat one pea on his plate before he asked him the next one. Normally, a plebe was asked to respond to only one or two questions during a meal so he'd have time to eat. Steinway made Bankroft recite all thirty. By the time the plebe answered them, mealtime was over. The boy could never get to his food—other than the few peas allotted to him by Felix Steinway. This game was also played at breakfast and lunch."

"Was this legal?"

"There were no rules against it. But it was frowned upon by the Point. The boy had to sneak food into his room to stay alive. All the cadets knew about it. Bankroft became the laughingstock of the academy."

"How did you find out about it?"

"There was a parade, right on this field. Parents and girlfriends were invited. During this parade, Bankroft passed out in front of the entire school and his family. He was taken to the hospital, where he was diagnosed with a severe nervous disorder. He refused to talk to the school doctor about it. He did, however, talk to his mother. She wrote me, telling me what had been going on. I was outraged. This sort of thing had never happened before. I met with First Classman Steinway and told him to stop the hazing at once."

"What did he say?"

"Nothing. He just stood at attention, waiting to be dismissed. I remember his face." Cherney shook his head. "I never saw that kind of anger before in a man."

"Why didn't Bankroft turn him in?"

"He was afraid of the code of silence that would be imposed on him by the other cadets. Steinway was the top student in his class, popular, a regimental commander."

"Did Steinway do this kind of hazing to the other plebes?"

Cherney shook his head. "No. He was strict but fair to the other ones. I found all this rather puzzling. Bankroft was a so-so student, nothing special. But so were a lot of other cadets. I asked Steinway that same question. Why only him?"

"What did he say?"

"He said the boy showed cowardly conduct during a field-training exercise at Camp Buckner."

"Did you believe him?"

"No. Camp Buckner is where the cadets go for summer training. The cruel form of hazing that Steinway imposed on

Bankroft didn't start until right after the Christmas break, four months later."

Something must have happened during or around Christmas, she thought. She looked at the old retired general. "Was that the only thing he did to Bankroft?"

"No. After I talked with him, he let up on the plebe, at least in the dining hall. But there were other incidents . . . very subtle and ingenious ones. The boy was methodically being torn apart. For what reason, I don't know. During the spring break Bankroft committed suicide."

"Where was Steinway at the time?"

"In Iowa."

"Do you believe that the general drove him to it?"

A bitter smile appeared on his face. "I'll tell you what I believe, young lady. Listen carefully, because I'll only say it once, then I'll deny this conversation ever took place. I believe your future commander in chief was directly responsible for the boy's suicide. He understood the psyche of a cadet better than any man I ever knew. That son of a bitch killed the plebe, as if he put the belt around his neck and kicked the chair away himself."

Malia sucked in a nervous breath. "Why didn't you ever make your feelings known?"

Cherney closed his eyes for a second. His face looked pained as the shame of his silence from forty years ago resurfaced. "Felix Steinway's father was a good friend of mine. I couldn't disgrace his son. God knows I wanted to. I just couldn't." His back was now hunched over, making him look older than his eighty-some-odd years.

His father again, she thought. "Did you ever talk to him about his son?"

"No. It would have stirred up a hornet's nest if I said anything. Looking back, I may have done the wrong thing."

"Was your silence about Steinway also part of the army's code of honor, General?"

"What's done is done," he whispered again.

That part of the conversation was over, she realized.

"You said you knew his father."

His bushy brows arched upward. "What about him?"

"What was he like?"

"He was a good man. Not much of a sense of humor. Very serious . . . very determined."

She already knew that part. There had to be more to him than that. "Where did you meet him?"

"In Washington—at the start of World War Two. We were both in the Intelligence branch, working with OSS operatives in Germany. Otto was a brilliant cryptographer. Eventually, he was switched over to the South Pacific arena."

"Why was he moved?"

"It smacked too close to home. The same reason Japanese-Americans were only allowed to fight in Europe during the war."

"Because Otto Steinway came from Austria?"

"Yes."

"He was just a child when he left."

"It didn't matter. If you believe the man you're aiming the muzzle of your rifle at could be a brother or a cousin—you're not going to shoot. That's how the army thinks."

"How did Otto Steinway feel about the change?"

"He was upset. He felt that his loyalty was being questioned. But he was a soldier. He did as he was told."

"I heard he went to Berlin after the war."

"Yes. He spoke fluent German. He understood the people." Cherney turned and peered at her. "Are we finished?"

"One other question. When I called yesterday, you said I was the second one to ask about the general. Who did you speak to before me?"

"Your predecessor, I assume."

"Jasper Rhodes?"

"That's who he said he was. I've read several of his books. A good biographer. Very competent. What happened to him?"

"He was fired."

Cherney let out a snicker. "Maybe he was *too* competent."

Malia hoped that wasn't meant as a slur on *her* capabilities. "Did you tell him about Bankroft?"

"It was only a short phone conversation. He didn't ask about the cadet."

"What did he ask about?"

"He wanted a list of West Point graduates who served with Steinway in Vietnam."

"Did he say why?"

"No. But I could tell by his attitude there was some kind of turmoil going on inside him."

"In what way?"

"Rhodes sounded impatient on the phone. Like he already knew something and was just looking for confirmation about it. I told him he'd be better off calling Steinway's home base, Fort Bragg, for that information. He said he did and they weren't very helpful."

"Why wouldn't they give him the information? He was the general's authorized biographer. He should have had a free hand in getting anything he wanted."

Cherney smiled at her naïveté. "Maybe, for some reason, our general didn't want him to have the list. Let me ask you a question: Do you actually think *you* have a free hand?"

Malia understood his point. No, she didn't, or she wouldn't be secretly meeting with Cherney right now. She stood up. "You've been very helpful," she said, shaking his hand.

Cherney smiled for the first time. "You're a beautiful woman. Probably very talented. A shame you have to waste it on a man like Felix."

Malia ate dinner in the hotel's restaurant that night, thinking about her conversation with Cherney. Steinway drove the boy to kill himself. Her feelings were right about that all along. But why? What did Bankroft do to him? The old man said the hazing began right around Christmas. Something had to have happened then. What? She was also convinced that Jasper Rhodes was fired not because he was a worthless hack like Steinway said but because he might have been doing his job too well and stumbled onto something. He wanted the names of the officers who'd served with the general in the war. What for? What had he found out?

She was thinking about contacting Rhodes when she locked eyes with an army major sitting at the table across from her. He was eating by himself, and Malia noticed he had been staring at her all through his meal.

He worked up a weak smile and leaned over. "Two people eating alone is not a good thing." A nervous chuckle emanated from his throat.

"Are you affiliated with West Point?" she asked him.

"Yes, ma'am," he said, with a Southern accent. "I teach electrical engineering there."

Malia smiled back at him. "Then move your chair over here, Major, and join me."

He was a heavyset man in his mid-forties. Picking up his snifter of cognac, he went over to her table and eagerly sat down. "Can I buy you a drink?"

Malia waved her hand. "Thanks, I have to work tonight."

His eyes lit up and he moved his hefty body into the table. "What kind of work do you do, ma'am?"

Malia smiled. The man thought she was a hooker. She sipped her coffee, then said, "Not what you think, Major. I work for General Felix Steinway." She waited for his reaction. It came immediately. The lights went out in his eyes, and he moved back in his chair.

"What do you do for the general?" he asked, nervously clearing his throat.

"I'm his personal assistant."

"Is he at the Point?"

"No. I came here on business for him."

He let out a deep, shaky whistle. "Excuse me, ma'am. I didn't mean to intrude on you." He started to get up.

Malia laughed and waved him back down. "That's okay, Major. I understand where you're coming from. Do you mind if I ask you something?"

He straightened his tie. "No, no. Not at all."

"What happens during Christmas time at West Point?"

He looked baffled. "Excuse me?"

"Is there something special that happens here around the holidays?"

"Not really. The academy closes down. The cadets and the instructors go home to their families."

She looked disappointed.

He swished the cognac around in the snifter. "You talking about the party? Is that it?"

"What party?" she asked.

"Every year the Point throws a Christmas party. Dancing, food, the usual. Cadets can bring their girlfriends. Sometimes we invite one of the all-girl colleges from around here."

"Is there anything special about the parties?"

The major shrugged. "Not really. It's a party for all the cadets and the instructors. It happens right before the break. Everyone gets real loose. Heck, the kids have been cooped up like robots for several months. They need it."

"Plebes and first classmen can intermix then?"

"Sure. Mostly they don't. The difference about that night is that the plebes don't have to walk around like they got poles stuck up their you-know-whats. Everybody has a good ol' time, then everyone goes on home to wherever they came from for the break."

Did something happen that night between Steinway and Bankroft? she wondered.

"Are you sure I can't buy you a drink?" he asked. "I don't know General Steinway personally, but I heard him speak at a commencement here and I'm a big fan of his."

Malia shook her head no. She waved to the waiter for the check. "Major, you've been delightful company."

He quickly stood up, took her hand, and shook it. "My pleasure, ma'am. When you see the general, tell him the boys at the Point love him."

Sitting in the corner of the dark hotel bar, Taang had a good view of the major and Malia. He wondered what they were talking about. A shame he couldn't hear. He was to report to the general everything Malia did. This evening, he had followed her through the gates of the Point and watched from a safe distance as she talked to that old man. He later found out that he was the retired superintendent of the academy. What was she doing with him? he wondered. Cherney was not on the general's list of people she was to interview—nor was she supposed to be here.

He was about to go to his room and call Steinway when the major sauntered into the bar. The man moved his big rear onto the stool and ordered another cognac. Taang got up from the table and sat down next to him.

The major glanced over at the small Montagnard dressed in a suit and tie, with his hair tied into a chignon, eyed him up and down, and made a face.

Taang smiled inwardly. Caucasians always looked at him strangely. He was used to it. Motioning to the bartender, he ordered an iced tea. When it came, he took several bags of sugar from the holder, tore them open, and poured them into his glass.

"Like some tea with your sugar?" the major said, snickering.

It was a tired old joke that Taang had heard a thousand times before, but he laughed along with him. "Where I come from, we like our tea sweet."

"Yeah? Where's that?"

"Vietnam."

The major furrowed his brow. "I did two tours there. You don't look Vietnamese."

Taang continued to keep a friendly smile, pushing down the desire to snap this man's neck. He could do it in seconds and walk out of the bar without anyone knowing. "I come from the mountains."

The major opened his fat mouth in surprise. "You one of those Montagnards?"

"Yes, I am," Taang said.

The major nodded in appreciation. "I heard you guys were something in the war."

Taang sipped his tea, hiding his distaste for it. He missed the wonderful teas that were grown in his beloved mountains. "The war was a long time ago," he said, putting down his glass.

"I heard General Felix Steinway talk about you fellas. He said you guys were the greatest fighters that ever walked this earth."

This was his opening. "The woman you were with tonight—she works for this general, you know."

"I know. She told me. Said she was his personal assistant. You know her?" He finished off the cognac in one gulp.

His assistant? The Hawaiian woman had lied to this man about her job. He wondered why. "I've met her," he said.

"Pretty lady." He turned to the bar, looking at the bottles behind the counter.

Taang knew he was thinking about having another one. He would make it easy for him. Pointing his finger at the empty snifter, he motioned to the bartender. "It's on me," Taang said to the major.

The major let out a wide grin. "Say, that's awful nice of you."

Taang grinned back, showing his large false teeth. "You two seemed to be in a heavy conversation," Taang said, leaning into the bar and fondling his glass.

"I wouldn't say heavy. The girl wanted to know what the Point did for the cadets at Christmas. I told her we threw a party."

"Is that all?" Taang asked.

"That was the whole conversation. She didn't say why she wanted to know. Lucky I found out she worked for Steinway. She was so darn cute, I was ready to hit on her." He chuckled, poking Taang in the arm with his elbow. Then he picked up his new drink and finished that one off.

The girl was not asking the questions the general wanted her to ask, Taang thought. Something was wrong here. General Steinway would have to know about this. He took a wad of bills from his pocket and tossed a twenty on the bar.

"You leaving?" the major asked.

Taang hopped off the stool. With his eyes disappearing into his cheeks, he smiled and said, "Time for my beauty rest, Major." He pointed to the twenty. "Have another drink on me," then walked quietly out of the bar.

Three hours later Taang dialed the general's private line in the Pentagon. He was sitting with his back against the headrest of the bed in his hotel room, wearing only a towel around his waist. His thick, muscular thighs rippled every time he moved. The TV was on, showing an old black-and-white Randolph Scott western.

"Where are you?" Steinway said on the other end.

"West Point."

"What the hell are you doing there? You were supposed to watch the girl."

"I *am* watching the girl. She didn't go to Fort Bragg."

"I already know that. She postponed all her appointments until tomorrow. Why?"

Reaching in back of his head, Taang took out the small bone knife from his chignon. He tucked the phone under his chin and began to clean his long nails with the tip of the blade. "She came to see an old man who lives at the Hotel Thayer."

"What old man?"

"A Major General Cherney."

"My—my God!" Steinway stuttered.

Taang heard the fear in his friend's voice, something he'd never heard before. This disturbed him. "I was too far away from them and couldn't hear what they were talking about."

"I *know* what they were talking about!" he snapped.

"She also talked to a major who she met over dinner. I spoke with him. The only thing she asked about was what the Point did for the cadets at Christmas."

"Oh, Christ!"

There was that fear again. Taang sat up, plucking the tip of the knife with his thumb. "Are you all right, sir?"

"Where is she now?"

"In her bed . . . asleep."

"How do you know that?"

Taang smiled. "I went into her room a half hour ago. I sat on her bed and watched her. Trust me, she's sleeping." Moving his mouth into the phone, he said, "Is there something you want me to do, General?"

"Not now, Taang. There may come a time, but not now. Do you understand me? Just follow her and keep me informed."

"I understand," Taang said. Again he touched the tip of the blade.

"There are papers in a wall safe in my bookshelf. I want you to take them out. You are not to look at them. You are just to take them out. Do you hear me?"

Taang said he heard.

He gave the Montagnard the combination, which Taang memorized.

The Pentagon

"Damn!" Steinway screamed, slamming his fist on the top of the metal table in the small cubicle. His face was scarlet and his lips were trembling. The girl must have found out about Cherney and Bankroft from the letters in the safe. It was locked. How did she open it?

"Damn it!" he yelled again.

He took several deep breaths, trying to compose himself. First that wimp Rhodes, now her. He had an invasion to help plan. He didn't have the time for this.

Chapter Eighteen

MALIA FLEW INTO Fort Bragg on Tuesday and met with Billy Doyle, the national security advisor. He was a cheerful man, big and extroverted. Doyle went to West Point with Steinway and was one of the cadets seated around the dinner table in the yearbook photograph. Later, he took her on a tour of the base, introducing her to the other officers who knew and fought with the general.

Over lunch in the mess hall, Malia turned to Doyle and approached the topic of Steven Bankroft. Doyle's face darkened and he immediately changed the subject without answering.

He had been warned by Steinway, she thought.

After the interviews were finished, she was driven to the airport by one of Doyle's aides. When they arrived at the terminal, he insisted on walking her to the gate. At first she thought he was being gallant, then she realized he was just following orders. Steinway was making sure she didn't have any "wiggle room" to get lost again. The soldier stayed with her until she boarded the plane to Los Angeles, where she would take a connecting flight to Hawaii.

Too bad, she thought, as she strapped herself into her seat. Holyfield, Virginia, Steve Bankroft's home, was only an hour's drive from here. She would like to have called the three Bankrofts who lived there to see if they were related to him.

The lights and the air-conditioning suddenly went out in the aircraft. The pilot came on over the loudspeaker and said that there was a temporary power failure, the delay might be an hour, and that everyone should disembark for their own comfort.

Back in the terminal, Malia went over to the phones. She had an hour to see if she could contact the Bankrofts. Malia opened up her wallet and took out the numbers given to her by the operator. Fishing around for change at the bottom of her purse, she grabbed a handful of coins and dropped them on the metal counter under the telephone.

The first name was Lilly Bankroft. After several rings, an answering machine came on. Malia hung up and tried the next name, Robert Bankroft. The man was friendly but said he'd just moved to Holyfield and had never heard of Steven. The last one was a Dr. Stanley Bankroft. She dialed the number. A woman's voice answered. When Malia mentioned Steven's name, she acted surprised. Yes, she knew about him. He was Stanley's cousin.

"Poor man died years ago," she said.

Malia asked to speak with her husband.

"He's feeding the horses," she said. "Do you need to talk to him about Steven? I could have him call you."

She told her she was at the airport. Perhaps she could come and see him. It wouldn't take very long.

"Come on over, then. He could use the company. Stanley sold his medical practice five years ago. He spends all his days now with his horses. A woman doesn't stand a chance against those dumb animals."

Malia got the address and directions from her, then hung up.

She first checked the TV monitor to see when the next plane departed for Los Angeles. It was at seven the next morning. That meant she'd have to spend the night in South Carolina. Steinway was already suspicious of her movements. Well, she'd just have to take that chance.

She rented a car again. It took a little over an hour to reach Holyfield. It was a nice quiet town, the kind that Frank Capra used to make movies about.

Following the woman's directions, she drove to the outskirts and turned left at the water tower. Stanley Bankroft's farm was a half mile down the road.

When she drove up, she saw that it was more of a colonial mansion than a farm, made of red brick and big white pillars. She parked the car in the driveway.

A broad-shouldered, white-haired woman, wearing jeans and a flannel shirt, came out of the house.

Her smile was warm and inviting. "Hi, I'm Jane Bankroft. You must be the one who called." The woman extended her hand to Malia.

"Malia Rico."

"Nice to meet you," she said. Her voice was intelligent. "Stanley is still out at the barn." She pointed to the wooden structure a hundred feet away. "He's expecting you. Good luck in prying him away from his animals."

She took the path over to the barn. The double doors were open and she saw a light coming from within.

Dr. Stanley Bankroft was kneeling down by one of his horses in the stall, fitting the steed with shoes. He was a lean man, with a full head of snow-white hair. Several horseshoe nails dangled from his mouth. He took one out and banged it into the hoof with a hammer. Not looking at her, he said, "I hear you knew Steven."

Malia knelt down next to him. "I'm afraid not. I was a long way from being born when he died."

The man glanced up. When he saw how young Malia was, his eyes opened wide in surprise. "Why . . . you're just a kid," he uttered. "Why are you asking about him?"

"Look, Dr. Bankroft, I'll get down to it. I work for General Felix Steinway."

The man's face hardened and a red flush came over it. "What do you want with me? Hasn't that bastard done enough to my family!"

She held up her hands. "I may work for that bastard. That doesn't mean I'm here on his behalf."

"Then whose behalf are you here for?" He banged in the next nail hard, as if to emphasize his question.

"For me," she said. She waited for him to say something else, but he didn't. "I've been commissioned to write the general's life story."

Bankroft let out a harsh laugh. "What do you want? A testimonial on the man's character? He killed my cousin. My aunt, Steven's mother; never got over it. She died of a broken heart a year later. Do you want to put that in your book?" He banged in another nail.

"I just might," she said softly.

Bankroft pulled the horse's hoof off his lap and looked at her. There was confusion stamped on his face. "Does he know you're here?"

She shook her head. "I would be fired if he did."

He stared at her for a long time, trying to read her face, then said, "You hungry?"

"Starving," she answered.

They left the barn and walked back to the house.

"Let me warn you," Stanley said. "My wife made some low-fat Indian cuisine tonight. She takes these damn cooking classes in town, then tries out her experiments on me. If you don't like it, and I suspect you won't, keep it to yourself. She's very sensitive in that area."

Stanley was mistaken. The food was delicious. Malia ate two helpings and was contemplating a third when the doctor turned off the lights.

He started up the eight-millimeter movie projector sitting on the coffee table. Grainy black-and-white images of two laughing boys building a large sand castle on the beach popped out on the white wall.

"That was Steven and me at Hilton Head," Stanley said. "His parents had a summer home there. We used to go all the time. After Steven died, I put together all the film we had of him on one reel. Steven and I . . . we were very close."

The movie jumped to a Little League baseball game. Steven was at bat and struck out. The small, thin boy dropped the bat and stuck his tongue out at the camera.

Stanley laughed. "Steven was not your star athlete, but he had determination. He tried hard."

The film spanned Steven Bankroft's life: summer camp; family functions; high school graduation.

Stanley explained them all in detail. What emerged was the story of a healthy young man who loved life.

"He seemed happy," Malia said.

"Steven? He *was*." He stopped the machine and turned on the lights. Then he lit up his pipe, puffing on it to get the tobacco glowing.

"The only image I have of Steven was at the cadet dining table at West Point. He looked gaunt and depressed."

He nodded. "I also saw that photograph. That was taken after Steinway had already gotten his hooks into him. Before that, Steven was anything but a troubled lad."

Jane brought in a bowl of fruit and a pot of tea. She sat down with him. "It's after midnight," she said. "I think it's silly for you to go back to the airport tonight. Stay here. We have plenty of room. Drive back in the morning." Her voice was crisp and clean, like the tinkling of the silver jewelry adorning her wrists.

"I don't want to put you out—" Malia said.

"Don't worry, you're not," Stanley cut in. "My wife saw how much of her food you ate. That's all it takes to get her on your side."

Smiling, Jane sat on the armrest of his chair and stroked his white mane.

These were good people, Malia thought. She would have traded in her aunt and uncle for them in a second. Her eyes glanced over the interior of the house. It was warm and alive. The living room was filled with photographs of their children, paintings, and wall-to-wall books. A Brahms piano concerto played on the stereo. "If you don't mind, I'd like to spend the night. It's been a long day," Malia said.

Stanley went out to her car and brought in her bag. When he came back in, he sat down and poured the tea.

"I'm turning in," Jane said to Malia. Then she stood up, kissed her husband on the cheek, and went upstairs.

Stanley examined the bowl of his pipe and waited until he heard the bedroom door close. He then turned to Malia. "You say you're working for that man. Obviously something bothers you about him or you wouldn't have put your job in jeopardy by coming here. What is it you think I can do for you?"

Malia sipped her tea. It was jasmine, her favorite. "I believe General Steinway deliberately wore down your cousin. In fact, there's no doubt in my mind about it. I just don't know why. The torture began around the time of the academy's Christmas party. I thought perhaps you could shed some light on what may have happened."

Stanley's eyes narrowed as he thought about it. He slowly knocked his pipe embers into a copper ashtray. "Did you know Steven was engaged to be married?"

"No, I didn't."

"Her name was Melissa. A beautiful woman. She was from Boston. Whenever she came to the Point to visit Steven, all eyes turned on her." He took in a deep breath to stifle the anger that was erupting inside of him. "Steven made the mistake of taking her to that Christmas party you were talking about. Because that was the night Felix Steinway discovered her."

"Are you saying Steinway *caused* Steven to kill himself because he wanted his fiancée. That's hard to believe."

Stanley had a bitter smile on his mouth. "That's exactly what I'm saying."

She knew the general was a bastard and a liar, but this was something else entirely. "Did they have an affair?"

"Melissa and Steinway?"

"Yes."

His grin grew wider. "I would say so."

"He must have been a busy man in his senior year, because that was also the time he met his wife, Peachie."

Stanley closed his eyes and shook his head. "My God. You really don't know, do you?"

"Know what?"

He went over to the credenza and took out an old photo album. He brought it over to the table, turning the pages until he came to a black-and-white glossy of Cadet Steven Bankroft with his arm around a young lady. "This was taken of Steven and Melissa by the academy's photographer the night of that Christmas party."

Malia turned the book around to get a better look. What she saw was a smiling, proud cadet showing off his fiancée. When her eyes moved over to the girl, she finally understood.

"Peachie was Melissa's nickname, given to her by Steven. When Steven died, that son of a bitch took that name for himself, too," Stanley said.

Yes, now she understood. Brinks, the president of the War College, told her that Steinway was secretive during his senior year. No wonder. He was having a clandestine affair with Steven's girlfriend.

"The man always gets what he wants, doesn't he?" Stanley said, between clenched teeth.

"He must have been madly in love with her to do something like that," she said.

"Love? I don't think love was the motivating factor in his move." He looked upstairs, making sure his bedroom door was closed, then turned to Malia and whispered, "Did you see his ranch on Hawaii? Hell of a spread, wouldn't you say?"

"Yes, I would. I'm staying there," she said.

"What about his Polynesian art collection? Have you seen that, too? Most of it is priceless. Where do you think the money for all that came from? Certainly not from his military salary."

"Peachie is an heiress to a supermarket chain," she said, suddenly understanding.

"As I said, the man takes what he wants."

Taang sat on top of the water tower, his feet dangling under the guardrail. He watched the lit window of Dr. Bankroft's house through night binoculars.

The old man was talking to the Hawaiian girl, gesturing with his hands. Whatever they were saying had to be important, he thought. Then they stood up and the lights went out downstairs. A moment later he saw a light go on in one of the upstairs bedrooms. He could make out Malia's figure through the lace curtains. He watched her undress, then get into bed and turn off the table light.

When the house was in total darkness, he put the binoculars down. Instead of being on a plane to Hawaii, she was staying with these people. Once again she went against the general's orders.

Taang liked the girl. Though she was frightened of him, she treated him with respect—not like the general's wife. But this girl now wanted to destroy his friend. Why couldn't the general see that? Why didn't he fire her like he did the other writer?

His false teeth were beginning to hurt his gums. He took them out and ran his tongue over the sharp points of his real ones, which he had filed down when he was a boy. In his old village, it was a Montagnard sign of virility.

He removed his shirt and leaned back against the tower, letting the wind drift over his body. How good it felt to be free of Western clothes!

A ravenous hunger swept over him. He reached into his knapsack and took out the rabbit he'd killed in the bushes right before he'd climbed up on the tower. He wished he could light a fire and cook this strange creature, but he couldn't chance it.

Taking the bone knife out of his chignon, he turned the dead animal on its back and began to skin it.

Chapter Nineteen

BEN SAT IN his truck—across the street from Honokaa's police station—until nightfall. When the town grew quiet, he got out of the vehicle and made his way around the side of the building, toward the small metal shed in the back. It was where the police kept physical evidence that was no longer needed. He groped for the door, then for the padlock. Working in the dark, he placed the head of a screwdriver between the clasp and the jamb and yanked down. The screws easily broke from their confinement. He pushed the creaking door open and went inside.

Closing it behind him, he turned on the flashlight, catching particles of dust and cobwebs in its beam. He moved the light over to the stacks of boxes on the floor and on the smaller articles jamming the shelves.

Ben stifled a cough as he waved away the dust. Holding the light in one hand, he began to sift through the boxes. He silently cursed the police for not dating the cartons.

It took twenty minutes of digging until he found what he was looking for—the box containing his brother-in-law's galoshes and a slab of cement with the boot imprint made at the pond. He'd poured the cement cast himself the day after the murders.

He then left the shed with it. There was no reason to screw the clasp back on the door. It would be weeks before the police discovered the break-in. They'd think vandals did it.

When he arrived back at his house, Ben opened the box on the kitchen table and removed the dirt-caked boots and the cement impression. Taped on top of the carton was Police Officer Isaac Yamaguchi's twenty-year-old report. Ben tore it off the cardboard and read it. He'd given the cast and the boot to

Isaac right after the murders to see if they matched. According to this report, they did.

He placed the left sole of the boot with the raised diamond shapes in the impression. They locked together like two pieces in a picture puzzle.

At first glance everything seemed right—the boot and the mold were the same size. Yet something bothered him about it.

Turning the boot over, he closely examined the rubber diamonds jutting faintly up on the sole. Etched between the sole and the heel was the name of the company who made the boot. CLAYBORG.

Ben moved the left-foot cast under the strong ceiling light by the table. The name of CLAYBORG was also molded in the cement. Everything looked right, yet he could feel something was wrong here. What?

Same patterns . . . locking together . . .

That was it! They locked together!

You're getting old, Lopaka, he said to himself. *It was there all along, staring you in the face.*

Once again he put the left boot into the cement cast.

They were telling you why they didn't match and you weren't listening. You really are pupule!

Panali's galoshes had slightly raised diamond configurations on the soles, so then the shapes in the cement cast should *also* be raised, not indented. They shouldn't lock together. That meant the patterns on the boots worn by the killer were inverted, not elevated. The footprints were not made by these boots.

Two soles with exact patterns, both made by the same company, yet the reverse of each other. *How interesting.*

Early the next morning, Ben drove to Isaac Yamaguchi's house and parked his truck in his driveway. The police captain had done all right with his life, Ben thought, looking up at the house. It was a large, well-kept home in a nice neighborhood, with a beautiful lawn and pretty flowers surrounding it. He grabbed the carton from the backseat and climbed up the porch steps.

Before Ben got to the top, Isaac's wife, Mary, opened the screen door and came out. She was a small, attractive Japanese woman in her mid-forties, with streaks of gray sprouting from her thick black hair. Her ancestors came over from Kyoto one hundred years ago to work in the Hawaiian pineapple fields.

"Ben, how nice to see you," she said, smiling.

"Good seein' you, too, Mary."

"You never come around," she said, chastising him with a mock scowl.

"Been busy, Mary." The truth was that he and his wife, Sarah, used to come around all the time. She and Mary had quickly become the best of friends. When Sarah left him, he was never invited back. Ben knew the reason—married friends didn't feel comfortable being around the lone spouse. It reminded them of their own shaky marriages.

"When was the last time you were here?" she asked.

"You had me over for Thanksgiving once."

Her eyes fogged, trying to remember.

"That was eighteen years ago, Mary."

She put her delicate hand to her mouth. "Oh, sweet God, Ben. Has it been that long? I feel terrible."

"It happens," Ben said, smiling. The box was heavy. "Is Isaac around? I know it's his day off."

"He's in back, working on his orchids, like he always does on Tuesdays. Come on in," she said, holding the door open for him.

They walked through the house. The inside was as neat and orderly as the outside. She opened the back door for Ben. He could see Isaac working in the glass greenhouse he erected in the yard.

"Would you like some breakfast, Ben?" Mary asked, still embarrassed.

Ben shook his head. "Thanks, Mary. I already ate. I jus' need to talk to Isaac for a few minutes."

"If you want some coffee or lemonade, give a yell."

"You know I'll do that," Ben said, walking over to the terrarium.

Isaac Yamaguchi was bending over one of his prized orchids, clipping the leaves with a pair of shears.

These flowers were now his only passion in life, Ben thought. His only other love was for his son, who died eighteen years ago after a lengthy fight with leukemia. He spent every dime he had trying to keep the boy alive.

"Mornin', Isaac," Ben said.

The police captain looked up and frowned at the intrusion. "I didn't expect you, Ben."

"I know that." He put the box down on the counter next to several pots of orchids, took off his sweat-stained hat, and wiped his brow with his bandanna. "Gonna be a hot day."

"It's always a hot day on the island," Isaac said blandly.

"Sorry for surprisin' you like this. If you got a couple of minutes, I want to show you somethin'."

"Show me what?" Isaac stood up. He was wearing Bermuda shorts that exposed his long, spindly legs.

Ben opened the box and put the shoe on the cast. "They don't go together, Isaac. See?" He held Isaac's old report out in front of him, making sure he saw his signature on it. "You were wrong."

Isaac put the shears down on the counter, removed his gloves, and walked over to the table. "They look right to me," he said.

"Look at the shoe, goddamn it, Isaac. It don't fit the cast. They shouldn't lock together like this. I don't know who was at the pond that night, but it sure as hell wasn't Panali!"

"Where did you get these?"

"From your storeroom."

"You had no right—"

"To hell with right! You didn't do your job back then. Do it now! Open the case back up."

"Ben, it's been twenty years."

"No, it hasn't. Remember Lupe Maile? That was only a week ago. He's still out there. The son of a bitch framed Panali with the bracelet and his neckerchief. He also knew you'd go after Sam Pua for the murder of the girl. This guy thinks, Isaac! Except he made one mistake." Ben slammed the boot down on the table. "He didn't see the directions the diamond shapes went—same as you."

Beads of mist formed around the police captain's upper lip. "They looked so much alike, I—I just thought they went together."

"I ain't blaming you, Isaac. You were new on the force. I should have overseen you. I didn't. But that was twenty years ago. I'm talkin' 'bout today. Now you either open up the case or I take it to the media."

The police captain glared at him. His eyes were like dark steel balls. "I can spare one officer. I'll have him look into it."

"One officer? You're a generous man, Isaac."

"That's the best I can do."

"Right. I know what you're doin'. Puttin' one man on it would be enough to cover your ass in case this ever became public."

Isaac moved closer to the evidence. "Go back to your taro fields, old man." He motioned to the boots and cast. "That's police property. I suggest you leave it."

Meeting his eyes, Ben said, "You're not goin' to do much, are you?"

"I'm going to do whatever I have to do. That's how I keep my job; that's how you should have kept *yours.*" His tone was cold and unyielding.

Ben left the police captain in the greenhouse and went outside. His face was grim. Mary stopped him at the gate. She was holding a glass in her hand.

"You just got here," she said, sounding disappointed. "I brought you some lemonade."

Ben tried to smile pleasantly. "Got to go, Mary. Give it to Isaac. I think he might need it right now."

Chapter Twenty

BEN DROVE TO Hilo to see Paul Nani. He asked the coroner for the old photographs of the Ricos' tissue samples and everything else he had on Lupe Maile's murder. After Paul dug them out, Ben went over to the fax machine and sent everything to the National Crime Information Center in Washington. It was a large computer median that compiled material on all kinds of criminal activity and furnished them to law enforcement officials all over the country.

He then called John Borshardt, the director of the organization, and told him to look for the material. Ben and the director had worked on a drug case together many years ago and remained friends. He told Borshardt that he needed to know if there were similar murders committed in the past thirty years. He also wanted to know if his computer had anything on an anthropologist from UCLA named Daniel Keahi. Borshardt told him he'd have his answers within twenty-four hours.

When he got off the phone, he and Nani walked over to the local diner to grab a quick bite to eat.

The coroner sunk his big frame into the red Leatherette booth and loosened his tie. "Does Isaac know you're doing this?" he asked Ben.

The old man shook his head while glancing up at the entrées on the blackboard by the counter. "It's out of his hands now," he said. "How's the *ahi* in this place?"

"As bad as it was twenty years ago." Nani unfolded his napkin and put it on his lap. "Isaac's not going to like this."

He turned and smiled at the coroner. "I got nothin' to lose. I already lost everythin' a long time ago. How's the chili?"

"Very suspect."

"The way chili ought to be. I think I'll have that," Ben said.

After lunch, Paul went back to his office and Ben drove to the excavation at the *heiau*.

He parked his truck at the edge of the jungle and traipsed through the underbrush. His legs felt as if someone had stuck pins in them. When he reached the clearing, he saw Daniel standing on top of the west wall of the stone structure. He was helping several students lift out a vat of freshly dug earth with a pulley.

"Can I help you?" a man's voice said from behind him.

Ben turned around and looked up at a face sporting a straggly beard with white patches and eyes hidden under sunglasses.

When the tall, angular Hawaiian saw Ben, he suddenly paled. He mumbled something, then turned away and hurriedly walked over to the group of students taking a break by the tent. He knelt down among them, keeping his back to Ben.

Do I know the man? Ben wondered. Then he heard his

name and looked over at the temple. Daniel was calling him from the top of the *heiau*.

"You want to see me?" Daniel shouted.

Ben nodded. He watched with interest as the anthropologist skillfully grabbed the cragged edges of the stone wall, locked his feet into the crevices, and climbed down. Daniel's movements were quick and gazellelike. He wore a tank top and shorts, and his arms and leg muscles undulated from the strain of his own weight.

Ben thought about the small ledge where Lupe Maile landed after being thrown from the cliff. The killer scaled it to toss her the rest of the way down, then climbed back up. Daniel looked as if he could do that in his sleep.

When he was ten feet from the ground, Daniel let go of the rocks. He landed on his feet, bending his knees to break the fall. For a brief moment his face contorted in pain, then he reached around and rubbed his left side.

Continuing to massage his back, Daniel bent down next to the water can at the base of the temple, scooped some of it up with the ladle, and gulped it eagerly. His body was glowing with a sheen of sweat.

Ben walked over to him. "Workin' hard?"

Daniel looked up and smiled. "Always."

"How'd you hurt your back?"

"Skiing." He dipped the spoon into the can again, then poured the water over his head. "Hot day," he said. He repeated the action several more times, until his hair was soaking wet, then he shook the excess out, ran his fingers through it, and stood up. "You interested in digs? Is that why you're here, Ben?"

The heat was also getting to the old man. "You think we could talk in the shade?"

Daniel took him over to the leeward side of the *heiau*, where the stone wall offered some relief from the sun.

Ben glanced over at the tall, thin Hawaiian squatting down with the students. The man was also staring back at him. When he caught Ben's eyes, he nervously shoved his sunglasses up the bridge of his nose and quickly looked away.

"Who's that man?" Ben asked.

"His name's Roger Alika. He also teaches at UCLA."

"He ever live on this island?"

"I don't think so. Why?"

"He thinks he knows me."

"Why do you say that?"

"The man lost his color jus' now when he saw me."

"I doubt it. Roger grew up in San Francisco."

"Really? I thought I detected a Hawaiian accent when he spoke."

"People pick up accents when they live in a place. Happens all the time."

"Not Hawaiian ones," Ben said. "That's one kind that don' rub off on mainlanders so easily."

"Look, I have to get back to work. Is there something you want?" Daniel didn't try to hide his impatience.

Ben reached into his pocket and removed a Xeroxed copy of the photograph of the sharks'-tooth club. "You know what this is?" he asked him.

Daniel curved his head around to look at it. "Yeah, I know what it is."

"There are only two of them in existence. One of them was stolen from the Natural History Museum in Honolulu."

"That happened a long time ago," Daniel said.

"How do you know?"

"I'm an expert in the field of Polynesian weaponry. I thought you knew that. You seem to know everything else."

"That's what killed Lupe Maile."

Daniel cocked his head. "Really?"

"It also killed the Ricos. I watched you climb down that *heiau*. I was impressed."

"Glad I made your day. Mountain climbing is a hobby of mine."

"A skier *and* a mountain climber. My oh my. And I thought anthropologists jus' liked to dig in sandboxes."

"Not all. I have to get back to work." He started to move away, but Ben put his body in front of him.

"You know when Malia's comin' back?"

Daniel was surprised at his question. "No, I don't," he said coldly.

"No? I thought you two were a combo?"

Daniel's eyes grew glassy and distant, like those on a dead fish. He suddenly spun around and dug his face into Ben's. In a harsh whisper, he said, "Stay away from things you know nothing about, old man." Then he limped off and knelt next to the other anthropologist, Roger Alika. He said something to him and the thin man with the sunglasses glanced around at Ben, then looked quickly away again.

That bearded fella thinks he knows me. Do I know him? Ben thought.

Driving back to Honokaá, Daniel's warning played in his head. "Stay away from things you know nothing about." *Hmm ... Now what is it that I don't know anythin' about?* he wondered.

He stopped off at a drugstore and faxed another letter to Borshardt at the NCIC. Before he gave it to the clerk, he re-read the message.

While you're digging up the other information, see if you have anything on a Roger Alika. He's about thirty-five to forty years old, Hawaiian, black hair, tall and thin. Teaches anthropology at UCLA.

When Malia arrived back at the ranch late that afternoon, she found a pouch from the general on the vestibule table containing more answers to her questions. She half expected to find a message inside saying she'd been fired. There wasn't any. *Odd.* He'd warned her about deviating from his schedule, yet he was acting as if she'd done nothing wrong.

The house was deserted. Malia went upstairs and peeked into Peachie's bedroom. It looked as if no one had slept there for days. Was she in Honolulu again? Too bad. She wanted to ask her about Steve Bankroft.

She changed into a Hard Rock Cafe tank top and her favorite shorts, which were nothing more than frayed, cut-off jeans that she had since her days at Columbia. Then she went down to her office.

There were several messages on her machine. Two were from Ben and three from Ciji. She secretly hoped that one of the calls would be from Daniel. Well, what did she expect? Why should he phone her, especially after the way she'd treated him the day of Lupe's funeral? She was good at pushing men away. That was her one true accomplishment. She wanted to kick herself.

Taking a deep breath, she called New York.

Perhaps the ax was going to come from Ciji. She was immediately put through to the editor of Baronin Books.

"Where the hell are my five chapters?" Ciji asked curtly.

Not even a hello, how are you? "I mailed them last night."

"All five?"

"Seven. I'm ahead of the game."

Ciji grunted in surprise. Then she said, "General Steinway is not happy with what you're doing."

"What *am* I doing?" Malia asked.

"It seems like whatever you want. You were not supposed to go to West Point and see his old superintendent."

How did she know about that? "I was hired to write Steinway's story. If it takes me to the Point, then that's where I should go."

There was a long silence on Ciji's end. Malia could almost feel the heat of this woman's anger tearing through the lines.

"I want you to stick to the schedule he gave you," she eventually said. Her voice crackled like wood snapping in a fire. "You are not to veer from it, is that understood?"

"You've made yourself clear," Malia said. She wanted to tell her about Steven Bankroft, but decided against it. The woman wasn't interested in the *real* Steinway, only in the image she wanted to foist upon the public.

"I have another writer waiting in the wings in case you don't work out," Ciji threatened.

Malia knew she was bluffing. Why wasn't she being let go? Ciji wasn't calling any of the shots, she suddenly realized. Who was? The general?

"I want to know where you are at all times. You're to phone me every day. I want the next three chapters by the end of the month." She hung up without saying good-bye.

Malia dropped the phone in the cradle and sat back. If Ciji knew she'd seen Cherney, then surely the general also knew. How? Surely the retired superintendent didn't tell him. Was Steinway having her followed? If he was, then he also must know that she was in Holyfield, talking with Bankroft's cousin.

She then called Ben. There was no answer. He must be in the fields, she thought. Suppressing a strong desire to phone Daniel and apologize for her behavior, she went into the general's office and went through his Rolodex, hoping he had Jasper Rhodes's home number. He did. The biographer lived in Waynesville, a small town outside of Key Largo, Florida. She pulled out the card from the stack, took it into her office, and called him.

After several rings a man's voice, hoarse from too many cigarettes, answered. "Yes?"

"Is this Jasper Rhodes?"

" 'Tis I. Who's this?"

"My name is Malia Rico."

"Ah, yes. Mr. Steinway's new immortalizer." A small chuckle, followed by a phlegm-coated cough. "I heard you won the lottery for the job. How's Alexander the Great doing these days?"

Under his sarcasm, she could detect a slight tremble in his voice. Was it fear? "The general is at the Pentagon," she said.

"Of course . . . the North Korean crisis. The Pentagon is not a good place for an obsessive-compulsive to be. Too many pretty buttons to push. The temptation for him must be overwhelming. If he had his way, he'd nuke our little yellow brothers into oblivion."

"You sound as if you don't like him."

"Not much. The last time I got fired from a job was twenty-five years ago. I was busing tables in a restaurant while waiting for my first book to sell and I dropped a pitcher of ice water on a patron's head."

"You weren't busing tables for the general. Why *did* he fire you?"

That nervous laugh again, then that cough. "I don't think I was macho enough for him. He's a Hemingway man. Likes his writers with bushy beards and flannel shirts."

"I don't have a beard and I wear a skirt. He hasn't fired me. What's the real reason, Mr. Rhodes?"

"What does it matter?"

"I read the research you did on him. It was precise and professional."

"Maybe I didn't have enough military savvy."

"I also read your book, *Loss of Innocence,* a chronology on the Vietnam War that won you the Pulitzer. You know the military infrastructure better than any four-star general. He dismissed you for another reason." She waited for a response. He didn't give one, but she could hear his uneasy breathing on the other end. Then she said, "There are over a hundred pages missing in your documents."

"Really?"

"Did you remove them?"

"I left everything at the ranch. That Hun gave me ten minutes to clear out after he canned me."

"From what I can gather, those pages dealt with some of the years Steinway was in Vietnam."

"My dear. I was paid in full after departing. Those notes now belong to Felix and Baronin Books. Ask them about it."

"I went to West Point. I spoke with General Cherney. He told me you had been in touch with him."

"And?" His voice quivered once more.

"And you asked him if he had the names of West Point graduates who served with Steinway in Vietnam." Malia waited. Again no answer. She continued. "That should be public information. Yet when you went to Fort Bragg and asked them for the same list, they closed up on you. How come? Was it because Steinway told them not to give it to you?" She heard metal clicking on the other end, then Rhodes letting out a deep breath. He had just lit up a cigarette with a lighter.

"Miss Rico. You sound like an intelligent woman. May I offer you some advice?"

"Of course," she said.

"Drop it."

She ignored his remark. "What happened in Vietnam that Steinway doesn't want known, Mr. Rhodes?"

"I'm not sure," he whispered.

"But you have an idea."

"Ideas aren't proof. Without it, I could be looking at a multimillion-dollar lawsuit for maligning a war hero."

"That hasn't stopped you before. In *Loss of Innocence* you maligned several war heroes, including Westmoreland."

"Westmoreland didn't have a Montagnard as a playmate."

"Taang?"

"I see you've met him."

"Did Taang threaten you?"

"Taang doesn't need to threaten. His very existence is enough to cause one to swallow their tongue. I hope for your sake that you understand that."

"I understand it very well," she said.

"Let me just say that I have my own sources at the Pentagon. Sources that are high up. They gave me some information on the general. These people don't like Steinway—and are deeply disturbed at the thought of him becoming the next president of the United States."

"Who are they?" she asked.

"My dear. You're a writer. You should know better than to ask for another writer's 'Deep Throats.' "

"What did they say?"

"It was all hearsay, so it doesn't matter, does it? There's really no proof. Believe me, I spent every spare moment I had checking it out. Let's just say that your great war hero has more of an affinity with Count Vlad than with George Washington. Now I'm going to get off the line. Nothing personal. I'm sixty years old. I want to enjoy what little time I have left. Seeing Taang at my door one morning would certainly shorten that time span."

With that, Jasper Rhodes hung up.

Malia put the phone back on the receiver. He said that Steinway had a lot in common with Count Vlad. If she remembered correctly, Vlad was the prototype for Bram Stoker's Dracula. He was a Transylvanian count, cruel and ruthless, who impaled thousands of his subjects on poles.

Malia rubbed her arms, trying to stifle a chill that was seeping under her skin. What happened in Vietnam? Rhodes knew, but was too frightened to tell. He was not a man to scare easily. Taang must have done some number on him.

The dark side of Steinway was slowly being pried open. Did she have the nerve to stick her head in and peek inside?

Chapter Twenty-one

BEN WAITED IN the early morning mist for Malia at the foot of Waiemi Falls. When he called her last night, she sounded evasive, hinting that they could no longer meet in public places. He suggested the falls because of its remoteness.

Looking out into the forest, he caught a glimpse of her head passing through the tall ferns as she jogged down the trail toward him.

"You ever walk?" he said, when she came to a stop.

"Not if I don't have to," she gasped. She bent forward, holding onto her knees, waiting for her breath to return.

Ben smiled inwardly. He liked this girl. Aka, his dead daughter, had the same kind of spunk. He leaned against a boulder, unconsciously tapping the bowl of his pipe against it. "You think you're being watched, *wahine*?"

"I'm sure of it," she said when she could finally breathe. "The man knows everything I do, everyone I speak to. For all I know, he even has my phone tapped."

She went over to the edge of the river and splashed water on her face and arms.

"Were you followed now?"

"Probably."

Ben grunted. "Then it has to be Taang."

"I never saw him."

"He won't let you see him." Ben looked out into the dense tropical jungle. "He's probably out there now, watching us."

Malia glanced around, trying to fight off that tingling sensation in the back of her neck. "That man scares me."

"He scares everyone on the island. It doesn't matter if he sees us, as long as he can't hear us. I faxed a letter to the National Crime Information Center in Washington. I asked if they knew of any murders that were similar to Lupe's and your parents'."

She wiped the water off her face with the front part of her blouse. "Did you get an answer?"

"Sure as hell did. Got it this morning." He took the return fax from his back pocket and unfolded the paper. "In 1985 a young girl in Guam was found murdered in her bed. The forensics report on her was the same as Lupe's and your parents'."

Malia stared at Ben for a long time, letting it sink in, then she slowly got up. "Who was she?"

"A servant girl, like Lupe. She worked for the French ambassador. Took care of his house. They faxed me photographs of what she looked like after they found her. I didn't bring them with me 'cause I didn't think you'd want to see them."

"Was the weapon the same?"

Ben nodded. "Right down to the missing tooth."

"Were there any arrests?"

He shook his head. "Nope. I checked with the State Department to see if Sam Pua was ever in Guam. He wasn't. Four people were killed with the same ancient club. Three of them were Polynesian women. Your father was the only male and the only *haole*."

"Is that important?"

"Could be."

"Was there a link between the women?"

"Jus' that they were all poor, Polynesian, an' uneducated. Two of them worked as servants."

"My mother wasn't a servant girl, but she had a low-paying job at the sugar mill," Malia said. "If this angel wanted the women, why kill my father? The bastard planned everything out so beautifully. He could have waited until my mother was alone."

"I still feel he wanted both of them. It's jus' too much of a coincidence that your father was murdered right before the strike at the sugar mill."

An uneasy look came over Ben's face.

"There's more, isn't there?"

"I asked my friend to check on Daniel and another man who's workin' up at the *heiau*. His name's Roger Alika. Ever meet him?"

Malia wrinkled her brow, thinking. "Yes. Daniel introduced me to him at the excavation."

"This is what I got back about them." He looked at the report. "Daniel seems legit. He's been teachin' for the last ten years at UCLA." He peered up from the paper and saw Malia's face relax.

"Was he ever in Guam?" There was a tinge of nervousness in her voice.

Ben cleared his throat. "Yes, he was. In the summers of eighty-three, eighty-four, an' eighty-five."

Malia's shoulders sagged. "Damn! Was the girl killed in the summer?"

"I'm afraid so," he said. "Daniel came over during the summer breaks. He was in charge of excavatin' an ancient village."

"That still isn't proof, Ben."

"I know that. I'm just showin' you how Daniel seems to be around every time someone's hacked to pieces by a *lei o manō* club."

"But why kill Lupe?" she asked.

"I think you already know the answer to that. Lupe was seein' someone other than Sam Pua."

"And you think it was Daniel?"

"I wouldn't bet my house on it yet, but I'm leanin' that way. Lupe knew Daniel because he was always comin' over to see the general. Accordin' to Pua, she may have had a crush on him."

"What about this Roger Alika?"

"Here comes the strange part. There was nothin' on him in the computer."

"There has to be. He teaches with Daniel at UCLA."

"No, he doesn't. Nobody by the name of Roger Alika ever taught at UCLA or any other university."

She was taken aback by that. "Then who is he?"

"I asked my friend in Washington that. He could find nothin' on him. He said the man has to be usin' an alias."

"He doesn't look like the kind of man who would use a made-up name," she said skeptically. "He looks more like someone who's had his head buried in excavations for the last fifteen years."

"I know." Ben then told her about the boots not fitting the cement cast. "Whoever set Panai up for the murders must have known him . . . knew what size shoe he wore, knew all about his unstable makeup."

"Did Daniel know him?"

"Maybe. Panali was about ten years older than Daniel. Honokaá is a small town. They could have known each other."

Malia had to get back. Ben told her he'd let her know if he found out anything more.

She then jogged through the jungle to the highway. The path was deserted, but she could feel someone's eyes on her. Her body pulsated with fear. She broke into a run, keeping up the pace until she reached the highway.

She stayed on the shoulder, walking the five miles back to the ranch.

Another murder. Christ!

Ben had hit upon something—all three women were Polynesian and unsophisticated. Did the angel just want the women? Was her father just in the wrong place at the wrong time? Ben didn't think so. He still felt the strike against the sugar mill had something to do with it.

She remembered her mother looking up at the angel, smiling. *Why the hell did she smile?* Did she know him? Did all the women know him?

Then Daniel entered her thoughts and her stomach knotted up. He was in Guam at the time of the girl's murder. Her choice in men seemed to be rapidly deteriorating.

When Malia arrived at the ranch she found Peachie's suitcases in the entranceway. The airlines stubs attached to the handles said she'd been in Honolulu. She suddenly heard the sound of the sliding glass door in back of the house open, then close.

Malia went over to the window and looked out at the lanai. Peachie, with a mug of coffee in her hand, was sitting on a lounge chair, facing the sun. The woman's skin was sagging and yellow. *She's been on another binge,* Malia thought.

She went into the kitchen, poured herself a cup of coffee, then stepped out on the lanai.

"May I join you?" Malia asked her.

The general's wife turned her head weakly in Malia's direction and smiled through jagged lips. "Of course." She motioned to the chair next to her.

Malia sat down. She could smell the stale odor of last night's vodka emanating from the woman's pores. "Nice morning," she said.

"All mornings are nice here. Boring, but nice." Her hand shook as she brought the cup to her mouth.

"Don't you like the island?"

She made a face. "If you like to watch coconuts fall off trees, then I'm sure Hawaii can be fascinating. I grew up in Boston—where there was culture and history all around me. Here there's nothing but leathery-skinned cowboys and volcanoes. *My God!* Sometimes I wonder how this all happened to me."

"You could move."

Peachie gave a short laugh. "Move? My place is with my husband. Didn't they teach you that in school?"

"No, they didn't, Melissa."

Peachie looked at her in astonishment, then she broke into a modest smile. "I haven't been called Melissa in years. Not since . . ." Her voice trailed off and her eyes took on a distant glow.

"Not since Steven Bankroft started calling you *Peachie*," Malia said.

The woman stared at her. "How did you know that?"

"I know you were engaged to be married to him."

Peachie's pink, swollen eyes moved down to her cup and stayed there. "Yes, we were to be married," she said, emitting a quivering breath of air. "My hair used to be naturally golden then." She dabbed at her dyed bubblegum hair with her fingers, smiling. "Steven used to say it was the color of a Georgia peach in full summer. That's why he called me Peachie. How did you know my name?"

Malia shrugged. "Research can be pretty dull. The perks come when you discover things you weren't looking for. You met Felix Steinway at a West Point Christmas bash. I remember you telling me about that party, except you called it a hop."

"Did Felix tell you that?"

"No. I found out through Dr. Stanley Bankroft, Steven's cousin."

Her eyes opened in disbelief and she sat up in her chair. "You met him?"

"Yes."

"Does Felix know?"

"I think so."

"I suppose the man still hates Felix."

"He does."

"I could understand that. Dear, sweet Steven," Peachie whispered, closing her eyes and leaning back down in the seat. "He was a wonderful boy. We met on a summer vacation in Nantucket."

"But you fell in love with Felix."

A thin smile cracked the skin on her sallow face. "Who wouldn't? He was everything a young, sheltered woman dreamed about. Handsome ... dashing. There was an edge to him, something Steven never had. Steiny could make you laugh one minute and cry the next. Do you know what I'm talking about?"

Malia nodded in recognition. She knew that kind of man too well.

"With Steven, there were no surprises. It was like following the dotted lines. I needed the highs and lows to feel alive."

"Have you ever regretted your decision?"

"No," Peachie said, shaking her head. "No, I've never regretted it." Then she paused, thinking. "I just feel a sadness sometimes."

"Because Steven killed himself?"

"Yes."

"Do you blame yourself for it?"

Peachie fingered the top of her cup, thinking about the question. "In some ways I do. He must have guessed about my relationship with Felix. I don't know how. I never told him."

Malia was surprised. "Why not?"

"I was going to wait until after Felix graduated from the academy. It would have been easier on Steven if Felix was no longer there. Steiny felt the same way. Unfortunately, he died before I had a chance to break it to him."

Felix didn't wait for graduation, Malia wanted to tell her. He probably made sure he knew. That conniving bastard didn't want to take the chance that she'd change her mind. "When did the affair start?" she asked Peachie.

"I don't know if I should be talking about this. Felix wasn't proud of our affair. He's a man of honor. Affairs were something he frowned upon. He went through a great deal of turmoil over it."

I bet, Malia thought. Trying to reassure her, she said, "What's said here, remains here."

Peachie picked up a bottle of aspirins from the table, shook three tablets into her hand, and swallowed them with her coffee. Finally she said, "You want to know when my affair with Felix Steinway started? I'll tell you. It began the night of that Christmas hop."

"You came with Steven."

"Yes. I told Steven I wasn't feeling well and he drove me back to my hotel. The truth was that I made plans to meet with Felix later on that night. I drove back to the Point about one in the morning and met Felix at a bar across from it. We had a few drinks ... talked ... laughed, then we took a walk along the river. The man was intoxicating. I'd never met anyone like him before. He took me on an old fishing boat that was beached along the bank. We made love on its rotting hull, under the stars. It was the first time I'd ever been with a man."

"You never made love with Steven?" Malia was somewhat amazed.

Peachie laughed at her reaction. "No, my dear, I never did. I was brought up in a different generation than you. Ladies of my class did not make love with their beaux until *after* they were married. They especially didn't fornicate on hulls of dirt-infested boats with men they'd just met a few hours before." Peachie's face glowed with the memory. "After being with Felix that night, I have to say my generation missed out on quite a lot." She then stood up and went over to the cabana bar and poured herself a vodka tonic. Peachie turned to her and lifted an eyebrow. "Would you like your usual, dear? Orange juice, wasn't it?"

"No, thank you," Malia said.

Peachie sat back down again and sipped her drink. "Now where were we? Oh, yes. Fornication. Felix and I met almost every day, either at a cheap motel or in a deserted field outside of town. I couldn't get enough of him. He was like an addiction. It was the most exciting time of my life. I was doing everything I was brought up not to do and I loved every minute of it. I never thought love and sex could be like that. In fact, I never even thought they went together. Everything was perfect"—a dark shadow suddenly swept over her face—"everything ... except for Steven." She quickly shook off the shameful feeling, looked up at Malia, and smiled. "Felix and I were married right after graduation."

"When did you get your inheritance from the supermarket chain?"

Peachie looked quizzically at her for a second, then said, "When I turned twenty-one. Steiny and I certainly didn't starve. I had a nice little trust fund."

"Is there enough left to support his run for the presidency?"

She gave Malia a knowing glance. "There's no reason to

touch that. There are very rich men in this country who believe in him."

"A war with North Korea will probably help loosen up their purse strings."

Peachie smiled secretively. "People love a good war, darling. Especially one they know they're going to win." She put the glass next to her ear and shook it, listening to the ice cubes tinkle. "Forty years and a half-dozen wars later, Felix and I are still together. That's the important thing." She gulped down her drink.

When she moved the glass away from her lips, she had a sad, bitter look on her face. Malia couldn't tell if it was from the taste of the alcohol or from their forty years together.

Peachie then mumbled something unintelligible under her breath.

"I didn't hear you," Malia said.

She spoke louder, repeating herself. "Poor Steven. He deserved better." Her tongue was beginning to thicken.

Later that afternoon, Malia went into the general's office, planning to go through the files in the safe. She'd only looked over a few of the letters, but there were other papers there, too. The man killed Bankroft. Something bad also went down in Vietnam. If only she could find proof in the documents to substantiate these allegations.

She moved the books away from the shelf and opened the steel door. To her despair, she found that the safe was now empty.

Chapter Twenty-two

AFTER MALIA DISCOVERED the papers missing from the safe, she tried to work but couldn't concentrate. Her fingers remained frozen on the keyboard. Giving up, she slouched down in her chair, leaned her head back, and closed her eyes.

This goddamn book was a sham! Continuing to write it would mean she'd be living Steinway's lie with him.

She was convinced he knew she'd seen the letters. That meant everything was now out in the open between them and they could no longer pretend with each other. She remembered Jasper Rhodes's warning about dropping her investigation. Well, it was too late now. Jesus! What the hell was she going to do? Where would she go? Her stomach was tying itself into knots. The office was beginning to suffocate her and she needed air. Malia closed down the computer, grabbed the keys to the general's Jeep, and left the house.

She didn't have a destination in mind. All she knew was that she had to get away from the ranch so she could think. She took Highway 19 past Honokaá and continued driving west, through the town of Ka'ohu. When she reached the outskirts, she saw the road leading to her parents' house and turned onto it.

She parked the car by the side of the road but didn't get out. Did she really want to go inside the house again? What for? That broken-down structure only brought back painful memories. Why had she come?

The sound of a tree being chopped down echoed through the hills. Malia realized it was coming from Daniel's property. A sense of dread came over her. He must be home, she thought. Why wasn't he at the *heiau*? Had he seen her?

She turned on the ignition and drove back up the path. As she rounded a curve, Daniel's body suddenly loomed up in front of her truck. He was standing in the middle of the road—cradling a long-handled ax. A tank top covered his muscular, sweaty torso, and slivers of wood stuck to his skin and hair.

Her stomach shriveled in fear as she jammed on the brakes.

"Hi," he said, smiling. He made no movement to get out of the way.

"Hello," she said back, trying to steady her voice. Her breathing was coming out in loud, jagged puffs.

He moved the ax to his right hand, pointing the blade to the ground, and walked over to the driver's side of the Jeep. "You look pale. What's the matter?"

"I almost hit you," she said. Her mind was moving fast, trying to figure out how to get away.

Putting his hand on the base of the driver's window, he leaned down and stuck part of his head inside. Again that smile. "What are you doing here?"

Her eyes stayed on the road, refusing to meet his. She could smell wood from the newly cut tree intermingling with his sweat. "I wanted to come back to the house."

"Why?"

"I'm not sure. Maybe to look for something I missed."

"You didn't go in."

"No, I didn't. I changed my mind."

"I thought maybe you came to see me."

"I thought about it," she lied. "But it's getting late. I really have to get back to work."

"That's crazy. All you ever do is work." He inspected her face, saw the fear in her eyes, her trembling lips. His expression turned solemn. "You and I need to talk," he quietly said. He opened the door and edged his body into the driver's seat, tossing the ax in the back. "Move over."

She found herself being pushed over the gearshift and into the passenger seat. "Look, I really need—" Before she could say anything more, Daniel closed the door, put his foot on the gas, and drove the Jeep up the path.

He stopped the truck in front of his driveway and got out. Going around to her side, he opened the door, grabbed her arm along with the ax, and pulled her from the vehicle. Holding her arm in a tight grip, he dragged her toward his house.

"Let go of me!" she yelled. She tried to break away, but his hold on her was strong.

He raised the ax over his head and brought the blade down on the cord of wood by the side of the house. Then he went around to the front and pushed the door open with his foot, shoving her roughly inside.

She stumbled into the living room, then quickly turned around and glared at him. The fear inside her turned to rage. Without thinking, she rushed at him, swinging her fist at his face. He quickly sidestepped her punch, grabbed her hand, and brought it down behind her back. With his other arm, he reached around her body and lifted her up. He carried her into the living room and dropped her onto the couch.

She tried clawing at his face, but he held her wrists, bringing them down on the arms of the divan. His knee was buried in her chest, preventing her from getting up.

"Stop it!" he growled. "Just stop it! Okay?"

He continued holding her down, letting her curse and squirm as she tried to break loose. After a few minutes, her body sagged and her head dropped down on the pillows.

"If I let you up, will you stop?" he asked.

Glaring up at him, panting, she refused to answer.

"Come on, Malia. I don't want to sit on top of you all day. But I'll do it if I have to."

Malia thought about her options. He was too strong, and no one would hear her screaming up here anyway. Eventually she nodded acceptance.

He let go of her arms and removed his knee from her chest. She sprang up, moving her body away from him. Kneeling down next to her, he put his hand on her leg, but she recoiled from his touch.

"You have some temper," he said.

She moved farther away from him, digging her back into the armrest.

"Listen to me. I didn't kill anyone," he said. "Ben is crazy."

"Is he?"

"The guy's been on my case since I've met you."

"You were in Guam," she blurted out. Her eyes were burning with distrust.

Daniel's eyes clouded in confusion for a second, then he shrugged. "So what?"

"A girl was murdered on that island when you were there."

"People get killed all the time. What does that have to do with me?"

"She worked for the French ambassador."

"So?"

She didn't answer.

He looked at her strangely. "Was she killed with that ancient weapon Ben's carrying on about?"

"Yes."

He stood up slowly, looking genuinely surprised. "Well, I didn't do it. Sure, I've been to Guam. I've been all over the South Pacific islands digging up the past. That's what I do for a living. Why would I possibly want to kill anyone?"

"You tell me!" she snapped. "Were you ever at the French ambassador's home?"

"Maybe. I don't remember. I've been to the homes of many bored diplomats. They were always throwing parties, inviting any foreigner who was white. It gave them someone to talk to other than their wives."

"Then you could have met the dead girl."

"I honestly don't know," he said. "If she was working there at the time, the chances were good that I did meet her. Maybe she was passing by me with a cheese tray," he said glibly. "I don't know."

When Daniel went to sit down next to her, Malia arched her back like a trapped cat.

"Look, there are things you don't understand," he said gently.

"I'm sure there are *lots* of things I don't understand."

He reached for her. "Malia—"

She clenched her fist, glaring at him. "I don't want you touching me, Daniel."

"All right," he said, with resignation. He moved away from her and leaned his elbows on his thighs. "I told that old man to back off. Why the hell didn't he listen!"

"You said there are things I don't understand. What things?" Her eyes caught the front door. She was thinking about making a run for it.

"Things," he said, quietly. "Just things." He sounded frustrated.

How far would she get, once she got past him? Not very, she realized. *Better stay here . . . talk to him.* "Who is Roger Alika?"

Daniel's head jerked in her direction. He looked at her hard. "He teaches at UCLA. I already told you that."

"No, he doesn't. Stop lying to me, Daniel. There are no records of anyone living called Roger Alika. Who is he? What's his real name?"

Daniel stood up, went over to the sliding screen door on the other side of the room, and looked out at the sugarcane fields. His troubled voice was barely audible. "Damn that meddling old man."

The late afternoon sun filtered into the house, causing harsh shadows to fall on his brooding face. Still staring out at the fields, he said softly, "I was falling in love with you. That was not supposed to happen."

Those words caused her heart to race. She stood up and looked over at him. The world seemed to weigh on his shoulders right now. Was this man a murderer? Christ! How would she know? What did a murderer look like anyway?

She stood up and walked over to him. "Who is Roger Alika, Daniel?"

"*Trust* me; he's an anthropologist."

"No, he isn't."

He turned away from the window and stared at her for a long time. "Look, if you want to go back, I won't stop you."

She was surprised. "Are you letting me go?"

He shook his head in disbelief. "My God! What the hell do you think I am?"

Malia looked at the door. It was open. She was free to leave. Instead, she turned to him and said, "I have no place to go."

Daniel looked down at her face. "What are you talking about?" His hands went up to her shoulders, softly tracing her smooth skin with his fingers.

She didn't move away. His touch sent shivers through her body. "I don't have anyplace to go," she said again.

"You have a job . . ."

"I don't want to work for that man."

"Why?"

"There are reasons. *Trust* me."

Daniel smiled. "I guess I deserved that."

"You do."

He leaned over and kissed her forehead. She didn't stop him.

"I'm sure it must be very confusing right now," he said. His hands stroked her hair, moving down to her neck.

She closed her eyes. "It's more than confusing, Daniel."

"I didn't kill anyone," he whispered in her ear.

"I'm trying to believe you." His touch felt so damn good.

"Are you going back to the ranch?" he asked, his lips now on her cheek, her ear.

She lifted her head to him. "To get my things."

"Talk to me," he said, tracing the enclave of her neck with his tongue.

"About what?" Her voice began to tremble.

"About why you want to leave Felix." His lips were moving to her mouth.

"It's personal." She reached up and held his face, moving her lips to his, then kissed him hard on the mouth. Peachie was right, she thought—certain men can do it to you.

Taang sat high in the tree and watched the two coupling together in the man's bedroom. He didn't need the night scope because they never bothered to shut off the lights.

A feeling of melancholia suddenly came over him. Seeing them like this made him think of Piing. They used to rub together like that. She was the only woman he had known—would *ever* know.

Did these two love each other like he and Piing had loved?

He quickly erased the dead, beloved woman from his mind and concentrated on the couple. Once again she disobeyed the general's orders. She was not supposed to see this man. He could easily do something about that, but the general told him to only observe and report back to him. Too bad, he thought, with a sense of disappointment. This anthropologist was well built and in good physical condition. He might have offered him a challenge.

He leaned back against the branch of the tree, chewing on a twig, wondering what they had been talking about before the rubbing began.

"Why don't you want to work for Steinway anymore?" Daniel said to Malia, stroking her face with his fingers. He had his elbow propped up on the mattress and was looking down at her. Their naked bodies were still locked together, coated in sweat.

"He's not the man I thought he was. He's a fake . . . so is the book."

His fingers now traced the lines of her jaw, then circled her lips. "Tell me about it," he whispered.

"Why?"

"I want to know you."

She shook her head, smiling. "Tit for tat, *brah*."

"Not fair, Malia. Talk to me. You need to talk to someone."

"I talk to Ben."

"He hasn't done the things I've just done to you."

She giggled. "I don't think anyone has."

"Tell me about him."

"The general's a shit."

"Why?"

"Because."

"Talk to me."

She did.

When she finished telling him everything, they made love again. This time their movements were gentle and synchronized, like a dance that was in no hurry to reach a finale.

Daniel held her to his breast, stroking her thigh, which was wrapped around his waist. "You have to go back."

"Why?"

"Because you still work for the man."

"I told you, I'm quitting."

He put his fingers to her lips, stopping her from talking. "Go back. You're a professional. You just can't leave like that."

She frowned. "I don't understand you, Daniel."

"I hope someday you will."

"I keep going up and down with you."

"I know."

She licked his fingers, which were on her mouth, tasting the salt. Feeling him getting aroused again, she turned over on her back and waited.

Malia woke up and glanced at her watch. It was well past midnight. She looked at Daniel sleeping next to her. The pale, yellow-gray light filtering through the room from the full moon illuminated his body. He was on his stomach, his face buried in the pillow. Smiling, she leaned over and kissed him on the shoulder. Her fingers moved slowly down the sinewy muscles of his back. They stopped when they came to a small, rough circular scar. Her eyes moved down to it and her body suddenly froze. She'd seen that type of scar before. It was the night her uncle came into her room drunk and showed her the bullet wound on his stomach.

Daniel had lied to her. He was in no skiing accident. This was a bullet wound. Malia felt an immense rage—not toward him but toward herself. She'd allowed herself to be taken in by him again.

Holding her breath, she quietly slid off the side of the bed, gathered up her clothes, which were scattered on the floor, and went out of the room. She got dressed in the hallway.

How much more had he lied about? she wondered.

She slowly opened the door, so it wouldn't creak, and left the house. Holding her sandals in her hands, she raced barefoot down the hill toward the Jeep.

This island is made up of liars! She got into the truck and drove back to the ranch.

Something must have frightened the girl to make her leave like that, Taang thought. He sat up on the branch, looking through his night field glasses at the girl driving away. Turning them to the window, he focused on Daniel, lying naked in bed.

This Daniel Keahi takes care of himself, not like those puffy, smooth-skinned men the general usually associates with.

Now what did she see that disturbed her?

He moved the binoculars slowly over Daniel's frame, stopping when he came to the scar from the bullet hole in his back. From its size, he surmised it had been a fairly large-caliber weapon.

Taang shook his head as he climbed down from the tree. There was never a dull moment working for the general.

Malia went back to the ranch and faxed a letter to Ciji Brown, telling her that she was quitting. Then she went to her room and packed her bags. She didn't know where she was going; she just wanted to get away from the ranch.

The phone began to ring. She knew it was Daniel and didn't answer it. What was she going to tell him? That he'd lied about the skiing accident? He'd just come up with a new story to cover the old one? She'd heard enough untruths in the last few weeks to last a lifetime.

Malia quickly undressed, went into the bathroom, and turned on the shower. She let the water get to a scalding temperature, then scrubbed her body raw for almost an hour, trying to rid herself of Daniel's smell.

Chapter Twenty-three

BEN SPENT SEVERAL days trying to get an address for Clayborg Boots, but came up with nothing. Finally he called the United States Patterns Office in Washington to see if they knew something. They did. Clayborg was out of business. They'd filed for bankruptcy in 1974.

That was twenty years ago.

There was that round number again.

He then phoned his friend, Borshardt, at the NCIC in Washington to see if he would use his influence to find out why Clayborg closed their doors, and why the same diamond-patterned sole was reversed on one of their models. Borshardt said he'd try. When he received an answer, he'd get back to him.

Ben hung up. Hopefully he'd soon have an answer. But now it was time to go back to work. The crop was full this year because of the rain, and the taro ripe for harvesting. For the last several weeks, the murders had filled all his time and he'd neglected his fields. If the taro stayed in the ground much longer it would be a hard winter for him.

He put the large taro sack around his shoulder and went outside. As he cut the stalks, Loke Rico crept into his thoughts. She was eight months pregnant when she died. Who was her doctor? Ben tried to remember who was practicing in Hilo and Hāmākua.

Just one name came to mind: Dr. Buddy Singer. He was the only gynecologist in those districts at that time. He delivered all the babies back then, including his own. Loke Rico had to be seeing him.

Ben left the sack in the field and went back into his house to call him. The taro would have to wait another day.

* * *

Dr. Buddy Singer lived alone on the gold coast of Kona. It was a sun-drenched point that butted out into the ocean. Rich *haoles* from the mainland, drawn to the island with the illusions of mangoes and serene tropical breezes, built million-dollar vacation houses on it. Most of them were now uninhabited. After a few trips, *haoles* found island life boring and returned to the nightlife of Aspen for their holidays.

Ben found Singer's house. It hung on a bluff overlooking the Pacific. Compared to the garishness of the other structures, it was small and nondescript, hidden behind large Indian banyan trees. Buddy, a Jew from Dayton, moved to the island after medical school.

Singer, wearing only a bathing suit, came out of the house to greet him. He was small and thin, somewhere in his late seventies. Overexposure from the sun gave his tanned skin the texture of raisins.

"I have the files on my back porch, Ben. I went through them while waiting for you. What are you looking for?"

"I don't know yet," Ben said.

They went around to the back and sat by the pool next to the cliff. Except for the sight of the large hotels dotting the coastline, the view was breathtaking.

"How's your daughter?" Ben asked him.

Singer shook his head. "She moved to New York. Said she had rock fever living here."

"Mine, too." Ben sighed. "Give them paradise and they opt for the concrete jungle."

The ex–police captain talked children with Buddy Singer for ten minutes, then he asked about Loke.

Looking uncomfortable, Buddy ran his hand over his thin jaw. "You know, I'm not really sure I can talk about Loke Rico."

"Why not?" Ben asked, curious.

"Patient-doctor confidentiality."

Ben leaned over and patted the doctor on his knee. "Come on, Buddy. The woman and her husband have been dead for twenty years. What's to keep confidential?" He told him about his suspicions regarding the murders of Lupe Maile and the Ricos.

"You think the killer is still alive?" Buddy asked.

"I know he is," Ben replied.

Buddy clasped his hands on the table, thinking about it. Letting out a deep breath, he finally said, "I suppose you're right. They're dead. It doesn't matter." He reached down to the cardboard carton by his leg, took out a manila file, and opened it on the table. "These are her records. The last time I saw her was two weeks before she died. She came to my office and asked for an abortion. The girl was as naive as they come. I had to tell her that she was five months too late."

"What was her state of mind?"

"Not good."

"You know why that was?"

"Yes." Another pause. "She wasn't sure if James was the father."

Ben automatically reached for his empty pipe, stuck it in his mouth, and puffed heavily on it. "Did she say whose baby she thought it was?"

"No," Buddy said. "She didn't tell me and I didn't ask."

"I'll be goddamned," Ben muttered.

"She said she couldn't live with what she'd done. The woman was guilt-ridden. She cried for over an hour in my office. Said she needed to know if it was James's child."

"Was it?"

"I took a blood sample from the fetus. It was something I didn't like doing. It was a bit dangerous back then, but she insisted. She said if I didn't do it, she'd go to one of the local doctors and have it done."

"Was James the father?"

Buddy nodded. "Yes."

"What was her reaction?"

"She threw her arms around me, laughing and crying at the same time. She said she'd been a fool. What she'd done was a mistake; she loved James."

"Did she say anything about the affair?"

The doctor looked over his notes. "Only that it lasted for two months."

"Nothing about the man?"

He turned the pages over in his yellow pad, then shrugged. "No, nothing." Singer suddenly pointed his finger in the air and shook it. "Wait a minute. I do remember one thing. Her mood changed. She became frightened. She asked me not to say anything about this. I didn't . . . until now."

"Frightened of who? James?"

"I don't think so. I think she was scared of the other man."

"Why?"

"I remember her telling me she was the one who broke off the relationship."

"Did she say why?"

"No. She didn't want to talk about it."

"James never knew that Loke was having an affair?"

"He didn't get it from me. Honestly, I don't think he ever knew," Buddy said. "I bumped into him in town right afterward. He was with his daughter. I forget her name."

"Malia," Ben said.

"That's it . . . Malia. I talked to him for a while. He seemed happy that he was going to have the baby. The man loved children." He shook his head and smiled. "Loke Rico was not exceptionally bright or educated. But she was beautiful. James was in love with her."

"When you examined her that day, what was the condition of her body?"

"What do you mean, condition?"

"Did you see any marks or bruises?"

Buddy looked at his notes again. "Ah, yes. There were faint scars on her stomach and left shoulder that resembled teeth marks."

"Now you know why she broke off the relationship," Ben said, biting down on the stem of his pipe.

Singer looked up at Ben, surprised. "How did you know this?"

"The other two female victims had the same kinds of teeth marks, Buddy."

"I remember asking her if James did it. She said no."

"It had to be the other man."

"A great tragedy," Buddy said, sitting back in the chair.

Ben thanked Buddy and left.

Driving back to the valley, Ben thought about the frozen smile on Loke Rico's face the night she was murdered. She knew her killer. Obviously, in her way, she still cared for him. Ben was positive the killer had sexual encounters with both Loke Rico and Lupe Maile. Did he also have one with the girl from Guam? He was sure the answer would be yes. But why kill them? Affairs happen all the time. Was the angel ashamed of those encounters? Did he try to cover them up by murder? That still didn't explain why he'd killed James Rico. Again he thought about the pending strike at the sugar plant. Was that it? Or was it something else?

His mood suddenly turned bleak. He had killed the wrong man, and everything he knew and loved was taken away because of it.

The image of his wife's handsome, brown face suddenly loomed large in his head. When she was alive, he always believed one day they'd get back together. A malignant tumor found in her pituitary gland seven years ago quelled even that. *Forgive me, Sarah. Forgive me.*

Instead of turning left on the path leading to his home in the valley, he continued north on Route 250, heading toward Hāwī.

Paul Nani walked into the local saloon, said hello to some of the regulars, and took off his wet rain slicker. It was coming down hard outside. Just as he was about to grab a stool at the bar, he saw Ben sitting at a table in the back. The old man was hunched over, holding a glass in both hands. Paul went over to him and sat down. Noticing several empty glasses on the table, he frowned. "When did you become a drinking man again, Ben?"

Ben looked up at the coroner. " 'Bout three hours ago."

"What's it been? About eighteen years now?"

"Nineteen," Ben said.

"Can I buy you a cup of coffee?"

"You can buy it, but I ain't drinkin' it."

The bartender came over with a Bud and a glass, putting it down next to Paul. The coroner poured the beer into the stein until the foamed head touched the brim. "Rough day?"

"You could say that," Ben mumbled.

Paul nodded. "You need a wife. There are a lot of good single women on this island, Ben. Any one of them would marry you. Maybe it's time you started looking."

Ben smiled at his friend. "Who's gonna match Sarah? When you're used to drivin' a Cadillac you don't settle for a Ford."

"Let me get you a cup of coffee."

"Screw you and your coffee, Paul."

"Hey, I'm your friend, remember? You don't know the shit

you caused me with Isaac when you tried to open up the Rico case again. The captain found out I was helping you and nearly tore my head off."

"Sorry 'bout that, Paul." He finished off his drink and waved to the bartender for another.

"I heard that friend of yours, that Rico woman, left the island this afternoon."

Ben looked up from his glass. "What do you mean she left? She works for the general."

"She quit. I bumped into Steinway's driver. He said he took her to the airport. She was taking a plane back to New York."

"Damn!" Ben hit the table with his open hand. When he calmed down, he uttered, "Well ... I can understand it, I guess. She was never an islander. Jus' surprises me she left, that's all. I thought she had more spirit than that." A sadness crossed his face. "I'll miss the girl."

"Want to play a game of gin rummy, old man?" Paul said.

Ben shook his head. He twirled the glass around in his fingers, thinking. "Remember the night of the murders, Paul? I've been sittin' here reminiscin' a lot about it. It was rainin' hard, like it is now. You came over to the car where I was sittin', talkin' to the Rico girl. We went under a tree, and you showed me the shark's tooth and Panali's bandanna."

"What about it?"

"You said you found the bandanna in the hallway of the house."

"It wasn't me who found it. It was given to me by one of your officers. Why does it matter?"

"I never saw Panali without it. The man slept with that damn neckerchief. I don't think he ever took it off, even when he showered. What was it doin' conveniently sittin' on the floor, waitin' to be picked up?"

Paul shrugged. "My job is to slice open bodies and see what they died from. Finding out who killed them was your domain."

"Do you remember the name of the officer who gave it to you?"

"Hell, that was twenty years ago." He stared at the jukebox near the wall, trying to remember. "Oh, yeah," he said, after a pause.

Ben looked up at him. "Oh, yeah, what?"

"It was Isaac. The reason I remember was because he made such a big deal about it. He wanted everybody to know that he found it. The man was trying to make a name for himself, going for your job even then."

"Well, he got it, didn't he? That's who I thought it was. I had to be sure." Ben got up from the table.

"You going out in that rain, Ben?"

"That I am, Paul."

"Have some coffee first."

"No reason to. I've been sittin' here tryin' to get drunk. 'Cept, the more I drank, the more sober I was gettin'. I guess it doesn't work for me like it used to in the old days."

Ben drove through the pouring rain to Hilo General Hospital. He thought about Malia leaving. Yes, he would miss her. Why didn't she let him know? That girl was hard to understand, like his daughter Aka.

The lot next to the hospital was only half filled with visitors' cars. He parked his truck in one of the spaces. Ignoring the pain in his knees, he ran over to the back entrance used by the staff, opened the door, and went in.

The offices in the hallway were deserted. Most of the night shift was in the other end of the building.

Ben knew this hospital like the back of his hand. Aka, after the car accident, was brought here to the intensive care unit from Kaua'i. For two months he stayed by her side, every waking moment, until she died.

He walked down the corridor until he came to the file room. Hoping it wasn't locked, he turned the knob and pushed. The door swung open.

Ben closed the door behind him and switched on the lights. He went around the milky partition glass of the admittance desk and into the back room. It was filled with metal file cabinets laid out in alphabetical order. Ben found the *Y* box and opened it up.

He scanned through the files of past patients until he came to an old one with Noah Yamaguchi's name on it. Noah was Isaac's son—the one who'd died of leukemia eighteen years ago.

He sat down at the desk, turned on the lamp, and opened the folder.

Five minutes later he saw what he was looking for. He wished he was wrong, but there it was in black and white. Part of the puzzle was beginning to come together.

Ben took the file with him, leaving the hospital the same way he came in.

The lights were out in Isaac Yamaguchi's house.

Sitting in his truck, Ben looked at his watch. It was only a few minutes after nine. He knew the police captain had just gone to sleep; he always did at nine o'clock. The man never veered from his schedule.

The rain was coming down heavy, sounding like jackhammers pounding away on the roof of his truck. Ben got out and hobbled over to the door. He rang the bell a couple of times, then banged on it with his fist. A few minutes later a hall light went on in the house.

Mary opened the door. She was wearing a cotton robe over her nightgown. When she saw Ben standing there, her eyes fluttered in surprise.

"I know it's late, Mary. I need to talk to Isaac."

Her face creased in annoyance. "Ben, he's asleep. Can't you come back tomorrow?"

"No, I can't." He held up the wet folder from the hospital, so she could see it. "This is Noah's medical history. Wake him up."

"Ben—"

He pushed past her, into the hallway. "I know all about it, Mary. Now wake him up, or I'll go upstairs and wake him myself."

Mary stared at Ben, her eyes filled with confusion, then went upstairs.

While waiting, Ben went over to the floor heater in the anteroom and stood over it, trying to warm himself. He heard whispering above him, then the bed creak. Isaac was getting up.

A moment later the police captain, wearing a Japanese kimono over his pajamas, came downstairs. His hair was mussed and his eyes caked with sleep. When he saw Ben standing by the heater, his lips curled. "What do you mean by coming to my house at this hour?"

"Hell, Isaac; it's only a little after nine. The world don't fold up its sidewalks when you go to sleep."

"You said something to Mary about my son?"

"These are his hospital records." Ben held out the folder and dropped it on the foyer table next to Isaac. "He had a bone marrow transplant at Hilo General."

"I know. I did what any father would do to keep his child alive. Say your piece, then get out of here."

"That was twenty years ago. Bone marrow transplants were in the experimental stages then."

"I know that. It kept Noah alive for two more years. He would have died without it."

"It was a dangerous operation. No insurance company would cover it."

For a brief moment Isaac's face seemed to sag and the life went out of his eyes.

Ben opened the folder and took out a photocopy of a check. He held it up to the police captain. "This is a personal check made out to the hospital by you. It's for thirty thousand dollars. That's what you paid for the transplant. You jus' got out of the army and you were on the force for only a month. Where'd you get that kind of money?"

Isaac took a step forward, then stopped. His fists were clenched. "I don't have to answer to you."

"I think I know where it came from, Isaac. I think it was given to you."

"My wife and I had family who cared about Noah."

"They were poor ... laborers who worked in the fields. None of them had that kind of money."

"Maybe some of it was a gift from an anonymous donor. So what?"

"According to the paperwork, Noah had the operation in October of seventy-four. That was two months after the Ricos were murdered."

Isaac's stare was as hard as porcelain. "What's your point? I told you ..."

"... it was a gift from an anonymous donor. I know. What did you have to do for it?"

Isaac didn't answer. His face was white and his breathing irregular.

"You were the one who found Panali's bandanna in James and Loke Rico's home. You made a big deal about it so everyone would see you findin' it."

Isaac let out a forced laugh. "Are you now saying that I killed those people? Why not! You've already accused everyone else on the island."

Ben saw Mary standing on the top step of the landing. Her eyes were moist and sad, and she was wringing her hands together.

"No, you didn't kill them, Isaac. Someone else did. You simply placed the bandanna there when no one was lookin', then pretended to find it. You were paid to finger Panali. You're the one who went to his bunkhouse and found Loke Rico's bracelet under his bed. You were also the one who discovered Panali's boots in his car. The boot size was right, so was the company who made them, but the sole patterns were reversed. You didn't know that. I remember thinkin' at the time that you were a good, conscientious policeman. I didn't know you were also an accomplice."

"You're a crazy old man." Isaac tried to sound hard, but his voice didn't carry much conviction.

"I understand why you did it, Isaac. But it's over now. He's killed again. Who gave you the money?"

"Get out of here."

"I can go to the bank and look up the check you deposited."

"There was no check," Mary said, slowly coming down the steps. Tears ran down her face.

Isaac turned to her, holding out his hand to keep her quiet.

She walked past him as if he wasn't there, stopping when she was next to Ben. "Thirty thousand dollars in cash was deposited in the bank."

"Mary, get back upstairs," Isaac said tautly.

She looked at her husband. "Enough, Isaac, please! We've lived with this for so long. He'll find out. Just tell him."

Ben looked over at the police captain.

Isaac slowly sank down on the bottom step and put his hands to his face. His body began to tremble. "I didn't know there were going to be any killings. That's not what I was told."

Ben sat down next to him. "What were you told?"

He wiped his sweaty brow on the sleeve of his kimono. "Two weeks before the murders I received a call."

"Was it a man or a woman?"

"A man, I think. I can't be sure. The voice was muffled."

"Young or old?"

"I couldn't tell. He offered his condolences about my son. Said it was a pity he was going to die because I didn't have the money for the transplant. He sounded sincere. I was angry about being turned down by the hospital. I offered everything I had as collateral but they still said no. He then suggested a way I could make the money. I listened."

"What was his offer?"

Isaac let out a long sigh. "He asked if I knew Panali. I said sure, everyone knew him. When I asked who *he* was, he told me he was a cattle rancher on Maui. He said Panali had been stealing his cattle and was bankrupting him. He went to the police, but without proof, they couldn't arrest him. I remember saying that stealing cattle was something Panali would do. He said he'd heard there was a rash of burglaries on the Big Island and that Panali might have been behind them. I told him he was probably right, but we also had no proof. That's when he suggested a way of getting rid of him that would be beneficial to both of us."

"Is that when he offered you the money?"

"Yes." Isaac didn't say anything more. He stared through the screen door, out into the wet night for several seconds, then he continued. "He said if I broke into the Rico house earlier that evening, on August twenty-first, stole something of the woman's, then planted the object under Panali's bed, we could arrest him for burglary once the theft was reported."

"Is that what you did?"

"Yes."

"Did you believe he was a rancher?"

Isaac shook his head and shrugged. "I just thought he was someone who wanted Panali out of the way. Everyone did." He looked at Ben. "So did you."

"The boot cast and Panali's galoshes were the same size. How'd he know that?"

"He wanted to know what size boot Panali wore. I told him I would check the police report we had on him. He said he would get back to me the next day."

"Did he call?" Ben asked.

"Yes. I told him Panali had a size ten foot. The only thing he said then was, 'Perfect.' I didn't know what he was talking about."

"Didn't you think to ask?"

"Yes. But when you need thirty thousand dollars to keep your son alive, you hold in those kind of questions."

Ben nodded in understanding.

"I broke in that afternoon, when they weren't home. I found the bracelet, then went over to the ranch Panali worked on. I made sure he wasn't around and left the bracelet under his bed." His hands were balled up. "I figured the Ricos would report the robbery later on that day. Except they didn't. They were killed a few hours later."

"This cattle farmer got you at the right time, didn't he?"

"Jesus, Ben! My son was dying. You saw your daughter die. You know what it's like."

Ben knew. "How'd you get his bandanna?"

"You arrested him for drunk-and-disorderly a few days before the murders. While he was sleeping it off in his cell, I went in and took it from around his neck."

"After you saw the Ricos mutilated, why didn't you say anythin'?"

Isaac rubbed his weary eyes. "It was too late. I already had the money. I was now an accomplice and had to play it out. The murders were carefully planned. Whoever did it knew there would be lots of blood on the floor and there would be footprints in and around the house."

"Did you ever check to see if there was blood on Panali's boots?"

Isaac glared at him. "No. Neither did you."

Ben sighed. Isaac was right.

The police captain continued. "I figured Panali was set up by the mob in Honolulu. Maybe he stole from them or got in their way. When Panali died, I thought it was over."

"You still think it was the mob, Isaac?"

He lowered his head. "No," he said softly.

"So you tried pinning Lupe's murder on Sam Pua."

"So what? If he didn't kill her, he'd eventually kill someone. I didn't feel any guilt over that."

"Where'd you pick up the money twenty years ago?"

"On the black beach in the Pololū Valley. It was the day before the Ricos were murdered. I was told not to bring a flashlight. There was no moon; you couldn't see an inch in front of you. It was the perfect place to meet if you didn't want to be seen. I stood by the lava rocks, like we had planned. Whoever it was, came up behind me. He told me not to turn around and to put out my hands. I did. A paper bag with thirty thousand dollars in one-hundred-dollar bills was handed to me. When I finally turned around, the person was gone."

Ben didn't believe him. He was too good of a policeman and would have wanted to know what the person looked like. He decided not to pursue it for now. "Was his voice muffled like the times on the phone?"

"Yes."

Ben stood up and looked down at Isaac. For a brief moment a rush of immense anger swept over him. This fool had helped destroy his life. Then his rage abated as suddenly as it appeared. He did it to save his son. Ben understood that.

Mary grabbed his arm. "Ben, what are you going to do?"

He looked at her frightened face. " 'Bout what, Mary?"

"Who are you going to tell? He did it for our son, Ben." Her voice was desperate; tears stained her cheeks.

Ben let out a deep breath and ran his hand through his thinning, gray hair. "I'm *pupule*, Mary. Nobody listens to me. Isaac's got a spotless reputation. I'm sure he could think of a million reasons how he came by that money." Then he turned to Isaac and said, "You saw who gave you the money, didn't you?"

Isaac's face turned white. "I told you, Ben—"

"I know what you tol' me," Ben said softly. "You're not a bad man, Isaac. Keeping all this inside you for twenty years must have been a livin' hell. Now you sleep on it. 'Cause I'm gonna come back tomorrow night and I'm gonna ask you that same question. I hope you have an answer for me."

Ben walked out into the rain and got into his truck. He felt no hate for Isaac. Hate wouldn't bring back his wife or his dead daughter. Besides, if push came to shove, Ben knew he'd have done the same thing to save one of his children.

He thought about the boots. The killer believed he was wearing same kind that Panali wore. But the sole configurations were different. It was the killer's only mistake.

* * *

By the time Ben drove down into the floor of the valley, the rain let up. In the distance he saw his house, with the lights on inside.

He never left the lights on.

Ben slowed down and turned the headlights and the motor off, then coasted down the hill, stopping when he was about fifty feet from his door. The window curtains were drawn.

Inside, he heard rock-and-roll music blasting from his radio. He grabbed a tire iron from the backseat, quietly opened the truck door, and got out.

He could see movement through the lace curtains. Someone was in there.

Ben slunk over to the door, his back pressed against the side of the house. His shotgun was on the wall and loaded. He wondered if he could get to it.

The music ended and a deep-throated announcer came on: *". . . and that was Pearl Jam. Yessiree, wahineee! The best of the top five!"*

Tightening his grip on the tire iron, Ben grabbed the door handle and pushed it open.

"Hey, where've you been?" Malia's voice shouted over the music.

With the bar cranked over his head, Ben looked toward the kitchen. Malia, smiling at him, was standing over the sink, wringing out her soaked jeans. She wore only panties and a tank top. Her wet hair was matted to her face. "Sorry about this. I'll try not to make a mess."

He slowly lowered the iron, reached for the old Emerson on the shelf, and turned down the music. "I—I thought you left the island," he stammered.

"I hope you're not the only one who thinks so. I faxed a note to my publisher and told her I quit. Then I had Thomas drive me to the airport. I even let him watch me get on the plane. I left before it took off, grabbed a cab, and came here."

"You're wet," was all that came out of his mouth.

"Yeah, I know. I couldn't get the cab to take me into the valley. I had to walk down in the rain."

She came into the living room, unrolled the wet jeans, then put them on top of the bureau to dry. Turning to him, she said, in a determined voice, "I'm not leaving the island until I find out who killed my parents." She plopped down on the couch, putting her feet over the armrest. "I hope you don't mind if I stay. I need a place that's out of the way, so no one knows I'm still around."

A warm glow came over him, like the rush of a tropical breeze. He smiled. *My Aka has come back,* he thought.

After Malia changed into a pair of dry shorts, Ben went into the kitchen. Using a pie roller on his counter, he mashed up the vines and yellow flowers of a *Kūkae pua'a* plant, mixed them together, then put the paste over two strips of cloth with a spatula. He brought them into the living room, sat down on his couch, and began rolling up his pants over his thighs.

Malia grabbed a Diet Coke from the refrigerator, came back into the room, and slid into the love seat. She watched with amusement as the old man tied the wrappings around his knees. A smile played around her mouth. "A folk remedy, Ben?"

He emitted a loud *"Ahhhh."* Then he said, "It's the only thing that helps these damn legs of mine."

"Whatever happened to aspirin?"

"*Kūkae pua'a* has been 'round a lot longer than aspirin. Burns like hell, but does the job."

Malia giggled.

"You can laugh, but it works. *Kūkae pua'a,* translated into English, means pig shit. I don't even want to think about how that name came into bein'." He propped his legs up on the ottoman and slumped down on the couch, puffing on his empty pipe.

"This what you do on rainy nights?"

"This is what I do *every* night. This and Jay Leno."

She glanced at the old gun on the wall. "You keep it loaded?"

"Don't see any sense keeping an unloaded one. Does Daniel know you're here?"

Her eyes darkened.

Ben could feel the tension inside her. "You want to talk to me, *wahine*?"

She sighed, then told him about the day she was with Daniel, including the bullet hole she saw in his back.

Ben lowered his eyes in her direction. "You sleep with the man?"

She gave an embarrassed shrug, then quickly looked down at her Coke can. "Don't give me any shit, Ben."

He grinned. "Hell, when I was young I once bedded down with a woman who killed her husband with a machete. 'Course, I didn't know it at the time."

"Gee, Ben. That helped a lot," she said wryly.

He thought about telling her of his conversation with the gynecologist, Buddy Singer, but decided against it. At this point, there was no reason for her to know that her mother had been with another man. Instead, he said, "Daniel and this Roger are an interesting pair. One has a bullet wound and lies, the other doesn't even exist according to Washington."

She yawned. "The second you think you have Daniel figured out, that slippery bastard changes skins on you."

He saw that she was tired. "Grab the bed," he said. "We'll work out livin' accommodations tomorrow."

"I can't do that. The bed's yours."

"I ain't sleepy yet. It's only twelve-thirty. I can still catch the last half of Leno. Go on."

Malia was too exhausted to argue. She got up off the couch, kissed the old man on top of his head, and went into the bedroom.

Ben didn't turn on the TV set. Instead, he sat on the couch, puffed away on his empty pipe, and thought about Daniel and Roger. Something wasn't right about them, but he couldn't put his finger on it. Why would anyone shoot a college professor? And who the hell was Roger Alika?

Chapter Twenty-four

THE PHONE WOKE Ben up. He'd fallen asleep on the couch with the bandages still wrapped around his swollen knees.

Groping for the receiver on the coffee table, he found it and put it up to his ear.

"Yes?" he said, clearing the sleep from his voice.

"Borshardt, Ben. Did I wake you? It's nine o'clock in Washington. I keep forgetting what time it is in paradise."

Ben looked at his watch. It was three in the morning. "I'm up now, John."

"I have some info on Clayborg Boots. You still want it?"

"Damn right."

"They went under in seventy-four."

"I know that."

"Seems they got a contract to make rubber combat boots for the army and overextended their resources to keep up with the demand. After a few months, the army dropped them."

"I thought the army believed in leather boots."

"It was an experiment. The Special Forces in 'Nam were the first to try them out. Those were the paratroopers. Our boys in Vietnam were getting all kinds of foot diseases traipsing through rice paddies. The army thought that rubber boots, like the type your cowboys wore in Hawaii, were the answer to the problem. When the war ended, there was no need for them. Clayborg found themselves without their major source of income. They folded right after that."

"What about the configurations on the soles?"

"They were the same diamond-shaped kind you asked about, except for one thing—the diamonds were inverted so our boys could march in them. The ones your cowboys wore were raised so their feet wouldn't slip out of the stirrup irons. Does any of this help?" Borshardt asked.

"I think you narrowed down my killer to 'bout half a million soldiers who went through Hawaii durin' the war." He thanked the man and hung up.

Ben unwound the bandages on his legs, thinking about his conversation with Borshardt. The killer was a soldier, a paratrooper. He had to be in good physical shape, or they wouldn't take him. Not too many men made airborne. That shortened the number. Then he thought about the murder in Guam. How many U.S. soldiers went to that remote island? Not a lot. The list was getting smaller.

Daniel crept back into his mind. Too many contradictions with this man who had a bullet wound in his side.

Then he thought about Roger Alika—the nervous fellow who came from the mainland, yet talked with a Hawaiian accent.

Something clicked in his head. Pieces were coming together, forming a picture. The image was vague at first, like a shadow floating across a room. Then it began to steady itself. It was the only thing that made sense, he thought.

Ben stood up and rolled his pants back down. He quickly put on his shoes, then peeked in the bedroom to see if Malia was still asleep. The girl was wrapped up in the sheet, with her long black hair flowing over the pillow.

Let her sleep. There'd be plenty of time later to tell her what he'd just figured out.

He quietly left the house and drove to the *heiau.*

The rain had calmed to a steady drizzle, but Ben knew that it was only a lull before another storm.

By the time he arrived at the edge of the jungle, the clutch on his truck was beginning to slip badly. He cursed himself for not taking it in and getting it replaced.

He parked the truck and got out. The ground was knee-deep in mud. Ben turned on his flashlight and walked through the mire toward the excavation.

When he came to the clearing, he saw the tent. He crept over to it, pulled back the flap, and went in.

It was dark inside. He moved the beam over the interior until he came to Roger's sleeping body lying on a cot. The man had fallen asleep with a book on his chest; his glasses hung crookedly on his nose.

Ben stuck the light directly on his face. Roger opened one eye, saw Ben, and shrunk away from him.

"I figured it out, son," Ben said. "I remember where I know you from."

"You figured what out, Ben?" Daniel said from behind.

Ben turned around, shining the flashlight in the direction of the voice. Daniel stood next to the open flap of the tent—holding a triangular-shaped trowel in his hand. He wore rubber boots and a white slicker with the hood drawn over his head.

When Daniel turned around to close the flap, Ben saw something that resembled feathery white plumes on his back. Before he could get a better look, Daniel turned to him.

Licking his dry lips with his tongue, Ben touched the side of his head with his index finger and said, "I figured it all out, my friend."

Daniel glared at the old man with hard, dark eyes. Touching the sharp point of the trowel with his thumb, he said, "I'm sorry to hear that, Ben. I truly am."

Malia awoke to the neighing of the wild horses on the valley floor. She got dressed, went into the living room, and looked for the old man. He wasn't on the couch. The wraps for his knees were on the coffee table and the blanket was neatly folded on the divan. She went outside and saw that his truck was also gone.

Perhaps he went into town to get some supplies, she thought.

Malia went back inside, found the percolator and a can of Kona grinds, and brewed a pot. As tired as she'd been last night, sleep hadn't come easy. Every time she closed her eyes and began to drift off, she saw that circular bullet wound on Daniel's side. *He had lied to her.*

After finishing off three cups, she glanced at her watch. It was almost seven-thirty. That meant people were already up and working in Los Angeles. She grabbed the phone and dialed L.A. information, requesting the number of UCLA. When she called, she asked for the Anthropology Department and was put through to one of the instructors.

"Hi, I'm calling from Hawaii. I know Daniel Keahi is on the island. Do you know where I can find him?" She put her feet up on the ottoman. "I'm doing an article for *National Geographic* regarding ancient *heiaus.* I heard Mr. Keahi is working on one."

"He sure is. Probably the biggest one ever unearthed on the islands," the instructor said.

"Really? Sounds fascinating. Can you give me some background on Mr. Keahi?"

"Ask away."

"How long has he been associated with UCLA?"

"Ever since he received his doctorate from here. I'd say about ten ... twelve years now. He's probably the foremost expert on Polynesian culture there is."

"Does that include their weapons?"

"There's none better. He owns a huge collection."

Malia was stunned. She didn't know he also collected them. "Where does he keep these weapons?"

"Most of them are here, in our department's museum. He keeps the more valuable ones in his home in Brentwood."

"Do you know if one of them is a Hawaiian club with sharks' teeth?"

"Sharks' teeth? I've never seen it. As I said, he may keep it in his house."

"Has he ever been to Aspen?"

"I doubt it. Why?"

She took a sip of coffee. "I was told he hurt his back in a skiing accident there several months ago."

The instructor laughed. "Daniel's Hawaiian. Hawaiians don't like snow. I doubt if he's ever been on skis in his life."

She thanked the instructor and got off the phone with him.

Daniel owned Hawaiian weapons. He'd never told her that, she thought.

Ben was right. Everything pointed to Daniel as the killer. Except she refused to believe it. She knew he could lie . . . but kill? No, it couldn't be true. Jesus! She'd slept with him!

She wondered if he was at the *heiau*. That meant his house would be deserted. She wanted to go there and look around.

How would she get there? She had no car. If she took the short cut through the valley, it would be a six-mile walk up mountainous terrain. Malia didn't see that as a problem; she'd run the New York City Marathon three years in a row.

Taking out her shorts and running shoes from her suitcase, she put them on and left the house. It had stopped raining, but the clouds were still dark and ominous. She hoped she'd make it before it poured again.

The climb up the valley wall was rough. She slipped and fell several times, scraping her knees. Thorns from wild bushes scratched her legs and arms.

Two hours later she stood in the sugarcane field, looking up at Daniel's house. She first checked to see if his truck was parked in the garage. It was gone. Then she tried the front and back doors. They were locked.

Nobody locks their doors on the island. The windows were also bolted closed. *The man doesn't want anyone in here,* she thought.

She grabbed a lawn chair off the balcony, lifted it over her head, and slammed it against the mesh door. The screen tore away from the molding. She stuck her hand through, released the latch, and pushed the door open.

Entering the stark living room, she went around to the staircase. Her heart was pounding. What if Daniel came back?

She climbed the stairs and walked down the hall. Passing his bedroom, she glanced in. They'd made love here a couple of nights ago. In the daylight, the room looked as barren as the rest of the house. There was a made bed, a night table, and a dresser, nothing else.

She went into the room and opened up the chest of drawers. Socks ... shirts ... underwear. Nothing of importance.

When she reached the bottom drawer, she found a small box made of koa wood and inlaid with Hawaiian petroglyphs. She tried opening it, but it was held in place with a small brass clasp. She looked through the drawers for a key but couldn't find it.

Too bad. She banged the box several times against the hard wood floor until the hinges broke. Sealed envelopes and faded lined paper fell out of it and scattered on the ground. She picked them up. The envelopes were all addressed to her mother.

Tearing one open, she read the letter inside.

June 12, 1973
My dearest Loke,
The love I feel for you just keeps growing. How much longer can I keep this secret?

Daniel

Holding the letter in her trembling hands, she looked at the date. It was written fourteen months before her mother was killed. Daniel was in love with her! How old was he then? No more than sixteen, she thought. It was possible. Her mother was not even twenty.

She tore open the other letters and read them. They were all in the same vein. The last letter was dated two weeks before she died. None of them were sent. Did she know about his love, or did he keep it to himself all that time?

The yellow lined paper contained poems to her mother,

scribbled in an almost illegible handwriting. They were awk-wardly written, but the pain over his love for her leapt out of the pages.

Trying to control the shaking in her hands, she put the letters back in the envelopes, then back into the container. After placing the box where she'd found it in the drawer, she left the room.

At the end of the hallway she saw a closed door made of thin slats. It was Daniel's office. She turned the knob, but it was locked.

Malia stepped back, brought her leg up, and thrust her foot into the frame, splintering the wood. She kicked it several more times, until the door broke loose from the jamb.

It was a windowless room, dark and musty inside. She felt for the light switch on the wall and turned it on.

There was a makeshift desk made of plywood, a file cabinet next to it, and an old swivel chair. Black-and-white eight-by-ten photographs were pinned to a corkboard that covered most of a wall. Over in the corner, on top of a counter, were chemical pans, a sink, and a negative enlarger.

Daniel was also into photography. One more thing she didn't know about him.

She went over to the wall and looked at the glossy prints. Most of them were candid shots of General Steinway, taken at the ranch before he was called to Washington. This was not the charismatic face the public knew. He seemed self-absorbed, tired—a man who no longer had a purpose in life.

There was no depth of field in the photos, suggesting they were taken with a telephoto lens and without Steinway's knowledge.

Several of them were also of Taang. In one shot, the Montagnard was standing naked, fishing by a small stream. He was staring intently down at the water, holding a spear. In another one, he was wearing a loincloth, sitting cross-legged on top of a crag and smoking an oddly shaped pipe. She could see the volcanic mass of Mauna Kea looming up in back of him.

Taang wore westernized clothing when he was in public, but reverted back to his Montagnard customs when he was alone, she realized.

How did Taang let Daniel get this close to him without his

knowledge? The Montagnard's senses were abnormally sharp. Daniel must have talents she knew nothing about.

Rain suddenly came thundering down on the roof. The downpour was starting again.

There was another stack of photos on his desk. She picked them up and thumbed through them. These were more recent. Several were of her and the general talking on the porch or walking in the fields together. Daniel had been spying on her, too. Why?

She dropped the photos on the desk and opened the drawer. There were several thick folders inside. Some contained more photos, others were filled with papers. She took the files with the photographs out and opened one of them up.

What she saw made her body contract in horror and buckled her knees.

These were old black-and-whites of her parents, taken from different angles right after the murders. Their bodies were sprawled across the bed, the sheets stained with their blood. Some were close-ups of her mother's belly, torn apart with the sharks' tooth club, exposing the fetus.

She had to sit down. Hot flames swirled through her stomach and she felt as if she were going to be sick. Her forehead broke out in a cold sweat and beads of perspiration formed around her top lip. She sat there, with her eyes closed, fighting down the bile that was threatening to come up.

When she felt better, she opened her eyes and forced herself to look at the other photos. They were of a young Polynesian woman, murdered in the same terrible way. The girl's body was also laid out awkwardly on a bed. Her arms were flung across the mattress and her legs were crunched up to her stomach. There was no doubt in Malia's mind that she was the French ambassador's servant in Guam.

Ben was right all along! Daniel was the killer!

With trembling hands she took out another file that was filled with papers. As she unwound the rubber bands, she suddenly heard a car coming up the hill.

Was it Daniel?

She dropped the file on the desk and ran out of the office toward the window. Pressing her body against the wall, she parted the curtain and peered out.

It *was* Daniel. He was driving up the hill in his Jeep. When he reached the driveway, he stopped and turned off the motor.

Daniel was getting out of his truck now. Through the water-streaked pane, she saw that he was wearing a white rain slicker and black boots. He walked toward the front door, then changed his mind and made his way around to the back of the house.

Terrified, Malia clutched the curtain. She heard his heavy footsteps coming up the wooden porch, then they abruptly stopped.

He has to be looking at the broken screen door, she thought. Then she heard the door thrown open. *He was inside the house now!* His footsteps were frantic, running through the downstairs rooms, searching for whoever was here.

He'll be coming upstairs any moment. She couldn't stay in the hallway.

His footsteps were now on the bottom step.

She raced into his bedroom, furiously looking for a place to hide.

The closet door was ajar. Just as he reached the top landing, she went inside and quickly closed the door. She ducked under the pole and snuggled in the corner, concealing herself behind his clothing.

He was racing down the hallway, bypassing the bedroom. "Damn it!" she heard him scream.

He's looking at the door to his office—the one I kicked in. She crunched farther down in the darkness, her body shaking with fear. *Oh, God! He sees the files I didn't put back.*

He was out of the office now, his footsteps heading for the bedroom.

Then he was inside. She could heard the wood floor creak next to the closet. Putting her head against the wall, she prayed he wouldn't look in here.

The door opened and a triangle of light from the bedroom touched down on her face. She saw his searching hands pushing aside the clothes on the hangers. Holding her breath, she waited to be found. His fingers were only inches from her body now. Just as they were about to touch her, he abruptly stopped and walked out of the closet.

From the crack between the clothing, she could see him looking around the room. His back was to her.

What she saw made her shriek out loud. There was nothing she could do to stop it. She was screaming now, just as she did when she was that four-year-old girl in her mommy and daddy's bedroom the night they were murdered.

The plumed white wings protruding from Daniel's sides made it all come back like a tidal wave crashing onshore.

Chapter Twenty-five

D ANIEL FLUNG OPEN the closet door, reached in, and tore the clothing off the pole, trying to get at whoever was inside.

Then he saw Malia crouching down in the corner, staring up at him, her eyes filled with terror. Her hands were pressed over her mouth, trying to stop the screams.

"Aw, Jesus!" he muttered. Reaching in, he grabbed her arm and dragged her out of the closet, flinging her on the bed.

She hit the mattress hard, then turned over on her back and stared up at him.

"What are you doing here?" His voice was low and threatening, his skin tightly drawn over his face.

She didn't answer him. Her mouth jutted open, but no words came out.

"Talk to me, goddamn it, Malia." He leaned over and reached out for her.

She balled her body up to avoid his hands, then rolled over to the opposite end of the bed and jumped off. With the mattress separating them, she arched her back and stared at Daniel, watching for what his next move would be. Her eyes flickered over to the door. In order to get to it, she'd have to somehow get around him.

He spread his lips, forcing a smile while he edged slowly around the foot of the bed. Holding up his hands, he said, "Malia, look . . . I know you're scared right now. I don't blame you. There are things you don't understand. Let's talk about it." His voice was calm, trying to reason with her.

Her body was tense and her breathing heavy, like a rabbit watching a coyote to see when it would pounce. She forced herself to stay completely still while he moved around to her side of the bed. When he was close enough to reach out for her, she threw her body on the mattress and bounced off, landing on the other side. He was no longer blocking the path to the door. She raced for it and ran out of the room.

She was in the hallway now. From the bedroom, she heard Daniel screaming her name.

Get to the staircase!

Malia took three steps at a time. When she reached the bottom floor, she saw gray daylight flowing in through the back sliding door.

Daniel was now in the corridor, racing toward the staircase.

Malia was a fast runner. If she could only make it outside, she'd have a chance.

Just as she reached the entranceway, Daniel leapt from the bottom step and tackled her, wrapping his arms around her ankles. She tumbled out the door onto the lanai. The rain was coming down heavy, drenching her in a blanket of water.

She spun around and looked up. Daniel was on his stomach, still holding onto her legs. From the corner of her eye she could see some kind of insignia embroidered on the sleeve of his white slicker. She kicked at him, trying to free her feet. He held on tight, slowly crawling up her legs toward her torso, all the time pleading with her to stop fighting. She couldn't let him get on top of her or it would be all over.

Malia punched and clawed at his face. Daniel let out a scream as her nails dug into the skin under his eye. He let go of her legs and put his hand up to his cheek. She thrust her foot as hard as she could into the center of his face. A dull grunt sprang from his throat.

She leapt to her feet. Daniel was curled up on the ground, holding his bloodied mouth.

Remembering what she'd done to her uncle when he'd forced himself upon her, Malia went around to his back and kicked him hard on his wound. Daniel rolled around the wood porch in agony.

That would only hold him for a few seconds, she thought.

She ran down the steps to the front of the house. Her heart sank when she saw the road leading to the highway was once again a raging river. The only route out was the way she came, through the sugarcane and down into the valley.

Malia climbed the hill and sprinted into the field. The tall, sharp stalks lashed out at her face and arms. She heard the sounds of cane being brushed aside. Daniel was coming after her.

Over the thunderous noise of the rain, he was screaming out her name.

. . . Everything was repeating itself.

Twenty years ago she was running through these same fields, trying to escape the same man.

She drew back in horror when she came to the black lava rocks forming the fish pond. The rain cascaded down on it, causing the murky overflow to spill onto the field.

All repeating itself.

No, she was not going into those dark waters again.

Malia raced around the perimeter of the pond and back into the cane field. When she reached the cliffs overlooking the ocean, she retraced her steps, then ran parallel toward the rim of the valley.

He was closing in on her now. She could hear the stalks cracking directly in back of her. There was no way she'd make it. Dropping down on her hands and knees, she hid behind the cane shafts and began to crawl. She dragged herself through the field until her lungs were ready to burst. The hard rain stung her skin.

No, she didn't see an angel that night. What she had seen was Daniel—dressed in the same white slicker he had on now, with the wings embroidered on the back. The reason she didn't remember his face was because she couldn't see it; it was hidden under the peaked hood of the same parka.

Hearing the sounds of crunching footsteps behind her, she stopped moving and dug her face into the damp ground.

"Malia!" he was screaming. "Goddamn it, will you stop this!"

Malia knew he was only several feet from her now. She kept her head down, held her breath, and clutched the broken cane in her fists. Her heart was pounding so loud that she was afraid he'd hear it through the rain.

The footsteps finally moved away, going toward the cliffs. She waited a minute longer, then looked up. She saw Daniel's figure standing on the rim of a boulder; he was scanning the field.

The tropical forest was only a few hundred feet away. It was the only way out. She took a deep breath to get up her nerve.

Now! Now!

Malia stood up and raced for the trees.

"Malia! Stop!" Daniel yelled.

He'd seen her. Without slowing down, she turned her head in his direction. He jumped off the lava rock and ran after her.

She put her head down and sprinted through the fields until the cane gave way to dense trees.

She made it into the forest.

Get back to Ben's house! The old man had a shotgun on his wall. He said it was loaded. If she could reach the house, she might stand a chance.

The earth was soft from the rain, slowing her down. She fell several times, tripping over broken branches.

A mile into the forest, the ground suddenly gave way, sloping down into the valley. It was slippery and treacherous. She grabbed onto branches and rocks, trying to keep her footing. At one point, she lost her balance and slid thirty feet down the muddy incline, saving herself by reaching out and clutching the twisted trunk of a hala tree.

Daniel was only five hundred yards behind her now. He was an expert climber and gaining ground.

When she reached the flat grassy terrain, she turned around and saw Daniel swiftly descending the slope and clutching his side in pain.

The house was about two miles away. It was now going to be a race. She prayed the pain from his wound would wear him down.

The grass was only a foot tall here and there was no place to hide. She ran full speed through a herd of wild horses grazing on the plain. They whinnied in fear and took off in a full gallop.

She spotted the path leading to Ben's house. Her sides were on fire and her legs were numb. It was like the wall a marathoner hits when reaching the twenty-mile mark. If she didn't give in to the pain, she'd make it.

The road turned into a small stream. She plowed through the water.

A half mile down, the path arched around a bend. Turning the corner, she saw the roof of Ben's house nestled along the ledge of the mountain. Just fifty feet more and she'd make it.

When she reached the clearing, she saw a four-wheeled vehicle parked out front. It wasn't Ben's truck.

Thank God there was someone inside!

Her legs gave way and she dropped to the ground before she could get to the door. She tried to stand but her muscles were cramped. Daniel had already reached the clearing and was only a hundred yards back.

Move, girl! a voice inside her said. She crawled to the door, pushed it open, and pulled herself inside the house. Gasping for breath, she peered up and saw the shotgun on the wall.

Where was Ben?

Dragging herself over to the wall, she clutched the top of the table and hoisted herself up.

"Malia!" Daniel was screaming. He was outside the door now.

Get the gun!

Using the strength she had left, Malia reached up and grabbed the shotgun. It was an old pinfire with a double hammer and two triggers. The barrel was partially rusted and she prayed it worked like Ben said.

Just as she cocked both hammers, the door flew open. Daniel was standing by the archway, covered with mud and drenched to the bone. His breathing was raspy and he gulped for air. When he saw the gun pointed at him, he held out a hand. "Malia . . . please . . . let's talk."

Holding the stock to her shoulder and her finger on the first trigger, she aimed the barrel at Daniel's chest.

"Malia . . . you don't understand." He took a step forward.

She tightened her grip on the trigger.

He took another step. "Put it down . . . listen to me." He was only six feet from the barrel of the gun.

Oh, Jesus!

Just as she closed her eyes and pulled the trigger, a hand

came from behind and grabbed the muzzle, pushing it toward the wall.

A huge explosion.

The recoil knocked her back against the table. She opened her eyes and saw the jagged hole the shotgun blast had made in the wood wall.

Whoever was behind her was still holding onto the barrel, trying to rip the gun away from her hands. She held tight, her finger finding the second trigger.

Daniel leapt on top of her, reaching out for the weapon. His weight pinned her against the table. Hands came at her from all directions, holding her shoulders, her legs.

There were men's voices speaking all at once.

The gun went off again, hitting the ceiling and knocking Daniel to the floor. Pieces of plaster fell on her face. She was kicking furiously now, screaming, trying desperately to get up.

Daniel was on top of her again, yelling something, but she couldn't hear because the loud explosion had clogged her ears.

Then she saw the face of Roger Alika standing over her.

Another face ... Ben's. His lips were moving.

Her ears began to clear and she could hear some of the old man's words. "It's all right, *wahine*. It's all right."

"He killed my parents, Ben!" she screamed. "I saw the letters ... the photos!"

Malia tried to move, but her legs and arms were held down by all three men. She glared at Daniel, breathing hard, her eyes filled with hate.

"You don't understand," Daniel said, trying to calm her down.

"I read those letters you wrote my mother!" she shouted at him.

"You don't understand," Daniel repeated again.

"He didn't write those letters," the one known as Roger Alika said. His voice was low, muffled with embarrassment.

Malia thrust her head in his direction.

The man moved his eyes away from her stare and glanced awkwardly down at the floor. "I was the one who wrote them," he whispered.

Chapter Twenty-six

S TEINWAY, WITH HANDS folded behind his back, stood by the large monitor on the wall of the Pentagon's War Room, looking at live satellite reconnaissance pictures of the southern portion of North Korea. A heavy thunderstorm hung over most of the Yellow Sea, but a high-pressure system was building from the west. The weather would clear in the next couple of days.

It would be perfect timing for a strike.

The excitement of what was going to happen caused his ulcers to act up. Grimacing, he picked up the glass of Maalox from the large rectangular table and drank it. He then glanced up at the digital clock above the screen. It showed fifty-five hours and counting down. The invasion, if the forecast held, would begin two nights from now.

His body tingled. He'd fought Congress and the president for this invasion and won. The war would be a quick one. He was riding a wave of popularity with the American public that could only grow larger with this victory. The presidency would soon be his.

Everything on this end was going like clockwork. The only kink—and it was a minor one—was this Hawaiian girl. Ciji told him she received a fax from Malia saying she was quitting, and his driver had seen her board the plane to New York. But when Taang checked the passenger list from the incoming flight at Kennedy, she'd never arrived. What happened to her? Was she still on the island, digging into his past?

Taang was right: it was a mistake to have kept her.

The Montagnard said he saw a large bullet wound on the side of Daniel Keahi's back. This bothered him a great deal. Anthropologists don't usually get shot. Also, during the past few months, Keahi had been asking him too many personal questions. He hadn't really given it much thought until now. Why was he so curious?

His aide, a young blond lieutenant, walked over to Steinway. "Sir, the computer is available now."

"Thank you," the general said.

They took the elevator to the second floor and went into a massive room as big as a football field. It was filled with mainframe computers. When the technicians saw the general enter, they stood up.

"Sit down," Steinway said, smiling.

The men, ill at ease at seeing someone of his stature coming into their enclave, sat back down and continued working.

Steinway and his aide walked over to a computer programmer seated behind a monitor on his desk.

"Can you get me into the main database of the Department of Motor Vehicles in California?" Steinway asked him.

"Yes, sir. That shouldn't be a problem." The technician patted the large mainframe.

Steinway stood over him as the programmer tapped some code words on the keyboard. Unix symbols sped across the large monitor.

"It'll be a few minutes, sir. Who are we looking for?"

"We're looking for a man named Daniel Keahi." The general spelled it for him. "I want to see the photograph on his driver's license."

"Piece of cake, sir," the technician said. "There can't be too many Keahis living in Los Angeles." His fingers continued to dance across the keyboard.

The computer asked several questions, which were answered by the programmer. Several minutes later, a photo of a California driver's license appeared on the screen.

Steinway moved his head closer to the monitor. "I can't see the face," he said, with impatience.

The technician moved the mouse onto the photo of Daniel Keahi, clicked it, then sat back as the facial features on the license zoomed out to cover the entire screen.

The general's expression turned grim as he stared at the picture of a gaunt-faced man with white patches in his beard; he was wearing thick glasses. This was not the Daniel Keahi he knew. This was the anthropologist who assisted Daniel at the *heiau*.

"Would you like a printout of this, sir?" the programmer asked.

"I would like that very much." Steinway's voice was almost inaudible.

Taang, wearing an identification tag clipped on his shirt, stood outside the computer room and watched the general through the thick-plated window. He knew every inch of the man's soul—knew what he was thinking, what he was feeling. This was the first time he'd seen him this upset.

His lips curled over his false teeth. It was the girl! She was the one who was doing this to him!

He put his short, stumpy fingers up to the window and pressed them against it. Feeling the anguish of his friend made his eyes tear.

The general, pale and shaken, walked out of the room and went over to the Montagnard. "I need your help," he said in a tired voice.

"You wrote those letters?" Malia said, stunned, looking up at Roger.

"There are things you don't understand, *wahine*," Ben said, putting his hands on her shoulders.

Malia's eyes darted from Ben back to Roger.

"I'm Daniel Keahi, not him," Roger said, pointing to the man Malia knew as Daniel.

"What's going on here?" she uttered.

"It's true," Ben said.

"Who the hell are you then?" she said to the man she thought wanted to kill her only a few minutes ago.

"My name is Erik Young. I'm with the Criminal Investigation Division of the army." He wiped his bloody lip with the back of his hand.

She suddenly felt numb inside. "Army Intelligence? You're not an anthropologist?"

He shook his head. "No. Anthropology is only a hobby of mine. I'm a psychologist and a major in the United States Army."

She rubbed her brow, feeling dazed and confused. Glancing at Erik's arm, she now got a better look at the patch on the shoulder of his slicker: 175TH AIRBORNE. White wings jutted out from the sides of the emblem.

"Erik took on Daniel's identity to get close to the general," Ben said to her. "I figured part of it out last night and went to the *heiau* to confront them. They filled in the missin' pieces for me."

She slouched against the table, looking lost and helpless. "What's going on here?" she managed to say again.

"A lot," Ben said. He took the blanket off the couch and wrapped it around her body. Shivering from the wetness, disoriented and frightened, she reminded him of that little girl who sat in his truck twenty years ago.

"Why did you write those letters to my mother?" Malia asked the bearded man.

He pushed his loose glasses up on his nose and cleared his throat in embarrassment. "Because I was sixteen and didn't know how else to express my feelings." He laughed nervously. "Love can be all-consuming at that age. When I wrote those letters and poems, I was caught up in its emotional spin. But I never sent any of them. I wrote them for a release. Your mother never knew of my feelings."

"You used to watch our house all the time."

The bearded man let out a soft groan. "I know. I was a stupid kid. Shy and innocent. She was beautiful. I had a crush on your mother. But that's all it was. My family moved away to San Francisco after the murders. I went to Stanford. There I met the woman who became my wife. We're divorced now. I have a daughter."

She looked at the man who now called himself Erik. Her expression was one of disappointment. "That's the same story you told me."

"I know," he said. "I lied to you. I had to. I was telling you Daniel's life story, not mine. I've never been married." He began to wipe the water and mud from his face with a towel Ben gave him.

"What's this all about, Erik—or whatever the hell your name is?"

He wrapped the towel around his neck. "It's Erik Young," he said. "That's my real name."

"I remember the night in my parents' bedroom. I remember everything. What I saw then were the same embroidered wings on back of the raincoat you're now wearing. I was four years old . . . they looked so damn *real*."

"It was dark," Ben said. "They'd look real to anyone."

"What are those wings?" she asked. Her voice was filled with revulsion.

"It's the insignia of the 175th Airborne Division of the U.S. Army. It's *my* division. The raincoat is issued by the 175th for the tropics," Erik said.

"The man who killed my mother and father was wearing the same thing," she said.

"I know that," Ben said. "The killer was a paratrooper in the same division."

"Why would a soldier kill my parents?"

"There's something I haven't told you about your mother," Ben said. "Something I only recently found out."

She glanced up at him, pulling the blanket further around her shoulders.

Ben let out a long sigh. He dreaded this moment. "Let's get you out of those wet clothes first. Then we'll talk, little one."

After changing into jeans and a sweater, Malia went over to the roaring fire Ben had lit in the hearth and sat cross-legged on the floor. The old man gave her a cup of coffee to warm her up, then told her about her mother's indiscretion.

She stared at the flames, trying desperately to digest everything Ben had just said. "Why didn't you tell me this before?" she whispered to him.

Ben, holding his pipe, was sitting on the couch with his arms on his knees, bending over her. "You've been through enough hell. I didn't want to add to it."

She angrily turned to him, the fire from the hearth reflecting like mirrors in her dark eyes. "You didn't want to add to it? Jesus Christ. I had a right to know."

"You did. I was wrong 'bout that," he said.

"Do you know the name of this paratrooper she was seeing?" Her voice cracked with contempt.

"No, but the 175th is a handpicked, elite group of fighters. They're not your everyday, average enlisted men. We need to find out the names of the soldiers who were stationed on the islands in 1974."

She looked over at Erik, who was sitting next to her. "The 175th was also General Steinway's division," she said. "He

was their commander in Vietnam. I interviewed many of the
general's associates, including the head of the Security Council, who was attached to that division."

"Like Ben told you, it was an elite group," Erik said. "If
you were a career man, you wanted to be in the 175th. It
pushed you way up the ladder."

"What do the wings on the back of the jacket mean?" she
asked him.

"We were nicknamed Death's Angels," Erik replied.

"How appropriate," she said coldly. Still looking at Erik,
she asked, "Why did you take on Daniel Keahi's name to get
close to Steinway?"

"That part is classified," he said.

"The hell it is!" Ben growled. "Enough secrecy! Better tell
her. She's been diggin' around in Steinway's past an' comin'
up with similar results as you. She knows more about him
than you fellows in Washington do."

Erik thought about it, then nodded. He turned to Malia. "I
see we need to talk."

"Good. You go first. This time try to keep it honest, okay?"
Her voice was filled with sarcasm.

"Fair enough," he said. "I'll start at the beginning. I was a
major in the 175th. In 1991, I was wounded in Desert Storm
and had part of my hip replaced . . . in the same spot where
you kicked me." He patted the area on his side.

Her eyes narrowed. "I thought you were in a skiing accident."

"There was no skiing accident. I think you already know
that. After I got out of the hospital, I was transferred to the
Criminal Investigation Division in Washington. I trained at the
FBI Academy in Quantico, then later on at Scotland Yard. Six
months ago I was summoned to the office of the Army's Chief
of Staff."

"Why?" she asked.

"Steinway was thinking about running for the presidency."

"So what?"

"There'd been rumors circulating around the Pentagon for
years that the man committed certain atrocities in Vietnam
when he was head of the 175th Airborne."

"What kind?" she asked.

"That he murdered innocent Vietnamese whom he suspected

of harboring the enemy. Many 'friendlies,' including women and children, were supposedly massacred."

"Why wasn't this made public?"

"No proof. With Mai Lai, there were newsmen present. If there weren't, trust me, none of that would have surfaced either. Most of Steinway's missions in 'Nam were covert. They never made the five o'clock news. With Steinway thinking about running for president, those rumors began to take on a whole new light. A retired general might get away with blowing up friendlies twenty years ago, but not the president of the United States. My job was to investigate him."

"By getting close to him?"

Erik nodded. "Right."

"Surely some of his troops would have talked."

"You have to understand the mentality of the 175th. They're a closed society composed of the best soldiers in the world. They protect their own ... always have. Not many of them under Steinway's command survived the war. Those who did would never have turned him in. They admired him. He had that kind of effect on soldiers."

"I know what kind of effect he had on soldiers," she said bitterly, remembering what he did to Steven Bankroft. Then she thought about Jasper Rhodes. He was fired when he tried to get a list of soldiers that were under Steinway's command in Vietnam. Had he also heard about the rumors?

She pointed to the bearded Keahi sitting on the sofa. "Why did you take on this man's identity?"

Erik said, "Steinway was a man who studied the tactics of ancient armies. He used many of them on the battlefield. Most times he was successful. The terrain of Hawaii was similar to Vietnam. Steinway became an expert on Hawaiian warfare and employed some of their methods to defeat the Vietcong. Years after the war, he contacted Daniel at UCLA. Daniel was also an authority on the ancient Polynesians and the ways they fought. They began to write to each other. Several months ago I read in an archaeological magazine that Daniel was going to Hawaii to excavate the *heiau*. I knew he was my ticket to Steinway. I did research on Keahi, found out everything I could about the man, then contacted him."

Daniel moved down onto the floor and sat next to them. Scratching his beard, he said, "Erik came to UCLA, showed me his credentials, and asked me if he could take on my name and pretend to be me while I was in Hawaii. At first I thought he was crazy and almost threw him out of my office. I told him the general would see through him in a second. Then he convinced me to go out to dinner with him." He put his hand on Erik's shoulder. "I must say the man was quite a charmer."

"He certainly tries." There was a sting in her tone.

"We talked about Polynesian history," the bearded anthropologist continued. "I was impressed. The man knew his stuff, but not enough to fool a man like the general. That's when he asked me if I'd give him a crash course, enough so he could get away with it. At first, I refused. Then he told me the reason and I began to have second thoughts. I was against the Vietnam War as a kid and Erik knew that. When he told me Steinway might have killed innocent people, then was going to run for president, it went against my grain. I didn't think Erik would get away with deceiving the general, but I told him I'd go along with it. We barricaded ourselves in my house for two weeks. I worked eighteen hours a day with Erik, teaching him everything I thought the general would ask him about Hawaiian warfare. He had a mind like a sponge—he learned fast."

"What about the students working at the temple site? Didn't they know what you were doing?"

The bearded man shook his head. "No. They're anthropology students from Hawaii University, not from UCLA. They knew of me, were familiar with my papers, but they didn't know what I looked like. Erik spent much of his time at the excavation, and he was good enough to fool the kids. I pretended to be his assistant and was always at his side, in case there was a problem. They never suspected. If Erik was to be me, then I had to tell him everything about me when I was living on the island. That included the night I found you in the fish pond."

"That's how I knew about it," Erik said to Malia.

The real Daniel slapped his hands together and gave a boyish laugh. "We actually pulled it off. Incredible!"

Malia turned to Erik. "I saw those photographs in your house you took of me. Why?"

"I took pictures of everyone at the ranch who knew the general," Erik said. "I'm sorry, but that was my job."

"How did you get away with photographing Taang?" she asked. "I didn't think anyone could do that."

"I have to thank General Steinway for that one. He was fascinated by the Montagnards—the way they fought and how they stalked their enemy. After the war, he incorporated their techniques into the basic-training program of the 175th. In a roundabout way, it was Taang who taught me how to stalk *him*."

"What about those photos of my parents and that murdered girl from Guam?"

"My job was to investigate the genocide in Vietnam, that was all. But when I heard about the wings you saw on the murderer and about those boots, I began to suspect that the killer may have been in the 175th. I called the FBI and asked for everything on your parents' murders. They fed the information into their computer. Based on the way they died, it also spit out the dead servant girl from Guam. The wounds were the same. Ben was on the right track."

Understanding, Malia nodded. "Your airborne division were paratroopers."

"Right," Erik said. "The killer knew the boots the *paniolos* wore and the ones his airborne division wore were made by the same company and had the exact same sole patterns. What he failed to notice was that the patterns were subtly reversed. Ben and I were following the same leads, only independent of each other. When I told my superior what was happening, he told me to drop investigating those old murders and concentrate on Steinway. . . . Except I couldn't do that."

"Why not?" she asked.

"Because of you. They were your parents," he said softly. "Then Ben came to my tent at the dig last night and told me what he suspected."

Massaging his knees, Ben said, "If you're from Hawaii, a Hawaiian accent is somethin' you carry with you the rest of your life. Jus' like your New York accent, sweet *wahine*." He motioned with his head to the bearded anthropologist. "This fellow here, who called himself Roger Alika, said he never lived in Hawaii, yet he had an accent." He then gestured toward Erik. "He told me he grew up on the island, but he sounded like a mainlander. Somethin' jus' wasn't right about it. The one thing I remembered about the Daniel Keahi I interrogated twenty years ago was that he was as blind as a bat. He was always pushin' his glasses up the bridge of his nose. When I went to the dig a couple of days ago, the real Danny saw me and ran away—but not before he did that same thing with his sunglasses. It took me a while, but I finally figured out who was who. That's when I realized I'd been suspectin' the wrong man of murder."

"Were you ever in the army?" she asked Daniel.

The bearded man shook his head and pointed to his thick glasses. "I'm lost without them. They wouldn't take me."

Malia turned and glared at Erik.

Erik said, "I know. I lied about that, too. I don't wear glasses. You asked me about my eyes that day you first came to my house, and I had to make something up." He laughed, then quickly grimaced from his split lip. He put his fingers up to it, dabbing for fresh blood. "You kick hard."

"I intended to," she replied.

"I wasn't the one chasing you in the sugarcane field that night," the bearded man said to her. "Everything I told Ben that night was the truth."

Malia looked at him doubtfully. "Ben brought up a good point the day of Lupe's funeral. He said you also told him years ago that you saw a car parked next to my house the night of the murders and you saw the figure of someone getting out. It was dark and raining. My house was a quarter of a mile away. How could you see?"

The real Daniel coughed and pushed his glasses up his nose. "I saw no lights on in your house when I was up on my roof. At first I figured everyone was asleep. Then I heard the car with no headlights. I got down from the roof and followed the sound to your house." Again he cleared his throat. "I thought it might have been Loke . . . your mother. I stood across from your house and saw the parked car. I couldn't make out its type because it was dark, but I could see by its shape that it didn't belong to her or your dad. Then I saw the shadow getting out. It happened very fast. I didn't see who it was. I didn't think anything of it at the time and went back to my house. A short time later I heard your screams coming from the fish pond."

"Why didn't you tell Ben the truth about following the car?" Malia asked.

Daniel shrugged. "I was confused . . . scared. I thought Ben might have felt I was the kind of person who spied on people."

"Or that he would have found out about your feelings for my mother," Malia said.

"Probably," the bearded anthropologist answered.

"He told me all about it months ago," Erik replied. "He's telling the truth."

Daniel continued. "When I heard you screaming, I ran into the field, following the sound of your voice. My parents called the police."

"You saw no one?" Malia asked.

Daniel Keahi shook his head. "It was pitch-black out in the field. The only way I could see a little bit in front of me was when the fireworks went off every couple of minutes. When I got to the pond, the glare from a rocket exploded in the sky. Otherwise, I never would have seen you."

"You were lucky, son," Ben said to him. "I don't think you'd be here today talkin' about it if you *did* see anyone." A somber look suddenly came over his face. He turned to Erik. "Isaac Yamaguchi saw the killer's face. I tol' him I would be comin' back tonight."

"Isaac saw him?" Malia said, astounded.

"Yes," Ben said.

"You mean he knew all the time it wasn't Panali?"

Ben nodded at her.

"Why didn't he say something before?" she asked, confused.

"Long story," Ben said. He turned to the bearded anthropologist. "My car's still at the *heiau*. The damn gears don't work. I need a ride."

Daniel nodded and got up from the floor.

"Let me go with you," Erik said, starting to get up.

Ben shook his head. "He won't talk if you're there. I'll be back later an' let you know what I've learned."

The anthropologist dropped Ben off in the driveway of Isaac Yamaguchi's house. It was dark inside, but he could see flickers of light coming from the greenhouse around the back.

"Do you want me to wait?" Daniel asked.

"No. I'll call for a cab after I talk to Isaac." He got out of the truck and hurriedly walked across the flowered path to the glass nursery.

When he was ten feet from the door, he saw the shadowy figure of Isaac through the streaked glass.

Ben quickened his pace.

He reached the door and flung it open. The smell of incense and blood permeated the nursery. His eyes caught the glow of burning candles on the floor. Mary was sitting on her knees next to them. Her closed, swollen eyes told him she'd been there for a long time.

Then he saw Isaac. He was holding his stomach, doubled over in the corner, lying perfectly still. A serrated kitchen knife protruded from his belly. His pale face was twisted in pain and his vacant eyes stared lifelessly at a pot of African orchids in front of him.

The color of his skin told Ben he'd been there for over a day.

By committing *seppuku*, Isaac did what he thought was honorable, Ben thought. *The man may have been third-generation Hawaiian, but he was still Japanese.* He should have remembered that.

Ben then noticed that Isaac was wearing his old army uniform. It was bloodied but pressed. The pants were tucked into highly buffed paratrooper boots.

He slowly walked over to the body, stooped down, and looked at the emblem on his arm. It was the insignia of the 175th, with white angel's wings embroidered into the shoulder.

Isaac was also in the 175th. Not only did he see the face of the killer . . . he also knew who he was, Ben said to himself.

Chapter Twenty-seven

MALIA WOKE UP in Erik's bed. When Ben didn't return last night, Erik talked her into going back to his house. He didn't feel comfortable with her being alone in the deserted valley.

Looking at her watch, she realized she'd been asleep for over ten hours. The rain had stopped and the morning sun glared through the window, forming a warm yellow rectangle on the wood floor.

She slowly got out of bed, rubbing her shoulders. Every part of her body ached from yesterday's chase. She shuffled into the bathroom, pulled back the cracked, floral plastic curtains around the tub, and turned on the water. When it was filled, she stepped in and sat down. The water stung the cuts on her arms and legs, but she could feel her bruised muscles beginning to loosen up. Lowering her body, she put her feet up on the rim of the tub and closed her eyes. She stayed that way until she began to feel weak from the heat.

Malia dried herself off, tied her hair into a ponytail, then took out a pair of jeans and a T-shirt from her suitcase.

She went downstairs and looked for Erik in the living room. He was already up; his crumpled sheets and pillow were on the sofa. The agreement they made before they left Ben's house last night was that she got the bed and he the couch.

Smelling the rich aroma of coffee brewing in the kitchen, she turned and went toward the source.

"Good morning," Erik said when she walked in. He was wearing shorts, thongs, and no shirt. Grabbing two cups from the pantry, he filled them with coffee from the percolator. "Sleep well?"

"It was the sleep of the dead," she said, plopping down in the chair next to the table and rubbing her arms.

"Milk and sugar?"

She yawned. "Black."

He handed her the cup and sat down next to her.

"How was the couch?" she asked.

He smiled. "Not as comfortable as my bed."

She ignored his innuendo, put her arms on the table, and cupped her hands to her face. Narrowing her eyes, she stared at his rugged features for a long time, thinking.

"Want to let me in on it?" he said, sipping his coffee.

"You sure your name's Erik?"

"I'm sure."

"I mean, I'm not going to look at your driver's license and find out you're Ted Bundy, right?"

"Right. It's Erik. No more surprises."

"You had me going for a while."

"Sorry," he said.

"You know, it's strange," she said, shaking her head.

"What is?"

"I slept with someone that didn't exist. I never did that before."

"But I *do* exist," he said, reaching for her hand.

She let him stroke her fingers for a few seconds, then pulled them away and hid them in the fold of her arm. "Who the hell are you?" she asked finally.

He puffed his cheeks up with air and let it out slowly. Putting his arms on the table, he touched his fingers together to make a V shape and leaned in. "I was born in Merritt Island, Florida. My father worked at the Cape . . . helped propel astronauts into space. He died in the same fire that killed Grissom. I was just a kid then. My mother was a schoolteacher . . . taught English to fifth-grade students."

"And who were *you*?" she said.

"Me?" He rubbed his cheeks, thinking about it. "I was a kid who was scared . . . alone . . . angry."

She angled her head in confusion. "Why?"

"Merritt Island had some of the greatest scientists in the country working there, but it was basically an undeveloped dung hole. The residents of the island had a problem with me."

"What kind?"

He let out a short laugh. "I'm a half-breed, like you. You lived in New York where it didn't matter. Where I lived, it *did*. The locals looked and acted like extras in *Deliverance*. I was constantly tested. Every other day I'd come home with a new face. Eventually I started rearranging theirs. I got to be real good. When I graduated high school, I enlisted in the army to get away from that kind of bigotry. The army put me through college, then grad school."

He reached out for her hand again. This time she didn't take it away. "I know I lied. I don't feel good about it. I'd like to make it up to you."

"Oh, yeah? How?" She slouched down in the chair and put her knee up on the ledge of the table.

"Let me start by making you breakfast. Nobody scrambles eggs better than a 'lifer' in the army."

"Eggs? I'm exhausted, my body hurts like hell, and you want to make me eggs?"

"Yep."

She gestured with her head to the pots hanging over the stove. "Get going, then. I'm starved. If they're not as good as you say, expect another foot in your side."

The wall phone next to the kitchen door rang.

Erik got up and picked up the receiver.

Malia watched the smile on Erik's lips fade and the muscles in his cheeks tighten as he clenched down on his jaw. He mumbled something to the person on the other end, then hung up.

Grabbing the frying pan off the wall, he placed it on the stove, then opened the refrigerator and brought out half a dozen eggs, Swiss cheese, scallions, butter, and milk.

"Who was that?" Malia asked.

"Ben. He's coming over."

"Did Isaac give Ben a description of the killer?"

"No." He turned on the flame, dropped a slab of butter into the pan, then expertly cracked open the eggs on its rim, letting them slide down and float over the butter. His expression remained grim while he worked.

"You look like you lost your best friend," Malia said to him.

"Isaac Yamaguchi was not a friend. I hardly knew him." He chopped up the scallions and sprinkled them over the eggs.

She put down the coffee cup and went over to him. "What happened?" she asked.

Tearing the slices of Swiss cheese into small pieces, he tossed them into the pan, then added pepper. "Ben was up all night with Isaac's widow and the police. Isaac committed *seppuku*. Hara-kiri to you mainlanders."

Her jaw dropped. "Why?"

"The Japanese do that sometimes. Ben said he'll explain." He turned on the flame, put the pan over it, and began to beat the ingredients with a wooden fork. "You like them soft or hard?" He couldn't hide the strain in his voice.

She leaned against the refrigerator, folding her arms. "I don't think I'm hungry anymore. That kind of news doesn't go well with eggs."

"I agree," he said. "Isaac was our one link. Damn!" He took the pan off the fire and dumped the eggs in the sink.

Twenty minutes later, Ben walked in. His face was sunken from lack of sleep. He sat down in the kitchen chair and rubbed his bloodshot eyes.

Malia put a cup of coffee in front of him. He took several sips, trying to clear the fuzziness from his brain. Then he looked up at Erik and said, "Isaac Yamaguchi was in the 175th Airborne Division, same as you."

"When?" Erik asked, sitting down next to him.

"'Bout twenty years ago. He was discharged a couple of months before he joined the police."

"Then he must have known the killer," Malia said, slowly walking over to him.

Ben nodded. "That would be the correct assumption."

"Are you sure it was suicide?" she asked him.

"Yes. His wife watched him do it."

"She didn't try to stop him?"

He sighed and shook his head. "Strange people, the Japanese."

"Is it possible that Isaac killed Malia's parents?" Erik asked.

Sipping his coffee, Ben said, "No. I checked to see if he was ever in Guam. He wasn't."

Erik leaned forward and put his arms on the table. "I want to go to Pōhakuloa Military Base. You think you're up for it?"

"What's there?" Ben asked.

"A list of every soldier that went through Hawaii in 1974."

Ben looked up from his cup and stared at him. "There must have been thousands. That's goin' to be one tough job."

"Maybe not. The soldiers I'll be looking for will have the 175th Airborne written next to their names. We were a special force, remember? There weren't many of us."

Ben scratched his weary face, thinking about it. "Is it okay if I finish my coffee first?"

Pōhakuloa was a small army base not far from the foothill of Mauna Kea. During World War II, the area surrounding it was an artillery training ground, and the infertile brown terrain was pockmarked with craters from old bombshells.

Erik showed the guard at the gate his credentials. The soldier saluted him and let them through.

He parked next to the main building, which housed the records for the base. It was an old wooden structure in need of paint.

Inside, Erik talked to the sergeant at the front desk, asking to see the files of all the 175th Airborne servicemen stationed here in 1974. The sergeant, a slightly built man with a large chipped front tooth, took them down to the file room in the basement. Several rows of metal shelves housing old manila foldouts filled the room.

The sergeant went around the counter, bent down, and removed a ledger from the back shelf. "These are the names containing the divisions stationed here for the last fifty years. I'll be honest with you, sir," he said to Erik. "I've been here for fifteen years, and I don't remember the 175th ever being on the island."

"I don't either," Erik said. "But I need to make sure."

The sergeant ran his fingers down the page containing the paratrooper divisions. When he reached the bottom, he shook his head and closed the book. "No, sir. No one from the 175th was ever stationed at Pōhakuloa."

"I was afraid of that," Erik muttered.

"Wait a minute, my friend," Ben said. "Wasn't Hawaii used as an R and R drop off for soldiers fightin' in Vietnam?"

"You mean, was this where they came for fun and games?" the sergeant said, grinning, exposing his big chipped tooth.

"That's what he's asking," Erik said stiffly.

The smile disappeared. "The Americans were out of the action in seventy-three."

"We still had a large force in Southeast Asia," Erik said.

"Normally, the army went to Bangkok for R and R. It was closer, the women more plentiful, and the booze a hell of a lot cheaper. 'Course that didn't apply to the officers." The sergeant squatted down to put the book back under the desk.

Erik leaned over the counter. "Army officers were sent to Hawaii for R and R during the war?"

The sergeant stood back up. "During and right after. But they were only officers of your stature, sir. There wasn't much to do here, except relax in the sun. The army didn't want their top brass getting into the type of trouble they might get into if they went to Bangkok."

"Were records kept of the names of those officers?"

"Sir, this is the army. We keep records of everyone who goes to the bathroom."

Erik smiled. "I'd like to see those records, Sergeant."

"Just of the 175th?"

"Yes," Erik replied.

"That shouldn't be a big list, sir. There weren't many of you boys of the 175th who stayed alive long enough to earn any R and R."

The sergeant reached down and brought up another ledger. This one was old and frayed. It took him a few minutes to find the page containing the 175th Airborne Division. When he did, he turned the book in Erik's direction. "As I said, sir . . . there weren't many. There are only about fifteen names in all."

They scanned the list. Many of the names were familiar to Malia and Erik: Billy Doyle; Thomas Brinks; and several others.

"Look here," Ben said, pointing to the last names on the list. "Sergeant Isaac Yamaguchi and a colonel by the name of Felix Steinway."

Malia and Erik glanced up at each other.

Erik then turned to the soldier behind the counter. "I think we can take it from here. We won't be needing you anymore, Sergeant."

"When you're finished just leave the ledger on the desk. I'll put it back, sir." He gave a quick salute to Erik and went upstairs.

"Isaac was a sergeant in the 175th," Ben said.

Erik read the ledger. "He was Billy Doyle's aide-de-camp. Officers were allowed to bring their aides with them."

"Did Isaac and Steinway know each other then?" Malia said.

Erik nodded. "Maybe not that well, but they most likely met." He turned the pages in the book, writing down the dates he saw next to Steinway's name on a yellow notepad. When he finished, he looked at Malia. "How many tours of duty did our general do in Vietnam?" he asked her.

"According to him, five," she responded.

"Officers were given two weeks R and R after every tour. According to these records, Steinway was on the island a total of six times during the years 1969 to 1974."

"What were the dates?" Ben asked.

"He was a man of consistency. He always came on August tenth and returned on the twenty-fourth."

She could feel the blood rushing to her head. "My parents were killed on August twenty-third, 1974. Steinway was on the island then. What about Doyle?"

He looked at the dates next to his name. "He was on the island in seventy-two of June and seventy-three at the end of July. He wasn't here in seventy-four."

"And Brinks?"

His fingers moved to the president of the War College's name. "Yes, he was here in seventy-four—but in March, not August."

"What about the other officers in the 175th? Were any of them here at that time?" she asked uneasily.

Erik went through the list and shook his head after each name. When he was finished, he glanced up at Malia. "Only Steinway was here on August twenty-third. Where was the general when Lupe Maile was killed?"

She swallowed hard, knowing where he was going. "Logistically, it won't work, Erik. He was at Fort Ord, California. He had meetings there."

"Are you sure?"

"I'm sure. He left early that morning with his entourage after his speech at the War College. I had to interview Brinks, so I took a later flight back to the islands."

Erik tapped the counter with his fingers, thinking. "Fort Ord is only three thousand miles away from Hawaii."

"That's too far. It's a five-hour plane trip from California to the islands. They'd have known he was gone," she said.

"Not necessarily," he replied. "When the Korean crisis hit, the Defense Department gave him a modified four-passenger Blackbird and a pilot. It's a jet plane that can fly upward to two thousand miles an hour and has a fifteen-thousand-mile gas tank. He could have made the flight in less than two hours, then returned. She was killed at night. No one would have missed him."

"Where would you land one of these planes?" Ben asked.

"Here, at this base." Again, he began to think. "I want to talk to the sergeant again."

They walked upstairs to the front desk.

The sergeant looked up and smiled. "All through?" he asked.

"Not quite," Erik said. "I need to see the arrival and departure flight records of September twelfth."

"They're kept at the radar tower, sir."

"Get them. I'll wait."

Ten minutes later the sergeant returned carrying two large loose-leaf books. He handed them to Erik.

He opened the one stamped ARRIVALS and turned the pages until he came to the date he wanted. His finger swiftly moved down the page. "Here it is," he said, showing it to Malia and Ben.

FLIGHT NUMBER: 10743
TIME OF ARRIVAL: 2312 hrs.
PILOT: CAPT. EUGENE SANDERS
NUMBER OF PASSENGERS: (2) GEN. FELIX STEINWAY; TAANG (no last name)

Erik muttered, "Twenty-three twelve. That's military time for eleven-twelve at night."

"How long was he here?" Ben asked.

Erik grabbed the book with the departure times, opened it up, and leafed through it. "I found it," he said. "They left for Fort Ord on the same night, at two hundred hours. That's two in the morning."

They stared at each other for several seconds, letting it all sink in.

"He was probably back at Ord before anyone knew he was gone," Erik said.

On the drive back from the base, Malia said, "Taang was with him."

"Lucky for the general that he was," Ben said from the backseat.

Malia turned to him. "Why?"

"When they tossed Lupe's body off the cliff, she landed on

that small precipice. Steinway was too old an' too overweight to climb down. Taang could have done it easily."

"Could Taang have committed the murders?" she asked.

"I don't think so," Erik answered from behind the wheel. "He certainly didn't kill your parents. It was hard for Montagnards to get visas to come to the States. Even with the general's pull, Taang wasn't issued one until 1976. That was two years after the murders. No, it was all Steinway."

"But Taang knew," she said.

Again he nodded. "Taang knows everything about the general. The Montagnard was the only one he trusted."

"And Isaac . . . he also knew," she said.

"Steinway didn't know he saw him the night he received the money on the beach. If he did, I doubt he would have been allowed to live," Ben replied. He glanced out the window and saw Mauna Kea's snow-covered dome off to the side. "We can prove Steinway was on the island, but we can't prove he was responsible," he said.

She looked confused and angry. "He killed my parents. Why did he pick me to write his autobiography?"

Erik thought hard about that question. He was a trained psychologist, and he was using it now to pick through the psyche of the man. "Steinway has a reputation in the Pentagon for being a megalomaniac," he finally said as he made a right turn on Saddle Road.

"You mean he thought he was God?" Ben asked.

"If not God, at least his right-hand man. He didn't tolerate failure in others, but he also didn't tolerate it in himself. Hence, the man never failed at anything he did. He was the complete success."

"But why me, Erik?" she asked again.

"When success is easy, you begin to push the envelope back just a wee bit farther, testing yourself to see if it's still as easy."

Malia looked at him in amazement. "You mean, that's what I was—a test to see how far he could go?"

"Remember, he's never failed. That type of achievement can breed a form of arrogance. He planned what he thought was the perfect murder when he killed your parents. Someone else died for the crime. He had nothing to fear. It all happened twenty years ago. Except he never felt it was perfect because you had gotten away."

"I don't think he planned on killing me when I came back to the island," she said.

"No. There was no reason to anymore. What he wanted was something much more subtle than that. What he wanted was your adoration."

"What?"

"Sure. Why not bring the daughter back and have her under his roof working for him, writing his autobiography, extolling his accomplishments to the world."

"This is some kind of sick joke," she murmured.

"Did you respect him?"

"Yes."

"Perhaps idolize him in a way?"

Her breathing was labored. "Yes."

"Did you ever see him as a father figure?"

She thought about it. "I guess there were times I did," she admitted.

"That's what he wanted you to feel."

"I don't understand," she said.

"He wanted you to transfer the love you had for your parents onto him. Only then would it be the perfect crime. Your father and mother would no longer exist spiritually as well as physically. It's a form of total control."

"My Hawaiian ancestors practiced that form of control," Ben said quietly. "When they killed an enemy, they ate his brain so they could possess all of him."

Erik emitted a bitter smile. "You've got it, my friend. Only in those days they called it tradition. Today it's labeled sociopathic behavior."

Malia let out a long sigh, put her knees against the dashboard, and hugged them to her body. "How the hell do you prove Steinway knew my mother twenty years ago? They didn't run in the same circles."

"The sugar mill," Ben said in a low voice. His eyes turned back to the volcano.

"What about the mill?" Erik asked.

Ben turned to Malia. "Your mama worked at the sugar mill along with your father."

"Yes, so what?"

"Would there have been a reason Steinway would be at that mill?"

"You mean, he may have met her there?"

"That's what I mean."

"I don't see how. The plantation was in a small town, away from the tourist areas."

"You tol' me it was illegally owned by the Comport conglomerate. Franz Hauptmann, the retired CEO, has a home on Diamond Head an' spends most of his time there," Ben said.

She began to think. "Hauptmann told you he'd never heard of my father when you brought his name up. You thought he was lying."

"Did you think he was lying, Ben?" Erik asked him.

"I still do," Ben said.

Erik looked at his watch. "Let's find out for sure. A plane leaves for O'ahu every hour."

Chapter Twenty-eight

ERIK DROVE THE Ford he rented at the airport past million-dollar homes lining the bluffs of Diamond Head. Ben didn't come with them. The exhaustion from being up all night had taken its toll on the old man.

Before they left for O'ahu, Erik called Hauptmann's number to find out if he was in Honolulu. A woman answered and said he was. Before she could ask his name, he hung up.

Hauptmann's estate was located on a cul-de-sac overlooking the ocean. It was surrounded by a white plaster wall, with an old-fashioned wrought-iron gate at the entranceway. Erik got out of the car, unlocked the gate, then drove onto the grounds.

The gravel pathway leading up to the mansion was surrounded by tropical flowers and exotic shrubbery. A large Japanese koi fish pond, with a cobblestone bridge, snaked its way along the property.

Erik stopped the car in front of the pillared house. He and Malia got out, walked up the path leading to the door, rang the bell, and waited.

Seconds later, the housekeeper, a stout Hawaiian woman, opened the door a few inches, keeping the chain lock on. "Can I help you?" she said. Her tone was filled with caution.

"Let them in," a woman's voice said from inside.

Malia knew that voice—knew it well.

When they entered the marble anteroom, Malia saw Peachie standing by the staircase, one arm on the banister and a smile stretched across her mouth.

Peachie looked at Malia, then at Erik. Her eyes widened. "Ah, the anthropologist. What a pleasant surprise."

"I'm not an anthropologist," Erik said, astonished at finding her here.

Her brows puckered in amusement. "No? What a shame. No matter. I've always liked you anyway."

"I'm surprised to see you here, Melissa," Malia said.

"Surprises are what you get when you don't let things alone." The smile remained on her face.

"Is this where you go when you're not at the ranch?" Malia asked.

"Yes. Always." She laughed. "Did you think I was off having an affair?"

"It crossed my mind," Malia said.

"Thank you for seeing me as a woman still capable of such things. Actually, I lead a very boring life. I just come to Honolulu when my general is away, relax in the sun, and talk to Franz."

The woman may have had a couple of drinks, but she was still sober, Malia realized. "How long have you known Franz Hauptmann?" she asked her.

"How long? Why, all my life, dear. You see, Franz is my uncle."

It was only a dim light breaking through Malia's head, but she was beginning to see the thin strands connecting Felix Steinway to the sugar mill in Honokaá.

Franz Hauptmann sat in his wheelchair on the back lawn, staring intensely at the koi fish in his pond, feeding them stale bread. When he looked up, he saw the two strangers walking

out of the French doors with Peachie. He folded up the bread
bag and put it on his lap. "Who are these two?" he said to his
niece as they approached.

"Most likely our herald of what is to come, Franz." She
picked up a half-finished glass of orange juice and vodka from
off the lawn table. "I'd like to introduce you to Malia
Rico ..."

Malia saw a stunned look cloud Hauptmann's face when he
heard her name.

". . . and this is—"

Before she could finish, Erik said, "My name is Erik
Young." He held out his hand to Hauptmann.

Peachie's mouth opened wide, then spread to a full grin.
"My, we are full of surprises today! Why, only last week your
name was Daniel Keahi."

Hauptmann didn't bother to shake Erik's hand or look at
him. His focus was on Peachie. "What do they want, Melissa?"

"Why don't you ask them, Uncle?" she said.

Hauptmann finally turned to Malia and Erik, acknowledging
their existence for the first time. He was a small man, withered
by age and corporate battles. His tan, bald head was spotted
with freckles. "All right, I'm asking. What do you want?" His
voice was cold, with only a vague trace of a German accent.

Erik instantly disliked him. "I'm in the same division of the
army that General Steinway was in," Erik said.

When he heard Steinway's name mentioned, Hauptmann's
eyes dimmed.

Without waiting to be asked, Erik sat down next to him.
Malia leaned against the cobblestone ledge of the pond.

"A while back, someone called you and asked about
Comport's involvement in a sugar mill in Honokaá," Malia
said.

"Yes, I remember. He said he was from the EPA. How do
you know about that?"

"It's not important how I know. The mill was supposed to
have gone on strike in 1974."

"Is that a fact?" Hauptmann said.

"Yes. How was the strike averted?"

"Comport is a civilized company. We worked things out with our employees."

"How?"

"We compromised."

"I don't think so. It was averted because the leader, James Rico, was murdered along with his wife only days before the strike," Erik said.

Hauptmann gave Erik a condescending smile. "I assure you we don't kill disgruntled employees."

"Don't you?" Malia said.

Hauptmann glared at her. "That's a libelous insinuation, young lady!" His face reddened with anger.

"Let's not get into a scruples mode here," Malia said. "That's something you've never been concerned with in the past."

"How dare you say that to me!"

"Easy. In 1973 you hired a bunch of thugs to break up a strike in the Loire Valley. Three workers were killed in the melee. You've had the Environmental Protection Agency on your back, and your company illegally owned a sugar plantation in Hawaii for tax purposes. I found all that out without digging very deep. Imagine what I'd find if I did."

Hauptmann's mouth began to twitch. "I never hired anyone to kill this Rico."

"Maybe you didn't—at least not directly."

"Just—just what the hell does that mean?" he stammered.

Erik cut in. "When did you first meet Felix Steinway?"

The old man's tanned face turned scarlet.

A knowing sadness engulfed Peachie's features. "Answer him, Franz," she said.

"At their wedding," he spat out.

"You don't seem thrilled," Malia said.

"I was . . . at the beginning. Two great families coming together. If only I knew . . ." He looked away and didn't continue.

"If only you knew what?" Malia asked.

"Nothing," he whispered. "Nothing."

"When did you and the general meet on Hawaii?"

"Never. Because I've never been to the Big Island," he sneered.

"You owned the sugar mill and never visited it?" Malia asked, surprised.

"I own many companies. I buy and sell them like a child trades baseball cards. That doesn't mean I have to visit every one of them."

Erik turned his head and looked at Peachie. "You were a supermarket heiress when you met Felix?"

"I still am," she said flippantly.

He then turned back to Hauptmann. "Was the supermarket chain part of Comport or independent from it?"

Hauptmann didn't respond. His lips were clamped shut with a hidden anger.

"Answer the man," Peachie said again.

"It was part of Comport. My company owned the controlling shares. My brother—Melissa's father—owned the other forty-nine percent."

"So Felix not only married into a chain of supermarkets, he married into Comport," Malia said to Franz.

"So what?" Hauptmann growled.

"Did Felix ever go to that sugar mill on Hawaii on behalf of Comport?" Erik asked.

Hauptmann's eyes darted from Peachie to Malia, then back to Erik. "He may have. I don't remember."

"I think you do," Malia said softly.

"Do I?"

"Yes. I suppose I could find some of the old employees who worked at the mill and ask them."

"All right, yes. He went there once, as a favor to me."

"What kind of favor?" Erik inquired.

The old man brushed his fingers over the top of his bald head, wiping away the beads of sweat. Malia noticed that his hand was shaking.

"Several months before the strike, sometime in 1973, word filtered down to us that there was talk of a walkout. Felix happened to be on the island at that time."

"On R and R?"

"Yes. I asked Felix to go to the plant. Felix had a natural ability with words. I thought he could calm the employees down, talk them out of it. He met with their leader. The strike was averted, at least for a year."

There it was, Malia thought. *Steinway's connection to the sugar mill.*

"What was this leader's name?" Erik asked calmly.

"How could I remember that? It was over twenty years ago," Hauptmann said.

Malia's nostrils flared in anger. "I think you do remember. It was James Rico, wasn't it?"

"Perhaps," Hauptmann said.

"Where did they get together?" Malia asked.

"I don't know. I think they went out a few times . . . talked. Felix was good at talking."

Malia's heart was beating fast. "Did they go out alone? Just the two of them?"

A confused look came over Hauptmann. "I didn't ask. Felix had a job to do. How he did it was his concern."

Erik turned to Peachie. "Was it a couples thing? Did you and Felix socialize with James Rico and his wife?"

"Several times," she said, with a smugness that attempted to veil her anger. "Winning James Rico over was a coup for Felix."

"Why?" Malia asked.

"James Rico did not like my husband . . . not at first. Actually, I think he was frightened to death of him. He wouldn't meet with Felix. He even stayed away from the factory when he knew he was coming."

"Obviously that changed," Erik said.

"Yes, that changed," Peachie replied. "Eventually he succumbed to Felix's charms . . . like everyone else." Without looking, she reached for the vodka bottle on the table, found it, and unscrewed the cap. She poured the Stoly into her empty glass, then put the bottle back down.

Erik asked, "Where did you four go when you went out?"

"To expensive dinners at some of the resort restaurants. Felix always insisted on picking up the bill. It seemed to embarrass the mill worker."

Malia glared at her. Peachie didn't even bother to give her father a name. He was just a mill worker to the woman. "Did it also embarrass my mother?" Malia asked.

Peachie's head swirled in her direction, her eyes meeting Malia's. "No, darling. It didn't embarrass your mother. She seemed to enjoy it. One got the feeling that she wasn't used to money."

"She wasn't," Malia said.

"She was a simple, beautiful woman. I was told she had a beautiful daughter. Are you surprised? You see, I always knew who you were. Do you know you resemble your mother a great deal." She tried to sound caustic, but her bitterness overrode it.

"Nothing surprises me anymore," Malia said. She went over to the woman. "How did my mother react to your husband?"

"Like I wasn't there. She was smitten with him, right from the beginning. You could feel the intensity between them . . . like two dogs in heat." She smiled at Malia. "Are you offended by what I'm saying? I hope not, dear. At least you didn't have to watch it. I had to sit there all those nights and watch my husband's cock grow hard every time he looked at her."

Malia glared at her. "You could have stopped what was going to happen between them."

"Oh, you think so?" Peachie suddenly laughed. "You don't know Felix. He takes what he wants, regardless of who he hurts."

"That's a truism, if I ever heard one. He took you and hurt Steven Bankroft in return."

The wind seemed to be taken out of Peachie. She sat down and stared vacantly at her glass. Then she slowly looked up at Malia and said, "I let Steven down. I was responsible for whatever happened to him."

"You said my father was frightened of Felix at first. Why?"

"I don't know. He wouldn't see him."

"My father, what I know of him, wasn't a frightened man. He was the negotiator for the sugar mill. If Felix was the company's arbitrator, then it would have been in the interest of the workers that my father talk with him."

Peachie's eyes blazed with an inner knowledge. "You don't know the depths of my husband. He can frighten the strongest of men."

Malia believed her. Jasper Rhodes was also frightened of him, to the point where he discontinued an investigation that would have garnered him another Pulitzer.

Malia stared at Peachie, wondering what secrets were in that tortured head. Then she understood. "It was you who left the safe open. You wanted me to find those letters."

"And so you did," Peachie said in a low voice.

Erik stood up and went over to her. "Where are those letters now?"

Peachie finished off half her drink in one gulp, wiped her mouth with her fingers, then said, "I have absolutely no idea what happened to them. I simply opened the safe and walked away. Whatever went on after that was in God's hands, not mine."

"Why did you want me to find them?" Malia asked.

Peachie's red eyes began to mist over. "To still this wrong that was eating me alive. Steven was a good man. He deserved better than to die like that. I lived with that guilt for over thirty years. When Felix told me he hired you to write his book, I couldn't believe it. You coming to live in our house was like opening up old wounds, bringing everything back. I asked him to please reconsider."

"What did he say?" Malia asked.

"He got angry. He said he'd do what he wanted to do."

"You wanted me to find out about Felix and my mother, didn't you?"

She smiled through her tears. "And so you did. Are there any other questions?" She stood up and went back to the table, grasped the bottle of Stoly, and looked at it with fondness. "If you don't have anything more to say, then I'd like to get on with whatever's left of my life."

"Put the bottle down," Hauptmann commanded her. "The hell with your husband! That man's destroyed you!"

Peachie put on a fake pout. "Felix took away my dignity, now you want to take away my last true friend. Not fair, Franz."

"I think the questions are over," Franz said to Malia and Erik.

Malia didn't move. She was lost in thought. Then she looked down at Franz and said, "Comport also owns Baronin Books."

"What about it?"

"They're doing the general's autobiography."

"So?"

"Did you have a hand in making the deal?"

"What if I did?"

"Seven million dollars is a lot of money to pay for a life story."

"Felix is married to my niece. If I chose to give that bastard seven million dollars so he could revel in his glories, that's my business," he snapped. "It won't happen again. Not after what I've learned today."

Malia's eyes fogged over for an instant, then the cloud lifted. "I always wondered why Baronin hired me. It was because you told them to do it."

"Felix was the one who wanted you. Not me! He insisted that you be hired. No one understood why."

Malia smiled down at the CEO. "Maybe I'll write a book on you, too, one day. How a man who started with a simple tool shop made a fortune using slave labor from the camps to make arms for the Nazis."

Hauptmann's lips trembled with rage. "I want you to leave or I'll call the police."

"Too bad you couldn't have used the same kind of labor in the sugar mill and at the winery in the Loire Valley. That way, you wouldn't have had to deal with strikes."

"Get out of here!" Hauptmann screamed. His body was shaking uncontrollably as he clutched the arms of his wheel-chair.

Erik stood up and grabbed Malia's arm. "We're leaving," he said, pushing her toward the front of the house.

"I do have one other question," Malia said to Peachie, free-ing her arm from Erik's grip.

Peachie's face was drained. "What is it?"

"When Felix made love to you, did he bite?"

At first the general's wife seemed surprised by the question, then she grinned bitterly. "Felix is a passionate man. One gets used to it."

Malia and Erik caught the next shuttle back to Hawaii.

On the plane, Erik grabbed a handful of peanuts, tossed them in his mouth. "Killing your parents was a duel operation for him. With your father dead, he saved Comport from ruin. Because if Comport went, so did Peachie's inheritance. Also the affair he had with your mother could have gotten embar-rassing for him, especially if the army found out. His career would have been over. Career officers, especially in those days, did not screw around with other men's wives."

"What about the servant girl from Guam? And Lupe? Was he screwing around with them, too?"

"I'm sure of it. You asked Peachie the right question. 'Did he bite?' All the women had teeth marks on their bodies."

Malia shuddered. "The night I heard Lupe being beaten . . . he was speaking to her in Hawaiian."

"Felix has a photographic memory. He speaks many languages."

"He seems to be attracted to native women."

"Again, it has to do with control. In his mind, those women were below him. They were sex objects, not human beings. If they died, it wouldn't matter."

"But why kill Lupe?"

"Sometimes, when you're dealing with the human factor, things go wrong. Lupe probably gave him a hard time and threatened to expose him. He couldn't afford that when he was going to run for the presidency."

"Why would she do that?"

"When Ben interrogated Sam Pua for Lupe's murder, Pua said he thought Lupe was seeing someone other than him. She told him that she was tired of being poor—that she was going to have money soon. Ben thought Lupe was talking about me. She wasn't. She was talking about Steinway."

"Did the girl actually think Steinway would submit to blackmail?"

"The kid didn't know who she was dealing with. I'll bet you anything he had the same problem with the girl from Guam."

"If you wanted to kill someone, why use that kind of weapon?"

"Hawaiian chiefs were considered gods. Only they were allowed to use that club. Steinway fancied himself a great warrior. He had a God complex, remember?"

Malia bit down on her thumbnail, thinking. "Peachie knew about my mother and Felix. Did she also know he killed them?"

"I tend to doubt it. Felix kept that dark part of himself well hidden."

She looked out the window. The shadow of the plane's wing

was directly over the island of Maui. "Peachie said my father was frightened of Felix when they first met."

"Felix can be intimidating."

"My father was not that kind of man. What scared him?" Turning to Erik, she said, "Taang told me he and the general were the same. I don't think that's true. Taang had a reputation during the war for being a cold-blooded killer, but he killed out of vengeance and loyalty, not out of greed and fear like Steinway. In his own way, the Montagnard had morals."

Erik said, "If we're going to nail Felix, I need those letters from the safe and the shark weapon."

"I may be able to help you with the first part," Malia said. "If Peachie didn't take those letters from the safe, then Taang did. They must still be at the ranch."

"Then that's where we're going," Erik said.

Chapter Twenty-nine

TAANG LOOKED OUT of the Blackbird's cockpit and spotted the 737 flying over Maui. He didn't know it, but it was the same plane Erik and Malia were on.

No one knew Taang was on the Blackbird, and the pilot was ordered by the general not to tell anyone about picking up a passenger at Andrews Air Force Base. The blood rushed through Taang's veins as he planned his moves.

He waited until the pilot radioed the control tower at Pōhakuloa that they were ready to land, then reached into his chignon and took out the curved blade.

The jet nosed downward as the island came into view. It flew over Hilo, then arched right toward the military base. Below, Taang could see the treeless barren terrain surrounding Mauna Kea's volcanic mass.

They were now at the spot.

Taang unstrapped his safety belt and leaned forward in his

seat, until he was only inches from the pilot's head. He grabbed the airman's neck in his muscular arm, pulling it toward him. With his other hand, he reached around with the blade, felt for the jugular, and slit it open.

The pilot's body went into convulsions, his arms and legs flailing in all directions. His blood pumped out of his artery and splattered onto the console and cockpit. Taang held him tightly in the headlock, until there was no longer any movement. He then let go. The airman's body slumped slightly forward, hanging suspended by the belt around his chest.

The Montagnard reached around the body and grabbed the control stick. He pushed it down, causing the plane to go into a nosedive. He then sat back and waited until the jet dived below Mauna Kea's snowcapped mountain, hiding it from view of the tower at Pōhakuloa. When he was ten thousand feet from the ground, he pushed the Eject button. The cockpit casing flew off, and he shot out into the lapis-colored sky. Within seconds, his parachute opened. Taang moved the cords, angling his descent away from the base.

In the distance he could hear the loud crash of the Blackbird as it plowed into the side of the volcano. There would be an investigation, the mishap would be blamed on pilot error. In a few days it would all be forgotten.

He dropped down onto the soft volcanic ash, landing on his feet. First he looked around to make sure that no one was there, then he quickly unhooked himself from his parachute and unzipped his bloodstained flight suit. Under it, Taang was wearing army fatigues. Gathering up the chute and the suit, he walked over to the lip of a volcanic cone and threw them in.

A tinge of sadness swept over him when he thought about what he did to the pilot. He liked the man. But some things had to be done for the higher good. No one was to know he was on the island.

The pilot soon faded from his mind as he began to jog toward the *heiau*. The general gave him a free hand. Taang knew what had to be done.

He ran twelve miles through volcanic ash hills, then into the jungle. His pace was uniform, never varying. When he reached the periphery of the excavation, he knelt down behind a tree and watched the students digging around the *heiau*. His damp fatigues clung to his body, but his breathing was steady.

He moved his eyes over the area, scanning the faces of the people, looking for the man who pretended to be Daniel Keahi. He wasn't among them. Then he saw the tall, bearded one whose picture appeared on Keahi's license. He was squatting by the side of the temple, teaching several of the young students how to dig around a petroglyph etched in the black stones of the wall.

Taang dropped to his stomach and crawled closer to the perimeter, hiding behind the tall grass.

An hour later, the students began to disperse. They walked up the incline toward their cars. The bearded man stood up, wiped the dust from his jeans, and went into the tent.

Quitting time, Taang thought.

He waited until all the cars left the area.

The Montagnard snaked his way around the trees on his stomach until he came to the back of the canopy. He pulled out one of the stakes that held the tent in place and stuck his head inside the canvas tarp.

The bearded man's back was to him. He was sitting at a small desk looking over ancient artifacts found at the temple. Every few seconds he'd push his loose, thick glasses up the rim of his nose. Eventually he stood up, stretched, picked up a book, and lay down on his cot.

Taang silently slithered into the tent and crawled over to the bed. As he rose up, his body blocked out the overhead light from the suspended oil lamp, casting a shadow over the book.

Daniel glanced up and saw Taang. His face turned pale and he immediately propped himself up on one elbow.

Taang sat down on the cot next to the anthropologist, took the book from his hands, and placed it on the floor. "I want to know where the other man is," he said, without emotion.

"Who?"

"The one who pretends to be you."

Daniel stared at him, trying to hold in his fear. "Look, I think you'd better leave." Then he noticed the dried blood on the Montagnard's hands.

Taang followed the path of Daniel's eyes and glanced down. A joyless smile came over his face. "It isn't mine. It belongs to another man." He moved his head closer, until he could smell Daniel's terror. "I asked you where the other one is."

Daniel edged his body away from him. "I—I don't know," he sputtered.

"You know," Taang said, reaching up and removing Daniel's glasses. He dropped them next to the book on the floor.

"I swear to you, I don't know what you're talking about." He heard his own voice cracking.

"You know," Taang said again. He traced his thick fingers lightly along the ridge of the man's neck. When he came to the Adam's apple, he put his thumbs on both sides of the lump, pushing softly down into the supple skin. "You know. Don't make me hurt you."

Daniel's body quivered from the Montagnard's gentle touch, but he knew it would soon be replaced by something horrible. A feeble groan sprang from his throat.

Erik and Malia reached the deserted ranch an hour before sundown. Up in the hills, several *paniolos* on horseback were separating a herd of cattle that was to be shipped to Japan.

Ben was waiting for them on the lanai. When they'd landed in Kona, they'd called him from the airport and told him to meet them at Steinway's house.

The door was locked, but Malia still had the key.

"Where's his room?" Erik asked when they were inside.

"In the back."

"I'll look in the other rooms," Ben said, disappearing down the corridor.

Erik and Malia walked across the hallway to the rear of the house. She tried the knob on Taang's door. It was open.

Inside the darkened bedroom, Erik clicked on the light switch. The ceiling lamp didn't work.

There were a dozen unlit candles placed on the floor. Erik took the wooden matches off the night table and lit several of them.

Malia smelled the Montagnard's odor in the room, a mixture of damp earth and incense.

Erik began to go through the chest of drawers. Most of them were bare. Montagnard jewelry of bone earrings and beaded necklaces were neatly placed on top of the dresser.

Malia opened up the closet door. All she found was some military clothing cut to fit Taang's size.

"Those letters are incriminating. Steinway may have asked Taang to destroy them," Erik said.

"I don't think so," she replied. "If he wanted them destroyed, the general would have done that a long time ago. He's a megalomaniac, remember? Men with those kinds of delusions don't destroy anything that pertains to them."

It took them only a few minutes to scour the room. "They're not here," he said.

She looked up at the ceiling lamp. Why didn't it work? "Bring the chair over," she said.

Ben went through the living room searching compartments and cabinets. He found nothing. The next room was the general's dark oak-paneled den. He combed the desk drawers, then the bookshelves. Again nothing.

As he turned to leave, he noticed the wall panels. He crouched down and knocked on each one with his knuckles. The bottom one next to the window sounded hollow. He pushed it inward. The hidden latch gave way and the oak pane popped open, exposing a compartment inside. Ben reached in and took out a rectangular leather box. He undid the brass hook and opened it up. Lying on a bed of red velvet was the *lei o manō* club, with the sharp, curved teeth still stained with the dried blood of its victims.

Erik grabbed the chair next to the dresser, brought it over to the middle of the room, and stood on it. He reached up and unfastened the curved, antique glass shade from the fixture and handed it to Malia. The threaded bolts that attached the light apparatus to the ceiling were loose. He easily unscrewed them and lifted it from the frame.

Letters and files fell out from the cavity in the ceiling and dropped to the wood floor.

"That's what we're looking for," Malia said, bending down and gathering them up.

Erik jumped off the chair and helped.

"The blue envelopes are the ones written by Steven Bankroft's mother," she said.

They took them over to the bed and sorted them out. While Erik opened the letters, Malia went through the files held in place with rubber bands.

After reading the pleas from the cadet's mother, he turned to Malia. His face glowed with excitement. "I think I have what I need."

She looked up at him, her dark eyes also animated. "You only have the tip of the iceberg. Wait till you see this." She handed him one of the documents in the files. The official seal of the United States Army was on it.

The Montagnard reached the bluffs and saw Erik's Jeep parked outside the ranch. *They're inside,* he said to himself.

Taang had no idea they would be here. When he realized the bearded anthropologist didn't know anything, he stopped torturing him and snapped the man's neck, killing him instantly. He only came to the ranch to get the shark weapon. With them in the house, his work would be simplified.

He raced across the green fields, toward the open front door.

Once inside, he stood quietly in the hallway, moving his head from left to right, listening for sounds. His sharp ears soon picked up voices and noises from down the hall. Some were coming from his room, others from the general's study.

Going into the living room, he moved stealthily across the carpet to the adjoining corridor. He passed by the ancient Polynesian artifacts hanging on the wall as he headed toward the general's den.

Ben saw Taang instantly. Before he could stand up, the Montagnard was on him. He felt his hand being grabbed, then pushed backward. There was a sharp pain in his wrist and the hollow sound of the bone breaking. When he tried to open his mouth to scream, Taang clutched him by the throat, squeezing his windpipe, preventing any sound from coming out.

Ben saw the indifference in the Montagnard's black eyes. *They're not human,* he thought as the darkness began to overtake him.

Taang let go of Ben's throat, letting the body fall silently on the rug.

He picked up the sharks'-tooth weapon on the floor and carefully touched the points of the fangs. They were still as keen-edged as the day the general first showed him the club eighteen years ago. Steinway told him he hired a petty thief named Panali to steal it for him from the museum in Honolulu.

Clutching it by the koa hilt, he swung the club sideways. It made a *whoosh*ing sound as the teeth cut through the air. The general was right—*the perfect weapon*. Well balanced and deadly.

Now *he* had it.

He left the den, crossed the living room, and made his way toward his bedroom. The door was partly ajar. He heard the Hawaiian girl and the man inside talking in excited voices. Gripping the shaft tightly, he brought the club slightly over his head and quickened his pace.

Erik was the first one to hear movement out in the hall. He jumped up from the bed and turned his body toward the entrance.

The door crashed open, and like a blur, Taang was in the room, coming at him. The Montagnard's face was hard and determined.

Erik dropped the papers and threw himself against the wall . . . just as Taang swung the club. He felt the wind from the weapon tickle his neck as it passed by him.

Erik hurled his body on the ground, rolled over to the other end of the room, and leapt to his feet again. From the corner of his eye, he saw Malia getting up from the bed.

"Get out!" he screamed at her. "Run!"

The weapon was coming his way once again. He moved back, flattening his shoulders against the dresser. The teeth caught his shirt, tearing through the first layer of skin. He parried his body to the right, then to the left, trying to confuse Taang, but the Montagnard kept in step with him, all the time moving closer.

"Stop it!" Malia shouted, rushing over and putting her body between them. She was holding a piece of paper in her hand. "Read this!" she screamed at Taang.

For a moment, a confused look crossed Taang's face as he brought the weapon up over his head once again. Why would this woman step in front of the man to take the first blow?

"Read it!" she yelled again. "I know you can read! Read it, for God's sake!"

What difference would that piece of paper make? Taang

thought. He raised the club higher to get better leverage. Just as he swung the weapon down on them, he saw the embossed angel's wings of the 175th Airborne on the paper's letterhead.

The teeth of the great white stopped in midair, inches above their heads.

The Pentagon

General Steinway looked into the full-length mirror on the closet wall of his room. He *tisk*ed and shook his head. Undoing his tie for the third time, he began to knot it all over again. When the Windsor was finally to his liking, he stuck the end of the tie between the buttons of his razor-sharp-pressed shirt. Then he took his uniform jacket off the wood hanger in the closet, put it on, and buttoned it up. He hadn't worn it since he'd retired from the army, but it still fit like a glove. After flattening the collar, he brushed his fingers over the coat, wiping away imaginary lint. He counted the medals and ribbons on his chest, making sure they were all there.

The order for the invasion was to be given in ten minutes, and he never went into battle looking unkempt. Neatness, he believed, was part of an officer's preparedness for war.

He combed back his thinning hair with the silver brush Peachie had given him for his fortieth birthday, checked his face for razor nicks, then looked down at his paratrooper boots to see if there were any scuff marks on them. They were polished to a mirror sharpness.

Satisfied with his appearance, he left his chambers and walked down the corridor toward the War Room. His leather heels cracked loudly on the marble floor.

When he turned the corner, he saw several military men, two of them MPs, standing by the doorway, looking in his direction. He smiled when he saw that his friend Billy Doyle was among them.

"General Doyle," Steinway said, approaching him.

Doyle didn't return the greeting. Instead, the head of the Security Council cast his eyes down at the floor. The two MPs moved closer to the War Room entrance, blocking it.

"You have to come with us, Felix," Billy Doyle said with a dry throat.

Steinway noticed that the other officers didn't salute him.

"What's going on, Billy? I have a war to run." He tried to get in between the two military policemen, but they held firm, refusing to move.

"The war can wait. Come with us," Billy said, putting his hand on his arm.

He could feel the hand gently pushing him away from the door. "Is this important?" Steinway said impatiently.

"Very important, Felix," Billy said in a low voice.

The Secretary of Defense, Bernard Howe, sat at his desk looking up at Steinway. "Please sit," he said to him.

"I prefer to stand, Bernard. What the hell is going on here?" He looked at his watch. "An invasion was to begin five minutes ago."

The secretary took off his wire-rimmed glasses, rubbed his tired, nervous eyes, then put them back on. "For the time being, there will be no invasion."

"Who ordered this?" Steinway spat out.

"The President."

"When did this happen?"

"This afternoon. He established a dialogue with the North Koreans. They're talking."

Steinway's eyes were bulging. "That man never had a stomach for fighting!"

The Secretary took a photostat of a memo from his desk and handed it to him. "Read it, Felix."

The general snatched the paper from him and looked at it. The blood suddenly drained from his face.

"It's a handwritten order to burn a 'friendly' village in Vietnam. Your name's on it."

The head of the Security Council's saddened eyes stared back at his friend. "It wasn't done with my knowledge, Felix. I heard rumors about it, like everyone else. That's all. Nor was it done with the knowledge of any officer of the 175th," the Secretary said. "You used a handpicked unit of trusted soldiers who you felt would never talk. Their names are on the sheet I just handed you. We questioned some of them. They've admitted their part in it."

The general's face turned scarlet. "Christ, man! This piece of paper is twenty-five years old! What are you raking this shit up for? And of all times, *now*! You don't know who's friendly and who's not when you're in soup! You should know that, Bernard!"

"You knew," a voice said from behind.

Steinway turned around and saw Erik in army dress standing by the door. Next to him were Malia and Ben. The ex-police captain's hand was in a cast.

For a brief moment Steinway's face sagged at the sight of the three, then he composed himself. "What are you doing in uniform?" he said to Erik.

Erik glared at him. "I'm with the CID. I always have been. My assignment was to investigate your involvement in the extermination of the village. You seem surprised to see us alive, General."

"What does that mean?" Steinway growled back.

"We'll get to that." Erik fought down the desire to go for Steinway's throat because of what Taang did to his friend, Daniel Keahi. "It was a Montagnard village in Mbur you destroyed, not one belonging to Charlie. They were so primitive they didn't even know there was a war. Every man, woman, and child was killed in that attack. Everyone except for Taang." Erik paused for a second, then said, "For all these years you had Taang believing that it was the VC who massacred his people. He now knows differently. That's why we're still alive."

The general's face suddenly grew old; his pale skin drooped and hung loosely on his jowls. "Where is he now?" Steinway muttered.

"When Taang saw the orders with your name on it, he crashed his body through the window of your ranch and ran into the jungle," Malia said.

"I swear, I thought that village was harboring VCs," Steinway said to the Secretary of Defense.

Erik's lips curled. "You never even checked to see if it was true. You just went in like Rambo and blew them apart."

"There are other accusations, too," the Secretary said. Chagrined, he cleared his throat. "There's the matter of the murders of several people that the U.S. Attorney's Office wants to talk to you about."

"This is bullshit!" Steinway screamed, slamming his fist on the desk.

"I'm afraid that's going to be up to the Justice Department, then a military tribunal, to determine," the Secretary said coldly.

Chapter Thirty

THAT NIGHT BEN took a cab to Dulles to catch the red-eye back to Hawaii. Malia accompanied him to the airport. With Steinway in the hands of the authorities, he felt there was no reason to stay in Washington any longer. Besides, an autumn chill had taken hold of the city and his broken wrist was beginning to ache from the cold.

The soulful horn of Miles Davis coming from the cab's radio was suddenly interrupted by a news brief: the North Koreans had released the naval minesweeper. It was now in international waters, heading back to the States.

He turned to Malia and patted her leg the same way he had in his truck outside her parents' house twenty years ago. "At least somethin' good came of this," he said.

She looked at him, smiled, and squeezed his hand.

"Why don' you come back with me, *wahine*?"

"There's nothing in Hawaii for me, Ben," she said quietly.

"Nothin' here for you either."

"Not true. Steinway's here." The shadows of the passing headlights masked the rage in her eyes. "At this moment he's being questioned by the FBI about the murder of my parents. I want to see that bastard's face when they lead him away in handcuffs."

Ben sat back and nodded silently. He didn't have the heart to tell her there was no concrete evidence linking him to the murders. And Steinway, he knew, would never confess.

When the cab reached the terminal, she didn't walk him in. They said good-bye at the curb. She put her arms around the old man and held him tight.

"The offer to come back to the island still stands," he said.

"Maybe someday, Ben." She hugged him again.

When Malia returned to the hotel, she got undressed and was just about to step into the shower when the telephone rang. Grabbing a towel from the rack, she wrapped it around her body and went into the bedroom to answer it.

"Hi, it's Erik."

By his sluggish tone, Malia knew something was wrong.

"The FBI just released Steinway," he said.

She was stunned. "How the hell could they do that?"

"There's no proof that he was involved."

"What—what kind of proof do those boneheads need?" she stammered.

"They could place him at the locations, but they couldn't prove he committed any of the acts. There were no witnesses, no murder weapon."

"He had affairs with all three women," she said.

"No one ever saw him with them," Erik said. "Taang is the only person who could link him together with Lupe and the girl from Guam."

"He must still be on the island. Why don't they find him?"

"They've tried. If Taang doesn't want to be found, looking for him won't do any good."

"What's the next step then?" She was frustrated.

Erik sighed. "Unless we can get some tangible evidence on Steinway, we'll have to make do with the massacre of the Montagnard village."

"Oh, Christ. That's it?"

"Let's hope the army sees slaughtering women and children as murder," he said.

She could tell by his voice that he wasn't convinced.

"What will happen to him if he's found guilty?" she asked.

"A dishonorable discharge. That's about it," he said.

She kicked the nightstand. "That's not enough!"

"Steinway claimed he didn't know it was a friendly village. He said it was all a regrettable mistake. He's apologized. There's nothing more they can do to him. It happened over twenty years ago. He'll also lose his pension, if it makes you feel better."

"That bastard doesn't need a pension! He's got Peachie's money!" she yelled into the phone.

"I know that. Look, I'm not giving up. I've ordered all of Steinway's army files moved to my office. Maybe there's something in them. If you're not doing anything, come on over and help."

"Let me take a shower and get dressed. I'll be over in twenty minutes," she said.

When Malia walked into the Pentagon she found Erik waiting for her. He signed her in, then they took an elevator up to his cramped office on the third floor. Every inch of space was taken up by old cartons.

"These all belong to him?" she asked.

Erik nodded. "Twenty years of army service are in them." He picked up a box and put it on his desk.

"This could take days," she said.

"Probably will." He handed her a copy of the military magazine containing the article she wrote on Gen. Mortimer Crowe. "I found this in one of his boxes. Looks like Steinway was a fan of yours."

"So he told me." She tossed the magazine on the cabinet.

Erik opened up a box and spilled the files out on his desktop. Malia pulled a chair over to his desk and grabbed a pile.

They spent the next two days pouring over the general's old papers. Nothing proved to be of any value.

On the third day they took a break and went down to the cafeteria for lunch.

Erik watched as Malia played with the salad on her plate. "Not hungry?"

She shook her head and pushed the plate away. "I'm too pissed to be hungry. You just can't kill people and get away with it."

Erik poured catsup on his cheeseburger. "He's doing just that."

She looked at him. "How much does the damn government *need*? His foot size fits the mold Ben made at the fish pond."

Erik shook his head. "Millions of other men wear the same size boot."

"Even those letters from Bankroft's mother didn't do any good," Malia said, waving her hands in the air.

"No, they didn't. They just showed he was a bastard.

There's nothing illegal in that," Erik replied. "But until you found the document regarding his involvement in the destruction of the Montagnard village, that was the best we had against the general."

"Big deal!"

"No, it's not a big deal. Sometimes we have to take what we can get."

"That's not enough. Did you see the news polls on television last night? Many people still see him as a hero. They don't care about the massacre."

"He's out of the army for good," Erik said.

"So what? He's being inundated with offers for speaking engagements. He's like a termite who can survive any catastrophic upheaval."

"Let it go, Malia."

Tears welled in her eyes. "I can't let it go. He killed my parents. . . . He killed your friend Daniel."

Erik let out a deep quivering breath. "Let's go back to work," he said, dropping his unfinished burger on the plate.

They spent most of the night going through the rest of the boxes. There was nothing in them she hadn't already known from her past research on the general.

She reached into one of the last cartons remaining on the floor and picked up the top file. It was a tan manila foldout, older than the others. She half-heartedly started to sift through it.

The first papers she saw were army orders written out during World War II. There had to be a mistake. Steinway was too young to be in the Second World War. She looked at the name on the folder: OTTO STEINWAY.

Malia turned to Erik. "These are not Steinway's files. They belong to his father."

Erik leaned over her shoulder and looked down at them. "The clerk must have been confused by the same name and put them together." He reached for the phone on his desk. "I'll have someone take them back."

"No, don't," she said. "Let me take a look at them."

Sifting through the papers further, she found they contained Steinway Sr.'s orders to ship out to Australia after his stint with the OSS.

Then she came upon another order, one that sent him to

Berlin on January 12, 1946, to work on rebuilding the war-torn city. The documents were signed by Gen. Mortimer Crowe. Malia knew from Felix Steinway that his father went to Berlin after the war. What she didn't know was that he was working under his longtime friend, Crowe.

Malia sat up, stretched, and rubbed her tired face. She began to think about the old German detective she'd interviewed three years ago when she was doing research for Crowe's bi-ography. He was convinced that the gas line in his bedroom was tampered with. Then she remembered Steinway had told her that he'd visited his father in Berlin with his mother on two occasions.

Was he there when Crowe died? she wondered.

Right now her exhausted mind was grasping for straws, looking for anything. She went over to the file cabinet where she'd put the magazine with Crowe's article and opened it up.

"What are you looking for?" Erik asked, pouring himself a cup of coffee from the Krups machine.

"The date Mortimer Crowe died." She flipped through the pages until she found it. "July twenty-seventh, 1948," she murmured. Closing the magazine, she turned to Erik and asked, "Do you have any contacts at the State Department at this hour?"

Erik looked at his watch and smiled. It was almost four in the morning. "I have a friend there who works the night shift who owes me. Why?"

"Felix Steinway went to Berlin a couple of times to see his father. I'd like to see copies of his old visas and look at the dates."

Erik put his coffee cup down on the desk and picked up the phone. He spoke to his friend at the State Department for a few minutes, then hung up. Looking over at Malia, he said, "I'll have copies of Steinway's visas on my desk at nine o'clock. Want to tell me what this is about?"

"I'm not sure yet." She grabbed her sweater off the back of the chair, pulled it over her shoulders, and tucked the old mag-azine under her arm.

"Where are you going?" he asked.

"Back to the hotel. I wrote this article, now I want to read it." She leaned down by his chair, kissed him quickly on the lips, and left.

The phone woke Malia up. She'd fallen asleep with her clothes on and the open magazine draped across her stomach. Reaching over the nightstand, she grabbed the receiver and put it to her ear.

"Hello," she mumbled.

"It's me, Erik. I have the dates Steinway was in Germany." She cleared her throat. "Well?"

"He was there the months of July and August in 1947 and in 1948."

Malia sat up in bed. "Crowe died in July of forty-eight."

"Felix just started West Point. He probably went to Berlin to see his father during the summer break."

"Every time someone dies he seems to be there."

"It's a long shot on this one," he said.

"When Crowe was in Berlin, he had a servant—an Italian boy he found in the streets of Rome after the war. He took him to Germany with him. He disappeared right after Crowe died. I wonder if he's still alive."

"Did you try to find him when you wrote the article?"

"Yes. I ran a search with INTERPOL. They weren't too responsive."

"What's his name?" Erik asked.

Malia flipped through the magazine until she came to the page she'd dog-eared earlier that morning. "His name's Giuseppe Rigutini. When Steinway interviewed me for the job, he brought up this boy's name. He also wanted to know if I'd found him."

There was a long pause. Then Erik said, "Let me see what I can do. I'll get back to you later this afternoon."

"You need sleep. You've been up for days."

Erik laughed. "I think I could suggest the same for you, too."

After they hung up, Malia laid back on the pillows, telling herself she would only close her eyes for a few seconds. In less time than that, she fell into a deep sleep.

A knocking on the hotel door woke her. She looked at her watch—it was almost one in the afternoon. Malia crawled out of bed, yawned, and went over to the door. She looked through the peephole and saw Erik standing there.

As soon as he walked in she could see the grim expression on his face. He turned to her, putting his hands on her shoulders.

"What is it?" she asked.

"I found Giuseppe Rigutini."

"How?"

His somber look remained. "It wasn't hard. I called Immigration to see if he came to this country."

"Did he?"

He let out a nervous breath of air. "Yes. He came over with his brother in 1953. Crowe, before he died, helped push the paperwork through for them. Why did you think he was Italian?"

Malia shrugged. "I just assumed. I talked with Crowe's aides. They said he didn't speak any English, and that when he conversed with Crowe, it was only in Italian. Plus, Giuseppe Rigutini is a pure Italian name. What else could he have been?"

He paused, then said, "He was French."

She looked confused. "French? But he conversed in Italian."

"That's because he was from Corsica. The true Corsican language is a form of Italian."

"I know that. My father and uncle were from Corsica."

"The reason they spoke Italian was because the general didn't speak French and Rigutini couldn't speak English."

"But the name Giuseppe Rigutini . . ."

"Italy ruled Corsica for centuries before the French took over. Many Corsican names are Italian." Again he paused, then said in a solemn voice, "Giuseppe is Italian for James. Rigutini was shortened . . ."

". . . to Rico," Malia said softly, suddenly understanding.

Erik nodded. "Crowe's orderly was your father."

She slowly sank down on the bed.

"We had it all wrong. Steinway killed your father because of something to do with Crowe . . . not because of the strike."

* * *

They ate lunch in silence at a restaurant in Georgetown. Malia, deep in thought, stared at her plate of untouched veal.

"Peachie said your father was frightened to death when he first met Steinway. I wonder if he remembered him from Berlin?"

"He had to." She quickly finished off her glass of Burgundy. Exhaling nervously, she said, "I think I need another one." Malia caught the waiter's eye and pointed to her glass.

"You never knew your name was Rigutini?" Erik asked.

She shook her head. "My uncle never told me. I always assumed it was Rico."

"Did he ever talk about your father?"

"Very little. From what I could gather, they never liked each other very much. My father moved to Hawaii in the sixties. My uncle stayed on in New York. The only time he ever mentioned my father was when he was drunk. He hated that he married my mother."

Erik sipped his Heineken. "Why?"

"She was dark-skinned, a Hawaiian. When he had a load on, he referred to her as 'that nigger woman.' "

Erik twisted his lips. "Nice man."

"No, he was not a nice man," she said, remembering the times he'd put his hands on her. "I couldn't wait to get away from him. I haven't seen him since I was eighteen years old."

"Is he still alive?"

She nodded. "*He* is. My aunt died last year."

"You may have to see him again. Your father may have said something to him about Crowe when he worked for the man."

"I know." She emitted a caustic laugh. "I hated my uncle all my life ... now I have to turn to him for help. Talk about irony. Steinway may have been right."

"About what?"

"Whether someone's out there keeping the planets from banging together." She angrily cut into her veal and stuck a piece in her mouth.

Chapter Thirty-one

MALIA TOOK THE businessman's shuttle to Newark, then grabbed a cab across the Goethals Bridge to Staten Island. As the taxi passed old familiar neighborhoods, a heaviness clawed its way through her stomach. She never thought she'd be coming back—and never to see him.

She told the driver to stop at Richmond and Victory and paid him. As soon as she got out, she saw it: the old apartment building where she lived was wedged in between the small candy store and pizza parlor. It was more run-down than she remembered, and the brick facade was now sprayed with graffiti. The fire escapes were covered with rust and the windows had new iron bars over them.

Neighborhoods change, Malia thought. And this one was no exception.

With her heart beating rapidly, Malia walked the half block over to the building. She climbed the steps of the stoop and opened the black metal door leading into the hallway. Aromas of cooked food, lodged in the walls for generations, sprang from their plaster confinements and stung her nostrils.

As she turned to close the door, she saw him. He was shuffling slowly up the street, pushing a Wal-Mart shopping cart. His spine was bent and his right leg dragged behind him. Once again that cold nervousness swept through her. She waited on the steps for him.

Vincente pulled the cart up to the stoop, reached in, and took out three large paper bags. Holding them in his arms, he shambled up the stairs. His head was down and he didn't see Malia.

"Hello, Uncle Vincente," she said, trying to keep her voice steady.

When the old man peeked his head over the bags to see

who it was, Malia saw the hairy mole on his nose. It was bigger than she remembered. Had it grown larger, or had her uncle just gotten smaller? she wondered.

Vincente's dark Corsican face registered no surprise at seeing his niece standing there. His eyes were as dead and impenetrable as black space, and the right eyelid seemed to sag lazily over the pupil. He emitted a small grunt, then said, "What are you doin' here?"

"I need to talk to you."

He cackled. "You never talked to me when you lived here. Why now?" His vocal cords sounded unused, as if caked with rust.

"Let me take the bags, Uncle," she said, reaching for them.

For a second, he tightened his grip on the bags, refusing to let go, then he loosened his fingers and handed her two. Without saying anything, he turned and went into the hallway. She followed him.

They slowly ascended the steps to the third landing. When they reached the apartment, he put the bag down on the tile floor and fumbled with his keys. Malia took them out of his hand, found the right key, and opened the door.

Without bothering to thank her, he walked into the apartment. Malia reached down for the other bag, took all three inside, and went straight into the kitchen. She laid the bags on the table and removed the groceries, putting the milk and beer in the refrigerator and the canned goods in the pantry.

"You have a good memory," he said, standing by the kitchen door, watching her.

"That was my job ... putting groceries away." She neatly folded the empty bags and placed them under the sink to be used for garbage receptacles later on. Standing back up, she looked at the old espresso maker on the counter and asked, "Do you want a cup of coffee, Uncle?"

"I wanna beer," he grumbled.

Her lips tightened as she remembered the smell of beer on his breath and his rough hands slithering down her body. Opening the refrigerator, she took out a Bud and handed it to him. She watched him clumsily grope at the tab with his twisted fingers, trying to rip it open. Malia would be damned if she'd help him.

When he finally got it open, he put the can up to his mouth

and took several hungry swigs. Malia watched his massive Adam's apple bob up and down like a mouse trapped in the stomach of a boa constrictor.

He finished half the can, then went into the living room and sat down on his old recliner, which was stained with coffee and food. Grabbing his right foot with his good hand, he grunted as he brought it up on the ottoman.

Malia followed Vincente in and sat down on the hard couch opposite him. She scanned the room. Nothing had changed. It was still drab and cold, just like when she lived here. Warm laughter never touched this place.

She looked at her uncle. His body, much thinner than she remembered it, was sunken down into the chair. "Have you been sick?"

"I had a stroke."

"When?"

"Eight months ago ... after Rose died." He stared at her with a wry expression. "You care?"

"I didn't know."

"And if you knew ... would you care?"

Malia opened her mouth to protest, but no words came out. *No, she didn't care.*

"What d'you want here? When your aunt died, you never came to the funeral, never sent a fruit plate ... nothin'."

"I want to know about my father," Malia said.

He looked at her strangely from his good eye, then sipped his beer and shrugged. "He's dead." His voice was matter-of-fact.

No matter how many times she'd asked about her father as a child, Vincente would never talk about him. Frustrated now, she began to squirm in her seat. "He came from Corsica. What was he doing in Rome after the war?"

Again he shrugged. "It don't matter. He's dead."

The man was like a spiteful rock, she thought. If he felt someone wronged him, he'd hold a grudge for years. "He was my father. I have a right to know," she said forcibly.

"He may have been *your* father, but he was not *my* brother."

"Because he married my mother?"

He held the beer can in front of him, squeezing it until the sides slightly caved in. "Yes, because he married your mother!"

"He loved her," she said.

Vincente laughed. "Love? The woman was a . . ."

". . . nigger!" Malia hissed. "I know. You've told me that all my life. What was he doing in Rome?"

He snickered and waved his hands. "Jimmy was a dreamer. The Americans were in Rome. He thought he could make friends with them. Maybe even come to America to live. The tobacco fields of Corsica weren't good enough for him."

"His name was Giuseppe, not Jimmy," she said coldly.

At first he looked surprised, then his face broke into a crooked grin. "His name, Giuseppe, wasn't good enough for him either. When he came to New York he changed it. Everythin' American—that's all he ever thought about."

"You came with him. You also changed your name."

"Yes, he talked me into it. 'New York! What a city! Everythin's made of gold here,' he'd say to me." He waved his good hand around the room. "You see any gold here? I spent my life in the train tunnels like a rat . . . never seein' a piece of the sun."

"My father went to the islands—he saw the sun," she said through clenched teeth.

He nodded bitterly, then snorted. "And it also killed him." He shook his head. "Always the dreamer, Jimmy. When he couldn't find gold here, he went to Hawaii. I no longer could listen to him. I stayed. Sugar, that's where he said the gold was now. Some businessman, your father!" He grinned harshly. "He worked on a factory line in a hot sugar mill ten hours a day for peanuts. He was crazy!" He stared out the window, then said, "I need another beer."

Malia stood up, "I'll get it for you." She went into the refrigerator, pulled out another can from the six-pack, and brought it to him. This time she opened it. He grabbed the can from her and quickly downed several gulps.

She went over to the window and sat on the sill. Glancing down at the doorway of the pizza parlor adjacent to the building, she saw a young ponytailed Puerto Rican with a beeper on his belt handing a small Ziploc bag to a boy barely in his teens. The boy looked around nervously, then handed the Puerto Rican some dollar bills. *Yes, the neighborhood had definitely changed.*

She turned to Vincente. "How did my father meet General Crowe?"

His good eye widened. "How do you know about that man?"

"I just know," she said simply.

"He met him on the streets, near the Spanish Steps." Vincente smiled knowingly. "They say Crowe was a little . . ." He wiggled his fingers in the air.

"I know what Crowe was," she snapped. "Was my father using him in that way?" Her lips were trembling.

"No!" Vincente said strongly. "Absolutely not! Jimmy was many things, but that he wasn't! Your father was young, good-looking. People liked him . . . women liked him. They were taken by him. This Crowe liked him, too. He gave him a job as his valet . . . that's all. Nothin' funny! When he went to Berlin, he took Jimmy with him. Jimmy wrote and told me he was goin' to America to work for this general. He said I should come to Berlin and we'd all go to America together. Like a fool, I believed he knew what he was talkin' about. There was no money in Corsica. Everyone was starvin'." He scornfully shook his head. "So I went to Berlin."

"Then Crowe died," Malia said.

"Yes, he died. But before he died, Crowe did all the paperwork to get us to America. Only thing we needed was passports. But Jimmy didn't want to wait for them. He started acting *pazzo*—crazylike. He said we should hide aboard a ship . . . get to America that way. 'What's the rush?' I said. 'America will still be there!' But he didn't want to listen. He said we had to get out of Berlin right away. I couldn't talk him out of it. So we packed our bags and went to Rotterdam and got the passports there. Then we left for America by boat."

Malia walked over to Vincente and knelt down next to him. "Why was my father acting *pazzo*?"

Throwing his good hand up in the air, he said, "Who knows with your father? He was always makin' up stories." Vincente waved his fingers around his head. *"Pazzo!"*

"What kind of stories?"

He squinted his good eye and wrinkled the left side of his face, thinking about it. "Oh, yeah," he grumbled, remembering. Then he chuckled. "He thought the general didn't die by accident . . . that someone killed him. Real *stupido*, your father."

She clutched the old man's knee. "Did he say who he thought did it, Uncle?"

"I don' know who. He talked like a madman. I didn't listen. He said he heard things at the general's house—things that were bad. Then when the man died, he thought someone wanted to kill him, too." He laughed again, then finished off his beer. Foam escaped from the paralyzed side of his mouth and trickled down his chin.

She grabbed his knee harder. "Did he mention a young man? The son of another general? Think!"

There was a long pause as Vincente dug deep into his memory. "I remember Jimmy talkin' about a boy, an American."

"What did he say about him?"

Vincente broke out into a grin, his one eye glowing with spite. "You don't give a shit about me, yet you ask a lot of questions."

"I need to know, Uncle."

Hearing the desperation in her voice, he smiled shrewdly and put his hand on her head and stroked her hair. "I can't think on an empty stomach."

Her scalp crawled from his touch, but she didn't flinch. This was one of his old games—don't give anything away without getting something in return.

"What would you like to eat? I'll make you dinner," she said, forcing down the revulsion she felt for him.

"Before you got so independent and moved away, you used to help your aunt cook. Go find somethin'. I'm starved."

She removed his hand from her head and placed it on his lap. Rising, she went into the kitchen and flung open the pantry door. Roaches scattered from the light and ran into the dark corners of the shelves.

Tears stung her eyes. How she hated this man!

She grabbed a can of Progresso minestrone soup from the top shelf. Throwing open the drawer under the counter, she looked for the can opener, found it, then angrily jabbed it into the container. She bit down on her trembling lips, letting the salty tears drop into the open can. Taking a greasy pot from the dish rack, she poured the lumpy liquid into it, then went over to the stove and lit a flame under the pot.

When it was warm, she brought the plate out to the living room table, along with another beer and some stale rolls she'd found in the bread basket. Vincente sat down and forced the soup spoon into his crippled mouth. He ate noisily, not bothering to wipe his lips.

Malia sat on the chair next to him, waiting for him to finish eating.

Vincente took his time. He tilted the dish, making sure he scooped up all the limp vegetables in the watery broth. When he was done, he pushed the plate aside and looked at her for several moments. "Your father—the *romantico*—he used to fancy himself a writer," he finally said in a crusty voice.

Malia looked surprised. "What kind of writer?"

He smirked and shook his head. "He used to keep a diary."

She held her breath. "Where is this diary?"

Vincente pushed himself up off the chair and hobbled over to the rosewood sideboard. His back cracked and he let out a groan as he bent over to open the drawer. Tossing aside his dead wife's lace tablecloths, he pulled out a stained, crumpled notebook with half the cover torn away.

"Was this written when he was in Berlin?" she asked.

"Yes. Jimmy wanted to keep notes so he could tell his children about workin' for this famous general."

She held in her anger. "You never told me about this."

He shrugged. "What for? It's only junk."

Her anger erupted. "It belongs to me, that's why!" Malia held out her trembling hand for the book. For a brief second that spiteful smile played across his lips again, then he shrugged and gave it to her. She opened it up and scanned the creased yellowed pages.

"This is in Italian," she said, looking up at her uncle.

He laughed. "What else would it be in? Jimmy was a Corsican." He reached for the beer can on the table and sat down in his recliner.

She didn't speak or read Italian, but each of her father's entries was accompanied by a date. Flipping the pages, she saw Otto Steinway's name scribbled several times. She looked at her uncle. "Have you ever read this?"

"No reason to," he grunted. "It didn't put food on the table."

She held out the book to him. "Can you read it now?"

He pointed to his good eye. "I can't see well enough to read." He flagged his hand in the air. "Throw it away. It's all silly dreams."

Malia put the book in her bag, then walked to the front door.

"Where you goin'?" Vincente barked at her.

Malia stopped and stiffly turned to the old man. "I have to leave."

"Stay awhile. With Rose dead . . . nobody comes to see me." His voice was raspy and pleading.

She wanted to feel something other than hate for this pitiful man, but he'd given her nothing in all these years to warrant more. "Good-bye, Uncle," she said firmly. Malia left, closing the door quietly behind her.

She took the shuttle back to Washington that night and met Erik at the foot of the Lincoln Memorial. He was out of uniform, wearing jeans and a leather bomber's jacket.

Putting his arms around her, he held her tightly to his chest and stroked her head. "How was it?" he asked.

Her body shivered involuntarily. "It doesn't matter. I saw him; it's over." She lifted her head from his chest, reached into her bag, and brought out the diary. "Whatever my father heard and saw is in here."

He took it from her, fingering the book. "I'll have one of my people translate it."

They bought hot dogs from the street vendor, sat on the steps of the Memorial, and ate them.

"Steinway is going back to Hawaii on Wednesday," he said, licking the mustard off his fingers.

She was surprised. "Why?"

"Kitsobi Cooperation of Japan is having a business function there for their employees. They hired him as the speaker."

"Isn't that dangerous? Taang is somewhere on the island. He knows Steinway destroyed his village."

"Kitsobi offered Steinway a six-digit sum for one night's work. For that kind of money he figured he could take the chance. Security's going to be tight."

She finished off her hot dog. "Why does he need the money? Peachie has millions."

Erik gave off a secretive smile. "The word around town is

that Peachie left him. His military trial is in three months. He needs the money to pay for his lawyers."

Malia had a shocked expression on her face. "I never thought she'd leave him."

"It happened. She used liquor to block out his infidelities. I guess it stopped working."

"The man's broke?"

"Dead broke," Erik said, still grinning.

"He was paid half of a seven-million-dollar advance from Franz Hauptmann's publishing company for his autobiography. What happened to it?"

"Frozen by the court."

Malia nodded in understanding. "I guess Franz Hauptmann also didn't like the fact that the general had been playing around on his niece."

"Or that he may be a murderer. Bad for business," Erik added.

She stood up, wiping the crumbs from her sweater. "Let's find that translator. I want to know what's in this diary."

Joseph Grazzi read the diary, carefully turning the pages so they wouldn't fall out of the broken binder. He was a naval ensign who worked night duty at the Pentagon. When he finished the journal, he looked up at Malia and Erik seated on the other side of his desk. "Is this thing for real?" he said, his eyes wide with amazement.

"I can't answer that. We don't know what's in it," Erik said.

Letting out a low whistle, Grazzi leaned back in his chair, put his feet up on the desk, and locked his fingers around the back of his head. "If this is true, then I'd say some of the history books will have to be rewritten."

"What are we talking about?" Erik asked.

"According to this, General Otto Steinway—Felix Steinway's father—was working for the Germans during the war."

A look of disbelief crossed Erik's face. "He was a spy?"

"You got it. He was an OSS operative, a cryptographer. You couldn't ask for a better place to be if you're working for the other side. Every time we broke one of their codes he'd pass the information on to the Germans and they'd change it.

He also passed our codes on to them. A lot of our men probably died because of that."

"Did Crowe find out?" Malia asked.

"He certainly did," Grazzi said.

"How?"

He pointed to the diary under his desk light. "Otto Steinway worked as Crowe's aide in Berlin after the war. Some high-ranking officer in the SS, who was wanted for war crimes, got in touch with Crowe. He was tired of hiding out and wanted to make a deal."

"What kind of deal?" Malia asked.

"He told him he'd turn Steinway Sr. in for a reduced sentence."

Eric's face lit up. "Did he offer Crowe any proof?"

Grazzi nodded, grinning. "Enough to put General Steinway in front of a firing squad a thousand times over. He gave Mortimer Crowe a notebook containing the names of every Allied operative working undercover in the German-occupied territories for the year 1942. He told him the Nazis obtained the information from Otto. I remember learning in Military History 101 at Annapolis that 1942 was not a good year for our boys in counterespionage."

"Oh, Jesus," Erik muttered.

Grazzi looked at Malia. "Your father, Giuseppe Rigutini, wrote that Crowe called Otto to his house and confronted him. Rigutini overheard everything."

Erik unzipped his jacket. "Did Otto Steinway confess?"

Grazzi picked up the diary and turned to the page. "It says he did right here. He had no choice; the proof was so overwhelming that Crowe had him pretty well nailed. Rigutini says Otto Steinway broke down and cried like a baby."

"Then what happened?" Malia asked.

Joseph Grazzi shook his head in disbelief. "Nothing happened. Crowe died that night from gas fumes."

Erik turned to Malia. "You researched Crowe. Did you ever hear about this notebook?"

Malia shook her head. "Never. If there was a notebook, then it disappeared the night Crowe died. I know my father didn't believe his death was accidental."

"It looks like he might have been right," Grazzi said.

"Does my father talk about his suspicions?" Malia asked.

Grazzi nodded. "Steinway Sr. and his son left that night through the front door of Crowe's office. They caught your father with his ear pressed against the rear door, listening to the whole conversation."

Malia and Erik looked at each other for a moment, then turned back to Grazzi. "You said his son. Are you saying that Felix Steinway was also at the meeting?"

"That's what I'm saying," Grazzi said. "According to your father, Crowe suspected the boy knew about Otto's ties to the Germans. Let me read you the last paragraph of your father's entry from that night." He turned the pages until he came to the one he wanted.

I don't think Felix Steinway could have been more than eighteen years old. He was well over six feet, with a long, thin body. When he caught me listening at the door, his eyes filled with such rage I thought for sure he wouldn't hesitate to kill me if we were alone. I never felt such dread in my life. My mouth went dry and I couldn't swallow. I was mesmerized by his hate. His father was sobbing. Never taking his eyes off of me, the boy put his arm around the man and led him out of the house.

Grazzi looked up. "The next time your father wrote in the diary was after Crowe died." He flipped to the page and read:

The general is dead. They say it was an accident, but I don't believe it. I also read in the newspaper this morning that this SS officer was found with his throat cut last night. It was either the boy or his father who killed them. I can't stay in this city any longer. Too dangerous. They know I heard everything. I'm taking Vincente and leaving Berlin.

Erik took the diary from Grazzi and thanked him for his time.

Walking toward the elevator, Erik turned to Malia. "No wonder your father was frightened of Felix when they met in Hawaii. He remembered him."

"Felix must have been some salesman to convince my father that the SS officer was wrong about Otto and that General Crowe's death was purely accidental."

"Steinway didn't get to where he was by *not* being a salesman. Except he couldn't take any chances with Giuseppe. He killed him. With him dead, the secret would be safe."

"The night Steinway quizzed me about Crowe's article, he really wanted to know how much I knew about Giuseppe Rigutini—my father."

"Fortunately, you didn't know much, including your real name."

Malia shuddered at what might have happened to her if she had.

Erik pushed the elevator button.

"Franz Hauptmann said the marriage between Felix and Peachie united two great families. What did he mean by that? The man had been a Nazi during the war. Did he know Otto was one, too?" she asked.

"He may have known Felix's father was a double agent, but I don't think he knew about any of the murders. He never would have allowed his niece to stay with Felix."

The elevator came and they got in. Malia leaned against the metal wall watching the floor numbers change. She seemed disturbed.

"What is it?" Erik asked.

"Like everything else, my father's diary is also no proof."

Erik put his arm around Malia. "No, it's not proof. Taang is the only one who could put the general away. It keeps coming back to one man."

"Good luck finding him."

"I may just do that." He kissed her lightly on top of the head.

Looking up at Erik, she smiled. "Our general is a multilinguist. I wonder if Italian is part of his repertoire?"

Chapter Thirty-two

Hawaii

BEN LOPAKA REACHED the clearing near the *heiau* just as the sun was coming up over Mount Kilauea. His shotgun was nestled firmly in the fold of his broken arm and he held the ax in his other hand. The morning mist floated along the ground, clutching at his legs.

After Daniel Keahi was killed, all work at the temple was halted. Weeds and moss were beginning to sprout through the cracks in the stone walls.

Ben stopped by a young tree and looked around nervously. He didn't like coming here alone because he knew the Montagnard was somewhere out there. His eyes flickered over the jungle, scanning the mountains and the trees for movement, but he saw no one. Ben removed the knapsack from his back, then put the shotgun on the ground, keeping it at arm's length. Grabbing the ax in his good hand, he began chopping down the thin tree. No, he didn't like being out here one bit.

Erik called last night and told him Steinway was coming back to the island. He said they needed Taang taken alive if they were going to convict the general of murder.

"Once he knows that Steinway is here, he's going to go after him," Erik said.

"You sure of that?"

"I'm sure."

"How do you let the Montagnard know he's coming?" Ben said skeptically.

"We tell him." Erik had an idea on how to do that. "Montagnards left gifts for their people on top of poles. I think we should give Taang a gift."

"An' since you're in Washington, that means I'm the one to do it, right?"

"You're the only one, Ben."

Ben continued to hack at the tree until it wavered, then snapped from its own weight. He wiped the sweat from his face with his sleeve. Getting down on his knees, he took the file saw from his back pocket and began to cut away at the limbs. When he finished, all that remained of the tree was a large, thin pole.

Ben put the knapsack back over his shoulder, grabbed the end of the shaft, and dragged it to the top of the *heiau* wall. He removed some of the lava rocks until there was a deep hole in the structure. Then he took out the plastic package of rice flour and bran from the knapsack and strapped them to the top of the pole with a rope. Opening up the plastic flap, he put an envelope inside, then resealed the bag. He placed the pole vertically into the hole and stabilized it by shoving rocks around the base.

Stepping back, he looked up at the offering. Erik said that Montagnards made a potent brew from rice flour and bran. He said it tasted like shellac and would knock most westerners on their asses.

Taang finding this gift was a long shot, Ben thought. The island was big. He could be somewhere on the other side. Erik wasn't so sure. He believed Taang was living somewhere close to the ranch, in case the general came back.

Ben didn't want to stay here any longer than he had to. As he climbed down the *heiau*, he spotted some white matter near the base of the stone altar. He knelt down to get a better look. They were patches of sheep hair, along with gnawed bones. Next to them was a man-made circular fire wall. The ashes inside were still warm. Someone had killed a sheep, cooked it, and eaten it right on this spot.

He looked out at the dense forest again. Erik was right, Ben thought. His stomach began to knot up. *He's out there, all right. In fact, he's probably watchin' everythin' I'm doing right now.* He cocked both hammers of the shotgun. Keeping it out in front of him, he hurriedly made his way back to his truck.

The next morning Ben reluctantly returned to the *heiau* to see if the package had been touched. Looking up at the pole, he saw that it was no longer there. Taang got the message Steinway was coming, all right. For the first time in two days Ben allowed himself to smile.

The Dynasty Hotel on the Kona Coast resembled Disneyland more than it did a resort. It was three hundred acres of sprawling complexes, with trains and gondolas hustling guests from place to place. Diamond- and heart-shaped swimming pools, golf and tennis courts, water shoots and large colorful fountains dotted the grounds.

It was a large resort, almost too large for the private security force Kitsobi Cooperation hired for this occasion. They'd spread themselves paper thin, attempting to cover the enormous area. Roadblocks were set up at the entranceway and at the back roads; men were stationed in the lobbies, the elevators, and at the doors of the massive ballroom where Steinway was scheduled to speak tonight.

The general arrived late in the afternoon by limousine. He was directly escorted by two muscular Samoans to the penthouse suite.

When he was safely inside, he took off his jacket, loosened his tie, then poured himself a Johnnie Walker tall from the bar. He brought it over to the couch, sat down, and opened his attaché case on the coffee table. His speech for tonight was inside.

It wasn't until he sank into the couch that he noticed the Federal Express package on the stand by the window. He stood back up and went over to it. Looking at the label, he saw that it was for him. It was sent from Washington with no return address. Steinway ripped open the package and took out several Xeroxed handwritten pages. He went over to the window and held them up to the light. It didn't take him long to notice that the faded handwriting was in Italian.

Malia, wearing a stringed bikini and a wide-brimmed straw hat, sat on the chaise longue next to the pool sipping a watered-down Bloody Mary. From her angle, she had a perfect view of Steinway's penthouse suite. She could see the man standing by the window . . . reading the pages from her father's diary. In fact, she could almost hear him gasp when he came to the part about himself.

Smiling, she unfolded her Ray•Bans and put them on. She then lay back on the longue and tipped the hat over her eyes to block out the sun.

By seven o'clock the ballroom was filled to capacity. Malia, dressed for the event, with her old press pass hanging around her neck, stood in back of the room. She hid behind the television cameras, so Steinway wouldn't see her.

Malia's eyes darted across the floor to the partially open door next to the stage. She saw Erik and Ben looking out from behind it. The general didn't know they were here.

Steinway, wearing a tuxedo, sat at the main banquet table on stage. Next to him were the cooperate heads of Kitsobi. Although he was laughing and drinking along with his hosts, he seemed uneasy. Occasionally he would peer out at the audience, scanning the Japanese faces sitting at the dinner tables.

Malia knew he was searching for her. She was strongly tempted to step out in front of the spotlight, so he could get a good look at the woman who sent him her father's diary.

Standing in back of Steinway were the two large-bodied Samoans he hired as private security guards. Their muscular necks seemed ready to burst through their collars as they moved their heads.

Steinway would be introduced in a few minutes, then he would get up to speak. *Where the hell was Taang?* she wondered.

The Montagnard, illuminated in a fluorescent glow of ceiling lights, sat cross-legged on the floor of the structure that housed the hotel's generator in back of the main building. The *lei o monō* club lay across his lap. He was surrounded by monitors, push buttons, and levers. A myriad of thick metal cables snaked and crisscrossed their way across the walls.

His hair was scraggly and dirty, hanging down past his shoulders. Except for the ragged shorts he stole from the clothesline of a coffee farmer, he wore no other garment. Carved earrings, made from the rib bones of slaughtered sheep, dangled from the large holes in his lobes. He no longer used false teeth, and his filed-down ones were blackened with lacquer.

Next to the large fuse box over in the corner, the body of

the electrician who worked the night shift was lying in a pool of his own coagulated blood. He'd been dead for over two hours.

Taang had slipped into the resort before dawn that morning. He knew he'd be spotted if he tried to pass through the guard gates or came over the barren lava fields from the east. Instead, he came from the one place that couldn't be secured: the sea.

He'd fought the deadly neap tides, swimming three miles with the club strapped to his back. Dawn was beginning to break when he made his way onto the man-made beach. Crouching low, he ran over the sand and into several acres of a dense tropical garden that separated the golf course from the hotel. He crawled under the drooping fruit leaves of a large mango tree, climbed to the top, and stayed there until this evening. When the throngs of Japanese businessmen went back to their rooms to shower and change for tonight's festivities, Taang left the garden and made his way to the generator room.

In front of him, the multitude of flickering, small black-and-white monitors showed different areas of the resort. But Taang's eyes were only focused on the one displaying the interior of the ballroom. It offered a clear shot of the head table onstage. In the center seat was the guest of honor, Gen. Felix Steinway.

He also saw that Hawaiian girl, Malia Rico, standing with the rest of the press. Hiding behind the stage door was the man who used to call himself Daniel Keahi and the ex–police officer. He'd watched the old man leave him the present of rice flour and bran, along with information on where the general would be tonight.

It was a generous gift by Montagnard standards, but he knew that the gift came with a price: his freedom. He understood the minds of westerners all too well. None of them had ever given him anything without wanting something bigger in return.

Ever since he'd seen the document that told how his village was destroyed, everything Western in him was cleansed from his soul. He was all Montagnard now, and he would soon join his beloved Piing and his ancestors, never again to be tainted by these deceptive demons.

But first he needed to find out the truth about their deaths.

He had loved the general, trusted him. The idea that his friend would ever lie to him had torn his heart out. Soon he'd find out what really happened. But now he had to get ready. The general would be speaking shortly.

Steinway, sitting next to the president of Kitsobi, laughed at something he said. The general picked up his wineglass, bowed his head, clinked his goblet against his Japanese host's to show that he appreciated a good joke, then sneaked a look at his watch. It was almost time to deliver his speech. When it was over, he'd immediately be taken to the airport by helicopter. In two hours he'd be on a night flight to Australia for another speaking engagement.

Though he laughed hard over dinner and told humorous stories, his stomach was in knots. He hardly ate anything and had to down several stiff drinks over the course of the evening to dull the tension raging within him. That damn half-breed! She'd sent him that diary. He should have taken care of her a long time ago.

He then thought about Taang. If Kitsobi hadn't offered him all that money, he would never have come to the island. He knew Taang, knew what he was capable of when turned loose. In war, he'd seen the bravest of prisoners beg for death and curse their sons and wives after being left alone with the Montagnard for only a few minutes. His speech tonight would be an abbreviated one. If they didn't like it, too bad.

The head of Kitsobi stood up and went over to the dais. In Japanese, he introduced the general.

Steinway rose from his chair to a hailstorm of applause. He raised his hands and the sound became louder, more deafening. No, it wasn't the same as the acclaim he'd have gotten if he was President, but it would do for now. While smiling out at the sea of Asian faces, he noticed the large amount of security positioned around the room. He nervously put his hand up to his breast, feeling the hardness of the Walther PKS tucked away in his shoulder holster, and walked over to the podium.

As he adjusted the microphone to fit his towering height, he spotted Malia standing in back of the crowd, glowering at him. So she *was* here. He forced down his anger. One day he would take care of her, but right now he had a speech to make. Once again, he looked at his watch. Then he smiled at the audience and opened his mouth.

The lights suddenly went out, leaving the ballroom in total darkness. People yelling orders in Japanese came from the tables below. Steinway tapped the microphone with his fingers, hearing only a thin, dull sound.

He looked out the bay window and saw that the lights around the grounds were also out. The fear inside him returned. Reaching for his gun under his jacket, he flicked the safety off with his thumb. He abruptly felt the strong hands of the Samoans clasping him on the biceps and moving him quickly away from the podium.

Manny Lanakila, a security guard for the hotel, stood alone next to the perimeter of the tropical garden. When the lights went out, he nervously fingered the stock of his Smith & Wesson resting in his holster. His breathing was unstable, and his eyes darted restlessly over the blackness around him.

The chief of security gave him this out-of-the-way post because he was new at the job.

Manny suddenly heard gentle rustling in the ivy nearby. Was it the wind? No. He had grown up with the trade winds; they made a different kind of sound. These were too erratic, like the movement of an animal. He reached for his flashlight on his belt, fumbled with the switch, and sprayed the garden with light.

The beam caught Taang. He was jumping over bushes, rushing at him, holding something that resembled a club.

Jesus! Oh, Jesus! He thought about the two-way radio in his hip pocket. Should he call for backup? No, there was no time. Manny took the gun out of his holster and tried pointing it at the figure, but the Montagnard was zigzagging through the flowers, coming at him with a speed that was nearly impossible for a human. The screams this creature emitted pierced Manny's ears.

He was only fifty yards away now. Squinting, Manny tried to get him in the gun sight, but his hand was shaking too badly. He'd never shot a man before, never even shot a gun. *Oh, Jesus!*

Taang stopped twenty feet in front of Manny. The Montagnard's eyes, like raging fireballs, were caught in the glow of the flashlight. He raised the club above his head, opened his mouth, and screamed louder, once again rushing at the security officer.

When Manny saw Taang's blackened filed teeth, he began to scream along with him, emptying his revolver as he did.

Malia and Erik heard the shots. People in the ballroom emitted a cacophony of panicked cries and ducked under the tables.

Erik grabbed Malia's hand and ran out the stage door into the night.

More shots cracked through the air, illuminating the blackness like a strobe light.

"I hit him!" Manny Lanakila's voice screamed over the din.

Racing around the side of the building toward the garden, Malia and Erik found several more security men, guns drawn, flashlights angled in every direction, scouring the grounds.

"I saw him go down!" Manny yelled. The young security guard, his face flushed with excitement, hopped nervously back and forth on both legs.

"Who went down?" Erik said to him.

"Some little guy with a club. He looked like an ape."

"I wanted him alive!" Erik shouted.

"Over here, fellows," a uniformed officer said, standing by the foliage. His flashlight was directed on the ground.

Erik, Malia, and Ben joined the crowd of officers who were gathered by the brush looking down.

The ferns were covered with blood.

"Where's the body?" someone screamed.

"This was where he went down," Manny Lanakila said, breathing hard. "I saw the guy fly ten feet in the air and hit the dirt."

"There's more blood over here," another voice rang out. About twenty yards away, an officer was shining his light on a cluster of flowers.

The guards moved into the tropical garden, trampling over the foliage, making their way to the spot. Their flashlights traced a trail of blood snaking across the tops of African tulips. At the edge of the garden leading to the beach, there was a small forest of date trees.

Spreading out, the men scoured the miniature jungle.

A plainclothesman walked under a giant koa and felt wet drops slapping him on his cheek. He brushed at his face, then brought the flashlight up to his fingers. It was blood. He leapt away from the tree and pointed the light upward, stopping when the beam rested on an immobile body wearing shorts twenty feet above him. It was wedged between two of the tree's forked branches. "He's up in the tree. He don't look alive," he yelled to the other men.

The officers converged around the tree, aiming their guns at the body. A young Hawaiian security guard with long hair and a tattooed cross on his earlobe took off his shoes and scaled the trunk. Crawling out on the limb, he reached out and grabbed the man's hair to dislodge his head, which was jammed between the branches. The body teetered for a moment, then fell from the tree, scattering the officers below.

With guns pointed at the tangled mass, the officers inched forward and made a circle around it. Erik bent down on one knee and turned over the bloodless, pallid body. Bathed in a mass of lights, Erik could see the man was Caucasian, not Asian.

"Christ, man! That's the electrician who works for the hotel!" Manny Lanakila whispered in a husky voice.

A sinking feeling suddenly came over Erik and he looked helplessly up at Malia.

A loud roar of chopper blades shook the earth. Malia peered up and saw Kitsobi's private helicopter ascending from the top of the main building.

"No!" she screamed. *"No!"* She clenched her fists and banged them powerlessly against her thigh as the rotating wings of the craft rose up and disappeared into the starless sky.

"We'll be landing in ten minutes," the helicopter pilot said to Steinway.

Sitting next to him, the general could only nod as he looked pensively out the chopper's window. He ran his hand through his thinning hair, sweeping in the loose strands. He turned to the two Samoans seated behind him. "You're to see me to the plane. When I've boarded you can leave."

One of them flexed his arm muscles, sending a ripple through his suit sleeve, as if to say, *Not to worry.*

The general leaned back in his seat and closed his eyes. Taang was the one who'd turned the lights out; he was sure of it. He knew he was lucky to get out of there alive. Fortunately, he demanded Kitsobi pay him before the banquet and not afterward.

His thoughts were interrupted by a dull *thump*ing sound in back of him. He quickly turned around. Both Samoans were still in their seats, their lifeless eyes drooping downward, their mouths hanging loosely from their jaws.

The general turned his eyes away from the dead Samoans and to Taang standing behind them. The Montagnard was totally naked and holding the blood-soaked *lei o manō* club in both hands.

Steinway knew instantly that the Montagnard used only one blow to kill both men.

With a quickness almost too fast to clock, the weapon came down, missing Steinway's head by inches. It sliced through the upper shoulder of the pilot, severing most of the rib cage. The airman let out a soft grunt as he slumped over the stick.

There was a combination of rage and sorrow in the Montagnard's face as he turned and glared down at the general. Like a child who'd been betrayed, tears sprang from his eyes and trickled down his cheeks. "Is it true?" he asked, with quivering lips.

The general stood up and held his hand out to the Montagnard. Although he felt sick to his stomach, he forced a weak smile. "It's all a lie. You know that. I would never hurt you. It's that damn girl. You were right. We should have gotten rid of her." He slowly began to slide his hand up to his chest, then into the breast part of his jacket.

Taang was not listening to the words. He was staring deeply into Steinway's eyes, down past the corneas, into the soul of the man.

"You're my friend . . . my brother . . ." Steinway could now feel the wooden grip of the PKS. "I would never kill your family. They were all lies, fostered by that half-breed." His finger slipped over the trigger and he leisurely brought the gun out of the holster.

Eyes never lie. The truth Taang so desperately wanted was there. *He now knew . . . he knew. "Moi!"* Taang yelled at the general in a trembling voice.

The gun was now out of Steinway's jacket. He turned the barrel in the Montagnard's direction.

Without taking his eyes away from the general's face, Taang quickly reached for the gun barrel and twisted it out of Steinway's hand, breaking his trigger finger.

Steinway groaned in pain and clutched his hand.

"Moi!" Taang shouted again, only louder.

Steinway understood the Montagnard's language. He was calling him a savage.

Taang leapt in front of the control panel and pushed the stick downward. The helicopter suddenly twisted and spiraled wildly in the wind, then nosedived toward the ocean. It tossed the general to the front of the chopper, banging him up against the seat of the dead pilot. Steinway could only look helplessly up at the Montagnard standing over him.

"Moi . . . Moi . . . Moi!" Taang screamed, raising the club over his head.

Steinway closed his eyes. As he waited for the blow, a vision suddenly erupted in his head, something that he had long forgotten—a small boy sitting in his father's lap, being rocked to sleep to a German lullaby. *"Mein kind . . . mein kind."* The voice singing the tune was soft and gentle.

Just as a smile started to break across the general's face, the vision shattered, replaced by nothing.

Chapter Thirty-three

New York City

C IJI BROWN SAT at her corner table at Antibes putting the tip of her cigarette out in the ashtray. She'd started smoking again after quitting three years ago. Glancing at her watch, she frowned, then finished off her second glass of Montrachet.

She peered over at the entrance one more time. There she was. Finally! Malia Rico had just entered the VIP room and was negotiating her thin hips between the crevices of the jammed tables. The Hawaiian girl wore jeans, a knee-length crewneck sweater, and an oversized man's trench coat.

Managing a forced smile, Ciji eyed Malia's dress code with controlled disdain. "The buses not running again?"

"Sorry. Had to find a home for my cat." Malia removed her coat, tossed it over the chair, and sat down. She ordered a glass of Burgundy from the waiter.

While still glaring at Malia, Ciji snapped her fingers at the waiter and pointed to her empty glass. She then lit another cigarette, took a deep drag, and let the smoke surge out through the corner of her mouth.

"You called for this lunch, Ciji. What's up?"

"Am I keeping you from something?"

"I'm moving to Hawaii, and I haven't even packed yet."

"Then I'll make it short. They located the helicopter last week."

"I heard."

"They can't get to the bodies because of the ocean's depth. Fortunately, General Steinway has officially been listed as dead."

"Fortunate? In what way?"

"Writing an unauthorized book about a man who is still

alive can be cumbersome," Ciji said, picking a piece of tobacco off her tongue.

Malia's eyes took on a playful look. "Are you now thinking
about doing an unauthorized biography on the man?"

"Yes."

"You won't be alone. I heard all the publishing houses in
New York are on a feeding frenzy over Steinway. What would
make your book different from theirs?"

Ciji nervously crushed her half-finished cigarette out. "I
spoke to Steinway's widow a couple of days ago. She's in an
alcoholic-recovery home in Miami."

"I know. I hope she makes it." Malia picked up the menu
and scanned the unpronounceable names of those same damn
dishes she had trouble with last time.

"I asked her if she would be interested in writing about her
life with the general when she got out."

"And she told you no, right?"

"I then asked her if the general left any personal papers that
might be of interest."

Malia didn't look up from the menu.

"She said there were lots of documents ... even jour-
nals locked away in his house in Iowa. You brought a lot of
charges against the man. None of them could be proven."

"No, they couldn't," Malia said casually.

Ciji cleared her throat and leaned into the table. "She told
me she'd been in touch with you."

"We talked." Malia looked over at the Prix Fixe section on
the menu.

"She told you where these papers were kept and gave you
permission to do with them as you wished. She said giving
them up was part of her Twelve-Step program—to free herself
from resentments." Ciji waited for an answer.

Malia didn't give her any. Eventually she poked her head
over the top of the large menu. "How's the *ris de veau finan-
cière*?"

"If you like sautéed brains, they're fine," Ciji said impatiently.

Malia made a face. "Is there a Cobb salad on this thing?"

The wine came. Malia sipped hers slowly, studying the editor's nails. They were like long red teardrops.

"The general was a very meticulous man," Malia finally

said. "He kept notes and diaries on everything he did. I found three file cabinets and a number of boxes in his attic."

Ciji's eyes widened. "Was there anything in them about those murders?"

Malia looked at her, smiled.

Ciji forced a returned grin. "I understand. Let's talk business first."

"Let's order first. I'm starved." Malia scanned the menu one more time, looking for something safe. She found the word *Salades*, and picked whatever the first thing was under it.

After Ciji gave the orders to the waiter, she turned back to Malia.

"I'm prepared to offer you a substantial amount for those papers."

"What's substantial?" Malia asked, picking up a breadstick from the basket and biting off a piece.

"Did you get an agent yet?"

"Nope."

Ciji slowly shook her head and sighed. "I usually work with agents."

"Sorry. I guess you're going to have to work with me."

The editor leaned back in her chair and smiled. "A half million dollars."

"A nice amount for another era. Unfortunately these are inflationary times we live in."

The smile evaporated from the editor's face. "You can't be serious."

"I'm afraid I am." She broke off another piece of breadstick.

"What makes you think they're worth more?" Ciji said.

"*I* don't. Croft Publishers thinks so. They offered me one million yesterday."

Ciji moved back in her chair. This impudent little twenty-four-year-old was now playing one house against the other. She fought hard to control her temper. "All right. Tell me what it is you want, then."

"First of all, I want to write the book."

"I have a Pulitzer Prize winner who is interested in writing it."

"Jasper Rhodes?"

"Yes."

Malia shook her head. "He had his shot. The papers stay with me."

Ciji closed her eyes, thinking, then opened them again and nodded quietly. "How about if you were to assist him?"

Malia dropped the bread back into the basket and looked defiantly at Ciji. "How about if I was to write it alone?"

They locked eyes for several seconds. Then Ciji broke the stare and nodded. "I suppose we'd just have to let you write it, then, wouldn't we? Do we have a deal?"

"We have a deal on *that* part. There's still the money to be worked out."

Stunned, Ciji cocked her head and whispered, "How much *do* you want?"

"With what I know, this book should knock the Bible off the all-time best-seller list."

"How much?"

"Three million," Malia said, not taking her eyes off Ciji's face.

"My God! What do you have that can bring in that kind of sales?"

"As I said, the general was very anal. He wrote everything down."

Ciji leaned over the table and pursed her lips. "Give me a token idea of what we're talking about."

Malia also leaned in, until their faces were only a foot apart. "I'll give you three token ideas."

"Go."

"Number one: The general loved his women, especially if they were Asian or Polynesian. I found a list with detailed notes and addresses on over fifty of them. The man not only liked to bite, but he occasionally beat them. Beat them hard. I located several of them who were willing to talk. One of them still carries around burn marks on her buttocks from his cigar."

Ciji's eyes were on fire. "What else?"

"Two: Steven Bankroft, the plebe at West Point, was methodically broken down by Felix Steinway."

"I know about those letters from Bankroft's mother," Ciji said, waving her hand in disinterest.

"I'm not talking about *those* letters. I'm talking about a diary, in the general's handwriting, giving joyous, detailed accounts of everything he planned to do—and eventually did—to Bankroft."

Ciji began to nibble on her thumbnail. "Did he say he did it because of Peachie?"

"No, he said he did it because of Peachie's money."

The food came. The editor waited impatiently as the waiter put the plates down on the table. As soon as he was finished, Ciji pushed hers away as if it was an intrusion. "And the third?" she asked in a hoarse voice.

"The general's father belonged to a group back in Iowa called the Bavarian Men's Club. I did some research on those good ol' boys. It started out as a social club for immigrants—a place where they could go to drink beer and tell dirty jokes in German. Then Hitler came into power and this little colony of Teutons turned into active supporters for the National Socialist Party."

Ciji wrinkled her mouth in disbelief. "Come on. Otto Steinway was an officer in the OSS. He never would have gotten clearance if the government knew."

"Otto Steinway claimed he resigned his membership in the club in 1929, four years before Hitler came into power. He said he had no contact with any of the members since that time, nor did he share in their political beliefs. In 1942, the army did a thorough investigation and could find nothing to show Otto was lying."

Ciji mildly shrugged. "You can't condemn the man for belonging to a club. He didn't know what they'd become four years later."

"No, you can't." Malia opened up her purse and took out the wallet-sized photograph of the Bavarian Men's Club and handed it to her.

Ciji put on her bifocals and held the snapshot at arm's length. "Who are these men?"

"The boys of the Bavarian Men's Club. The picture was taken during their anniversary picnic, so I'd say they were a bit tipsy at the time. The guy in the middle is Otto. The cute little tyke on his lap sucking his thumb is Felix."

Frowning, Ciji said, "What's so important about this photo? It was obviously taken before 1929."

"Then what's Felix's doing in it? He was born in 1931.

Now look at the date on the anniversary banner in the background."

Ciji held the photo up to the skylight. Her mouth suddenly jutted open.

"It says 1934. Otto lied to the army. He lied to everyone. He was very much in contact with those Third Reich sympathizers."

"How did you get this?"

"I found it in Felix's photo album was I was going through his pictures for the book. When I showed it to him, he stuck it in his jeans pocket instead of giving it back to me. For obvious reasons, he didn't want the picture in his autobiography. I went through his old clothes last week, looking for it, hoping those jeans hadn't been washed. I lucked out."

Ciji looked confused. "Why would he continue to socialize with these people?"

Malia didn't answer her. She waited for it to sink in.

Ciji's mouth dropped farther down. "My God! Are you implying . . . ?"

"I'm not implying, I'm saying it. Otto was a double agent and Felix knew it."

Ciji slowly took off her bifocals and lit up another cigarette. Her mind was racing. "What about the murders? Did he admit to them?"

Malia poked through her salad, pushing away the anchovies with her fork, looking for something edible. "That's four. I told you I would give you three."

A small whistle came from Ciji's throat as she nervously exhaled. "I can't make a deal like this without first talking to the president of my house."

Malia shook her head. "I guess I'll have to take Croft's offer. Franz Hauptmann would never go for it."

A small smile stretched across Ciji's thin, WASPish lips. "Franz Hauptmann sold Baronin last month to an American firm."

Malia smiled back. "It that case, take your time and talk to the new president. My plane doesn't leave for two hours."

Malia arrived in Kona at twelve o'clock that night.

Erik, wearing shorts, a tank top, and thongs, was waiting for her at the luggage carousel.

When she saw him, she ran over and threw her arms around his neck. She held him tight, kissing his cheek, his lips. "I missed you," she said when she finally let him go.

"You're here now," he said, running his fingers through her thick hair.

"Yes, I am. But I'll need a house if I'm going to stay. I heard the general's ranch is up for sale."

Erik grinned. "Does that mean you got your price?"

She giggled. "I hope you don't have a problem being with a rich woman."

"I think I could live with it as long as she doesn't punch and kick."

"She won't—not anymore."

"Welcome home, *wahine*," he said, putting his arms around her again.

Epilogue

Epilogue

WEEKS LATER, BEN drove to the graveyard where his wife and daughter were buried. It had been many months since he last visited them. He parked his truck by the shoulder of the road, then grabbed the batch of white calla lilies off his front seat. Before he'd left the valley this morning, he'd gone into the fields and picked them. Calla lilies were Sarah's favorite. Sometimes she would wear them in her long black hair at night, her way of saying that she wanted to make love. In all their years together, Ben never refused.

He walked over to their plot, which was covered with ivy and colorful vines. As he knelt down and placed the lilies on their headstones, an unidentifiable glass object buried inside the bedding caught his attention. Using his hands, he dug around the vines to remove whatever it was. Eventually he was able to make out the shape of a glass jar. Digging further, he could see that it was filled with a mud-colored liquid. Ben picked it up, unscrewed the top, and opened it. A dank odor abruptly sprang up from the container. At first he flinched from the smell. Then he realized there was something familiar about it. He took another whiff. Shellac, he thought. *It smelled like shellac.*

Ben put his nose closer to the opening. He immediately recognized the odor of bran and rice, like that Montagnard liquor Erik had told him about.

Was the jar put here recently? Or was it left after Taang died?

It *had* to have been Taang who left it, he thought. No one besides Daniel knew about this alcoholic brew.

He had given Taang a gift. The Montagnard had given him one in return.

But Taang was dead . . .

307

A dim light, the size of a pin, lit up in Ben's head. *Could he have survived the crash?* If anyone could have lived through it, it would have been him. The Montagnard was imperishable, like the ageless, turbulent mountains he sprang from.

The ex-police captain scanned the endless miles of thick jungle surrounding the graveyard. He slowly began to smile. *Is he still alive? Watching me right now?*

I'll never really know . . . nor do I want to, he thought.

Ben screwed the top back on and put the jar in the pocket of his rain slicker. Walking back to his car, he looked up at the sky—a gray, massive wall. It was going to be a heavy squall this time. He sighed, thinking about his knees and the inevitable pain that would follow.

GARY GOTTESFELD

Published by Fawcett Books.
Available in your local bookstore.